PASSION'S FLAMES

Mylan's gaze raked over Celiese slowly. "I did not think you would find my embrace so distasteful," he said wryly.

He reached for the clasp on the gold brooch that held her gown at the shoulder and undid it deftly. The silken folds slipped to the ground.

Celiese stood stiffly as he undressed her. Her hands shook with fear and she clenched them at her side. But as Mylan bent to remove her suede slippers, his soft curls touched the inside of her thigh and she gasped sharply, shocked by the sensation that brightened her pale cheeks with a deep blush.

He slid his hands to her knee, then higher still. She stood trying simply to breathe calmly as the warmth of his touch flooded her cool skin with a delicious rush.

As he carried her to his bed, he pressed his lips to her throat, his breath hot against her creamy skin. She had never dreamed a man could be so gentle, could arouse such unfamiliar longings deep within her. Too lost in his tender affections to remember her fears, she wound her fingers in his bright curls to pull his mouth to hers.

Their bodies seemed to burn with the heat of desire. The flames of their passion seared them to each other in an eternal bond that they would never break. . . .

PASSIONATE ROMANCE BY PHOEBE CONN

CAPTIVE HEART (1569, $3.95)

The lovely slavegirl Celiese, secretly sent in her mistress's place to wed the much-feared Mylan, found not the cruel savage she expected but a magnificently handsome warrior. With the fire of his touch and his slow, wanton kisses he would take her to ecstasy's searing heights—and would forever possess her CAPTIVE HEART.

ECSTASY'S PARADISE (1460, $3.75)

Meeting the woman he was to escort to her future husband, sea captain Phillip Bradford was astounded. The Swedish beauty was the woman of his dreams, his fantasy come true. But how could he deliver her to another man's bed when he wanted her to warm his own?

SAVAGE FIRE (1397, $3.75)

Innocent, blonde Elizabeth, knowing it was wrong to meet the powerful Seneca warrior Rising Eagle, went to him anyway when the sky darkened. When he drew her into his arms and held her delicate mouth captive beneath his own, she knew they'd never separate—even though their two worlds would try to tear them apart!

LOVE'S ELUSIVE FLAME (1267, $3.75)

Enraptured by his ardent kisses and tantalizing caresses, golden-haired Flame had found the man of her dreams in the handsome rogue Joaquin. But if he wanted her completely she would have to be his only woman—and he had always taken women whenever he wanted, and not one had ever refused him or pretended to try!

Available wherever paperbacks are sold, or order direct from the Publisher. Send cover price plus 50¢ per copy for mailing and handling to Zebra Books, 475 Park Avenue South, New York, N.Y. 10016. DO NOT SEND CASH.

CAPTIVE HEART

PHOEBE CONN

ZEBRA BOOKS
KENSINGTON PUBLISHING CORP.

ZEBRA BOOKS

are published by

Kensington Publishing Corp.
475 Park Avenue South
New York, NY 10016

First printing: April 1985

Printed in the United States of America

Chapter One

"Celiese!" Olgrethe's thick, honey-colored curls flew wildly about her shoulders as she turned to summon her servant. "Where are my new gold bracelets? I know I wore them only last night but they are nowhere to be found!" The high-strung beauty stamped her tiny foot in angry frustration as she demanded assistance.

Celiese lifted her cool green gaze from the hem of the silk gown she was mending, her steady glance sweeping the bedchamber with amused detachment before she nodded toward the young woman's clothes-strewn bed. "I believe they are still lying in the corner where you tossed them, Olgrethe. Do you see them on the far side of the bed?" Celiese bent her head to hide her impish smile as she returned to her sewing, using stitches so intricate they were invisible upon the sheer blue garment.

"You are supposed to gather my jewelry and return it to my case each evening, Celiese, not leave my things lying about in such a careless fashion!" Yet Olgrethe stepped over the heaps of clothing she'd thrown about the room to retrieve the bracelets herself. She slid them up her slender arms, but was no happier once she had them in place. Returning to an inspection of her clothes, she picked up first one shimmering garment then another, only to cast each aside in rapid succession. "I need a new wardrobe, Celiese, not one thing I have is worth wearing."

"All your gowns are new, none worn more than once or twice. Your father is most generous with you, but you should not expect a new gown to arrive each day with the certainty of the rising sun." Celiese tied a knot in her thread, snipped it off, then folded the blue dress neatly as she rose. She was the taller of the two, and even more fair, for her hair was a blond so pale it sparkled like the finest silver in the bright sunlight that filled the large chamber. After putting away her sewing basket she moved gracefully about the room, gathering the discarded apparel with the fluid rhythm that marked all her motions. Except for the slight difference in their statures and the shades of their blond hair, the two young women were remarkably similar, exquisite beauties both, with the regal bearing of their class, the delicacy of unmistakable nobility gracing their sweet features. Yet one was mistress and the other slave, a distinction that seldom crossed the mind of one but gave the other no peace.

"Take whatever you want for yourself, Celiese, it matters not to me what you choose. My gowns are all prettier on you anyway." Olgrethe flopped across her bed and made no effort to hide the sounds of her racking sobs as she wept on and on, her desperation too great to bear in silence.

Celiese ignored the weeping young woman until she

had returned the room to its usual tidiness, then she sat down beside her and gently massaged her back with a slow, gentle touch. "It is not the quality of your wardrobe that has upset you so, for your gowns could not be more lovely. Has your father proposed another suitor to whom you object as violently as you have to all the others?"

Olgrethe nodded and dried her eyes on the back of her hand as she sat up. "He has no end of men to whom he'd like to see me wed, and the sooner the better, it seems. Whatever shall I do?"

Celiese's pretty smile was sympathetic, "Has none been to your liking, Olgrethe? Has not one met with your approval? You know a Viking maiden is never forced into a marriage when she may divorce her husband whenever she chooses. Won't your father expect your consent to any marriage he proposes?"

Olgrethe chewed her lower lip petulantly before she responded. "I'll not consent to marry any man, no matter who he might be! What difference would it make, are not all men the same?"

Celiese's green eyes deepened in hue as she considered that question thoughtfully. "No, Olgrethe, all men are not the same. Some are fine and good, gentle, loving husbands and caring fathers, while others are unspeakably cruel in all they do, a disgrace to all that is human."

Olgrethe frowned, not readily comprehending her beautiful maid's words. "We have grown up together these last five years, Celiese, how can it be you know so much of the world while I still know so little?"

"I have had far more opportunity to consider life and

7

all its many situations than you have, but if you would but hold your temper and think before you speak, you would see the obvious also, Olgrethe."

"What should I see that I do not?" the pretty young woman asked skeptically.

Choosing her words carefully, Celiese attempted to make her point. "Your father will be certain your marriage enhances his own position, but you would be wise to see that the choice is yours rather than his. Now let us consider for a moment whom you might select. Whom among the men your father might wish you to marry would you accept for a husband?"

Olgrethe shuddered with revulsion, "None! They are all the same—loud, boastful tyrants or arrogant buffoons. I would have none as my mate!" She pounded her clenched fist angrily upon the bed to emphasize her disapproval.

"Perhaps they wish only to impress you with their bravery, Olgrethe, for a Viking takes great pride in being a valiant warrior, does he not?"

"Of course!" Olgrethe thought that a characteristic too obvious to merit discussion. "But I do not enjoy hearing an endless recitation of their raids, of how many men they have slaughtered in the glory of battle to gather their fortunes and bring home slaves to staff their farms!" Seeing her servant stiffen with sudden anguish Olgrethe reached out to embrace her closely. "Forgive me, Celiese, I never think of you as a slave, you are as dear to me as a sister would be, and no matter whom I marry I will take you with me when I go to his home."

Celiese returned Olgrethe's warm clasp and brushed

aside the hurt the young woman had inflicted so thought-lessly. "I do not ever forget I am a slave, nor how I came to be one—but let us not neglect our original purpose. You are of an age to marry, and we must choose your husband before your father does. If no one you have met is appealing then we will have to arrange for more young men to be invited here for you to meet."

Olgrethe's lilting laugh was spontaneous, "Do you really think we can find a man for me, Celiese, one who is brave and strong but does not continually boast of his prowess?"

"If such a man exists in this land then you shall have him, Olgrethe!" Celiese promised confidently, for truly she was as fond of her mistress as the young woman was of her.

"I will insist he provide a fine husband for you, too. We are the same age and if I must marry then you cannot be left alone."

Appalled by that suggestion Celiese rose from the soft bed and moved away swiftly. "There is no need for such generosity, I have no desire to marry some other unfortunate captive and provide our master with children who will live and die in bondage. No, I am content to serve you as I always have."

"Celiese?" Olgrethe went to her friend's side, encircling her slender waist tenderly with her arms. "I will set you free to marry a Viking. Your children will be free, and so will you."

"No!" Celiese responded with fierce pride. "I have no longing for a Viking's affections, no matter what the reward!"

9

"Do you hate us all, Celiese, for taking you captive and bringing you to our land? Do you hate us still?" Olgrethe inquired anxiously.

Celiese turned toward the narrow window cut in the thick stone wall and scanned the rocky countryside with an intense gaze. "It is pointless to hate your family, for they are no worse than any of their countrymen who make war on my homeland each summer with ceaseless vengeance—and I have never hated you, for you are not to blame for their horrible deeds." Wishing to push the terror of her memories aside, Celiese forced herself to smile. "Now, let us devote ourselves to finding a husband for you, Olgrethe, and allow me to meet my fate alone." As I always have, she thought sadly.

Olgrethe shook her head. "I'll give no such promise. Now brush my hair for me and we'll go riding, the day is too lovely to waste in worrying over the future."

When her mistress sat down Celiese took her hairbrush to groom her glowing tresses, pinning them atop her head in a profusion of curls, while she left her own hair hanging freely in loose curls that reached past her waist. "If we do not worry now, I fear you will have far more to worry about once you find yourself wed to a man you scarcely know and may soon grow to despise. Let us consider those who live closest first, the men you see frequently, before we discuss those who must travel a greater distance to visit you."

After a weary sigh Olgrethe complied, and she named each family with marriageable sons, dismissing them one by one as no better than loudmouthed boys she could not abide. "There are grown men too, Celiese, more than I can count, but this is simply pointless, for none has touched my heart, nor even caught my eye." After a moment's silence Olgrethe continued in a hesitant voice, "Aldred Vandahl has sons, handsome ones, I've heard, but my father would never suggest one of those men for my husband."

"Vandahl? I've not heard you mention that name. Who might they be?"

"It is a sad story. My Aunt Helga told me about them only once, but I have remembered her tale. It happened in my grandfather's time. When he was a young man, his best friend was a Vandahl. They were inseparable, closer than brothers, until they both fell in love with the same young woman and their rivalry over her led to the fiercest of fighting. They fought repeatedly and my grandfather finally won, but at the price of slaying his oldest and best friend. Our families have been the bitterest of enemies ever since. The Vandahls neither forget nor forgive that death."

Celiese stood back to survey her handiwork, fluffing Olgrethe's tawny curls as she spoke. "What of the young woman? Was she not heartbroken at the tragic death of one of her suitors?"

"She was my grandmother, Celiese, but she died before I was born. We will have to ask Helga to tell us more of her mother, for I knew her not."

"Would Helga not be a woman to whom we could turn for advice now? A marriage is too important a decision to be left to your father's whim."

"Of course! My father's sister is very clever. When next she visits, I will ask her. Now, please, let us forget

11

this tiresome matter until then, please, Celiese, please."
Olgrethe turned to look up, her blue eyes pleading for
agreement.

Celiese laughed as she laid the hairbrush aside. "As
you wish. Let us go riding and hope Helga arrives before
your father presents another suitor, perhaps one he will
not allow you the privilege of refusing." Although the
spring day was warm she reached for her cloak, pulling
the hood low to shade her face. She would accompany
Olgrethe, as she always did, like a shadow whose face was
never seen, a being who attracted no notice, which was
exactly what she wanted.

The two lovely young women teased each other playfully as they went skipping down the steps and out to
the stables, as they did nearly every morning when the
weather was pleasant. Their mounts were spirited, the
day drenched in brilliant sunshine, their lives were
placid, easy, for Olgrethe was the pampered daughter of
Raktor Torgvald, a Viking whose fierce reputation was as
well deserved as it was richly rewarded. He was not a man
of unlimited patience, however, and, while his daughter
spent the early spring days being fitted for new gowns or
riding through the expanse of rocky coastline that
bordered his vast farmlands, he spent many an hour con-
templating her future, and he had decided he would not
allow her to continue to flaunt his will.

Olgrethe found her father and brothers unusually
boisterous at the evening meal. She longed to return to
her chamber to retire and covered her yawn with no real
haste. When first her father began to speak she scarcely
listened, until she realized the import of his words.

"It is a well-known fact I have a daughter of astonishing beauty, a young woman who unfortunately finds all men unworthy of her attention. I have been lenient in the past, Olgrethe, not overly concerned with your willfulness, but I have received a most intriguing offer for you, my dear, from an enemy I respect too greatly to ignore."

Olgrethe held her breath, frightened by her father's stern tone, then asked, "Who might this enemy be that you would consider sending your only daughter to him?"

"Aldred Vandahl, and he suggests a marriage to rejoin our families in the bond of friendship my father severed with his uncle's death. You will become the bride of one of his sons, to put an end to the feud that has existed between us for half a century."

Olgrethe clenched her fists defiantly at her sides as she leapt to her feet. "How dare he offer such a bargain! We are strong, we need no such truce with the Vandahls as to require my marriage to one of them!"

Raktor frowned at his pretty child's outburst. She was the image of her mother, a lady whose death he still mourned, and he tried to explain his reasoning more clearly. "Our strength is considerable, that is true, but we are not so strong as Aldred, and he knows it."

"Then why would he have offered such a truce if he has no need? Is it a trap of some kind, a bit of treachery you do not recognize?" Olgrethe suggested the possibility in a valiant attempt to dissuade her father from the course of action she was afraid he had already chosen.

Raktor nodded thoughtfully. "Such a thought also crossed my mind, as his offer came so unexpectedly. I do not know what his purpose might be, Olgrethe, if it is not the one he declares it to be, but we must not refuse this gesture without considering it fully, when it may be more to our benefit than to his." The heavyset man leaned forward and gestured for his daughter to approach him. "Aldred has four sons, none married, so it is Mylan, his eldest, whom he has offered as your husband."

Olgrethe gasped in horror. "Mylan? But is he not the one who was killed, attacked by a bear and slain by the beast two winters ago? Was that not Mylan who died?"

Raktor waved aside her questions. "The man was not killed, only mauled. He has recovered sufficiently to wed."

"But was Mylan not engaged to another, to Remald's eldest daughter, Estrid? Surely Aldred wants Estrid for his son, not me!" Olgrethe could feel the net tightening about her and cried out in desperation to avoid a fate she wanted so greatly to escape.

Raktor seemed surprised. "How could you have heard such gossip? That engagement is long over, the girl refused to consent to a marriage with Mylan for some reason, and her father allowed it. I will not."

"Refused him? You mean she would not marry a man left so scarred by the attack of a bear he is no doubt hideous? That is the real reason Aldred has come to you, isn't it? He wants a wife for his son, and no other woman will have him! That is his trick, an enticing offer of peace to secure a wife for a man who can no longer win his own bride!"

Growing impatient, Raktor interrupted. "Aldred has four sons, I have only one daughter among my six children to offer as a bride to seal this bargain. If it is to our advantage to make this truce, then you will go. I know of no Viking who is without marks from one battle or another. Whatever the man's scars, they should not offend you. Now be still about it."

"No!" Olgrethe's fury blazed brightly in her deep blue eyes. "The Vandahls have never seen me, you may send them any woman and they will not know it is not me!"

Raktor scoffed at such an outrageous suggestion. "He offers a marriage to create a peace for all time between our families, and I send him a substitute for my daughter? Your treachery outstrips mine, Olgrethe, but no other has your beauty, and it is well known."

Seeing the light of possibility in her father's eyes, Olgrethe grew more bold. "There is one. My slave, Celiese. Shall I summon her?"

Raktor chuckled as he nodded. "Yes, I must see her before we continue to plan this deception you suggest." He laughed heartily then, pleased by his daughter's cleverness, for he greatly admired deceit as a tactic in battle and was glad to see she possessed such sharp wits.

Olgrethe rushed to her room and with no more than the briefest of explanations grabbed Celiese by the hand and dragged her hurriedly into her father's presence. "You see, she is a beauty, just as I told you. Although her hair is more blond, we are nearly the same size, our features are not dissimilar. In a fine garment there would be none at Aldred's home who could say she is not me."

Celiese was horrified by her mistress's words. She seldom left their quarters, did not pass through the large home without Olgrethe by her side, and had no desire to be shown off to the Torgvalds and hoped to be dismissed promptly.

Raktor's eldest son, a brute named Oluf, leaned over and whispered something that made the older man laugh out loud. "No, Olgrethe, we cannot send this girl, despite her beauty. She is not a suitable bride for any Viking."

"Why not? She speaks our language fluently, she has been with me for more than five years and knows all our ways. She could fool any of the Vandahls easily."

Raktor shook his head emphatically, "We need not discuss the reason. She will not be sent."

"Neither will I! I have no wish to wed one of Aldred's offspring, especially one half-eaten by a bear! You must send Celiese instead, that will satisfy Aldred, and me as well!"

Celiese's eyes widened in alarm as she realized it was her future that was being argued over so heatedly. What had made Olgrethe think of such an impossible deception? How could she ever pretend to be Raktor's daughter? Her cheeks burned with embarrassment, for she understood the Viking's objection to her, even though Olgrethe did not.

Olgrethe's favorite brother, Jens, attempted to end her confusion. "You will have to find another, if such a woman can be found in our household, but Celiese would not please Mylan, for she is no longer a virgin."

Olgrethe's cheeks flooded with color. "How can she not be one? You gave her to me when she was no more than twelve. Do you rape children when you raid?"

Raktor gave Jens a rude shove. "Silence, we need not speak of such things in front of your sister. It is not for her to know our deeds."

Olgrethe took Celiese's hand to draw her near. "Is that true? Which of my brothers abused you? Tell me now and I'll see he suffers for it immediately!"

As Celiese looked toward them the men gasped in wonder. They had not seen her in nearly five years and were stunned by the deep green eyes that regarded them so coldly from beneath a thick fringe of long, dark lashes. Her glance was defiant, so proud and filled with hatred that each felt its power and looked away rather than attempt to return her steady stare. The expression that graced her lovely features was sweet, her lilting voice as clear as a silver bell as she responded to Olgrethe's question. "All of them, mistress."

"All of them!" Olgrethe shrieked as her eyes widened in horror. "You gave this beautiful child to me as my personal maid after you had had your fill of her, is that what you beasts did?"

Raktor rose to his full height. A robust man, he presented a menacing sight, indeed. "How your slaves are treated before they are given to you need not concern you, Olgrethe. I will admit she was young for such sport, but your anger will not change what happened now. Take her and leave us. We will discuss this amongst ourselves, and if I decide upon this treaty when I think you can be persuaded to wed Mylan Vandahl without further argument."

Olgrethe knew better than to persist in her defiance when her father's blue eyes glowed with the same cold light as his burnished steel sword. He could make her life very difficult to live if he chose to do so, and she knew

17

that was exactly what he was threatening. Taking Celiese's hand firmly in hers, she withdrew to her quarters, where she quickly gave way to tears. "Why did you never tell me what happened to you? Oh how I hate them for what they did! You were no more than a precious child, Celiese, no more than an innocent child!"

Celiese pulled her hand away, not pleased by Olgrethe's actions that night. "They had forgotten me. Shall I tell you which one is first when they come for me later tonight?"

"They will not dare! I forbid it!" Olgrethe paced up and down her room with an angry stride. "What are we to do, Celiese? Our dilemma is the same, my brothers will take you, and Mylan Vandahl will have me!"

Celiese watched Olgrethe's frustration grow to a dangerous level before she spoke. "There is no time to lose. You must ask your father to send for his sister immediately. Helga may be able to help us both."

"Yes, that's it! I'll speak with him at first light." Olgrethe gazed into her servant's pain-filled eyes and shuddered. "You did not speak to me for more than a year. I was always kind to you though, wasn't I? I did not understand what they had done to you."

"You are the kindest of mistresses, Olgrethe, but I was free in my own land before your father slaughtered mine." Celiese turned to go but hesitated when Olgrethe called her name.

"Celiese, wait. You must not leave my side, not ever again. My brothers will not take you in front of me. You will sleep in my bed and stay with me until we see what will happen. Should I be sent to Aldred's house, you will go with me."

"As you wish, Olgrethe." Celiese returned and began to brush out Olgrethe's curling tresses as she did every night. Her hands shook badly, but she completed her task without complaint. She'd been safe with Olgrethe, felt secure for five years' time, but that complacency had been put to a rude end. She would be glad to go to Aldred's, for she would be unknown there and could avoid unwanted attention more easily. She wanted only to escape Raktor and his vicious sons, for no matter how easily they had forgotten her, she would never be able to forget them.

Chapter Two

Knowing his younger sister to be a practical woman who would give Olgrethe sensible counsel, Raktor sent for her immediately, wanting only to settle the matter of his daughter's marriage without further aggravation. Each day the hours of sunlight were growing longer, and he was anxious to leave his farm to begin the summer raids for which he spent the rest of the year in eager anticipation. When Helga arrived he sent her to Olgrethe with clear instructions to influence the young woman to wed Mylan Vandahl, and soon, so he could turn his mind to the sea and the riches that lay beyond it, but well within his grasp.

After hearing Aldred's proposal Helga considered it with her full attention. She was an ambitious woman, keen of mind and still quite beautiful, for the Torgvald women were fortunate in that they in no way resembled the men. While her brother was large-boned and coarse-featured, she was petite, as delicate a beauty as Olgrethe. She had seen her own daughters married into fine families and considered her niece's predicament thoughtfully. "Your father is right to be attracted to this match, dear child, for Mylan was well known for his handsome appearance as well as his heroic deeds." The slender woman turned slowly as she spoke. "He has not been seen by anyone I know in the last two years, however, in fact, until you spoke of him today, I believed him dead."

Celiese followed Helga's comments closely and seeing Olgrethe's confusion, asked a question herself. "Is it not possible that he is?"

"What?" Helga's bright blue eyes widened in surprise. "How can that be?"

"Olgrethe believes this proposal is a trick of some sort. A marriage to a dead man would be the ultimate betrayal, would it not?"

Helga dismissed Celiese's suggestion quickly. "Aldred's reputation with those not of our family is most favorable. Despite our suspicions, this appears to be a true proposal of marriage, one you might be foolish to refuse, Olgrethe. The Vandahls are wealthy, extremely so, prosperous traders, adventurers who sail far and wide in search of the finest wares. Yet I am confused as to why no word has been heard of Mylan for so long." Helga pursed her lips dramatically, her puzzlement clear.

Her aunt had been her only hope, and Olgrethe was near tears as she explained her fears. "He must be grotesquely scarred, hideous to behold no matter how fine he might have looked years ago. He must have been cut to shreds by the bear—perhaps he lost an arm or a leg. Oh Aunt Helga, I cannot marry such an ugly man, I cannot!"

Helga sighed regretfully. "Since he did not come to

21

you with his proposal himself, I am inclined to agree, Olgrethe. It seems likely he has suffered some impairment, but whether it is so considerable as you fear, I do not know. You are entitled to make your own decision in this matter, and if it is against the marriage then I can be of no further service and will return home. I had hoped to remain to plan your wedding, but if there is to be none—"

"Wait, do not leave yet, Helga. Olgrethe may change her mind in a day or two. Give her time to consider this more fully, please, before you depart," Celiese requested calmly.

"Never!" Olgrethe screamed defiantly, yet as soon as she and Celiese were alone she had no such courage and paced her room nervously, wiping away her tears.

When she could no longer bear to see her mistress so distraught, Celiese asked a question that had been weighing heavily upon her mind. "Olgrethe, why did you suggest that I go to Mylan in your place?"

"We are so much alike I was certain Mylan would never know he'd been fooled. I'm sorry, it was a wicked thing for me to do to you when you have always been so loyal to me, but I was desperate that night, Celiese, as I am still!"

Nodding sympathetically, Celiese began to propose a plan of her own. "If your father insists upon this match, I *will* go in your place, Olgrethe. Doubtless the man will be so drunk on his wedding night he will recall nothing. I can complain to him the next morning of how badly he hurt me, and he will never question what occurred and what did not."

Olgrethe's expression grew bright with excitement. "You would do that for me?"

Celiese shook her head emphatically, "No, for myself. I would be free, the bride of one respected man rather than the whore of your five brothers, which will surely come to pass if I remain here, despite your efforts to save me from that degradation. I will marry Mylan to protect myself, but you would be helped in the bargain."

"But what if he truly is ugly, horribly mutilated, what if—"

"Enough, Olgrethe, the poor creature may be hideous, but I will not despise him for his misfortune, I will ask only that he be kind, and if he believes me to be Raktor's daughter, he will not dare to be otherwise."

Olgrethe rushed to Celiese's side and hugged her warmly. "Thank you, thank you, for I have none of your sweet compassion and would make Mylan the worst of wives."

Celiese accepted Olgrethe's gratitude calmly, but in truth she was far more frightened of remaining in the home of the Torgvalds than of marrying the man Mylan Vandahl might be. Appearance was not the only consideration in a person; he could still be a fine man, no matter how severely he'd been injured. She was probably only fooling herself, she realized suddenly; regardless of the extent of his injuries he would be a Viking still, so what chance was there his heart would be a kind one? Pushing her mistress away gently, Celiese turned their conversation to the practical aspects of their plan. "We must prepare identical gowns, Olgrethe. If your father sees you clearly the morning of the journey to the Vandahls' home, he will not think it odd that we cover our heads in his ship. The wind would disturb you greatly, and you would not want to appear in front of his crew in full view." Celiese smiled slyly as she saw her mistress nod with approval. "We can trade places at the last possible moment. I will wear a veil for the ceremony, and it will be too late by the time your father realizes what we have done—I will be Mylan's bride by then, and he will never tell his enemy he has been tricked so completely. He will have to keep the secret as well as we do, for his own reputation will be at stake."

"Yes, that is the perfect plan." Olgrethe was so delighted to avoid such a disastrous marriage that she would have agreed to anything. "I will go to Helga's for a while, for a long visit, and if ever I do decide to marry people can be told my father had two daughters rather than only one, and none will dare dispute him!"

"That is true!" Celiese hugged Olgrethe this time, certain their plan would save both of them from fates they would not freely have chosen. They made their preparations carefully, considering each and every detail, every aspect of the deception, and they were far too clever to miss any necessary step. Olgrethe would be expected to be attended by her own maid for her wedding, but then she would simply send the servant back to her father's home when the guests departed, and then it would be Celiese who had wed Mylan and Olgrethe who returned to the home of the Torgvalds. They hoped that all would go well for both of them. Then one afternoon Olgrethe was summoned and told she was to become the bride of Aldred's eldest son, but that she would be sent to his home alone, without the company of her slave. She accepted her father's order demurely and returned to her room to give Celiese the startling news.

"He says you must be left behind, Celiese. He gave me no reason for his decision—as if I would not know it!"

"Then we will simply change places before the voyage rather than after. Our original plan will still work for us," Celiese insisted, certain it was far too late to change their minds about so important a matter now. "You will wear my cloak and I'll wear yours when I bid you good-bye. Surely the confusion at the beginning of such a voyage will make the switch easy to effect."

Badly frightened, Olgrethe clung to her friend. "It must, it simply must, Celiese, for if we are caught I dare not even imagine what my father will do to us!"

Knowing only too well exactly what Raktor would do to her, Celiese turned their conversation to Olgrethe's wardrobe, distracting the pretty young woman as well as herself from the fear that gripped them both. They retired early, escaping their fright in dreams, but Celiese was awakened at midnight, lifted from the large bed so quietly that Olgrethe did not stir as her faithful maid was carried away. Oluf's hold did not slacken; he held Celiese firmly, his right hand over her mouth to silence her screams as he shoved her inside Raktor's room.

"You must not be so rough with the girl; we want no bruises marring her lovely skin when she becomes Mylan's bride tomorrow," Raktor said.

Celiese wiped her lips on the back of her hand, disgusted by the man's touch. None of Raktor's sons were kind, but Oluf was not only mean but crude as well. He

25

reeked of beer and his tunic was covered with grease stains from the evening meal. That he'd brought her to his father rather than carrying her straight to his own room puzzled her greatly, as did Raktor's remark. "Is it not your daughter who is to become Mylan's bride? And did you say tomorrow? You did not tell her it was to be so soon."

Celiese was wearing no more than a light chemise, and Raktor walked around her slowly, enjoying her scantily clad beauty. Her figure was superb, her breasts high and full, her waist tiny, her hips narrow, the proportions of her long, slender legs perfect. "My daughter does not realize I raped you too, does she?"

"No, I spared her that grief," Celiese replied proudly.

"Why? Surely you have no love for me?" Raktor's eyes continued to rake over the slender girl before him. He licked his lips slowly, making no attempt to disguise his lust.

"No, my regard is only for Olgrethe, and for no other in this house."

"I have decided to send you in her place, after all. You will have to fool the man into believing you are a virgin, but it will not be too difficult, since you are so clever. There will be celebrating long into the night, and I will see that Mylan is so drunk he must be carried to his bed. That will help you trick him. Whatever you tell him when he is again sober he will believe. I have had gowns made for you, not unlike my daughter's. You will sleep alone tonight and we will leave at dawn. The voyage is not lengthy and Aldred will entertain us all until we are ready to go home."

26

Celiese backed away, not trusting the master of the house or his brutish son. "Shall I return to my own room, then?"

"Yes, the gown you are to wear tomorrow is there, and the rest are already on board my ship."

Celiese left quickly before the man could change his mind about how she should spend her last night in his house, but she heard Oluf begin to argue and ran to bolt her door against him in case he had convinced his father to give her to him. She sagged against the door and waited. Oluf was the strongest, too difficult for her to fight off for long, but Raktor could not send her if she were black and blue from the beating Oluf would have to give her before she'd submit to his attentions. As the minutes passed without mishap she began to relax. Raktor was no fool, and apparently he'd known his plan would be ruined if Oluf had his way. Taking no chances, she pushed her bed across the door before lying down upon it, but still she was too frightened to sleep and lay wide awake until dawn, when she got up to dress.

The silk gown that lay across her chair was a pale green that reflected the jade of her eyes, and she brushed her hair into the elegant style Olgrethe wore and secured it with the gold hairpins she'd found with the gown. There were gold bracelets for her arms and heavy gold earrings, too. Raktor had left nothing out, and when he came for her she was ready. He quickly handed her a fine woolen cloak.

"Cover your head, Celiese, none must know it is not my daughter who is leaving this morning, until we are gone. See that none of my men see your face while we are

27

on board my ship, either, as this is a secret that must be well guarded."

Still not understanding the man's reason for sending her in his daughter's place, Celiese knew better than to question his motives and did as she was told, following close behind him to his sleek vessel, which lay beside his dock, ready to sail. The finely sculptured prow was in the shape of a dragon's head, its large eyes seeing all in its path, and she shivered, remembering her last voyage aboard the evil ship as though it had taken place only the previous day rather than five years ago. The sea spray stung her eyes as she sat huddled in the stern, but she watched carefully. It took too many men to sail the dragon for her to dream of stealing it to make her way home. The work was hard even with the brisk wind, and the crew cheered when land came again into view. Raktor took her arm firmly in his hand to lead her ashore and whispered, "I did not think to ask, do you ride? They will expect you to manage your own horse for the journey to their home." Raktor shaded his eyes with his hand as he saw a band of riders approaching. "Good, they have seen our arrival and will soon be here."

"Yes, I rode frequently with your daughter. I will not disgrace you now."

"See that you do not disgrace me tonight either, Celiese!"

"You must call me Olgrethe, do not give away this deception with your own words!" Celiese answered reproachfully. As the horsemen drew near, she wondered which would be Mylan, and what his thoughts would be that day. Did he long for a bride, or was he as

28

opposed to this marriage as Olgrethe had been? Her eyes swept the faces of the approaching group. She found Aldred easily enough; he commanded the group and welcomed Raktor with a loud greeting, but none of the riders with him appeared to be his eldest son, for none came forward to meet her as she'd expected him to do. She looked down demurely as Aldred came forward, hoping to impress him with her modesty.

"I have long awaited this day, Raktor. My son remained at home, a condition upon which he insisted, but he should have come with me, I know." The man reached out to tilt Celiese's chin so he might see her more clearly, and he exclaimed with delight, "Ah, I had heard Olgrethe was a beauty, but not even my imagination provided such a splendid face as this. You are exquisite, and Mylan will be enchanted. Come to the horses, do not keep him waiting when he is so anxious to meet his bride."

Celiese smiled sweetly, "Not too anxious, I hope. Is there to be no celebration, no feast to mark this wonderful occasion?"

"But of course, you will not find my hospitality lacking, Olgrethe. Now let us make haste."

As Raktor helped Celiese to mount her horse he whispered, "Good, keep your groom celebrating until he is too blind to see the obvious, and I will reward you well, dear daughter."

Celiese turned her horse and took up a place near her future father-in-law. His hair and beard were a light auburn shade, only faintly streaked with gray. He was muscular, yet not thick through the waist as Raktor was, and she thought it likely Mylan might once have been as attractive a man as his father. They rode at a brisk pace and soon sighted their destination. Set upon a rise, the stone buildings of Aldred's farm spread over a considerable distance, dwellings and barns, storehouses, granaries. The main structure was an imposing one, and Celiese hoped she had not exchanged one prison for another.

"You ride well, did your father teach you?" Aldred held her horse's bridle as Celiese slipped gracefully to the ground.

"Yes, my father was—is a fine horseman, he taught me many things, Aldred." Celiese blushed with embarrassment, but the man had not noticed her slip, and she reminded herself to be more cautious in her replies, for she was now Olgrethe, and Olgrethe's father was very much alive.

"Mylan is most fortunate then. Come quickly, he insists upon meeting you the moment you arrive. But first I want you to meet Thulyn, his mother."

As they entered the large home a tall, elegantly dressed woman came to greet them. She smiled with the same delight as her husband as she saw what an astonishing beauty Olgrethe had turned out to be. Her eyes were an unusual light brown, amber in hue, while her once-blond hair now held more than a trace of silver. "I am Thulyn, Mylan's mother. Welcome to our home."

Celiese smiled politely as the introductions continued, but before she had time to draw a breath Aldred took her arm and led her down a long corridor and left her in front of a heavy door. "Do not bother to knock. Simply enter; my son is expecting your arrival and will be ready."

When he turned and left her, Celiese had no choice but

to go in alone. At first she thought the room empty, for it was unlit and quite dark. "Mylan?" she called in a whisper, afraid she might offend the man who would soon be her husband. But what if he were truly as hideously disfigured as Olgrethe had feared? He had not come to his father's dock to meet her—was he unable to ride? Did he spend all his time in darkened rooms so his appearance could be hidden? Would she be able to hide her revulsion from him for even one minute, let alone for the rest of her life?

"I am here, Olgrethe." When he turned toward the window only his silhouette was clearly visible, the bright outline of a tall man, powerfully built but lean, his broad shoulders tapering to a slim waist and narrow hips. He was leaning against the back of a sturdy chair, favoring his right leg slightly as he stood gazing out toward the sea. "What they have done to us is unpardonable. Our fathers have sealed a bargain of theirs with our lives, but I am a grown man, not a child who must do his father's bidding, and you need not marry me today, nor ever. I will release you from whatever promise you have made."

Celiese approached Mylan slowly, her fear of him replaced by a curious fascination, for the rich timber of his deep voice was mellow and very pleasing, even though his words were bitter. "Mylan, I—"

"No! Listen to me—if you will not refuse this match, then I will refuse you! I want no bride who has been forced to take me sight unseen. I want no part of our father's wretched pact!"

Certain what her fate would be should she have to return to Raktor's house, Celiese gathered all her courage and reached out to touch Mylan's sleeve lightly, but she felt him flinch before he drew away. "Mylan, please, will you not look at me while we speak?" She held her breath, terrified of what she would see as he turned slowly toward her, but as the light of the sun illuminated his face she gasped sharply, for never had she expected Mylan Vandahl's appearance to provide such a shock. His thick tangle of bright curls shone with copper highlights, yet his finely drawn brows and long eyelashes were dark. His eyes, which widened in surprise as he looked down at her, were the same sparkling light brown as his mother's, topaz in hue, with a compelling shine she could not resist, and she exclaimed with genuine delight, "Why Mylan, you are so very handsome, why would any woman refuse to marry you?"

Mylan frowned as he reached out to touch her silken curls. "You are very young, little more than a child, but how can you think me handsome?"

Celiese moved closer, turning so the light fell fully across his face. The scar that crossed his left cheek was a slight flaw in her opinion, but she was no stranger to the pain that filled his level gaze. She reached up to touch his cheek lightly, her fingertips tracing the thin scar with a delicate caress. "Your features are perfect, as finely carved as the most proficient sculptor could fashion, your coloring so unusual and attractive, why would this small scar disturb you so greatly?"

Mylan stepped back into the shadows as he drew his tunic over his head and then tossed it aside as he moved back into the light so she could see him clearly. The skin of his broad chest was horribly scarred, as if he'd been

32

flayed alive by some vicious giant who had lost interest in mid-task and pressed his victim's flesh back into place with no effort to make the pieces fit properly.

Celiese swallowed the painful lump that filled her throat and tried to smile but could not. "You must be very brave to have survived such a painful ordeal, Mylan, and surely courage and spirit are far more important qualities in a man than mere physical beauty."

"This is not the worst of it." Mylan brushed her sweet comments aside rudely as he gestured impatiently to the grotesque ridges that crisscrossed his torso. "My right leg looks no better, the short distance I can walk I cannot traverse without limping badly, I still tire much too easily and—"

Celiese stepped into his arms and lifted her fingertips to his lips to silence his confessions. "Scars matter so little to me, and you will recover your strength in time. If you do not want me, please speak the truth now, but do not wait for me to refuse you, for I will not do it."

Mylan stepped back, confused by the ready acceptance by the lovely creature before him. Her hair shimmered in the sunlight with a sparkle that nearly blinded him, but her large green eyes were cool, her open appraisal of him as curious as a child's. There was not the slightest trace of fear in her sweet expression, only a quiet anticipation, not the revulsion he'd come to expect from a woman. Why was she so different, her perceptions so acute? "How old are you, Olgrethe?"

Celiese smiled shyly. "I am seventeen. I hope you will not think that too advanced an age for your bride."

Mylan's troubled expression broke into an easy grin as

he laughed at her teasing. Her unexpected humor amused him greatly, and his spirits rose to match hers. "I thought you would be spoiled, Olgrethe, the only daughter of a man I've been taught all my life to despise. I thought you would be eager for any excuse to avoid our marriage, for I was certain you would hate me, if not for who I am, then for what I have become."

"And what is that, Mylan? You will have to explain what you mean, for I see only a man, and a most handsome and brave one." Celiese was amazed at how simple a matter it was for her to converse with him. She had hoped only to find a place in which to live as a free woman, a refuge from the lusts of Raktor and his brutish sons, a home she had been willing to share with any man. But the one who stood so proudly before her was not only attractive, but pleasant and bright. Far too bright, she realized with sudden sorrow, for the deception she would have to attempt later that night. With considerable effort she forced that frightening prospect from her mind and looked up at him, her head tilted at the saucy angle that was Olgrethe's favorite pose. "Well, will you not respond? Have you decided to send me home or make me your wife?"

Mylan frowned thoughtfully, then leaned back against the chair he'd used for support and folded his well-muscled arms over his bare chest. "I am still considering the matter. Turn around so I might have a better look at you." He regarded her critically, looking her up and down slowly, assessing her fair beauty with a practiced eye as she turned, then taking her small hand in his he sat down in the oversized chair and pulled her down across his lap.

"Mylan!" Celiese was appalled by his impertinence but found her struggle to rise swiftly ended as his arms encircled her waist with the force of steel bonds. "Is this your answer?" Her lips were a few scant inches from his as she spoke, and, although she tried to lift her gaze to his, she found the curve of his enchanting grin irresistible. When he raised his hand to the nape of her neck to draw her near she made no effort to fight him but relaxed in his arms, a willing prisoner in his strong embrace as his mouth brushed hers with the lightest of touches before lingering in a far more demanding kiss. She had not expected such tenderness from a Viking and drew back, her cheeks flooding with color as she did so.

Mylan chuckled as her pretty blush deepened, "I think your beauty surpasses even Raktor's boasts, for your face and figure are perfection, and you seem to possess wisdom far beyond your years, Olgrethe, but has no one taught you how a man likes to be kissed?"

Celiese looked away. She hoped he was teasing her, but the images that flooded her mind were horrible indeed, and she had no intention of telling him just how much she'd been taught nor how brutal the lessons had been. Raktor had never permitted any man to be alone with Olgrethe, nor had that young woman ever longed to be kissed, and, taking that knowledge as her cue, she replied softly, "Raktor is very strict, Mylan, he would not allow such a thing."

Mylan wound his fingers in Celiese's thick curls to force her gaze up to his. "You call your sire by his name, is he so formidable a man you dare not call him father?"

35

Too late Celiese realized her mistake, but she could not bring herself to call the hateful villain, Raktor Torgvald, father. "I call him by many names, but he is a most worthy adversary, and I do not take his commands lightly."

"Is that meant as a warning?" Mylan's golden eyes narrowed to vicious slits. "If you find me to be less than you had hoped as a husband, can I expect Raktor to punish me for my faults? Must I live only to please you or suffer the consequences at his hands?"

Celiese gasped in pain as Mylan tightened his grasp upon her, but gave no thought to begging him to release her. The last person in whom she'd ever confide would be Raktor, no matter what sort of husband Mylan proved to be. "No, you are mistaken, I issued no threat. I have left the house of the Torgvalds and will make my life with you, and you need never fear you will suffer any pain for accepting me as your wife." Yet as she spoke those words she knew she could not honestly give such a promise. Her very presence in his home was a lie, and she had scant hopes she could win his love when their marriage was based on so great a deception. As tears filled her eyes she tried unsuccessfully to hide them. "If you do not want me, Mylan, please say so now, it would be far better for both of us if you did not hide your doubts behind excuses." Celiese knew she had failed to please him, and she cared little what reason he gave to Raktor for refusing her.

Mylan's gaze grew puzzled. The young woman who sat perched so calmly upon his left knee was the most perplexing creature he'd ever met. He stroked her soft haze of silver hair lightly as he tried to consider which was the wisest course to take, but he found her stunning beauty a serious distraction to any coherent contemplation. She had the sweet, trusting heart of a child, and he'd hurt her. She had been willing to accept him, in spite of the grotesque horror his badly torn body presented, and he had been most ungracious. He had no fear of Raktor, surely the man's bellow was no more than the howl of the north wind, annoying but doing no real damage. He chuckled to himself then. What punishment could Raktor inflict to equal what he'd already suffered? He lifted his hand to tilt the lovely girl's chin and spoke softly as he leaned forward. "Kiss me like this, Olgrethe, open your lips."

Celiese obeyed Mylan hesitantly, not knowing what to expect as he drew her near. The expanse of his chest was warm to her cool breast and she rested her hands lightly upon his broad shoulders to steady herself. His kiss was light, as gentle as before, but as his tongue passed between her lips she grew frightened and drew away. "Please, please don't." Her heart was pounding so wildly in her ears she could scarcely think, and although she saw his lips move she could not make out Mylan's words. He appeared to have nothing in common with the Torgvalds, but as his arms tightened around her she was terrified, desperately afraid of the affection he seemed determined to give despite her reluctance to accept it. When the door flew open Mylan relaxed his hold for a moment as he turned to look over his shoulder, and Celiese seized that opportunity to leap to her feet and back away.

Aldred Vandahl laughed heartily at the intimate scene

before him. "I do not have to ask what you have decided, Mylan. It has been far too long since I've seen a beautiful woman in your arms, but can you not wait until Olgrethe is your wife?" He crossed the small chamber swiftly, and taking the young woman's trembling hand firmly in his turned toward the door. "Come, child, you must dress. Raktor will accept no excuse for postponing the ceremony beyond the agreed-upon hour, as indeed, neither will I."

Celiese glanced back at Mylan and was shocked by his furious stare, but whether his anger was directed at her or his father she could not tell, and she clung tightly to Aldred's hand as she was swept through the door and out into the hall where Thulyn stood ready to assist her.

Chapter Three

"Come, Olgrethe, your bath is waiting, and I fear it will grow cold." The friendly woman led Celiese up a short flight of stairs into a small, well-lit chamber. "Here is your trunk. The silk of your gowns is exquisite, but then, Raktor is very rich, is he not?"

Celiese nodded as she began to remove the jewelry the man had provided that morning. "Is Aldred not also? The fabric of your dress is as sheer as any of mine."

Thulyn smiled, pleased by the young woman who would become her son's bride. "You are bright, Olgrethe. I did not expect such a daughter from Raktor, yet you possess both grace and spirit. I pray you will give Mylan many sons."

Celiese paled noticeably at that remark and turned toward the steaming tub that had been prepared for her use. "Thank you. I am happy if I have pleased you."

Seeing the pretty young woman's discomfort, Thulyn was afraid she had offended her, but she misunderstood the cause. "Olgrethe, I know your mother is long dead, but you do understand the love between a man and a woman, do you not? I will try and explain, if you lack all such knowledge."

Celiese pinned up her hair so as not to dampen her long curls, using that activity to delay making a response while she considered how best to reply to that question. Thulyn seemed so sincere in her inquiry, so eager to offer advice, and she turned slowly, a demure expression gracing her lovely features. "I understand the act, but not how to accomplish it. I am most dreadfully ignorant of the ways to give a man the greatest pleasure. Is there not something you could teach me so I may please your son?"

Thulyn smiled graciously, happy to have won her future daughter-in-law's confidence. "I am certain Mylan is pleased with you already. Your beauty would delight any man, and he will be a far better teacher than I could ever be. Now step into your bath before the water loses its warmth."

Celiese smiled shyly, certain she'd convinced the charming woman of her innocence. She tossed her new green dress aside with the carelessness Olgrethe had always shown and sank down into the waiting tub. The heated water enveloped her in a delicious warmth, and she had no desire to hurry. The longer she remained soaking contentedly, the more time Raktor would have to fill Mylan with drink, which she desperately needed him to be. The truth of that thought saddened her greatly, for she had liked the golden-eyed young man from the first moment they'd met, and she was more frightened than she cared to admit that she would not be able to fool him so easily as she had his mother. But what if she did?

There was not only her wedding night to survive, but the rest of her life, as well.

"Why Olgrethe, you've no need to weep." Thulyn stepped closer, her voice filled with sympathetic concern.

"No, I am not crying." Celiese splashed her face with the warm water until her tears were lost from the perceptive woman's gaze.

Not convinced by that denial, Thulyn persisted in trying to reassure her, "Please, Mylan is such a fine man, he will never mistreat you. Do not be afraid of him, nor of what your life will be here, for it will be as pleasant as the one you've known."

Celiese did not respond immediately, since Thulyn's remark had been meant as encouragement rather than a threat, and she knew the considerate woman had no idea how terrifying a prospect it truly was. "Yes, your son seems most kind."

Thulyn sighed wistfully. "If only you had known him before the tragedy. His smile was as bright as the rising sun and his laughter never ceased. He can be that man again with your love, and that is why my husband pressed him so strongly to accept this marriage." Hesitating, Thulyn realized she had revealed too much, "I mean—"

"I understand, Thulyn. Mylan told me himself he was not eager to wed, but I will do my very best to make him happy." Celiese was overcome with longing then, for Thulyn reminded her of her own dear mother. She wanted so desperately to be loved and protected once again, to be surrounded with the joy she'd once known rather than the endless fear and peril that forced her to

41

use all her cunning simply to survive. She wished she were marrying a man she truly loved in a ceremony attended by her own family and friends, but she knew the beloved world of her parents was gone, ground to dust beneath the Vikings' violent tread. The bride she should have been would never have come to Mylan Vandahl, and the danger in the path she'd chosen closed in upon her with a dread so deep she could not hide her shudder. Pretending she had grown chilled, she stood up, letting the warm water drip from her slender figure before stepping out of the tub to take the towel Thulyn offered. She dried off carefully before selecting the gown Raktor had told her to wear for the wedding. The glistening ivory silk was shot through with golden thread, so the garment shimmered with the seductive glow of moonlight as she turned. With her hair freshly brushed and styled she had never been more stunning, her beauty soft and appealing, like that of the pretty child she once had been. She scarcely needed the heavy gold jewelry Raktor had provided, but she slipped it on again and was ready to go.

"My husband has looked forward to this day so eagerly. We must stop this senseless fighting amongst ourselves and learn to live in peace in our own land."

Celiese's green eyes burned with fiery light as she responded angrily, "To better make war on our enemies, to kill and rape those across the sea with all the bloody courage for which the Vikings are so justly feared?"

Thulyn shrank back in astonishment. "Why, Olgrethe, you sound so bitter! But your father's warlike ways are not ours. The Vandahls are responsible for no deaths on our shores or those across the seas. Did your father not explain that our men are traders only, men who barter the finest goods of one people for those of another?"

Celiese regained her composure swiftly and reached out to touch the older woman's arm lightly. "It is only that I long for peace more than your husband ever has. It is no mere dream to me, but a memory of all I hold dear." She knew she had been foolish to speak the truth, but she'd never stop screaming it in her heart. She relaxed when Thulyn smiled, placated by her more moderate tone. Helga had called the Vandahls adventurers, but why had she forgotten their interest was in trade, not murder?

Thulyn gestured graciously. "Everyone is waiting. Let us go." She followed Celiese down the stairs, then escorted her through the long hallway that led to the main hall where all were gathered to celebrate the marriage that would soon take place. The large room was crowded, the merriment already underway when they entered, and they stood unnoticed at the doorway for several minutes. While Thulyn scanned the faces of those present looking for her husband and Mylan, Celiese searched for Raktor and his sons. They were scattered about the room, all drinking and talking in loud, raucous voices to Aldred's far more reserved kin. As a hush spread over the room, Celiese was surprised to realize that she was the cause. She felt little like a bride, but she followed Thulyn hesitantly across the wide expanse to Mylan's side. She expected someone to shout, to scream out her true name and end her ruse before it had been completed, before she became the bride of a man who believed her to be another, but all were silent as she passed by with a graceful step that brought a look of envy to every eye.

She tried to smile as Mylan took her hand, but it was obvious to her that no matter how drunk the other men in the room might have already become, he had consumed little or nothing as yet. His glance was reserved, yet curious, as it swept over her. He also had changed his attire, and his well-tailored suede tunic and trousers emphasized his lean, muscular build handsomely. She had not realized he was so tall, but now he was standing upright, rather than leaning against a chair for support, and he was easily a full head taller than she, although her height was unusual for a woman. His expression held none of the anger she'd seen that afternoon, but she could not help but wonder what he would say should he learn that his bride was a Christian slave rather than Raktor's proud daughter.

As the ceremony began Celiese found she could understand little, for the Viking religion was not something in which she'd been tutored. She had difficulty following along, but hoped none would think her nervousness unusual, for surely no bride was calm on her wedding day. As the chanting continued, the low voices repeating ageless prayers, her fears grew, her deception gaining a horrible momentum in her mind until she was certain she would faint before another minute passed. But as she glanced up she saw Raktor leering at her, the lust plain in his evil expression, his desire no different from that which showed clearly on his sons' faces, and she stepped closer to Mylan, clinging to his arm. When he looked down she tried to smile, for the stranger who would soon

44

be her husband offered more in the way of security than
did the master of the house where she'd lived in hiding
for the last five years.

At the conclusion of the ceremony, Erik Vandahl,
Mylan's youngest brother, was one of the first to offer a
toast to the bride and groom. He was nearly as tall as
Mylan, not yet so well built, but a charming youth with a
ready grin who kept those around him laughing with his
easy humor. Aldred apologized for the absence of his
other two sons, but there were kinsmen aplenty to join in
the festivities, and the wedding feast continued for
hours. Although the mead was plentiful, Mylan drank
little of the fermented honey beverage, and Celiese dared
taste no more than a sip. He watched her closely, his
amusement at her discomfort undisguised as he remained
by her side, accepting the teasing as well as the kind
wishes for their prosperity, until a moment's lull presented him with the opportunity to draw her away from
the noisy gathering. He led her quickly up the side stairs
to his room, a chamber far greater in size than the one in
which she'd found him that afternoon.

"You do not wish to remain with your relatives,
Mylan?" Celiese hung back, knowing she would have no
defense against his certain anger, for he was far too sober
to be fooled by any ruse that came to her mind.

"No, I want only to be alone with you, to continue
what my father interrupted so rudely this afternoon." He
pulled her through the heavy wooden door, then bolted it
securely before he went to the hearth. He bent down to
add wood to the coals that glowed softly upon the stones
and soon had a blaze burning to his satisfaction. He

turned back to face his lovely young bride.

Celiese backed away, frightened more by his charming grin than by his height and obvious strength. He moved with ease, his limp slight despite his complaints about his health. He appeared to be most fit, vigorous, and strong, and she tried frantically to think of some way to postpone the inevitable humiliation she was certain to suffer that night. Her anxiety was clear in her expression, and Mylan came closer, a slight frown creasing his brow.

"Olgrethe? Why are you trembling so? You were not so terrified of me this afternoon. Are you only cold? Come closer to the fire." He reached out to take her hand and drew her nearer to the hearth. "This house is older than time, but once the stone walls draw in the heat of the fire they will remain warm all night. You will like my room, it is one of the warmest."

Celiese stood in his easy embrace and hoped he'd believe the tremors that coursed down her spine were due only to the chill of the night air. She held her palms out toward the flames and took several deep breaths, knowing Mylan was being kind because he believed her to be his equal. She dared not consider how he might usually treat pretty slaves. She straightened her shoulders proudly as she rejected that thought. What Raktor called her was one thing, what she truly was quite another, and she felt not in the least bit inferior to the handsome man who stood so near. "I was not all that certain how you felt about me this afternoon, Mylan. I was afraid I had angered you." She had run from him like the terrified young woman she was, and she had little hope he had understood her reticence to return his eager kisses.

Mylan's warm breath caressed her cheek softly as he replied with a low chuckle. He combed her shining curls away from her face with his fingertips, then bent down to kiss lightly the silken skin of her throat. "How could I ever be angry with you, Olgrethe? You seem to see in me the man I once was, as if—"

Celiese turned in his arms, captivated anew by his gentle manner, and her smile was wistful and sweet as she interrupted him. "I do not understand your sorrow, Mylan, but I am pleased to know I was not the cause of your anger." She thought again how handsome a man he was, and the charming sparkle that filled his amber eyes did not displease her. Raktor should have sent Olgrethe, she thought sadly, for the lively girl would have loved Mylan instantly, even if she had been unable to fathom his moods.

"You are far too lovely a young woman to inspire any emotion within me, save desire." Mylan drew her curls through his fingertips to pull her close. "Your hair is so very fair, like sunlight upon the snow. May I brush it for you? I do not want to send for a maid to attend you, not tonight."

Celiese forced back the guilt his tender tone evoked and nodded. "Yes, would you please? Do you have a hairbrush? I do not know where my belongings were taken after I bathed."

"They are all here." Mylan turned away briefly, then returned with her brush in his hand and quickly removed the gold pins from her carefully coiled tresses, spilling the luminous curls about her pale shoulders in a glittering

47

cascade. "I have never done this before, forgive me if I prove clumsy."

Celiese stood patiently while he brushed her hair slowly with long, even strokes, but finally she had to speak. "It is not like grooming a horse, Mylan, here let me show you." She took the brush from him and pulled it through her hair from underneath. "Do you see, if you hold your hand at my scalp you may use more force."

"Yes, I understand, but when have you ever brushed a horse, Olgrethe?" He scoffed at the ridiculousness of such a beauty's working in her father's stables.

"From time to time I have groomed my pets. They are gentle animals who welcome my touch." Indeed, Celiese had answered with the truth, the mares had belonged to Olgrethe not her, but they had both groomed them upon occasion.

Mylan took her thick curls in his hand and brushed out the ends for a moment, then let his fingertips stray along the graceful line of her bare shoulder. "Horses are not the only creatures who would welcome your attentions, Olgrethe."

His sensuous touch brought a shiver Celiese could not suppress, and she pulled away, then crossed hurriedly to the row of narrow windows on the far side of the room. "Is the sea visible from here?"

"What?" Mylan turned, startled by her sudden flight. "Oh yes, at night it is difficult to distinguish the sparkle of the water from that of the stars, but it is there." He walked up behind her again, but left his hands at his sides and followed her gaze as she studied the darkness with an intensity he could not understand. "Are you fond of the sea?"

"Yes, I have lived all my life within sight of the water." Yet Celiese found little comfort that night in the scent of the salt spray that filled the air. It was all she could do to stand calmly when she wanted so desperately to flee, but there was nowhere for her to run, and such foolishness would only make her plight all the worse. She stood trying to appear interested in the view, but she could not ignore the presence of the handsome man who stood so near. She could feel his warmth and his charm, which was almost a tangible force, and she wished she could return his attentions as honestly as he gave them.

"In the morning you will be able to see the coast clearly, but tonight you must trust my word that it is there."

Celiese smiled demurely as she turned to look up at him. "I am certain you know the view from your own room, Mylan, but I fear we will be unable to sleep here tonight with the noise our guests are making. Should we not return to the party and join them?"

Mylan laughed as if she'd told the most amusing of jokes, "Olgrethe, surely you did not plan to waste our wedding night in sleep!" He began to tug at the intricately carved gold bracelets that encircled her upper arms, and she helped him to remove them. "Good, I see you do know what it is I wish to do. Now give me your earrings as well."

Again Celiese obediently complied with his request, but each time she tried to step clear of his embrace he moved closer, until the backs of her legs brushed the furs that covered his bed and she had to stop abruptly, for further retreat was impossible.

Mylan grinned broadly at her predicament. "You may have escaped me this afternoon, Olgrethe, but you won't elude me tonight, nor any other night I want you. There is no need for you to fear me. I will be very gentle with you until you have learned all there is to know."

Celiese seized upon his words in hopes of delaying his promised lessons as long as she could. "I was also disappointed we had so little time to talk this afternoon. I have so many questions, will you not permit me to ask them?" She sat down primly on the foot of his bed and folded her hands in her lap, her wide, innocent gaze rapt upon his face as she did so.

Mylan frowned impatiently, annoyed by her unexpected request. "Olgrethe, let us talk on the morrow."

Celiese reached out to take his hand and drew him down beside her. "Please, we are strangers still, Mylan, neither of us prepared to begin a marriage. Will you not grant me this one small request?"

"If it is only one, I will indulge you, but then I will insist you repay me in kind." Mylan's glance was a mischievous one, but when he saw she did not understand the meaning of his teasing remark he put his arm around her shoulders and hugged her warmly. "I am sorry, Olgrethe, ask me whatever you wish, and I will try to satisfy your curiosity about me as best I can."

Now that he had agreed so readily Celiese realized she had no query in mind, then, remembering Olgrethe's complaints, she struggled to be coherent. "You are a grown man, Mylan, doubtless a veteran of many exciting voyages. Will you not tell me of some of your adventures?"

Mylan groaned in frustration, "Yes, I am a grown man, I am twenty-eight, and you expect me to relate so many years of my life in amusing tales on our wedding night? We will have our entire lives to discuss our pasts, but tonight I prefer to enjoy the present. I will say no more than that I will return to the sea as soon as I am able to command my vessel with my former strength and skill." Mylan's expression darkened as he admitted slowly, "Although I am afraid that day may never come."

Puzzled, Celiese continued to probe. "Why has no one seen you these last two years? You look very strong and fit to me, and your appearance could not be more pleasing." She had been observing him closely all evening, for it was a fascinating pastime, but now she hoped to keep him talking until dawn, if possible.

Mylan rose to his feet and pulled Celiese up with a forceful lift. "I have no need for pity, Olgrethe, especially not from you. Would you rather I did not disrobe fully?"

Celiese chewed her lower lip nervously as she considered his question; she knew she was attractive, and, as she was now his wife, he had asked for nothing that was not his right as her husband. If he had avoided his friends to escape their pity he was doubtless lonely too, and that was a feeling she could readily understand. She pulled her hands from his, then knelt at his feet and began to loosen the laces of his soft suede boots. "I have lived in a house filled with brothers, Mylan. The sight of an unclothed male will not shock me."

The tall man had to bend slightly to stroke Celiese's fair curls. "Even if you are not frightened by my manhood, I am certain my scars must revolt you."

Celiese hastened to disagree. "You did not believe me this afternoon? I will never mention your scars, if you will promise not to hate me for mine."

Mylan pulled Celiese swiftly to her feet and held her before him, his grasp upon her shoulders firm, as if he meant to shake her. "What scars? Your beauty is without flaw. Tell me what you mean!"

Celiese replied softly, "Not all scars are visible, Mylan, the worst disfigure the spirit, not the body."

"I am no coward, Olgrethe, is that what you mean? You think I have hidden like some quaking coward, so I need not see my family's anguish when they look at me?" Mylan asked in a hoarse snarl, the bitterness of his mood twisting his handsome features into a cruel mask.

Celiese's thick lashes nearly swept her brows as she stared up at him wondering how he could have misunderstood her remark so completely. "Mylan, I am delighted to have a man as fine as you for my husband. I most assuredly do not believe you are a coward and did not mean for you to think I had called you one. I was referring to my own faults, not accusing you of having any."

Mylan sighed dejectedly as he dropped his hands to his sides, "I am a great fool, Olgrethe, but the confinement I have been forced to endure has not been easy for me. I am angry only with myself, not with you. Please forgive me."

Celiese stood on her tiptoes to brush his cheek softly in a light kiss. "There is nothing to forgive, Mylan, but please try and remember that since we do not know each other well as yet, misunderstandings will be unavoidable. We must each be patient with the other."

Encouraged by the sweetness of her gesture as well as her words, Mylan drew Celiese into his arms and held her tightly against his lean body. He did no more than hold her, but she stiffened in his embrace, her anxiety increasing tenfold as the seconds passed and he did not release her. She could not bear to be held so closely, for it reminded her far too vividly of the brute force she'd been unable to escape. When Mylan at last relaxed she stepped back quickly, her smile slight, for she had no control over her emotions, and they tore away at her heart with the fury of vultures picking clean the carcass of some fallen beast. She began to shiver uncontrollably.

"I did not think you would find my embrace so distasteful." Mylan's gaze raked over Celiese slowly, but he did not seem displeased, only amused by her reticence to accept his attentions.

Not wishing to offend him, Celiese apologized. "No, it is only that I am not used to a man's affection, that is all. I know you do not mean to frighten me with your strength, but it is considerable." Celiese looked down shyly, wishing she could fill her mind with thoughts of him rather than the dreadful memories from her wretched past. He was kind and dear, not a beast who would abuse her, and she wanted so badly to please him, but knew she would not.

Mylan's expression softened instantly, her beauty enchanting him anew. "I have let you become chilled again. The furs of my bed are thick and warm, and that is where we both belong tonight." He reached for the clasp on the gold brooch that held her gown at the shoulder, undid it deftly, then laid it aside with her other gold jewelry.

Celiese stood quietly as he undressed her, but she jabbed her fingernails into her palms until she was certain they were bleeding to keep herself from screaming hysterically. Standing nude before him Olgrethe would have been embarrassed, nervous because she did not know what to expect, but Celiese was anxious because she knew exactly what was going to happen. When the blond man bent to her feet his soft curls touched the inside of her thigh and she gasped sharply, shocked by the sensation that brightened her pale cheeks with a deep blush, and as he looked up she could only stare into his amber eyes, too surprised to speak, for the pleasure his presence brought her astonished her. After he had removed her suede slippers he did not rise but lifted his hand to her knee, then higher, and she had no desire to push him away. She stood trying simply to breathe calmly as the warmth of his touch flooded her cool skin with a delicious rush, leaving her whole body as flushed as her cheeks. He caressed the length of her thigh lightly, then let his fingertips trace the line of her leg to the tip of her toes before he again stood to face her, his smile a mischievous one.

"You are supposed to enjoy my touch, Olgrethe, and you need not be ashamed that you do," Mylan offered sympathetically.

Celiese could not respond, for the beat of her heart roared like thunder in her ears, drowning out her efforts to compose a lucid response. She was captivated by the brightness of Mylan's ready smile, enchanted by his eyes' fiery brilliance, and she made no protest as he lifted her into his arms and carried her to his comfortable bed.

After casting off his own clothing swiftly, Mylan joined Celiese upon the soft furs, but when he pulled her into his arms the shyness of her hesitant kiss amused him once again. "How can any creature be so astonishingly beautiful, so sweet and bright, and yet so cold!" His lips brushed her flushed cheeks with light, playful kisses before he leaned back to look down at her, his golden glance caressing her delicate features softly.

"Cold?"

Celiese could scarcely breathe with her husband so near, but his sly grin inspired her trust rather than feeding her fears. "Yes, the room is still a bit cold."

Mylan chuckled at the innocence of her reply. "Olgrethe, when I kiss you, I expect you to kiss me, to accept my affection even if you cannot yet return it with any feeling for me. Until today I have had no desire to take a bride, but I find I want you most desperately now."

"You are wrong, Mylan, for although we have known each other for no more than a few hours, I do have feelings for you and very tender ones." That was part of her problem she knew, for she admired him greatly and did not want to trick him as cruelly as she had. As he leaned down to kiss her lips lightly she lifted her hands to his shoulders, caressing his warm skin slowly before she wound her fingers in his bright curls to pull his mouth down to hers. She opened her lips slightly, kissing him as he had kissed her that afternoon, her tongue teasing his playfully until at last he drew away.

"That is much better. Forgive me for teasing you when I promised to be a patient teacher." Mylan could not recall ever being with so shy a young woman and reminded himself to be more considerate lest he frighten her needlessly. "Now, please kiss me again." His mouth found hers warm and sweet beneath his own, her lips trembling only slightly this time, and he moved closer still, lengthening his kiss until he felt her acceptance along the entire length of her youthful body, for as she relaxed, the contours of her slender figure fit perfectly against his lean physique, as if she had been born to be his wife. The pleasure that flooded Mylan's powerful body was one he had not forgotten but had despaired of ever sharing again with a woman as beautiful as the elegant creature who was now his bride. "You see, is this not a far better way to kiss?" But he gave Celiese no time to reply before his lips again caressed hers softly, for he truly did want to teach her well, to create within her breast the desire that was already pounding with such insistence within his own. He made his voice a reassuring whisper as he began to pay her pretty compliments, wanting her to feel the delight her loveliness gave to him as he covered her delectable body with soft kisses. Her skin was smooth, creamy to the touch and as fragrant as the gardens of wildflowers that surrounded his home each spring. She had the gentle perfection of a clear spring day, all its beauty and sweetness, and he was lost in his own romantic dreams as he continued to savor the swells and curves of her splendid figure.

Celiese smiled contentedly as Mylan's lips trailed down her throat. She traced the ripple of muscles that moved across his broad shoulders with a slow, sensuous touch, for the skin of his back had been unmarked by the bear's claws and it felt smooth and alive beneath her fingertips. She held him in a tender embrace as his lips slid across her breast, too lost in his tender affection to remember her fears of his love. She had never dreamed a man could be so gentle. The longings he aroused within her were exquisite, and as unexpected as his handsomeness had been, a surprise too marvelous to contain, and yet, as his fingertips slowly moved over her soft curves, the feeling continued to grow and the desire to deepen. His knowing touch grew more intimate. His bed had the softness of a cloud at her back, she was floating in his embrace, adrift on the tide of his passion, and she drew him close to her heart, hoping to return the pleasure his warm, sleek body gave to hers. As his lips returned to her mouth his honey-flavored kiss led her further into the madness, teasing her senses as deftly as his slow, sensuous touch drew forth the deepest of pleasures until she shuddered with joy, her surrender to him now complete.

Mylan shifted his weight gradually, tenderly cradling the delicate beauty in his arms as he moved to possess her fully, to make her truly his wife, but as his first forceful thrust went deep within her he stopped abruptly, stunned by the ease with which her slender body had accepted his.

Celiese felt Mylan stiffen and dropped her hands from his shoulders to cover her face. She held her breath waiting for him to strike her, for a brutal beating was the very least of the punishments she expected from him, but he called her name softly, and when she lowered her hands to look up at him his mouth returned to hers with a soft caress that seemed endless in its delights. His desire drew her back into his dream of love, and she lifted her arms to encircle his neck as he began to move within her, his strength tempered with such easy grace that she wanted all he could give of this new and even greater pleasure. Her whole body seemed to burn with the heat he infused, the flames of his passion searing her to him in an eternal bond she would never seek to dissolve. She moved with a graceful rhythm to accept his loving, drawing him ever deeper into the magic he had created so thoughtfully for her, until at last he buried his face in her flaxen curls and she clung to him still, her heart too full of love to let him go.

When the bright haze of passion had at last cleared his mind Mylan covered Celiese's face with kisses as gentle as the summer breeze and drew her close to his heart. He had thought he'd married a girl little more than a pretty child, but had found his bride to be a woman of astonishing depth and spirit, and she simply fascinated him. "I will keep your secret, Olgrethe, if you will but tell me the truth."

Celiese drew her fingertips through his thick curls and along his cheek as she tried to imagine how she could possibly tell him the truth about anything. "Do not ask, Mylan, for I am yours now, and you must love me enough never to ask."

After a moment's pause, Mylan whispered softly, "Did you love him?"

"No." Celiese could not suppress the shiver of disgust that coursed down her spine. "No, there was no love

58

between us, never that."

"If you wish him dead, I will kill him gladly for your sake. You need but speak his name and his life is over." Mylan sealed his vow with a slow, deep kiss that left them both dizzy, entwined in each other's arms, too content ever to part.

Celiese could not accept his gallant offer, for she feared too greatly for his safety. His love now meant more to her than avenging her honor ever would, and she'd not risk his life for any reason. "No, our marriage was meant to bring peace, not further strife, Mylan." She snuggled against him, for she had found a paradise in his arms she'd not imagined existed on earth and knew he had shared the same exquisite joy he'd given to her. "Is this not enough, Mylan, am I not enough to make your life complete?" Her fingertips traced his scarred chest with a seductive caress before slipping down his flat stomach and encircling his waist to draw him near. When she lifted her lips to his he responded eagerly to her enticing affection, enveloping her once again in a passion-filled dream that left her glowing with the pleasure of his love. She was the most talented of pupils, the most loving of wives, and had learned swiftly how to please him as greatly as he pleased her. When at last she fell asleep in his strong arms she prayed their marriage would last forever, for she had never felt more truly a woman nor more dearly loved than she did lying in Mylan's affectionate embrace.

Chapter Four

Celiese awoke slowly from her beautiful dreams of love. She stretched languidly, pressing her lissome body closer to Mylan's to savor his comforting warmth. He lay sleeping so soundly that she did not try to wake him, but propped her chin on her elbow to study the planes of his attractive features in the dim glow that was all that remained of the once bright fire upon the hearth. The scar upon his cheek was faint, a wound suffered at an earlier time than the bear's attack, and she grew curious as to what had caused the mark he'd always carry. Perhaps it had been no more than a boyhood game that had ended too roughly, the result of a brawl with his brothers or some boisterous friends. She would not ask though, she'd wait until he wished to tell her, as it was so slight a flaw she'd not make him think it disturbed her by calling his attention to it. Her eyes continued to sweep his face with a loving caress. He had become so dear to her in the brief time they'd shared, and he would be the husband she had not dared hope ever to have. She could not stop smiling as she watched him sleep. His dark lashes were as thick as her own, and she leaned down to kiss his eyelids sweetly. Her light touch did not wake him, although a slow smile came to his lips. He had a marvelous smile, so charming an expression that she was tempted to wake him just to see it again, but she knew that would be foolish, since he'd surely smile at her whenever he chanced to wake. She laced her fingers in his as she moved closer to snuggle against the curve of his lean body, and yawning dreamily, she drifted over the edge of sleep before any thoughts save those of him could fill her mind.

It was not yet dawn when a piercing cry of alarm brought Mylan swiftly from his slumber. He looked down at Celiese for one brief moment, then sprang from his bed and reached for the clothing he'd discarded so carelessly upon the floor. "Stay here, Olgrethe, bolt the door and do not open it to anyone until I return."

Celiese sat up, clutching a soft fur robe to her breast as she watched her husband dress with considerable haste before he withdrew a sharp, double-edged sword from the wooden chest beside the hearth. "Mylan, what is it? I heard someone call—a scream—what could be wrong? What terrible thing could have happened?"

"Perhaps nothing." Mylan turned to smile reassuringly as he reached the door. "It may be no more than a guest rousing from a drunken stupor, but I will make certain all is well."

As he slipped through the door Celiese saw only the ease with which he carried his weapon, as if it were an extension of his arm, and she brought her hand to her lips to stifle her own cry of alarm. Dear God, why had she not understood what he was? Did his mother truly believe her sons traveled the world as honest traders and merchants rather than as the bloodthirsty pirates Vikings always were? She sprang from the ample bed and dressed quickly, cursing her own folly as the sounds from the great hall below continued to increase in volume. She was frightened by the suddenness of the activity that had awakened them so rudely, and despite Mylan's command she opened the door, hoping to discover what had happened. The sounds of battle surrounded her with a sudden horror. The clang of steel as swords clashed with brutal blows echoed up the stairway with a deafening roar, followed by the screams of both male and female voices. Smoke from fires set below stung her eyes and she had to draw back into the safety of her husband's room.

Celiese slammed the door shut and threw the bolt, then began to pace distractedly up and down. Blood-drenched scenes of battle and death raged through her mind with the indelible memory of her own people and how quickly they had died under Raktor's sword. Who could have attacked on this of all nights? Surely Aldred's forces combined with Raktor's could defeat any intruders, but the noise of the fighting continued until the rising sun spread crimson flames as vivid as blood across the morning sky.

When the door flew open with a mighty crash Celiese sprang back, ready to face her assailant, certain of what a beautiful young woman's fate would surely be at the hands of any enemy warrior. "Raktor!" Her voice filled with hope. "Have you beaten off the intruders' assault?"

The husky man threw back his head and howled with

laughter. "It is my own attack, Celiese. Did you not understand why I brought you rather than Olgrethe?"

"It was a trap?" Horrified by that revelation, Celiese ran toward the door in an effort to slip passed the despicable brute. "Where's Mylan? Where is my husband?"

"Husband? You fooled him then?" Raktor's face filled with glee. "We may do this again and again, Celiese, as my enemies are many. I may marry you off a hundred times, since it allows me such easy access to my foe's home."

"You coward! What have you done with Mylan?" Celiese slapped the villain's face viciously, but he grabbed her hand and twisted her arm cruelly behind her back to force her down the steep flight of stairs in front of him.

"There is your 'husband,' girl, bound with the other captives. Keep him alive if you can. I plan to demand a high ransom for his return, for him or his body, whichever I have!"

Celiese rushed to the young man's side. His tunic was torn and bloody, but whether the blood was his own or that of his adversaries she could not tell. "Mylan!" She whispered a desperate vow: "I will save you, but you must help me, my dearest."

Mylan opened his pain-filled eyes and hissed a venomous reply. "I'll see you dead first, you traitorous bitch!"

Raktor gave a hearty chuckle as he approached. "Well, Celiese, your husband seems displeased with you for some reason." As he drew back his foot to kick the helpless man, Celiese dove between them, taking the full

force of his vicious blow in her ribs, and she heard the
bones crack with a loud snap as she fainted across
Mylan's lap, the excruciating pain too great for her to
bear.

More than an hour elapsed before a forceful shove
jarred Celiese to consciousness. They had all been taken
aboard Raktor's ship, where she was lying wedged
between Mylan and another prisoner she couldn't name.
They'd not thought to bind her hands and feet as they
had the others. She tried to adjust her position to become
more comfortable, but the pain that shot through her
chest stopped her effort instantly. The sea had grown
rough, the cloud cover low and dense, and a light rain
splashed down upon the huddled group of captives,
making their confinement all the more miserable. Mylan
was asleep or unconscious, Celiese could not tell which,
but she moved slowly, just ahead of the pain, to untie his
feet before she reached for his hands. The guards were
laughing amongst themselves, drunk with beer as well as
with the ease of their surprise victory, and they paid no
attention as she freed her husband and then drew him
into her arms as the storm worsened, sending heavy cas-
cades of water upon them as the graceful ship continued
across the fjord toward Raktor's land.

Lightning burned fierce arcs through the clouds,
illuminating the red dragon emblazoned upon the white
sail seconds before the icy waves again crashed down
upon the ship, this time shearing off the mast and
sending the heavy sail down upon the hapless prisoners.
The next wave covered them with a sudden rush of water
that carried away the debris, and Mylan was swept from

his bride's arms, but she grabbed for the edge of his tunic with a desperate clutch and held on as they were hurled over the side of the ship and were plunged headlong into the storm-ravaged sea. Now fully awake, Mylan grabbed a length of the shattered mast and thrust it into Celiese's hands to keep her afloat in the mounting waves. They drifted together, unseen in the mist as the ship sailed on, her crew straining at the oars to control the vessel through the giant swells of the storm.

Celiese clung to the wood until she was so cold her fingers could no longer grasp, but Mylan reached out to catch her as she slipped away. He drew her back and held her head above the bone-chilling water until he could see nothing but the grim face of death hovering before his eyes.

Drenched by the rain, battered by the waves that had tossed her upon the rock-littered shore, Celiese had never been in such agonizing pain. She retched repeatedly, gagging again and again until all the salt water had poured from her shaking body. She crawled along the jagged shoreline until she found Mylan sprawled upon the sand, blood streaming from a slash above his left eyebrow. But his pulse was strong, and she was elated to find him alive. She pressed her palm against his forehead until the flow of blood had been stemmed, then lay down beside him and drew him close so they might share what little warmth their bodies still possessed. Exhausted by her ordeal, Celiese sank into a deep, dreamless sleep, but even then she did not let her husband go.

The sun broke through the thick gray clouds by late afternoon, and Celiese awoke to find Mylan's amber gaze intent upon her face. He was furious with her still, his anger undisguised, and she pushed herself up slowly into a sitting position while she tried to think of some way to make him understand she was not his enemy.

"What did Raktor call you? You are most certainly not his daughter, Olgrethe." Mylan was glad to see the young woman awaken, as he was filled with questions to which he intended to demand honest answers.

"I am Lady Celiese d' Loganville, a Frenchwoman of noble birth. The Torgvalds slaughtered my parents and kidnapped me five years ago."

"A slave?" Mylan's finely shaped mouth curled into an accusing sneer. "Were you Raktor's mistress?"

"No!" Celiese shouted angrily. She straightened her shoulders proudly, disgusted he'd even suggest such a revolting alliance. She longed to make him understand that her plight was every bit as desperate as his. She'd never forget what she'd suffered at that monster's hands, and she explained in a breathless whisper, "Just as they did in your house, the Torgvalds and the band of rogues who run with them attacked my family before dawn. The fighting was so fierce the bodies of those who had fallen littered each passageway, their innocent blood splattered upon every wall. Raktor himself carried me screaming from my bed, and because he thought me amusing I survived that terrible night." After taking a deep breath Celiese continued, determined to relate the whole disgusting tale now that she had begun. "The Torgvalds camped at the mouth of the Seine for more than a month and used the river to raid ever deeper into my homeland. The single advantage of my youth was that it was an impossibility for me to conceive a child that summer, for I was still a child myself, no matter how often they used me as though I were a woman. In the fall Raktor took me home as a present for Olgrethe, as if I were some exotic pet he'd captured simply to provide entertainment for her." After pausing a moment, Celiese continued in a soft, lilting voice, "I had been very gently raised, Mylan, and provided a far more suitable companion for Olgrethe than I had for Raktor and his vile offspring. I did my best to avoid all contact with those hateful men and they soon forgot me, although the only time I ever felt truly safe in that accursed house was in the summer, when they took to the sea to pursue their bloody thievery. I have been no man's mistress, for that term implies a knowledge of pleasure, and I did not even know such a possibility existed between a man and a woman until I married you."

"Married me!" Mylan scoffed contemptuously. He had listened with rapt attention to her story and found himself thoroughly confused, for she spoke with such obvious conviction that he knew she was either exactly who she claimed to be or the most talented actress ever born. He was inclined to believe the latter and snarled bitterly, "I have heard enough of your ridiculous lies. What did you hope to gain by telling me that pathetic tale? That the Torgvalds would rape children is no surprise, but how can you expect me to believe you are French?" Mylan laced his fingers in Celiese's tangled curls to draw her near. "Although I have no interest in setting foot upon the shores of France, I have seen enough of your countrymen to know they are dark, the women petite. You, however, are tall and fair, obviously one of our own, most probably one of Raktor's many bastards! Your blood is no more French than mine!"

Celiese yanked her hair from his grasp as she hastened to argue. "You are the one speaking lies—for I know who I am! You may have seen French peasants, poor country folk brought here as slaves to work the farms, but you know nothing of the d'Loganvilles and how we look!"

Mylan was astonished by her show of spirit, for no woman, least of all a slave, had ever dared raise her voice to him. "You have more courage than the French king, for it is said Charles will soon give away a portion of his land as appeasement, since Vikings cannot be defeated by so meager a defense as he is able to raise!"

"Never! The King of France would never be so weak as that. He would not give pirates so much as an inch of soil in the name of peace!" Celiese found his arguments as ridiculous as he found hers, and could not believe they could possibly be true.

Mylan sat back and stared at the bedraggled young woman before him. She had fared no better than he on their perilous voyage, but he found her beauty not in the least diminished by her disheveled state, and it was with considerable difficulty that he returned to their present discussion. "The king will soon give the land to one of my countrymen, a Dane by the name of Hrolf, and whether or not you believe it will happen does not matter, for it surely will. Now as to your tale, if any of what you say were true about how badly Raktor had mistreated you, you would have warned me last night to save me and my family from the same gruesome fate yours suffered. Your silence shows clearly where your loyalty lies."

Celiese clenched her fists in frustration as she responded with an anguished plea, "Had I known he planned an attack, I would have told you when first we met. I would have warned you immediately and helped you in every way I could, but I knew nothing of his evil plot. I was never told what was planned, and I am as shocked as you are by what has happened."

Realizing further argument would be pointless when she was being so obstinate, Mylan rose slowly to his feet. After stretching to work off his stiffness, he looked down at Celiese. "Can you rise, are you able to walk? We can prove nothing here, and I have wasted enough time listening to your endless lies."

Celiese waited for his hand, but he did not offer it, and when she tried to stand alone she could not. Her side was too sore, and she slipped back upon the damp sand, shaking with the sharpness of the pain her exertions had brought.

Mylan swore in a long string of bitter oaths, damning Raktor to the bitterest of fates. "Why did you let him kick you? That was lunacy, and now you're too badly hurt to be of any help to me. What possessed you to be so foolish?"

"He meant to kick *you*!" Celiese's pretty green eyes filled with disbelief. Her action to protect him had been instinctive. Why did he not understand that her devotion to him was real?

"So what? I am a grown man, and I do not need the protection of some lying female slave! That won't make up for your treachery. Had you wanted to help me you would have warned me of Raktor's true plans instead of deceiving me as you did." Mylan's expression was bitter. She was a rare beauty, but he was thoroughly disgusted with himself for falling so swiftly under her spell. It was a mistake he'd not make again, not ever.

"But I knew nothing of Raktor's scheme!" Celiese insisted once again, imploring him to believe her.

"You knew you were not Olgrethe! If nothing else, you knew that! Now cease your lying or I will kick you myself!" Mylan stepped forward, clearly ready to make good on his threat if she did not obey him.

Celiese stared coldly at the hostile young man. How could he not believe her after the night they had shared? Did he truly think she could have returned his affection so joyously if she had wished him dead? The truth was so plain she did not understand why he did not see it. Hiding her anger, since displaying it was futile when he was in so obnoxious a mood, she asked calmly, "If you will please help me up, I can walk."

"I should leave you here to fend for yourself after what you've done to me!" Mylan took a few steps away, then turned back. "Come, dear wife, I will help you stand, but if you cannot keep up with me I will leave you behind." Mylan reached down to lift her, but drew back when Celiese cried out in pain.

"Just give me your hand, do not touch me again." Celiese bit her lip in an effort to stifle the sob that came to her lips.

"Here then!" Mylan extended his right hand and waited as Celiese took a deep breath and grasping his outstretched arm rose unsteadily to her feet. But she took no more than two halting steps before she fainted, collapsing

70

in the wet sand at his feet.

Mylan lifted his gaze to the heavens to implore the aid of the gods, but he knew they would be uninterested in the fate of a slave, no matter how lovely she might be. He cursed his own luck that continued to run so swiftly to tragedy, and, scooping up the slender girl in his arms, he walked slowly down the beach in search of some shelter before the gathering clouds could again drench them to the skin with freezing rain.

The cave was small, no more than an identation in the rocks, but they were protected from the chill of the cold wind as they huddled inside. Celiese was grateful Mylan had not left her, but thought it wise not to inquire into the reason for his kindness.

"You are the most worthless of slaves, Celiese, more trouble than help!" Mylan was still scowling angrily, his mood not improved by the good fortune of finding shelter.

"Am I no longer your wife?" He seemed to use the words slave and wife interchangeably, but she could not believe he regarded her as a servant when she lay so lovingly cradled in his warm embrace. His hands were light upon her arms, his touch gentle still.

"It was Olgrethe I thought I'd married, to seal a treaty Raktor had no intention of honoring! How could you have expected to be my wife when you knew it was unlikely I'd survive our wedding night?" Mylan snarled impatiently, caring little for her reply.

Celiese sighed softly, "There is no way for me to prove my innocence if you will not accept my word. Raktor himself will never tell you the truth, but I did not know what treacherous scheme was behind his desire to switch me for Olgrethe.''

Mylan continued, his voice no less bitter, ''Even had he meant to honor his promise to my father, would he have sent her?''

Celiese licked her lips slowly, considering how best to answer that question, and chose the truth. ''He would have sent her, but it would have been I who arrived. Olgrethe and I had already planned to trade places, for I wanted to come to you and she did not.''

Mylan was astonished by her candor, ''So you admit you are a liar, as capable of tricking me as Raktor was?''

Again Celiese chose her words carefully. ''It was Olgrethe herself who first suggested the substitution, for there is such slight difference between us she knew you would be fooled. She has found no man she has met to be to her liking and was certain one who had not been seen in two years must have something truly horrible to hide. I thought only that I would be free if I married you. I have no hope of ever returning to my home, for all who I loved are dead, and it would be pointless for me to return to live alone amid so many painful memories. I knew you would not be displeased with my appearance, and I hoped you would be kind, no matter how severely you'd been injured by the bear's attack.''

''You are a slave, Celiese, how could you have believed I would accept such a woman as my wife?'' Mylan scoffed at the ridiculousness of that notion.

Celiese straightened her shoulders proudly as she argued. ''It is not uncommon for a Viking to marry a former slave, but *I* am the one who has married beneath my station, Mylan, not you. Had Raktor not murdered my family and stolen me I would now be the bride of a prince, for my father would have accepted no less for me. He most certainly would never have given me to a pirate such as you!"

Mylan laughed out loud, despite the severity of their situation. "Then we are both equally unhappy, Celiese, for I want no slave for a bride and you want no pirate for a husband." He continued to shake his head as he chuckled, "I am many things, but no pirate."

"And I am no slave!" Celiese insisted defiantly, her clear, sweet voice ringing with the unmistakable knell of truth.

After a moment's pause Mylan asked pointedly, "Surely there is one great difference between you and Olgrethe. Did you think me so great a fool I would not realize you were not a virgin? Not even a French prince would be that stupid."

"I thought you would be like Raktor's sons, oafs ruled by their own insatiable lusts, and to fool a man such as they would not have been difficult," Celiese pointed out logically.

"First you said you hoped I would be kind, and now that you thought I would be a drunken fool! You are a very poor liar, Celiese, for you cannot keep your stories straight. You would be wise to tell me the truth from now on, if you are even capable of it."

Celiese looked away, hurt again by his lack of sympathy. "I had both hopes and fears, Mylan, but those contradictions are not lies."

Surprisingly, Mylan tightened his embrace, shielding

her body with his own as a fresh gust of wind swept into the small cave. "We will have to find better shelter tomorrow, and something to eat. We are already too weak to survive much longer without food and fresh water."

Celiese was as amazed by his protective gesture as she was that his plans for survival seemed to include her, and she smiled as she looked up at him. "Have you any idea where we might be? Are we on your side of the fjord, or Raktor's?"

Mylan's curious glance swept her face slowly. "Where do you wish to be?"

Celiese's level gaze met his and held it. "I have no desire ever to return to Raktor's home, although Olgrethe was always kind to me. You say you do not want me, and there is no way I can reach France. I am lost and alone no matter where I am, Mylan, my future bleak no matter in which direction the storm has tossed us."

Mylan pointed to the mouth of the small cave. "The sun, when I could see it, was to our right, therefore we are on Raktor's side, but how close we are to his home I cannot say. We may be far from his docks, or they may be just around the next bend. In the morning I will go out and see what I can find." Mylan's voice softened as he explained, "That is what I do best, Celiese. I prefer exploring new lands to pillaging the known world."

Encouraged by his tender tone as well as his words, Celiese offered a plan. "We could steal one of Raktor's ships. They are not all as large as the Dragon, and perhaps there is one we could sail back to your home."

Mylan found her suggestion ludicrous. "I thought you were a lady's maid, not a mariner. Do you even know how to sail, no matter what size the vessel?"

Celiese blushed under his sarcastic teasing, but did not give in. "No, but I could help you. You could tell me what to do."

"Why would you wish to help me?" Mylan asked skeptically.

"I did not understand all the words of the ceremony yesterday, but is a Viking's wife not expected to assist her husband in every way possible?"

"That ceremony was a farce! I've been tricked most cruelly, Celiese. I am not your husband; you are a slave, and I will sell you at my first opportunity. You will command a high price, and I mean to receive it, although that won't begin to repay the wrong you've done me."

"I will leave you now then, go back into the sea to drown, since I have no future worth living!" Celiese attempted to rise, but Mylan gripped her narrow waist firmly to pull her back down beside him.

That Celiese was so spirited a creature continually amazed Mylan, but he found her far too fascinating to lose in so foolish a fashion. He kissed her cheek lightly before his lips found hers, and when she returned his kiss with an affection he found impossible to resist he drew away, sighing sadly. "If only it could have been real, Celiese, why couldn't you have really been my wife?"

Surprised by his suddenly subdued mood as well as by his unexpected kiss, Celiese whispered softly, then held her breath as his fingertips began to tease the tip of her breast. "I am really your wife, Mylan. Why do you insist I am not when we found such perfect happiness together?" The damp folds of her tattered dress offered little barrier to his touch, and the thrill was the same, a rush of warmth that began in her loins and spread the length of her chilled limbs. She drew him into her arms, covered his face with sweet kisses as his hands slipped beneath her gown. He knew her body well now, and his tantalizing caress grew more bold until she was lost again upon the tide of his cresting passion. She clung to him, no longer fearing his strength, for he gave such delicious pleasure before taking his own that she would never cease to adore him. Her sweet affection enveloped him in love, flooding his senses with a pleasure so deep he could not release her but kept her clasped in his embrace until the pale light of dawn entered their rocky confines, bringing the harsh reality of their situation into sharp focus, and the magic of the night receded to become no more than a lovely memory.

Mylan's lips brushed the ugly purple bruise that marred the creamy skin of Celiese's left side. "This is far worse than I had feared. Surely your ribs are broken, and there is nothing I can do to help you here." His tone was as tender as his kiss, smooth and warm, for he found her delicate body so delightful he did not want to see her come to any harm.

"The pain is not so intense today, a few broken ribs will not kill me." Celiese ran her fingertips through his thick curls to draw him near as his lips again caressed her breast in a lingering kiss. She longed to ask if he still meant to send her away, but could not bear to hear his reply. He filled her body so completely with his love, but had she still failed to move his heart? She held him tenderly in her arms and hoped he would speak of love, but he continued to savor her luscious curves without offering the slightest of compliments or promises, and when at last he drew away his mind was on far more practical matters.

"Here is your dress; there is little left of it, but put it on quickly." He watched closely as Celiese slipped on the pale garment, then took her hands to lead her out through the entrance of the cave. "If I climb the bluff just ahead I may be able to see. I know my own coastline well, but not this one, although I hope to see something that will help me establish our location."

"Be careful, Mylan, the way is steep and you might fall," Celiese cautioned anxiously.

Her comment brought a disapproving frown to Mylan's brow, "I will not fall. If I am no longer as agile as a spider, my leg will still hold up for that short climb. Do not tire yourself with needless worry about me."

"I had forgotten your injuries, I meant only for you to take care," Celiese replied softly, she found his height and strength so reassuring that she had forgotten his scars covered injuries not fully healed.

Mylan turned away without speaking, then did indeed go up the rocky incline above them with the ease he'd promised. But when he disappeared from view over the top Celiese was not at all certain he would want to take the trouble to come back for her. She couldn't climb unassisted, and for as far as she could see the shore was littered with rocks, making the walk along even the level terrain treacherous. She was afraid she'd have to remain where she was no matter where Mylan went. She rubbed her arms to ward off the chill as she gazed out at the water. The sea had grown calm again, but how could they catch any fish with no implements? They had not even a knife to fashion a spear if they could find a piece of wood.

When Mylan reappeared he scrambled down the rocks and ran to her side, his gait uneven but swift. "Come with me. There is a guard nearby—if you will distract him I can seize his sword."

"Distract him?" Celiese moved away from Mylan's grasp. "I can imagine how you wish me to accomplish that! What benefit will a sword be to us when Raktor sends a squad of twenty men to find the one who is missing?"

Mylan's amber eyes widened in astonishment. "The man let you plan his strategy for raids, did he? You are an expert on how to fight as well as making love? Why did you not kill me yourself when you had the chance, if you are so clever a warrior?"

Celiese shuddered at that gruesome query. "I am no expert on anything other than survival, Mylan, but think, if we kill one man and steal his sword how have we gotten any closer to your home? All we will have done is alerted Raktor to our presence!"

Mylan sat down, folded his arms across his knees, and glared out at the sea. "Raktor has warriors aplenty, and I have but one beautiful woman who refuses to help me disarm a man so I might have a weapon!"

"I would seduce Raktor's entire force if it would help you, Mylan, but it would not! If he has guards posted he must be expecting some retaliation for the attack upon your home. I didn't know the prisoners—whom did he take and whom were left behind who might come to our rescue—" Celiese knelt down beside her husband and waited patiently while he sat silently considering her question for several minutes before replying.

"Two of my brothers are away, gone trading to Kaupang. My father was wounded, but how severely I do not know. You met Erik, at sixteen he is not half the man I was at his age. He enjoys playing the jester to amuse us more than anything else, but he may be able to command such an expedition if my father is able to give him assistance."

"Will your brothers be home soon?" Celiese pushed her hair away from her face, but the breeze tossed her curls carelessly about, blocking her vision once again.

"No, not for weeks. They were journeying north and may be delayed time and again before they return. They knew nothing of the plans for our wedding before they left and have no reason to return home quickly."

Knowing that time was their enemy, Celiese hastened to warn him. "Mylan, the Dragon was badly damaged by the storm. It is Raktor's pride and he will make haste to repair it. That will mean activity on his docks, as he will lose no time in restoring his largest vessel to full use. The summer is nearly here, and he never remains at home. Surely this year will be no exception."

Mylan glanced at the lovely young woman, his expression filled with frustration. "If you think of any more problems, Celiese, I shall simply strangle you myself and swim home!"

Ignoring his threat, Celiese continued, "I meant only that we have no time to waste waiting for others to come for us. Perhaps we should break into the house tonight, free your kinsmen and murder all of Raktor's sons in their beds. Would you prefer that plan?"

"How can I devise any sort of plan when I have only a traitor to help me?" Mylan responded bitterly.

Shocked by that cruel insult, Celiese stood up and backed away. "Had Raktor raised his sword against you rather than his foot, I would still have blocked his way, and you see a traitor when you look at me? I am better off in the sea than married to a husband such as you!"

"I am not your husband!" The handsome man shouted defiantly, his light eyes blazing with a furious gleam as he denied her again.

Celiese turned and walked into the water. Her dress was wet clear past her knees when Mylan realized she would not turn back. He leapt to his feet and overtook her swiftly, sweeping her up into his arms. "Fool! I will not let you drown, not when you are the only help I have! Now come back and tell me how we might enter Raktor's house undetected."

Celiese leaned her head against Mylan's broad chest as he carried her ashore. When he placed her feet on the sand she did not move from his embrace but stayed close. "If you will help me up the bluff I will go to Raktor and tell him you drowned. Tonight when everyone is sleeping I will unlock the side door on the north and let you in. We can free your kinsmen and capture Raktor and his sons before they know the house has been entered. Your men are few, but we will have the advantage of surprise on our side and with Raktor taken prisoner his warriors will not fight. They are all cowards, without any spirit of their own."

Mylan's amber eyes searched Celiese's delicate features slowly as she outlined her plan, but he could detect no trace of deceit in her expression. She seemed serious and determined, but still he was unsure, "You expect me to trust you after what has happened?"

"You shall have to trust me, for there is no one else here to help you." Celiese could understand his hesitation. None of her story made any sense, no matter how true it all was. She waited, hoping only that he felt for her the deepening affection she could not deny she felt for him.

"What shall we do with Olgrethe? Is she truly as beautiful as all say?"

Celiese did not let her disappointment show in her eyes, but his question brought real pain, an anguish as deep as any she'd ever known. "Yes, and since you insist we are not married perhaps you will decide to take her as your wife. She will not disappoint you as I have."

With a rueful laugh Mylan drew Celiese close to his heart and hugged her warmly. "Disappointment does not begin to describe my torment, but we have no time to discuss emotions, Celiese. If we are going to attempt this deed we must begin without delay."

"Yes, that is true." Celiese stepped back from his arms and smiled bravely. "You will have to help me climb to the top of the bluff."

"You are not frightened?" Mylan took her arm as they moved across the sand.

"Yes, I am terrified, but I will not fail you," the pretty blonde vowed confidently.

81

"Celiese." Mylan spoke her name in a hoarse whisper as he drew her back into his arms. This time his passion was no longer tender, but violent as he crushed her slender body against his own. His deep kiss left her shaking in his embrace, her lips bruised by the savage force of his kiss. "You dare not fail me again, Celiese, or I will see you join Raktor upon his funeral pyre. Should you choose to serve him again rather than me you will continue to serve him in Valhalla!"

Celiese shook her head slowly, a sly smile coming to her lips. She knew the Danes comprised only one group of the men known as Vikings, but she found his beliefs as well as his threat ridiculous. "Your custom of sacrificing the living to serve the dead is foolish, Mylan, for I am Christian and would not willingly join Raktor in anything, most especially not your battle-filled vision of eternity. If you have so little faith in me, kill me now and be done with it. It will save me the pain of climbing this steep embankment, at least." Her defiant gaze dared him to end her life as he had threatened, but she stood calmly, her fear of him obviously slight.

Mylan's fiery gaze did not soften, for no matter how much he admired her bravery, he did not trust her one bit. "I will not destroy the only help I have, no matter how little faith I might have in you. Now let us cease this argument and hurry. We will have time enough to talk after I have captured Raktor."

Celiese did not speak again until she called to the man standing guard. Her voice startled him so badly he wheeled, sword drawn, ready to strike her down. Then he recognized her and ran forward. "We thought you had drowned—how have you survived?"

"I awoke on the sand after the storm, but I was too weak to climb the cliff until I had rested. Help me reach the house please, for my step is still unsteady, and I must tell Raktor that Aldred's son is dead."

Seeing a chance to gain favor with the powerful Viking, the man left his post to escort Celiese to her home, and Mylan crossed the deserted terrain swiftly to find a vantage point hidden among the thick stand of trees on the north side of the dwelling. His wait would be a tedious one, but he hoped it would not be futile.

Raktor leapt to his feet as Celiese entered the sun-drenched hall. "I thought we had lost you both, Celiese." He reached out and drew the trembling young woman near. "What of Mylan, do you have news of his fate?"

Celiese's eyes filled with tears at the memory of their ordeal and what was yet to come. Her downcast expression was most convincing in its sorrow. "We were together for only a short while. When he could no longer cling to the piece of mast we'd grabbed I tried to save him but could not. He is dead, drowned."

Raktor nodded as she spoke, considering her narrative carefully before he summoned another of his warriors. "Take this woman and tie her up with the other prisoners. They will all leave for Kaupang at nightfall. You have returned just in time to meet your destiny, my beauty. I am selling you, for I can no longer trust you, not even to serve my daughter."

"After I have been so loyal to her all these years?"

Celiese shouted angrily, arguing heatedly with the hateful man. Yet the fear that clutched her heart was overpowering. If she were gone Mylan would not know. He would come and find the door locked and think only that she had betrayed him! She screamed and tried to slip past the burly man who'd been ordered to remove her, but he only laughed as he swung his fist into the side of her head, sending her sprawling across the stone floor, where he scooped her up and tossed her limp body over his shoulder as if she were no more precious than a sack of grain.

Chapter Five

Celiese fought the man in every way possible, biting and kicking fiercely as he bound her wrists and ankles, but he paid scant heed to her heated protests at the injustice of her treatment and tossed her roughly into the room with the other captives. They all were bound as firmly as she was—to her advantage, as they turned hate-filled stares in her direction. Several started to complain.

One young man nudged another. "Look what Raktor has thrown away, is that not the woman who posed as Mylan's bride?"

"Aye, that is the slut." Clearing his throat so he could spit on her, the man realized just in time that their quarters were too confined for such a display not to splatter his friends as well, and he had to swallow rather than carry out his insulting gesture.

Celiese could not see if the guard had remained outside the door but dropped her voice to a whisper in case he might be listening. "I am Mylan's wife, truly I am. Why else would Raktor have decided to sell me too? He believes Mylan to be dead—but he is alive, waiting now to set us all free."

Celiese's words were met with loud jeers and rude insults from the prisoners, for none thought her words worth hearing. She counted quickly, there were twenty-six men but only three other women, pretty young girls who were doubtless slaves as she had been. "Will none of you help me? If we work together we can get free and overpower the guards when next they come!" She pleaded with them just as she'd argued with her husband, exhorting them to attempt an escape she was certain would succeed if they but worked to help each other. Unlike Mylan, this surly group would not listen to her plan. Every face turned away with a disgusted sneer, and she was left with no hope of ever seeing her dear husband again.

When the guards next returned they were heavily armed, ruffians who bullied the captives as they led them to the docks, where they divided them into two groups. From what Celiese could discern the other group were all warriors, Mylan's kin who'd come to attend the wedding, while she was pushed toward the captured slaves. In addition to the three women, there were seven men, two barely out of their teens, obviously fieldhands who'd somehow been caught during the fighting. She doubted they would be able to raise any sort of resistance that would enable them to escape. She looked back toward the house, praying Mylan would see her and understand what had happened, but it was nearly dusk and the visibility was poor, and she saw no sign he might be observing their departure. She was shoved into one of the Dragon's sister ships, a smaller but no less sleek vessel named the

Elk of the Sea, and left huddled with the three other girls
to endure a miserable journey that seemed to have no end.
The prisoners had all been fed before she had joined
them, and she was given nothing to eat when she asked
the guards for food. They only laughed at her and threatened to beat her senseless unless she were still. Silenced
Celiese could barely control her temper, for she knew
Mylan would rescue his kinsman somehow, but would
any of those hostile men tell him where she had been
taken? If she were sold more than once would he ever be
able to find her? More frightening still, would he even
want to try? By the time she finally fell into an exhausted
sleep she no longer cared what dreadful fate awaited her,
for if she'd lost Mylan the best part of her life was already
over.

Kaupang was a heavily trafficked commercial port, the
center of Viking trade, and by the time Raktor's ship
reached the city Celiese had confirmed her worst fears.
None of Mylan's family was on board. The people who'd
been sent to be sold had all been slaves in Aldred's home,
household servants and farmhands caught up in the net
thrown out the night of the wedding. She had no hope
anyone would come to rescue them now, for she overheard one of the guards saying all of Aldred's kin had
been taken only a short distance by ship and then
marched inland to be held for ransom, and she knew by
the time Mylan had secured their release her trail would
be impossible to follow. Her three female companions
cried pitifully at the thought of being separated after
several years of friendship, but they did no more than
spit upon her as they left the ship. The sorry group was

marched to the slave market where the slavemaster examined them thoroughly as if they were prize horses about to be traded for untold wealth rather than a bedraggled group of unfortunate servants who could be expected to bring little in the way of profit. Celiese's once beautiful silk gown was no more than rags, her superb figure now far too thin, but the sharp-eyed man stopped before her, shocked by her defiant stare.

"I am the wife of the Dane, Mylan, eldest son of Aldred Vandahl. If you but send him a message that I am here he will come for me and pay you any price for my safe return." Celiese had no hope that that were true, but any tactic that would stall her sale at a public auction was one she would attempt. "He will buy all of us at twice what others would pay. You must send for him at once."

The wiry old man raked his fingertip down Celiese's sunburned cheek, then tore off the remnants of her wedding dress with one swift tug so he could look at her more closely. He walked around her slowly, eyeing her reddened skin with disgust before he jabbed his bony fingers into her bruised side. "I have heard of the man, but how could Mylan's wife have come to such a sorry state?"

"I was kidnapped and beaten, but if you will but let my husband know where I might be found he will reward you well, for he loves me dearly." Celiese looked the man straight in the eye and made no effort to hide her nakedness, but her hopes for rescue were dashed when the three girls with her began to call her foul names, scoffed at her story, and said such vile things about her that the slavemaster gave her a rude shove and tossed her back her ragged dress.

"I will not trouble Mylan about you, for I know him to be a serious man who would not be amused by such a ridiculous tale." Surveying the lot of them he exclaimed sadly, "You are as poor a group of slaves as I have ever been forced to sell, but perhaps my wife can scrub you up so you will bring a fair price." He gestured toward a billowy figure in the corner and she came forward to offer her opinions, which were no better than his.

"Sell them tomorrow with the others we've gathered, they are scrawny enough as it is and I do not wish to feed them until they grow fat!" The hag sucked what few teeth she had remaining in her head and turned away, leading the group into the rude shelter that served as the quarters for the slaves being held for sale.

Celiese nearly fell asleep in the steaming tub, the warm water bringing a relaxing comfort she'd almost forgotten, but before she could enjoy more than a few seconds' pleasure the nasty old woman began to scrub her hair with a coarse-bristled brush. She cried out in pain and pleaded with her to stop, but that did not deter the unsympathetic creature from using her most diligent efforts to wash her clean. The tunic she was given was much too short, but Celiese was dreadfully afraid women were displayed nude before buyers and that worry kept her from eating any of the meager meal they were served for supper. Her female companions were varied, all as unhappy as she, but none spoke her native tongue nor appeared friendly, and the three girls from Aldred's home continued their spiteful insults for half the night, complaining to everyone how she had brought ruin upon their home.

At dawn Celiese vowed to endure whatever public humiliation she had to suffer with every bit of dignity she had left. In spite of the slavemaster's unkind words he apparently thought her worth a handsome price and kept her back until all the others had been sold. The sun was high overhead when she was brought out, and as she had feared she was quickly stripped naked, but she reminded herself as she always did that her blood was as fine as that of a princess and her appearance should be regal as well. She held her head proudly and scanned the crowd with a defiant stare, silently insisting the assembled group respect her. Her fiery emerald gaze had the same effect that day as it had had on the Torgvalds, and more than one man turned away, knowing he lacked both the skill and strength to tame such a vibrant beauty.

When a man standing just to her left spoke up she turned, startled by something in his voice. He was tall and well built, and his amber eyes could belong to only one family. Celiese whispered quickly while his attention was focused upon her face, "I am your brother's wife, Mylan's wife! Do not let one of the others buy me!"

The handsome young man gasped in astonishment, then called to the auctioneer, "Who is this woman?"

The old man smiled broadly, delighted to see the well-dressed and obviously wealthy man display such interest in the striking blonde. "What does her name matter? You may call her whatever you choose. She was a slave in the house of Raktor, that he wants her no more is your good fortune. Now what is your bid?"

"A former slave of the Torgvalds cannot possibly be

my brother's wife!" Laughing, the man folded his muscular arms across his broad chest and regarded Celiese's elegant figure with an appreciative glance.

"It is the truth!" Celiese insisted, incensed he did not believe her.

"My brother is not married, so how could you be his wife?"

Exasperated, Celiese attempted to prove she knew the man at least. "I do not know your name, only that you and your brother are here trading. Mylan is the eldest, while Erik, your younger brother, is sixteen. You have your mother's eyes, her name is Thulyn." Turning as she heard another man offer a generous bid, she urged him to help her. "If you are so foolish as to let another man buy me, Mylan will be furious with you! You can sell me yourself if what I say is not the truth, but what if it is?"

Not pleased by her taunts, the amber-eyed man waited a long moment before tossing a bag of gold at the auctioneer's feet. He then leapt up onto the raised platform where Celiese stood and wrapped his cloak around her shoulders. "There has been some mistake, this woman should never have been offered for sale, but my purse contains more than enough to cover any bid you could have hoped to receive." Not waiting for an argument from the elderly man, he picked up Celiese, carried her across the square and down a narrow street, laughing all the way at her keen embarrassment, for no matter how tightly she clutched his cloak to her breasts it continued to fall open, displaying her nakedness to all who passed by. When he reached his inn he took her to his room, where his brother answered his knock and exclaimed in horror.

"Andrick! What have you done now? You know mother will never permit you to keep such a woman!"

"Oh, yes, she will." Andrick placed Celiese upon her feet as he introduced her. "May I present our brother's wife, who somehow had the great misfortune to be put up for sale at the slave market this morning."

Celiese looked quickly from one man to the other. Mylan had not mentioned that these two brothers of his were twins, but clearly they were. Their hair, while blond, was not as fair as his, nor their features so finely carved. While they were a handsome pair they were clearly nothing alike in temperament, for while Andrick appeared to be amused, his twin clearly was not.

"What lie is that? Mylan does not even leave his farm—he'd not go seeking a wife for any reason!" Appalled, the young man snarled his question.

Not dismayed, Andrick proceeded with his introduction. "This is Hagen, and let me warn you now, dear lady, this is his usual mood. Had he seen you as I did he would have walked off without replying to your plea for assistance. Perhaps this morning was a more fortuitous one for you than you had imagined."

"Fortuitous indeed!" Celiese exclaimed, suddenly wondering if she were any better off than she had been. Taking a deep breath, she hastened to explain how she'd come to be in Kaupang and why it was imperative they return to Danish shores at once. She wanted to leave nothing to their imaginations, so she described the horrors she and Mylan had suffered in vivid detail, but she feared she was rambling in her narrative, telling her tale in too disorganized a fashion to be understood. But she was nearly faint from hunger and sick with despair. She was certain she was making no sense at all when Hagen interrupted her.

"Describe my brother's room to me, if you can. If you were married at our home as you claim, that should be a simple matter for you." His sneer made it plain he thought her incapable of producing such a description.

"His room is large, at the top of a narrow flight of stairs. The fireplace is opposite his bed, there is a row of windows, and although it was late at night when I was there he told me they faced the sea." She'd had far too much on her mind to notice the view at dawn, but hoped Mylan had not been teasing her, since Hagen seemed to regard his question as an important test.

Andrick laughed at her comment. "Did he now?" He glanced at his sullen twin and nodded. "We will take you back with us, because your tale is amusing, but if it is no more than a cleverly woven lie I'll warn you now that you will be very sorry."

"Did you not recognize any of the others from your household? There were others, both men and women, who were sold before I was." Celiese was surprised he'd not seen them, for their very presence in Kaupang would prove her point.

Andrick shook his head. "No, I had just happened by, we have finished our business here and are preparing to sail. I wanted to purchase no slaves, but something made me stop when they brought you out. The sparkle of the sunlight upon your hair perhaps, or—"

"You needn't say it!" Celiese cautioned him sternly.

"Mylan will be angry enough without your telling him you have seen me naked!"

"Yes, that is true. If by some strange happenstance you are actually Mylan's bride, his anger should be considerable." When Hagen offered no objection Andrick continued, "We had planned to leave in a day or two, but now we'll sail on the morning tide, as this will be worth rushing home to confront. I cannot believe a word you've said is true, not that Mylan would consent to any marriage, nor that even a villain so foul as Raktor would stoop to such treachery as you have described."

Exhausted and having no hope of explaining anything more coherently than she already had, Celiese yawned sleepily. "May I please go to bed?" Tossing Andrick's long cloak aside, she climbed into the nearest bed, pulled the covers up to her chin and was sound asleep before either of the astonished brothers could reply.

It was late afternoon when Hagen shook Celiese's shoulder to awaken her. "I've found all the others, and it was well worth the expense to hear what they had to say about you!" His menacing expression left little doubt that the people from his home had continued to blame her for their misfortune.

Celiese rubbed her eyes, trying unsuccessfully to make them stop hurting, but she ached all over, and the few hours she'd rested hadn't been enough to heal her many bruises. "I know exactly what they said. None believes in my innocence, but Mylan knows the truth, and he is the only one you must ask."

"I must?" the amber-eyed man snarled angrily at the sleepy blonde.

"Hagen, there will be time enough to question this young woman aboard our ship, let's not waste another moment in so futile an argument." Andrick stepped forward to end the bitter confrontation he knew was coming, for Hagen's fierce temper was not one he wished to see provoked needlessly. "We cannot delay now we know what has happened at home in our absence. We are sailing on the evening tide, and you must be ready to come with us."

Celiese looked up at the well-built brothers, uncertain as to what they expected her to do to prepare for such a journey. "As you know, I have no clothing, nothing at all. How am I to make my way to the docks?"

Andrick turned away briefly, then returned with a pale yellow gown, which he laid in her hands. "This is all I could find. Even if it does lot fit well, it will still far surpass my cloak as a garment."

"Why, this is lovely!" Celiese smiled widely as she thanked him. "You have been as good to me as if you were my own brother rather than Mylan's. I did not know such good men even lived in your land until I met your family."

Hagen frowned impatiently, certain he'd done nothing to deserve such a compliment, but when Andrick took his arm he turned around too in order to give Celiese some privacy in which to dress. "Did you think of shoes for the woman, or a cloak? It will be cold aboard our vessel. She will become too easily chilled and if she falls ill she will be an even greater burden to us all!"

Laughing, Andrick explained to Celiese, "You must ignore Hagen's rudeness, for clearly he is as concerned about your welfare as I am." He had to duck then to avoid a fist thrown in his direction, but he was light on his feet, and Hagen had had no real intention of harming him.

Alarmed by the roughness of their play, Celiese pulled the pretty gown over her head and secured the brooches that fastened the garment at the shoulders. "I will not need shoes, nor a cloak. Now let us hurry, for Mylan needs your help desperately, and I do not want to delay your departure if it can be hastened."

Andrick grinned at her spirit and reached out to take her hand. "I did not even think of shoes, but you are welcome to wear my cloak again." He picked up the soft brown cape from the bed where she'd dropped it and draped it over her shoulders before leading her toward the door. "You bring our belongings, Hagen, and I will see to Celiese's safety." Considering he had the best of that bargain, Andrick hurried the young woman through the door before his twin could offer an alternate plan. When they reached the dock where their merchant vessel lay at anchor, Celiese was greeted by insolent stares and coarse insults from the group of servants Hagen had reassembled. Neither man had expected such outrageous behavior from their slaves, nor would they tolerate it either.

"I do not want to hear another voice raised against this woman. I am content to let Mylan settle this dispute with his wife himself, and if there are any of you who would like to argue that matter with me, then step forward and say so now!" Andrick moved in front of Celiese, shielding her slender body from any attack, verbal or physical, but she slipped around him to confront the hostile group herself.

"You need not thank me for telling Aldrick and Hagen of your plight, since you undoubtedly have already expressed your gratitude to them for rescuing you from owners who could not possibly have been so kind as they!"

Amused by her spirited taunt, Andrick laughed loudly and gave Celiese a warm hug. "Come, let us begin this journey, for it can not end too swiftly to please me." He joined his brother in the last-minute preparations to sail, while Celiese stayed close by his side, unwilling to join the huddled crowd in the bow when she knew how greatly they despised her.

Celiese leaned against the rail near where Andrick stood holding the tiller and let the breeze blow through her long hair as if she were the most carefree of passengers, as the heavily laden ship left port on the rising tide. When Hagen relieved him, Andrick stepped up to her side, and she turned to thank him again. "I am as desperate to see this voyage end as you must be, Andrick, but I want to thank you again for not believing the worst of me, for I do not deserve the abuse your servants seem to delight in hurling at me."

Andrick had found the lithe blonde so sincere in all she said that he could not bring himself to believe his brother would rebuke her for her part in Raktor's deceit. "I am glad you could so readily see that our family is unlike the Torgvalds. We are hunters and traders, we do not raid your homeland as they often do. Mylan is a tireless hunter and explorer. I doubt he will ever be content as long as there is the prospect of new lands to discover, but he finds the bargaining we enjoy a tedious bore. He is adept at the excitement of adventure, while we are the ones considered best at shrewd trading."

Celiese found the charming young man's company most welcome and hoped he truly liked her, for she knew she would need all the help she could possibly gather to win Mylan's favor when next she saw him. "You do believe me, don't you, Andrick? I would never betray my husband nor allow him to suffer the smallest harm if I had any way to stop it. You have been so sympathetic and kind, but I can tell Hagen does not trust me, and I am greatly worried about what will happen when we reach your home."

Andrick tried to reassure her. He knew his brother had too quick a temper, but often when he had time to reflect more thoroughly he chose the right side to an argument. "Hagen is worried, as am I. It is his concern for our family that makes him so irritable, but do not judge him too harshly. Perhaps Raktor knew we were away when he agreed to my father's offer of a marriage between our families, but when we return home we will be swift to avenge this wrong, if Mylan has not already done so."

Celiese shuddered at his confidently voiced vow. "I cannot bear to think of any of you risking your lives now. Raktor's kin are not worth your trouble to kill, and I beg you to turn away from revenge, for you may not be able to escape harm yourself and I would always feel I was to blame."

Andrick shook his head as he disagreed firmly, "You must leave this matter for us to settle, Celiese, and do not waste another moment fearing for our safety, for we are all men who learned at an early age how to look after ourselves." Andrick continued to speak in a confident manner until he was certain Celiese believed him, and as soon as she had eaten and was resting comfortably he took Hagen aside to begin making their plans for an attack Raktor and his clan would never forget.

The Vandahl brothers sailed home far more swiftly than the men who had manned Raktor's ship which had carried Celiese and the others to Kaupang. She marveled at their skill in commanding their craft and wondered if Mylan possessed the same talent upon the seas. His name rang in her heart and echoed in her mind, but she was frightened for him still, despite Andrick's constant reassurance that he would see his brother and all his kin promptly returned to their home. If Mylan had somehow managed to free his relatives on his own, would any have told him where she'd been taken? She worried constantly about him and prayed fervently for his safety, not once stopping to consider how little respect a pagan would have for her God.

Aldred rode down to the shore to meet his sons' ship as it docked. His right arm was heavily bandaged but healing well, and he scarcely felt any discomfort until he saw Celiese, and then he could not suppress a cry of outrage as he withdrew his dagger from its place at his belt. "I would kill you now, but that would deprive Mylan of gaining satisfaction for your treachery!"

"No, you are mistaken, for I have done my husband no wrong!" Celiese was quick to defend herself for she'd expected his insult, but she'd not considered he'd be so incensed he might murder her on the spot.

Aldred shoved her rudely toward the waiting horses. "You were no wife to my son, only a spy sent to our home to destroy him! He will see that you are punished severely for your evil deeds!"

Celiese gasped as Hagen leaned down from his horse to pull her up in front of him. He gripped her waist tightly as he rode to the well-fortified stone dwelling upon the cliff, where he tossed her roughly to the ground at his mother's feet, his disdain for her clear in the cold gleam of his angry stare. "I will leave this woman in your care, Mother, for I do not trust myself to have the patience to wait for Mylan to see to her punishment!"

Thulyn greeted the disheveled blonde with a vicious whisper. "So they found you, did they? I will lock you in Mylan's room and he may do with you as he pleases when he returns. You will find no horror you can imagine will prepare you for the revenge my son will extract from you, but I will warn you now, no matter how loudly you scream for mercy, he will not hear you!"

Celiese rose gracefully to her feet, brushing the dirt of the path from her gown before turning to stare at the woman who had once been so kind. "You will never hear me scream, Thulyn, never!" She ceased to listen to the woman's cruel threats as she made her way to Mylan's room. The furs were soft upon his bed, and she thought only of the sweetness of her husband's kisses as she stretched out upon them. She had been loved for such a brief time, but it had been more wonderful than she had ever dreamed possible, a memory she would savor for the rest of her days, no matter how many or few they might be. When Thulyn shoved a plate of food in the door she did not get up to eat it, for if none there believed in her innocence she would not plead for their understanding. She planned only to die as proudly as she had lived and returned to sleep, lost in the memories of the love that filled her heart with such happiness that there was no room for any fear, not even of the gruesome fate that Thulyn and Aldred had promised awaited her with Mylan's return.

Chapter Six

Olgrethe bent down beside the large bed and caressed Celiese's tangled curls lightly. "Dear friend, I thought you were lost to me forever. I am sorry you have grown so pale and thin. I can see you have suffered dreadfully for my father's warlike ways."

Celiese sat up slowly, her voice filling with alarm as she pushed her long blond hair away from her eyes. "Olgrethe, who has brought you here to Aldred's home? Are you being held as a prisoner, too?" She had been asleep for many hours, days perhaps, but could not imagine how Olgrethe had come to be with her.

Laughing brightly, Olgrethe tossed her tawny curls at such a ridiculous thought. "No, of course not. I am to be married tonight, as it was agreed in the beginning, but now that I have met the man I am certain it will be for the best." Curling up on the foot of the bed to get more comfortable, Olgrethe began to talk in an excited whisper. "I wish you had been there to see the fight, Celiese. Aldred's sons agreed to pay the ransom my father had demanded for the safe return of their kin, but rather than hand over such a fortune when those men were brought forth they turned their swords upon us. There was not one of my brothers who could outfight them, and they soon made my father admit he'd not accepted the proposal for my hand in good faith. The Vandahls are so different from my family, every bit as brave, but with a kindness I have never seen displayed in my home. I do not think of myself as a prisoner, nor as a captive bride, and I know you and I will be very happy living here."

"You expect me to remain here with you?" Celiese was appalled by that possibility. How could she stand the sight of Mylan with Olgrethe after having known the joy of his love herself? "No, please don't ask me to stay here, I cannot."

"But why not?" Olgrethe's pretty features assumed the pose of a pouting child, frustrated by not having her way.

Celiese simply stared at her friend for a long moment, then shook her head sadly. "The Vandahls were all so quick to condemn me, to believe the worst of me, and I do not want to live where I know I will never be trusted." Celiese could say no more, her throat ached with the pain of unshed tears, and she turned away rather than let Olgrethe see the depth of her anguish.

Puzzled by Celiese's solemn mood when she was so happy, Olgrethe left the room quickly, intent upon making the final preparations for her wedding before she saw to her former maid's problems, which she was certain could not possibly be so acute as the young woman believed them to be.

When Olgrethe walked out leaving the door wide open,

Celiese wasted no time in leaving Mylan's room, for she had no desire to be found there when he came looking for Raktor's daughter. She pushed herself off the bed, and after a few moments' dizziness moved swiftly down the narrow staircase and out into the bright sunlight. She took the first path she found, following it down from the cliff to the flat expanse of plain that led to the sea. She walked until she came to the water's edge, then sank down in the soft sand and stared out at the distant horizon, wishing with all her heart there were some way for her to return to her homeland where she might live in peace, if not with love.

The setting sun cast long shadows across the path as Andrick drew his high-spirited mount to an abrupt halt. In his haste, sand shot up from the beast's hooves went flying all over Celiese, and she had to leap to her feet to avoid being trampled. Ignoring the danger his careless actions had presented he extended his hand as he issued a terse command, which he clearly expected to be obeyed. "Get up behind me, girl. Mylan allowed none to accompany Olgrethe, and she refuses to prepare for the marriage ceremony without you to attend her."

"Your mother must have someone who can serve as her maid, or why not Thulyn herself? She was willing to help me, will she not assist Olgrethe as well?" Celiese argued as she tried to catch her breath and shake the shower of sand from her hair.

Andrick shook his head emphatically. "She will not do, it is you Olgrethe wants and it's you I'll bring."

His stern tone and hostile glance offered no other choice but to comply, and Celiese took his hand to mount his powerful chestnut horse. When she was comfortably seated behind him she wrapped her arms around his waist and asked shyly, "Was Mylan pleased with Olgrethe?"

Amused, the blond man turned his horse toward his home as he gave a noncommittal reply, "Ask him yourself, if you are so curious as to his opinion."

Celiese's cheeks burned with a bright blush at that teasing rebuff. She'd probably never have an opportunity to speak with Mylan alone ever again, nor would she seek it. How could she inquire as to whether he preferred his second wife to his first, the real Olgrethe to her? The wind whipped her hair and stung her eyes, but she shed no tears. Her situation had been hopeless from the moment they'd met and she'd been a great fool to believe Mylan could have grown to love her as swiftly as she'd come to adore him. When they reached the house she slipped from the horse's back and ran inside before Andrick noticed she was gone, but she soon realized she was uncertain as to where Olgrethe might be waiting. Deciding Mylan's room was the most logical choice, she climbed the stairs. Hearing no sound as she approached the door, she opened it slightly to peer inside.

"You!" Mylan turned, an oath upon his lips. He stood stripped to the waist, clutching his left side as he attempted to stem the flow of bright red blood that oozed from between his fingers. "As long as you've seen so much, you might as well come in and help me. Bolt the door so I am not disturbed again."

Celiese entered the room quickly, shoved the bolt into place, then rushed to his side. "Why did no one tell me you had been wounded? Oh Mylan, this is dreadful, you might bleed to death!" She placed her hands over his to add more pressure in hopes of stopping the flow of blood. His flesh felt warm to her touch and filled her slender body with a longing that the severity of his injury did not quell. She had no right, she told herself, no right to want him so badly when he now belonged to Olgrethe, as indeed he had from the very beginning, but that realization did not lessen the force of her desire. She wanted to hug him tightly, to kiss him again and again and tell him how desperately she had missed him, but she dared not speak a word. His greeting could not have been more insulting, and she knew that no matter how she felt he was obviously not in the least bit pleased to see her.

"The Torgvalds got the worst of it. This is nothing, a mere scratch from a blow deflected off my ribs, but when I stepped out of my bath just now I tore it open again and cannot make the bleeding stop. I am expected to appear in the best of health tonight, not as a damn invalid!"

Celiese looked up, unable to comment upon how he would be spending his evening. "I did not mean to disturb you, please forgive me, I was looking for Olgrethe, as she wants me to help her dress."

Mylan continued in the same volatile mood, ignoring her apology as if he'd not heard it, "You will help me instead. There is linen in my trunk—tear enough into strips to bind my side, and make haste to do it before Andrick comes seeking my company and discovers what has happened."

Celiese rinsed her hands in the tub of water he'd used to bathe, then searched through the contents of the small chest for the clean fabric. When she turned with the cloth in her grasp she was startled by Mylan's insolent gaze, for his golden eyes raked over her slowly with a disapproval so scathing she could scarcely bear it.

"You are a sorry sight, Celiese, I am amazed Andrick was willing to pay so much for you. I would have given no more than—"

"Hush!" Celiese insisted angrily. "My appearance is of no consequence now, it is you who need immediate care." She ripped the cloth with vicious tears, then pushed his hands aside to inspect the gruesome gash more closely. "You call this no more than a scratch? Who did this to you, do you know the man's name?"

"What? You expect me to reveal the brute's name so you may avenge it yourself? My battles are of no concern to you, girl, I do not need your assistance to seek revenge, for I'll not risk any more of your tricks." Mylan drew his breath in sharply as Celiese began to wrap the linen around his ribs. "Your touch was tender when last we met, why is it so brutal today?"

"I am never brutal!" Celiese denied heatedly as she choked back her tears. Did the man think her devoid of feelings, incapable of offering the devotion he inspired? "I am merely trying to bind your side securely so you'll lose no more blood." Satisfied with her handiwork, she tied the end of the last linen strip in a firm knot, then stepped back. "There, that should hold for the night, and tomorrow you may find another to apply a fresh bandage, someone whose touch pleases you far more." She began to move toward the door, thinking her task was completed, but Mylan stepped quickly to block her way.

"I want no others to know of this, you must promise

your silence. If the dressing needs changing, then you will be the one to do it."

Celiese thought his demand unreasonable, for surely Olgrethe ought to be the one to tend him. She would be his wife and his care one of her rightful duties, but she had no desire to point out so painful a point to him if he did not see it. "I must go, Olgrethe sent for me and—"

Mylan moved closer still, forcing Celiese against his door, where he held her captive between his outstretched arms. "You have kept not one of your promises to me, but I'll see you keep this one, Celiese. No one must learn I have been harmed, no one."

The lovely blonde's eyes filled with a curious glow as she stared up at the man who had been her husband so briefly. "I have broken none of the promises I made to you, I—" She saw him incline his head, his intention clear but a surprise all the same, and his mouth covered hers, ending her protest with a soft sigh of surrender. She made no move to resist his forceful embrace, but lifted her arms to encircle his neck as she returned his deep kiss, unable to stifle the need his loving touch created within her heart. This kiss was as marvelous as all his others, soft and slow. It swept her ordeal from her mind, the days they'd been apart disappearing from her memory, and she was again his bride. Then as suddenly as he had drawn her near Mylan released her, shoving her aside as he backed away.

"Did you really think I'd be fool enough to wait at that door for you? Did you truly think you could hand me over to Raktor so easily as that?" Mylan's eyes grew dark with disgust. "Is there no end to your treachery?"

"I did not meet you because I couldn't!" Celiese grabbed his arm, imploring him to listen. "Raktor locked me up with those he'd taken prisoner the moment I stepped through the door. Did none of your kinsmen tell you I was with them, or that later they had seen me taken aboard the ship for the voyage to Kaupang?"

Mylan brushed Celiese aside, turning his back upon her as he began to sort through the clothing laid out upon his bed for what he wished to wear. "Another of Raktor's schemes, no doubt. My kin were too clever to believe anything you said after what you'd done to them. That he sold you is not surprising, for he knew you would betray him as swiftly as you had betrayed me!"

"Why is it you continually choose to ignore the truth in my words?" Celiese clenched her fists tightly at her sides, furious that he would not believe her. "I tried only to help you!"

"With any more help such as yours I'd soon be dead! Now go and find your mistress, and spin your lies together with her, as you have always done!"

Celiese dared not leave when he understood nothing about either her or the proud young woman who would soon be his bride. "Olgrethe is not like her father, Mylan. She is spoiled, for she has been pampered all her life by her family, but she is kind, her heart is filled with goodness. Please do not think ill of her simply because you despise me."

Mylan snarled through clenched teeth, "She sent you to me, did she not? You said it was her idea. Was that a lie also?"

"No, that was the truth, but I tried to explain it was

109

only because—"

"Get out! I have no further need of you, be gone!"

Celiese sped through the door as Mylan picked up a heavy brass box, clearly meaning to hurl it at her should she not obey him. She could not blame him for his anger, but neither would she remain and risk needless injury. She had taken no more than two running steps down the hall when Olgrethe opened a door and saw her.

"There you are at last! Come quickly, Celiese, for I cannot make my hair curl as it should, and I want to look my very best." The animated girl grabbed her longtime servant's wrist and led her into the room where she'd dressed. "Where have you been? I had to bathe and dress myself, but you must comb my hair before you dress." Olgrethe sat down and handed Celiese her hairbrush and golden pins. "Hurry, I am late already! This wedding will be nothing like yours, there will be no feasting, but I do want to look pretty even if I am not to be entertained as lavishly as you were. This is the only wedding I am likely to have, and I'll make a celebration of it even if the Vandahls will not."

Celiese fashioned the elaborate coiffure Olgrethe preferred without hearing any of the young woman's excited chatter. She was too hurt to contemplate anything more than the painful fact that her only friend was about to marry the man she had thought would be her own husband. It was all so unfair—none of the torment was her fault, and yet Mylan blamed her for deceiving him to aid Raktor, when she'd done nothing of the kind. Her work finished, she stepped back, hoping to be excused even if she had nowhere to go in the expansive home.

Olgrethe held her skirt daintily above her feet as she left her chair, "The bathwater is fresh; I had it brought for you. Now hurry and get ready. They will come for me shortly, and I do not wish to be married without you being there to see it, as I have no other friend in this household."

"Olgrethe, please—"

The high-spirited girl grabbed for the brooches that held Celiese's yellow gown and removed them with a swift tug. "Hurry Celiese, or I shall take you with me nude!" She shoved and pushed, argued and cajoled until at last she had her friend seated in the steaming tub. "There, now doesn't that feel good? Why don't you wear my blue dress—I brought along all my jewelry and I'll get everything out for you so we won't keep them waiting."

Celiese sank down into the warm softness of the large tub to wet her hair before lathering her thick curls with the perfumed soap Olgrethe had thrust into her hands. There was no way to escape the enthusiastic girl's plans, but once the ceremony had begun she knew Olgrethe would have eyes only for Mylan and then she could slip away, hide somewhere away from the Vandahls and their accusing stares. She turned as the door swung open, shocked as Mylan strode into the room and came straight toward her, but she had no way to hide her lissome figure from his hostile glance.

"Why are you blushing so deeply, girl, you've nothing I have not already seen—more than once—to say nothing of half of Kaupang, which had a full view of your charms! You have kept us all waiting too long, Olgrethe, you must come with me now." With no more than a brief backward glance, Mylan swept the startled young woman out of the room, leaving Celiese flushed with shame as she sat in the rapidly cooling water. His disgust with her could not have been more painful, and she had little reason even to leave the tub, let alone dress for an evening that promised to hold no joy for her. But as the water grew chilled her anger mounted, until she finally forced herself to rise, dried off carefully, then donned the silken gown Olgrethe had laid out for her. She fastened the gold brooches at her shoulders with shaking fingers and tried to dry her hair sufficiently to join the gathering for a few minutes, at least. She twisted her gleaming tresses upon her head and secured them with the golden pins Olgrethe had not needed. Furious at her own weakness that had allowed her to care so deeply for a man who thought so little of her, she vowed to show Mylan she still had her pride. His insults might hurt her terribly, but she'd not let him suspect she felt the slightest discomfort at his scorn. If he wished to reject her love then she would reject his hatred with the same cool disdain.

Lifting her chin proudly Celiese made her way to the hall where the marriage ceremony was already taking place. Many of those who had attended her wedding were there again, so while the atmosphere of the large room was not nearly as festive, it was no less crowded. Those who turned to note her arrival frowned angrily, but she stepped swiftly to move along the side of the room, hoping to find a place to stand where she would attract no notice. She would greet Olgrethe warmly at the close of the ceremony and then return to the room where she'd dressed and hope her presence in the house would be forgotten. As she edged along the back of the crowd, an arm suddenly closed firmly around her waist, and she gasped in surprise as she struggled to get free.

"Hush, I mean you no harm!" Mylan whispered sternly as he pulled Celiese close to his side. "Do you always dress as finely as your mistress, or is this yet another of your masquerades?" Truly he thought her as splendidly garbed as Olgrethe, and in his opinion she was far more lovely. That so pretty a woman could have such an evil heart confused him and his question sounded more like a rebuke than a query.

Celiese was so astonished to find Mylan at the back of the room that she stood on her tiptoes to see what had happened to Olgrethe. Had the ceremony not yet begun, after all? Her eyes widened further, her long lashes sweeping her delicately arched brows, when she saw the young woman standing in the center of the room with Andrick by her side. Turning so she might speak discreetly, she whispered. "Olgrethe is not marrying you?"

Mylan brought his fingertip to her lips to silence her. "No! I have no need for another bride! Now be still, you are disturbing everyone with your chatter!"

Celiese relaxed against him, forgetting his injured side in her amazement. Her body melted into the sleek line of his and she felt him draw away quickly, but not before she'd felt his body's involuntary response to hers, and when she looked up at him his blush was as bright as hers. His hand had not relaxed upon her wrist, but she was too relieved to find he'd not wed Olgrethe to complain over that slight pain. Her agile mind worked swiftly. What had

113

he said? He wanted no other bride? What had he meant by that remark—that he was finished with marriage, or was he only finished with her? She peeked up at him through her thick fringe of dark lashes. He looked far from happy, and she risked leaning close again to whisper, "Why is Andrick marrying Olgrethe?"

"Because I wouldn't!" Mylan snarled angrily, then pulled her around in front of him, keeping his arms clasped tightly around her slender waist so she could not escape his grasp. His embrace was confining, not tender, and the moment the ceremony concluded he dragged her along beside him to congratulate his brother. He mumbled a brief greeting, then left the large gathering with Celiese still firmly in tow as he climbed the stairs to his room. He pushed her inside, then turned to go. "Wait here, I will return in a moment with a more suitable garment for you to wear."

Celiese looked down at Olgrethe's lovely blue gown with a puzzled glance. "But why? This dress is so pretty, don't you like it?"

"No, it will not do for the journey to my home, nor for what you will do when we arrive." Mylan stood in the doorway, impatient to attend to his errand.

"You do not live here with your family, Mylan?" Celiese found each of his announcements perplexing.

"No. Now remove that dress quickly so I am not kept waiting!" He slammed the door as he went out, but Celiese sat down on his bed, unwilling to disrobe when she understood so little of his purpose. Where were they going, and what unnamed task must she change her

114

clothes to perform?

When Mylan returned he swore heatedly as he tossed her a coarsely woven gray wool gown. "Your modesty is misplaced with me, Celiese, now don this and let us go."

Celiese held up the drab dress and shook her head. "This is at least clean, but hideous. Mylan, why must I wear it?"

Mylan moved about the room collecting his belongings rapidly. "You must cease to concern yourself with beauty, Celiese. Practicality is the issue here; now dress or I shall leave without you."

Celiese ran her fingertips over the rough threads of the gray fabric and complained again as she slipped it over her head. "I cannot wear this next to my skin, Mylan, it is so poorly woven it would be unbearably uncomfortable."

"Your comfort is unimportant. Since I am ready, let us go." Mylan frowned with disappointment as he looked at her, for the ill-fitting wool gown did little to hide her beauty. Forcing himself to continue, he asked gruffly, "Can you ride?"

"Yes, of course."

"Of course? Not all women do. It will be dark—do you ride well enough to escape injury should your horse stumble?"

Celiese answered his question proudly. "My father taught me to ride shortly after I learned to walk. Olgrethe and I rode nearly every day in the spring and summer months, so it is not my skill or practice that will be a concern. I am far more worried over your well-being than my own. Can you ride with that gash in your side?"

Mylan brushed her unwanted sympathy aside. "I can sit a horse! Cease your ramblings and let us depart at once."

Celiese lifted the heavy gown above her feet and followed him down the back stairs and out to the stables where a groom stood holding the reins of two sturdy mounts. She was given the smaller of the two, a dapple gray mare, and with an agile leap she mounted the gentle horse. Holding the reins tightly in her grasp, she turned the mare to follow Mylan's lead.

The moonlight was pale, the shadows deep, but Mylan knew the worn trail well, and they traversed it for several hours without mishap. When at last he reached their destination he called over his shoulder, "Wait here while I light the fire, then you may come inside, too."

Celiese slipped down to the ground and stood rubbing the ache in her spine, for the trip had been a long and tiring one. She remained standing at the open door while Mylan bent over the hearth in the center of the small house. After a few moments he'd ignited a blaze that sent a warm glow clear into the far corners of the cluttered dwelling, and she gazed about in dismay as she entered. It was a farmhouse, no different from any other, but so ill kept that she was astonished to find it served as Mylan's home, when he was always so well groomed and finely clothed. "Is this where you have been living for the last two years?"

"Aye, this is my home." Mylan threw off his cloak and turned to face her, his frown again becoming his constant expression. "It needs a good cleaning, that I will admit,

116

so you need not think you will insult me by seeing to it at first light."

Celiese looked about the one long, narrow room again, hoping her poor first impression had been as a result of the flickering fire, but now that the wood burned with a steady glow the place looked no better. "You have brought me here to clean?" Her disappointment was obvious in her luminous green eyes, their color bright with unshed tears. She knew she was not a bride being welcomed into a home filled with love, but still she had hoped for better than this from him.

"To clean and to cook, indeed to perform any task I might assign. For the present you must tend the horses, they are doubtless weary, and so am I. The stable is in the rear. Well, run, I'll not have such fine animals neglected!"

With an angry glance Celiese left without arguing. She gathered up the reins and spoke softly as she led the two horses around to the small shed that served as the stable. "Mylan says you two deserve care, but what of me? Am I not to be shown even the slight amount of consideration he shows a horse?" Knowing the beasts would not reply, Celiese did her best to see they were cooled down properly and ready to spend a restful night. The shed was dark and she stumbled, bruising her shins cruelly as she missed her step at the door. That pain was the final assault on her spirit, and she burst into tears before realizing with a sudden flash of insight that she should be rejoicing that Mylan had not married Olgrethe as she had feared he would. Sitting up, she brushed away her tears, for why would he have brought her with him if he had not missed her as greatly as she had missed him? As she stood up she tripped again over the hem of her long gray gown. Gripping it tightly in her hands, she ran around to the front door, gasping for breath as she entered the large room, but all was quiet. Mylan lay sleeping, his deep breathing easy as if he'd fallen sound asleep the moment he'd sprawled across the heap of furs that served as his bed. She tiptoed to his side and slipped her hand under the soft suede of his tunic. His wound was apparently no longer seeping blood, for the linen bandage was still dry, and, satisfied that he was merely exhausted, not unconscious from loss of blood, she ceased to worry about him and looked about for a place where she might rest comfortably herself. Mylan lay at a diagonal, leaving no space for her upon his bed. She was certain that that had been deliberate rudeness on his part, but she was too tired to care. She leaned down to brush his tawny curls with her lips, her kiss a spontaneous gift of the affection she had no desire to hide regardless of the bitterness of his mood. "God bless you, dear husband, may your dreams be sweet."

As was the custom in a farmhouse, the platform that formed a bench around the interior walls served as seating during the day and as beds during the night. That Mylan had such a splendid mound of furs upon which to sleep was a tribute to his skill as a hunter, but she hoped he would not miss a few so she might make the hard wooden bench at least somewhat more bearable as a bed. After adding more wood to the fire, she gathered a few pelts from his generous supply, then lay down and closed her eyes wearily, for she was as exhausted as he was from the long day. Forcing all fear for the future from her mind, she smiled with a lazy satisfaction. She had never expected to be a farmer's wife, but now that prospect seemed most rewarding, for as long as Mylan kept her with him she cared not at all where he chose to live.

Chapter Seven

In the pale light of dawn Mylan's farmhouse was even more disorderly than Celiese had at first imagined. She lay upon her stomach on the wooden bench where she'd slept, her chin propped on her hands as she scanned the room slowly, amazed by the accumulation of clutter that littered the quaint little house. As was the Viking custom, it was sturdily built of tree trunks split into staves and then placed vertically in the ground to form the walls. Although it had been dark when they'd arrived, she knew this late in spring the thatched roof would be covered with a sprinkling of bright wildflowers, and with the cleaning Mylan had suggested she was certain the home could be a charming place. Since the fire that had burned on the hearth when she'd fallen asleep was now no more than ashes, she wondered if Mylan would soon rise to light another to help her prepare breakfast. Glancing over her shoulder where she expected to see him still sleeping, Celiese found only the heap of furs occupying the corner. Suddenly certain she'd been left in an abandoned farmhouse many miles from home, she leapt to her feet and ran out the door, sprinting around to the shed where she found the dapple gray mare she'd ridden with Mylan's roan stallion, both munching contentedly upon a fresh supply of feed. He had apparently fed and watered the animals before he'd left, but where could he have gone? Anxious to find him she circled the low dwelling, shading her eyes from the rising sun as she searched the surrounding fields for the tall, blond Viking. He was nowhere to be seen.

The landscape was a serene one, the fertile land flat, while nearby a stream ran with inviting swiftness beneath a thick stand of linden trees whose branches were topped with the new growth of spring. While not so immense an estate as the one owned by Raktor or Aldred, the farm appeared to be a prosperous one, and Celiese's mood grew more optimistic as she continued to survey her new home. When after a few minutes' time Mylan had still not appeared, she walked to the stream. Knowing she was quite alone, she slipped off the coarse woolen garment, then Olgrethe's blue gown. The chill of the water brought a bright blush to her cheeks, and she made haste to complete her grooming before her fair skin took on the same pale blue as the sky. Donning only the silk gown, she carried the gray one back to the house to search for a pail so she might carry water to begin the cleaning.

It was late afternoon when Mylan returned, limping badly. He carried two rabbits slung over his shoulder as the only evidence of his day's efforts. He hesitated at the door, clearly dismayed at the sight of the tidy household Celiese had managed to create in less than one day's time.

That she had obeyed a command he'd issued in such an offhand manner the night before amazed him, as everybody knew that slaves were completely devoid of such initiative. "I did not expect, I mean, you need not have—" He caught himself then—an order given should be obeyed, still, she had caught him off guard, and he was more confused than pleased by her unexpected willingness to clean his house.

Celiese approached the handsome man with an enchanting smile. "I have always preferred order to chaos, Mylan. Your house did not present too great a challenge for me."

Ignoring her friendly greeting, Mylan strode through the door, then tossed the limp animals upon the table. "I suppose this is the best you could do." He commented gruffly. "In time you will learn how I want my house kept."

Celiese's pretty smile of welcome vanished instantly at that rebuke, for she was shocked that he thought there was something she'd neglected to do. "I put fresh straw on the floor, shook out the furs of your bed, cleaned all your cooking implements, dusted all the furnishings—what more should I have done?"

Mylan turned away. His home was spotless, but he'd pay her no compliments that day or any other. "The fire has gone out. I expect my supper to be ready when I come home. Do not be so careless ever again."

Gesturing helplessly, Celiese explained, "It was out when I awoke. How did you start a fire so quickly last night? I have no idea how to do it." She'd worked so hard to please him and as usual had failed, but she knew the fact that the fire had gone out was not her fault and resisted assuming the blame for it. "I did bring in more wood," she offered quickly, hoping that might put him in a more agreeable mood.

Drawing a small leather pouch from his belt, Mylan removed a flint and bent down over the pile of kindling she'd laid. In a matter of seconds he'd ignited the dry wood and stood up to back away.

"How do you expect me to light a fire if you carry the flint with you?" Celiese asked indignantly.

Mylan drew himself up in a slow, menacing stretch, towering above Celiese as he regarded her with a contempt-filled gaze. "Just see that this fire is properly tended, so that it does not have to be relit! Now show me what you can prepare out of the rabbits. I have not eaten all day and am hungry."

"Cook those?" Celiese glanced at the small furry animals lying upon the table. "I have never cooked any meal, Mylan. I have no idea how to prepare those little beasts so that they will be tasty."

Shaking his head sadly, Mylan continued to scold her. "Then it is time you learned. I have no need for a maid here; your housekeeping is barely adequate, and if you cannot prepare edible meals then—" He broke off in mid-sentence, and when no truly horrible threat came to his mind he gestured broadly, "Then we shall starve!"

"We'll not starve!" Celiese laughed at his stricken expression, not caring if the sound of her merriment provoked him further. "How have you managed to survive these last two years? Show me how you have prepared rabbits yourself, and I will watch carefully so I might do it the next time. Won't you please show me?" she coaxed with an infectiously pleasant smile and bright glimmer in her sparkling green eyes.

Mylan pulled a razor-sharp dagger from his belt and with a few swift strokes skinned and dressed the rabbits. Cutting the carcasses into quarters, he offered scant advice. "Fill the iron kettle with water from the stream. There are onions and other vegetables in the garden, add them when the meat is tender. Since you did not have the water boiling it will be a long while until supper."

"Since I didn't know where you'd gone, or when you might return, how was I supposed to know you'd gone hunting and would expect the stew made before you'd arrived home with the meat?" His demands made no sense at all to her, but rather than argue she grabbed up the pail and ran to the stream to fetch the water.

Angered by the sharpness of her wit, Mylan jabbed his dagger into the table top with a vicious thrust before going out to check his horses. When he found both had been expertly groomed, their stalls cleaned, and their feed and water replenished, he swore under his breath. "Where does that woman find such energy?" He leaned back against the rough wall of the shed and held his side, for it ached badly and he knew the dressing needed changing. Closing his eyes he breathed deeply, trying to force away the pain with the power of his thoughts, but his confrontation with Celiese had provided such a distraction he could concentrate on nothing but her delightful image, and he was soon certain his decision to bring her along to the farm with him had been the wrong one.

When Celiese had the preparations for their evening

meal well underway according to Mylan's directions, she began to wonder if he'd bother to return to eat it. She looked about the one-room abode, searching for the flaws he'd noticed so readily, but she could detect none. Everything was in its place, all spotlessly clean and shining from her labors. Too nervous to rest, she waited at the door for a while, then went outside to look for her reluctant companion. He was still leaning against the shed where he'd stopped to rest, his face set in a mask of undisguised disgust, and she waited for a moment for him to notice her. When he did not, she spoke softly. "The horses are not in need of more care, are they? It is difficult to perform any task in that small stable after the sun sets, but I have the time now if—"

"What?" Mylan stood up too abruptly, then winced as the wound in his side caused him a new burst of pain. Unable to catch his breath, he could say no more and feared Celiese would think him a fool for not having heard her question.

Frightened he might be ill, Celiese lowered her voice to a sympathetic whisper. "You have done far too much today, Mylan. Do not exert yourself needlessly. Please come inside and I will see to your comfort as best I can." Another of her many failings, she realized, for she knew nothing of brewing remedies from herbs, but perhaps he might be able to prescribe something she could prepare for him.

Mylan offered no resistance to her suggestion, and when her arm encircled his waist he walked slowly back inside where he sank down into a chair at the table before pulling his tunic off over his head. "I am none too clean, but I'll not risk opening the wound again by bathing."

"That is wise, but I can help you to wash," Celiese offered agreeably without realizing what exquisite torture it would be to touch him. His skin was deeply tanned, golden-brown and warm beneath her fingertips. She had to force herself to concentrate upon the blood-soaked bandage at his waist rather than on his lean, muscular body, which reminded her far too vividly of the nights she'd spent in his arms. Concerned, she scolded him softly, "You must have been bleeding all day, you never should have gone hunting."

Mylan sighed wearily, feeling no need for her advice. "It is a slight injury, and we must have food to survive."

Celiese worked quickly to pull away the matted layers of cloth that covered the deep wound as she replied, "I can hunt for us, my father taught me how, and I've not forgotten his lessons."

"Why would Raktor teach you such things, when he has sons aplenty?" Mylan asked skeptically.

"He didn't, but he is not my father, in case you have forgotten," Celiese pointed out quickly. "Tomorrow you must simply rest, and I will kill a wild hen or two for our supper."

Snorting derisively, Mylan exclaimed, "I'd rather eat porridge!"

"Would it offend your pride so greatly to eat food I'd provided?" Celiese stepped back, insulted that her offer of assistance had been so rudely refused.

"I will not be able to eat anything if I bleed to death while you stand there talking! Find some linen to bind my

126

side and be quick about it!"

Complying rapidly, Celiese ripped a piece of cloth into narrow strips. "You brought me here to be useful, didn't you? What difference does it make what work I do? Since you find my housekeeping so disappointing, perhaps my hunting will please you more."

Mylan looked askance but made no comment as she bent down to tend him. She was wearing the blue silk gown he'd told her to leave behind, her hair was loose, curling softly over her shoulders, and he was disgusted with himself for finding her fair beauty so appealing when he knew full well she had the lying heart of a serpent. "You will do as I say, Celiese. I am the master here and I mean to be obeyed."

Celiese finished her task swiftly and turned away to hide the heartache that shone so brightly in her eyes. "Why don't you lie down for a while and I will call you when the stew is ready to eat."

Frowning, Mylan hesitated to agree with her suggestion. It was most sensible, but he did not want her to think he would do anything simply to please her. But knowing he was too tired to do much else, he walked the short distance to his bed without complaining and stretched out carefully so as not to aggravate the gash in his side. The aroma from the bubbling kettle was surprisingly enticing, and he realized it had been far too long since he'd eaten. He was dizzy and weak, more seriously injured than he wanted to let the graceful blonde see, but when she was ready to serve their supper he could not summon the energy to rise.

127

"Mylan?" Celiese did not want to disturb him, but she'd found only one bowl and his utensils were few. "Is there no more than one bowl?"

"I had several, have you misplaced them?" he responded accusingly.

Sorry she'd inquired, Celiese simply gave him a hostile glance, then noticed how pale he'd grown. She knew she hadn't mislaid any of his belongings, but excused his foul mood after considering the pain she knew he had to be suffering. "Well, since we have only this one bowl it will be difficult for us to dine together, but perhaps—"

"I don't share my meals with slaves!" Mylan shouted hoarsely, then fell back with a moan, sorry he'd been so nasty when it had caused him such agony to yell at her.

Ignoring his cry of pain, Celiese continued agreeably, "I see no reason for us to eat separately." She attempted to affect a calm she didn't feel, for if she called him husband and he called her slave their lives were never going to run smoothly. The point seemed to be a mute one that night, however, as Mylan appeared to be too ill to leave his bed to come to the table. "Since there is just this one bowl, I will sit beside you and help you eat. That way you will not have to tire yourself by rising from your bed."

Mylan shot her another disapproving frown, then decided not to argue; he was hungry, and his bed was suddenly too comfortable to leave. "I am no infant— bring me the bowl and I'll feed myself."

"As you wish." Celiese carried the steaming bowl to his side and waited for him to sit up.

Mylan struggled to shift his position but found it too painful and lay still. "It looks as though you'll have to feed me after all. Just be careful you do not spill any of that hot broth on me."

"I will be very careful, Mylan, I won't spill a drop," Celiese promised playfully, and after bringing a chair to his bedside she sat down and offered him a spoonful of the stew. It smelled delicious, and she tried to ignore her own hunger while she saw to his.

Mylan watched Celiese closely as she lifted another spoonful of the tasty stew to his lips. She had spent the day cleaning his home, but she'd obviously bathed and had washed her hair, for she appeared as well groomed and pretty as when they'd first met. The pointlessness of that tender meeting brought back his anger in full force and he nearly choked on his next bite. "Not so fast, give me a minute to chew, at least!"

"Forgive me," Celiese offered coolly, frustrated that he was being so totally unreasonable in his attitude. They were eating together as she saw it, though, and that thought pleased her. Thinking perhaps if she tried he would converse with her more agreeably, she asked sweetly, "Your farm seems to be a most prosperous one, Mylan, but how did you come to own land located so distant from that of your father?"

"You must know how land is acquired, Celiese, do not pretend that you do not."

Puzzled, Celiese persisted, "It can be bought, I suppose. Did you simply purchase this property because the land is fertile?"

Her question seemed so innocently asked that Mylan answered truthfully, "This farm was part of the land my mother gave to my father when they married, part of her dowry. Have you never heard of that custom?" It seemed unlikely that she had not, but the wife's goods belonged to the husband after the marriage, and every family increased its wealth in that fashion.

Celiese found it impossible to raise her eyes to his. She stirred the bowl of stew as though searching for a tasty morsel and asked shyly, "Were you promised land when you married Olgrethe?"

"Of course! Raktor is rich, the man who married his daughter could expect land and other valuables, as well. Did you think she would be prized solely for her beauty?"

"I gave such matters no serious thought, Mylan, but wealthy young women have attractive dowries in my country, as well." When she glanced up, her deep green eyes were bright with unshed tears. "I am sorry that you were disappointed in that respect, too, to not have the wife you thought you'd married, nor to have the wealth you'd been promised."

Astonished by her sincerity, Mylan changed the subject abruptly. That she actually seemed to care about his feelings had to be another trick, he knew it, and he was too clever to let her fool him again. "You needn't look so stricken, for Andrick now owns all that he should as Olgrethe's husband, and my family was cheated of nothing that was rightfully theirs. Now I am finished eating. That was not nearly as good as it usually is, but you'll learn how to cook with more skill in time." Closing

130

his eyes, Mylan considered their conversation, as well as the evening, finished.

Realizing she'd been dismissed without the courtesy of a thank you for her help, Celiese got up. She rinsed out the bowl and filled it with a portion of the savory stew and sat down at the table to eat. She thought the meal quite good, despite his complaint, and wondered if perhaps he weren't just being spiteful. She'd often eaten alone, for Olgrethe had joined her father and brothers for the evening meal. But this was different. There were only the two of them occupying the small house, and she couldn't believe he truly planned to treat her as a slave. She'd not take that insult from him—to be ordered about from dawn to dusk, made to eat alone and then made to share his bed whether she wished to or not, she thought angrily. When she glanced in his direction he'd not moved. Perhaps he was already asleep. She vowed he'd never have a worse slave. She was his wife and deserved to be treated with kindness, to be loved and cherished rather than ignored unless there was some menial task he'd not wish to handle himself.

While Mylan fell more deeply into the serenity of untroubled sleep, Celiese sat fuming with rage, watching the glowing coals upon the hearth until they were no more than a few bright embers. She wasn't a bit tired, in spite of the long hours she'd spent cleaning the small house and the stable. Too anxious to rest, she cleaned up the remains of their meal, then added more wood to the fire. She was confused and hurt by Mylan's continual criticism, but reminded herself he'd been through an ordeal every bit as harrowing as the one she'd survived. Perhaps if she held her tongue and was patient for a few more days he would recall the hours they'd shared as fondly as she did and again take her as his bride. If not, then she'd be forced to run away, for she had far too much pride to live as a slave in a house in which she was rightfully the mistress.

Chapter Eight

When she awoke before Mylan the next morning, Celiese hurried out to the stream to bathe as best she could while she tried to decide what to do. She'd boasted that she could hunt, but she'd been a child when her father had let her ride by his side. She'd been able to draw the small bow he'd made for her, but what of Mylan's far more powerful weapon? If it took all her strength to draw back the string she'd be unable to aim the arrow with any accuracy and never be able to provide meat for their table. "His table!" She corrected herself bitterly. Glancing up at the sun to judge the lateness of the hour, she returned to the small dwelling to begin making porridge for their breakfast.

Mylan opened his eyes slowly and for a brief moment could not recall why he should again be on his farm, when he absolutely despised the place. At least Celiese was there to tend the house and relieve him of the tiresome chores that entailed. He lay quietly watching her move about without letting her see he was awake. That she had begun preparing his breakfast without being told was a point in her favor, and he tried to recall where he'd last seen the pewter bowls he sometimes used, for even if he'd not eat with her he knew she deserved the courtesy of having her own dishes. "Look in the chest where you found the linen yesterday, Celiese, I must have a dish or two stored away there," he said suddenly, breaking the quiet.

"Oh Mylan, you startled me badly!" Celiese spun around to face him, happy to see he was well enough to consider her comfort for a change.

The pretty blush that filled the delicate blonde's cheeks surprised Mylan completely. He thought his request had been phrased casually and didn't understand why she'd reacted with such delight, as if he'd paid her the most flattering of compliments. Why was she blushing so attractively when there was not the slightest cause for such a reaction? "Well, go on and look, I'll not have you standing around waiting for me to finish eating when there is so much work to be done here!"

Celiese moved toward the ornately carved chest without any real haste, for she was embarrassed that her happiness in seeing him that morning had not been returned in kind. She bent down, lifted the lid, and after regarding the layers of apparel for a moment commented, "You have very fine clothing, Mylan, the smoothest suedes I have ever felt. But I do not see any bowls here."

Mylan pushed himself off his bed, and when his side gave him no pain he knelt down beside her to look for himself. "They would be along the side, not among the folds." Thrusting his hand along the wood, he withdrew first one bowl and then another. "There, now you need not wait for me when you prepare meals."

They were so close their shoulders were touching, and when Celiese turned to take the two bowls from his hands they slipped from her grasp and clattered to the floor. "I'm sorry." She grabbed them up quickly for his accusing stare made her acutely uncomfortable and she did not want to make him angry with her again. "I am not usually so clumsy."

Mylan turned away, as startled as she had been by the spark of excitement that had passed between them. Her fingertips had barely brushed his wrist and he could not even catch his breath. Disgusted with himself for having so little control of his emotions where she was concerned, he got to his feet and left the house, determined to remain outside until he could again convey the cool detachment he wanted to affect in her presence. He'd brought her with him to punish her, to make her work keeping his house and cooking his meals, but that was to have been the extent of her duties. He'd not realized how quickly he would again succumb to her charms, but she was the most attractive of women, a beauty of such grace and spirit he'd been a fool to think he could treat her with the indifference he usually showed a slave. He knelt by the stream, splashing the cold water upon his face until its icy chill had cleared his mind and cooled his blood sufficiently for him to think calmly. The problem was a simple one, he realized. Since he would not have Celiese for his wife, she would have to accept her place as his slave and consider providing him with the pleasure he craved as only one more of her duties. A small matter, he decided with a sly grin, and he returned to his house to see if she had prepared an edible porridge.

Celiese waited as Mylan ate, her smile shy. "Well, what do you say? I thought it quite tasty myself." He had finished one bowl of the steaming porridge and had then asked for another, so she was reasonably certain he liked it.

"I was too hungry to taste the first bowl, some honey might help, or fruit, if we had any." Making a face, he shoved the half-eaten bowl aside. "I will forgive you since you have no experience as a cook, but if you cannot do better than this tomorrow morning I will just throw it out." Without looking her way Mylan got up from the table, reached for his bow and quiver of arrows, and headed out the door.

Astonished by his abrupt exit Celiese ran after him, calling excitedly, "Wait, I can hunt even if I cannot cook! Please let me come with you!"

Mylan hesitated only a moment. The porridge had actually been quite delicious, and he was sorry he'd not thought of some way to finish his second helping before he'd said it was no good. "It is a proficient cook I need, not a hunting companion. And how can you hunt with no weapons?"

"I could make my own if you would help me. Let me come with you today and I will gather sturdy branches to fashion a bow and arrows of my own," Celiese offered eagerly. She'd cleaned his house so thoroughly the previous day she knew she would have little to do if he again left her alone until sunset.

"Your attire is unsuitable for walking through the forest." Mylan reached out to touch the soft silk of her

136

blue gown. "Since you'll not wear the garment I gave you, you cannot afford to ruin this one."

"If you'll but wait a moment I will put on the other one." The coarse wool would be uncomfortable, but she wanted to go with him too badly to worry over that discomfort.

"The morning is half gone already. I have no time to waste on a woman's whims!" Turning to hide his smile Mylan stalked off with a long, confident stride, his limp barely noticeable as he moved down the path that led to the woods. He took his time that day, knowing the longer he left Celiese alone the more anxious she would be for his company when he returned and therefore all the more agreeable to his demands. He could not understand her continual eagerness to please him, but knew he'd be a fool not to make that work to his advantage. He'd most certainly never allow her to hunt with him, but there were plenty of other chores to keep her busy. He'd forgotten to tell her to water the vegetable garden, but that was so obvious a task she'd undoubtedly think of it herself, and if she didn't he'd scold her sternly for being so negligent. That she had so few practical skills was annoying, but she was bright and would learn soon enough how to manage his farm so he could leave it in her care when he returned to the sea.

When he'd shot a plump bird for their supper he sat down under a tree and stretched out to rest, for he did not want to make the same mistake he'd made the day before of thinking he was more fit than he actually was. He was fortunate that the wound hadn't been far worse. Another day or two of rest were what he still needed. As he sat lazily in the shade he soon began to wonder how Andrick had fared with Olgrethe. He'd wished him luck and had meant it, but thought his brother had little chance of making the willful girl happy. She was no prettier than Celiese, in fact, he had found Raktor's daughter something of a disappointment after having known her maid. It wasn't so much that her features were any less attractive, nor her figure any less amply endowed, but her manner was not nearly so pleasant nor her smile half so sweet. Celiese had done him a great favor, he thought ruefully, for she had saved him from marrying a young woman who would surely have nagged him incessantly, always wanting to be kept amused, and he had no desire to be any young woman's pet. All women were troublesome, he thought suddenly, bothersome creatures he would sooner live without. He'd not make the mistake of ever trusting another female, but that did not mean he intended to enjoy what they did have to offer any the less. His frown deepened as he thought of his three brothers. As the eldest he was expected to be the leader, but he'd set a sorry example in the last two years. Perhaps with Celiese there to help him he would be healthy enough by the next spring to return to the sea with his former vigor. There was the matter of his ship— it needed to be completely refurbished. And his crew had been scattered when he'd had no work for them, but with a year's time to prepare he should be able to set sail again. His mind turning to the wondrous possibilities for adventure, he dozed for more than two hours before returning home to see what Celiese had accomplished in his absence.

Celiese had stood watching until Mylan had disappeared into the forest before she'd returned to his house. She could not see any task she'd left undone, so she had no idea why he'd been so terribly disappointed with her housekeeping when he'd given her no clue as to what had caused his displeasure. The house was small and his possessions many, but she'd done her best to see they were neatly displayed and had no intention of doing any of her work over again when he'd not explain why he'd been so angry. As for herself, she had almost nothing, and, wondering if he might not have some fabrics she could fashion into another gown, she opened his chest and began to sort through its contents, stacking the layers of his clothing in neat piles by her side. She'd meant her compliment when she'd paid it; all his clothes were very fine, and her fingertips brushed the soft suede fondly as she laid it aside. Rather than the few yards of silk she'd hoped to find when she reached the bottom of the chest, she discovered only a piece of heavy wool she recognized as being a small portion of a torn sail. Leaning down to touch it, she found it had been wrapped around some heavy object, and she lifted the bundle out to see what it contained.

The unexpected sight of the gleaming sword startled her badly and she drew back, ashamed now that she'd searched through Mylan's belongings, regardless of her purpose. The blade of the double-edged sword was decorated with the finest gold filagree, an intricate swirling design pounded into the steel to create not only a most deadly weapon but a magnificently beautiful one as well. It was a sword any Viking would prize, and she knew

139

he must have a suit of mail as well as a helmet and shield. The armor was expensive, but he was a wealthy man from a fine family and could afford all the necessary implements to make war. That he chose to reside on so distant a farm in such a humble abode was unusual, even perplexing, but she guessed he'd wanted to be left alone while he recuperated from the injuries he'd suffered in his encounter with the bear. Undoubtedly his armor and other weapons would be at his father's home, but for some reason he'd wanted to keep this sword close at hand, and with a shudder of contempt Celiese replaced it in its wrapping and laid it at the bottom of the chest. She put away his clothing as neatly as she'd found it, and, satisfied he'd not suspect she'd looked through the chest, she slammed the lid shut and turned away, as disgusted with herself as she was with him. There was a wicked-looking spear in the corner where he kept his bow and arrows, as well as a double-sided battle ax that appeared to have been used only to chop wood. But it was the image of the sword she could not clear from her mind. Repelled by that gruesome discovery, she went quickly to care for the two horses, As she returned to the house she noticed the vegetables in the small garden were in need of water and brought several bucketsful from the stream to quench their thirst. She then turned the wooden pail upside down to use as a stool and sat down to contemplate the vast expanse of grain that had begun to sprout upon the surrounding fields. Mylan must have sown the seed just prior to their wedding, she realized, and the bitter-sweet memory of that day filled her heart with despair. She sat gazing out over the countryside, her posture betraying her dismal mood.

Mylan paused as he rounded the corner of the house. Celiese was sitting so still that he approached her stealthily, uncertain why she should be observing his small garden with such intense interest, but she was concentrating so deeply that she did not notice his presence until he cleared his throat and spoke gruffly. "The plants will grow without such close supervision, Celiese, or is the knowledge of how to raise food for your own use also a skill you lack?"

"What?" Celiese leapt to her feet, picking up the pail by the handle as she replied, "I was merely thinking my own thoughts, Mylan, not wondering how these plants grow."

"At least you were clever enough to bring water, that is all the vegetables require for the time being." Mylan frowned with disappointment, for the young woman was obviously not in the least bit pleased to see him return home. She looked annoyed, impatient at having been interrupted when she'd been doing no more than staring at his garden! Thrusting the hen he'd shot toward her, he exclaimed, "If you have no idea how to pluck a bird, I suggest you learn before suppertime!"

Celiese backed away, not eager for such a duty, "Why couldn't you simply teach me how the fowl is to be prepared rather than complaining that I'm unable to do it? You have no reason to continually treat me so meanly!"

"No reason!" Mylan threw the limp bird at her feet, furious with her for being so stubborn. "That I speak to you at all should please you. That I have been so generous as to bring you here to live with me has clearly made no impression upon you!"

Celiese drew back her foot, tempted to kick the dead bird clear over the roof of the house. "Is it gratitude you want or simply obedience?" she asked defiantly. Mylan was looking extremely fit, and she knew he could silence her with one blow from his fist, but she was beyond caring.

For the first time Mylan stopped to consider the expert fluency with which Celiese spoke his language. There was no trace of an accent in her speech, and she never seemed to lack for the precise term she wanted to make a point. "Can you even speak the French tongue—"

"What?" Celiese was confused by the irrelevance of his question and could only stare up at him too dumbfounded to give a more sensible reply.

"Can you speak the language of the French? Yes or no?"

"*Oui!*" Celiese replied flippantly, tossing her fair curls for emphasis.

"What does that mean?" Mylan took a step closer, closing the distance between them to no more than a foot, and that space was occupied by the dead hen.

"It means yes, I am a Frenchwoman, and I speak the language of my people as easily as I speak yours."

That she could manipulate words so readily made him distrust her all the more. "I care not at all what you say or in what language you speak as long as you learn to prepare meals worth eating!" Mylan turned away, deciding Celiese was no easier to manage if left by herself all day. He swore under his breath. He'd wanted her to . . . to what? To learn her place; but he knew he'd taught her

142

nothing that day.

Perplexed by the bitterness of their angry encounter, Celiese glanced down at the feathered heap at her feet and decided the sooner she began the disagreeable chore of plucking the bird clean the sooner she'd be finished. Using the wooden pail again as a stool, she sat down and began to pull away the feathers, scattering them to the wind as she muttered a coarse string of oaths of her own.

Mylan warmed only enough water to clean himself thoroughly with a wet cloth before he peeled away the bandage that covered his side. The wound seemed to be healing well, but the scar would be as hideous as his others, he thought with a grim sense of humor.

Celiese stopped at the door, never having expected to find Mylan standing nude. She was uncertain whether to go back out or to simply complete the errand that had brought her inside. When he glanced over his left shoulder at her she continued to regard his lean physique with an admiring gaze as she explained, "I came to get a knife to dress the bird. Do you need me to rebandage your side while I am here?"

Mylan found the pretty young woman's level stare astonishing, for she seemed to be neither embarrassed nor repulsed by his unclothed body, and he was as uncertain as she as to what action he should take. He reached for his suede trousers and pulled them on without seeming to hurry as he responded. "No, it will be better if I do not cover it now."

Coming close, Celiese reached out to touch his ribs just above the gash. "Are you certain? It has just begun to heal. If you were to move too quickly it might tear open and—"

Brushing her hand away, Mylan laughed at her concern. "Just what do you think I'll be doing tonight that will prove so strenuous?"

Frightened by the taunting light in his golden eyes, Celiese blushed deeply as she backed away. He was right, of course, if he came after her now he'd cause himself far more pain than pleasure, but it was that threat that appalled her, and she could think of no ready retort to wipe away the smirk of triumph that lit his handsome features with such devilish glee. Turning away, she picked up his knife from the table. Suddenly noticing that it was decorated with the same rhythmic pattern of inlaid gold filagree as the sword she'd found earlier, she nearly let it slip from her grasp.

"Be careful with that! I'll not have the blade dulled by your carelessness!" Mylan called after her, but she was gone before he realized she could just as easily have turned in his direction and thrust the blade of that highly prized weapon clear through his heart. Appalled by his own carelessness, he vowed to be more cautious where she was concerned, for he knew he'd frightened her, and she was not the type of woman to take such an insult lightly. "A slave would not dare attack her master!" he said aloud. Knowing she still did not regard herself as a slave, he swore bitterly, and Celiese would have been pleased to see the mocking shine had left his eyes to be replaced with a far more clouded glow of confusion.

Celiese roasted the hen upon a spit over the hearth, and although Mylan paid her no compliments he did not complain about the meal she served him, and she considered that a victory in itself. There was still the matter of her sharing his table, however, and it was all she could do not to ask him why he wished to treat her so rudely when there was no one about to know or care if she dined with him. Not wishing to beg for his company if he'd not give it gladly, she cut off a tasty portion of the breast for herself and went outside to enjoy the coolness of the evening while he finished his meal. She then went for a walk before returning to the house, and to her relief found Mylan sleeping soundly. But it was a long while before she could rest, with the strain of their uncertain relationship troubling her so badly.

In the following days Celiese found her life no easier to live, for now she frequently looked up to see Mylan studying her actions with an interest she felt far from flattering. He would laugh at her blush, or remind her of some tiresome duty she'd neglected to perform, but she recognized the gleam in his amber eyes for the pure lust it was and knew it was only a matter of hours before he felt well enough to give vent to his passions once again. He had been so dear to her before, so gentle and sweet, but now everything had changed between them and she could imagine no torture worse than having Mylan treat her as a whore when she still wanted so badly to be his bride.

Her mounting fears compounded to terrifying proportions the afternoon she went to the door to shake out a fur and saw Mylan approaching with two strangers. The men were almost as tall as he, yet neither had a pleasing appearance. They struck her instantly as being of the same crude nature as Raktor and his kin, and she closed the door, looking about for someplace to hide herself, but there was none, and the men were too close for her to successfully escape them if she ran outside. She tossed the glossy pelt upon Mylan's bed and backed away into the corner, praying the strangers would not be invited inside, but in the next instant all three men came through the door.

"I can offer you some ale, at least while we discuss the reason for your journey here, but I can give you no hope that your proposal appeals to me." Mylan slammed the door behind his guests, using far more force than was necessary to emphasize his words. "I am not pleased to see you, nor would I welcome anyone now when I am busy with my crops and cannot spare the time for such an interruption as your presence here presents."

Celiese held her breath, for she knew Mylan was no farmer. He spent his time hunting or with his horses, and she doubted he did more than glance at his fields from the day he planted them until the harvest began. She brushed a stray curl away from her eyes, wanting only to disappear into the shadows, but to her horror Mylan called out to her in a loud voice.

"Have you no manners, Celiese? I would like my guests to be served as promptly as they would be in my father's home. Bring us some ale and be careful to spill none, for I have little to spare."

The strangers turned then, their mouths agape as they watched the graceful blonde prepare to serve them. Never had they seen such a treasure, and after they exchanged knowing glances one exclaimed, "So this is your woman, Mylan. No wonder you do not wish to be disturbed. I would never leave my bed were she to share it!"

Appalled by the boastful man's assumption, Celiese set the tray down carefully upon the table without daring to look up at Mylan. She knew him to be a proud man and she didn't want to hear his response, for she knew he would be no more pleased by his guest's teasing than she was. As she turned to go, the man who had spoken reached out to grab her wrist.

"What is your name, girl? The story is a confusing one, I'm told. Are you slave or wife? What do you call Mylan, master or husband?"

Celiese struggled to pull free, but the man held her too tightly and finally she had to look toward Mylan for assistance, her gaze imploring him to speak in her behalf. The look in his light eyes terrified her though, for his glance was filled with hatred, and she was certain it was directed solely at her. In desperation she gave the obnoxious visitor a hoarse command. "Unhand me, you swine!"

Astonished by the clear ring of authority in the young woman's voice, the startled man released Celiese with a quick slap to her fanny and gestured toward the pitcher of ale. "I like a woman with spirit, but there will be enough time for me to see to you, girl, after I have quenched my thirst. Well, Mylan, perhaps if my original proposition does not please you I can make another one that will!"

When the two strangers burst into deep peals of hearty laughter, Celiese did not tarry but reached for the pail and ran to the door. "I need more water to prepare our supper," she said breathlessly, then left the house. But the second she turned the corner she dropped the pail and fled for the safety of the woods on the far side of the stream. She ran on and on, not caring if her only gown were ripped or her arms and legs were scratched cruelly by thorns. She kept on running until she feared her lungs would burst, and she had to sink down behind a thick clump of bushes to try and catch her breath before she rose again to flee ever deeper into the forest to where she hoped the hateful men would never be able to find her.

When dusk fell and Celiese could no longer make her way through the dense underbrush, she crawled beneath the only shelter she could find, a tree uprooted by a long forgotten storm and left half buried in the earth. She was cold and tired, and desperately afraid, for Mylan had sworn once that he'd sell her at his first opportunity, and she was certain by now the money had already changed hands.

Chapter Nine

Mylan leaned against the doorway of his house, waiting impatiently as the sun rose, his keen gaze sweeping over the fields in the distance with the same care to detail he'd given the sea. The land was flat, uninteresting to view in the pale light of dawn, devoid of the constant motion that made the sea the most fascinating of sights. He cursed loudly, though no one would hear, and turned to pick up his bow and arrows, deciding if he had to search for Celiese he'd at least make good use of his time. He knew she'd never come back by herself; she was too willful by far to return on her own and beg his forgiveness for leaving his home without permission. He had apparently been much too lenient with her; she was more spoiled than Olgrethe, surely, for that haughty girl had the excuse of her class, but Celiese was no more than a slave. That word caught in his throat, for he knew he'd failed completely in his attempt to make her accept that lowly status. Nothing about the lovely young woman reminded him of other captives he'd known. She always looked directly at him, her gaze neither servile nor defiant, but curious, questioning, until he was usually the one to turn away first, for he found the clarity of her expression troubling. It disturbed him greatly that she had such a guileless glance when he knew her to be capable of the most treacherous deceit. Everything about her annoyed him, for she moved about his small house with the grace of a princess, as if she were the finest of ladies surrounded by luxury rather than the housekeeper of one young farmer who despised the land. Lady Celiese d' Loganville, he whispered to himself, her name rolling off his tongue like the melody of a favorite song, and he halted abruptly, realizing he was doing a poor job of tracking. Giving all his attention to his task, he returned to his home to begin anew. The pail lay where she'd thrown it, and when he found the trail of footprints ended at the water's edge he crossed the stream and searched carefully until he found the marks her tiny feet had made as she'd sped over the mud. He laughed to himself as he spied her path easily. She had moved too swiftly, carelessly leaving a trail of broken twigs and trampled grass. A boy could track so obvious a trail as the one she'd left, and he quickened his pace as his spirits rose in triumph.

The shrill call of the birds greeting the new day startled Celiese as she came fully awake, sitting up so suddenly she struck her head upon the tree that had provided her only shield against the chill of the night wind. She shivered and rubbed her arms, but as she attempted to rise Mylan's hand clamped down upon her shoulder, forcing her back upon the earth.

"How could you have become so lost while going to the

stream, Celiese? Is it not a straight path from my house to the water's edge?" Mylan asked sarcastically, his handsome features set in a taunting leer.

Celiese looked up slowly, fearing the worst. She saw the hopelessness of her fate clearly in his eyes. His fingers gripped her shoulder securely, but when she placed her hand lightly over his he drew away. She'd found the warmth of his touch irresistibly appealing, and even on that bitter morning when she sat cold and hungry she longed for the comfort of his embrace and marveled at her own weakness. At least he'd come for her alone, and she didn't have to face all three of them at once. "I am not lost," she replied calmly, turning his menacing question aside sweetly.

"Oh, but you must be, for surely you know the penalty for a slave who flees from her master, for one who runs away so foolishly as you did yesterday." As Mylan stepped back his curious gaze swept over her slowly. She looked as though she'd spent a most miserable night, and yet her confidence seemed undiminished by her ordeal.

Celiese lifted her hand to shade her eyes from the morning sun. Mylan carried only his bow and quiver, so what did he plan? "I have never been punished by a Viking for any crime, Mylan, I cannot even imagine what cruelty you might wish to inflict."

Her comment sickened him thoroughly, for there was not the slightest trace of fear in her gaze, only a sadness so deep he could scarcely bear to see it. When he tried to answer his voice broke, and he covered that display of weakness by clearing his throat with a deep cough before speaking again. "It is not cruel to teach a slave her place!

151

It is the right of the victor in any battle to make slaves of the defeated and bend their wills to his."

"You and I have fought no battles of any kind, Mylan. In fact, since my family was attacked by the same people who are also your enemies, why do you not regard me as an ally rather than a slave?"

"Get up!" Mylan commanded hoarsely, exasperated beyond endurance since her point was well taken and he had no way to refute it. "I have no desire to make allies of young women! Since you are so dreadfully ignorant, I will teach you that any slave who runs away can expect to be whipped, beaten severely when she is captured and returned to her master."

Celiese rose slowly and smoothed out the wrinkled skirt of her tattered dress. She was sorry to see the pretty garment had been ruined, since she had no other. "You cannot afford to whip me, for it would greatly reduce my price if you left me scarred, and I know you planned to ask all you could possibly receive for me. Is the matter not already settled?"

Mylan shrugged, perplexed by her query. "Who would buy such a continually troublesome woman as you?"

Now Celiese was the more confused of the two. Her eyes studied Mylan's expression closely, but she could discern nothing to help her understand his meaning. "What of your friends who came yesterday, did you not sell me to them?"

Amazed by the ridiculousness of her assumption, Mylan scoffed impatiently, "Those villains are no friends of mine! They wished to hire me to captain a ship for their raids, but I'd sooner rot here on my excuse for a farm than lead a band of pirates out to pillage. I gave them no more than one sip of ale and sent them on their way." Lying with what he hoped was convincing bravado, he continued. "They took scant notice of you, Celiese. Are you so vain as to think they'd have paid me for you?" They had, in fact, approached the subject, offering a more than generous amount, but seeing his total lack of interest, had not pursued it, despite their great desire to own such a captivating beauty. He'd forgotten he'd once threatened to sell her; the prospect was unthinkable to him now, and he was sorry to see Celiese had remembered his boast and had thought he'd carried it out. Knowing it had been her own fears rather than something he had done that had caused her to flee his home lessened his anger at her considerably.

Celiese looked away to hide her sorrow, but his criticism had hurt her far more deeply than he'd realized. "That I do know, Mylan. I know Vikings think nothing of asking their host for a pretty slave, and no man is so inhospitable as to refuse such a request."

Mylan clenched his fists tightly at his sides as he fought back the wave of red film that descended over his eyes, but he was so infuriated by her comment he could scarcely see. "Did Raktor make a practice of offering you as an entertainment to his guests? Is that what the bastard did to you?"

"No." Celiese replied softly. "Never." But only because she'd been clever enough to remain hidden whenever strangers were about, but she dared not reveal that secret to Mylan when he already thought her the most devious of creatures.

"Yet you thought I would give you to any man who knocked at my door?" Mylan stared down at her, horrified that she would rate him below Raktor in the manner of his conduct toward her. He'd made no secret of his desire for her, perhaps had been too obvious about it in the last few days, but he'd never meant for her to think he'd allow others to share her favors when she was his alone. She did not reply, but her unspoken answer was in the sorrow that filled her luminous green eyes, and he reached out to take her arm as he changed the subject abruptly. "Come, it is a fine morning for hunting, and I am wasting time here that could be better spent elsewhere. You are fortunate the bear that lives nearby did not perceive your scent, or I would have found little left of you this morning." Her skin was cool and he drew her close, hoping to warm her slender body as well as lift her spirits.

"Is this where the bear attacked you?" Celiese looked about them anxiously, certain the animal must be lurking close by.

"Yes, and he's a vicious beast who would have devoured you in no more than two savage bites. He is enormous and lives just beyond the rise. Would you care to see his cave?" Mylan pointed the way with a broad sweep of his arm.

"No!" Celiese backed away, still uncertain of his mood. "I believe you."

Mylan eyed her with a skeptical glance. "Then that is the first thing I've told you that you've accepted without an argument!" Delighted to have won even so small a concession from her, he started off in the direction he'd indicated without once looking back to see if she were following, but Celiese had no desire to be left behind and hurried to catch up with the tall man. He led her on a winding path through the trees, stepping so carefully that not a twig snapped beneath his feet to warn the creatures of the forest of his presence. When at last he had the cave in sight, he reached out for Celiese's hand and drew her close to his side as he whispered, "Do you see the mouth of the cave beneath that rocky ledge in the hillside? That is his lair. Bears are solitary beasts, preferring to mate then leave their females to have their young and raise them alone. He roams far and wide, so you must never stray so far from my house ever again, for you would be too tasty a morsel for him to resist." As Mylan glanced down at her frightened expression the stern line of his mouth softened to a teasing grin, but she was so intent upon spotting the ferocious beast that she didn't notice his smile.

Celiese scanned the rocky terrain, expecting the gigantic animal to appear at any moment, her tension mounting until it nearly suffocated her, and, at the precise instant in which she thought she'd surely faint, the stillness of the morning was shattered by a deep growl that could have come from no other animal. Mylan shoved her behind him as he withdrew an arrow from his quiver and set the notch in his bowstring, ready to attack should there be cause, but no other sound came, nor did the bear show himself. After a long moment Mylan relaxed his alert stance and beckoned for Celiese to follow as he started back in the direction from whence they'd come.

That Mylan had moved so swiftly to shield her body with his own at the first sign of danger had astonished Celiese, and she tried to stay in his shadow as they left the woods. Why had he done that? she wondered. Was it no more than a reflex, a man's natural instinct to protect a woman? She could not help but hope there had been some feeling for her in his action, but the events of the last twenty-four hours had confused her so completely she did not know what to think about him. She watched him closely as they walked along, his golden curls shining in the bright sunlight with a healthy sheen, the muscles that crisscrossed his broad back flexing and relaxing as he moved, his long legs swinging rhythmically from his narrow hips, his stride confident, despite the slight limp that marred his gait. In every way she thought him the most handsome of men. The sun was high overhead when they came upon a wide, sunlit meadow, and when Mylan paused suddenly to rest she was so lost in her own daydreams she nearly slammed right into his back before she realized he'd stopped walking.

"Why are we stopping here?" she asked softly.

Mylan brought his fingertip to his lips to warn her to be silent, and she stood quietly by his side, not wanting to disturb him when he seemed to be straining to hear something upon the morning breeze that she could not yet discern. She watched him casually take an arrow from his quiver and fit it against his bowstring, but when he began to pull back the string and turn toward her she gasped in horror. She saw only the gleaming tip of the deadly arrow as it flashed in the sunlight and shut her eyes tightly to force away the terrifying sight of her own death. The arrow sped by her cheek so closely she could feel the wind made by its path, and, fainting, she slumped forward upon the soft new grass.

Mylan threw down his weapons and gathered the slender woman into his arms, kissing her lips lightly before he called her name. "Celiese, Celiese!" He shook her, but she did no more than moan softly, and satisfied that she would soon revive he laid her down gently and walked across the meadow to the spot where the young buck lay and withdrew his arrow from the animal's neck. It had died instantly, which pleased him, for he derived no pleasure from making an animal suffer needlessly when death should be sure and swift. He wiped the arrow upon the grass to clean it, then replaced it in his quiver and walked back to find Celiese sitting up watching him. "I thought you enjoyed hunting, why have you been so anxious to come with me when you fainted at the death of a deer? That is the purpose of hunting, which I thought you understood, to kill animals for their pelts and for food." Mylan bent down on one knee and regarded her pale complexion closely before lifting his hand to caress the smooth curve of her cheek. Her face flooded with color as she blushed deeply, and he chuckled as he teased her. "That is better. I cannot carry you back home as well as the deer."

Celiese was dreadfully embarrassed to have been so foolish; it was obvious now he had been aiming over her shoulder and not at her at all. "I'm sorry. I have not been hunting in a long while, but I would not have fainted had I known that animal was your target rather than me."

"You?" Mylan laughed out loud as he got to his feet.

"Your imagination seems to know no bounds this morning, woman. Now, the hour grows late and we are a long way from home." Handing Celiese his bow and quiver to carry, he walked back to the deer, got a good grip on the carcass, and slung it over his shoulder. His burden was heavy and he kept his thoughts to himself as they returned home, but his mood was still a good one when they finally arrived. "We will roast some of this venison now and dry the rest to preserve it. I do not even hope that you know how to prepare hides."

"You know that I don't," Celiese admitted readily, for his smile did not waver, and she realized with delighted surprise that he was teasing her for a change rather than criticizing her for her many failings.

"I will prepare the meat. Heat water so I can bathe when I finish. There is a tub on the far side of the shed. Well hurry, fetch it so I'm not kept waiting!"

"As you wish," Celiese replied sweetly, but she feared she was the one in need of a bath. She found the tub, and after dusting it out rolled it into the house and placed it near the hearth. Since Mylan was going to skin the deer and carve up the meat she thought it only fair she help him in whatever way she could, but the buckets of water were heavy and she soon wished she'd known how to prepare the hide. When at last he came in she had the final kettle of water heated and ready to pour into the tub.

After pulling his tunic off over his head, Mylan sat down to unlace his boots. "I built a fire outside so we'll not fill the house with smoke. You know how to turn the spit, but it does not have to be done so often as with a bird."

"Yes, I understand." Celiese waited a moment, pleased he'd taken the time to tell her what to do in a pleasant tone, but when he stood up and reached for his belt she turned to go. It was his home, and he knew where to find soap or a towel to dry himself with, but before she reached the door he called her name.

"You may stay here with me if you like, Celiese, I have no objection to your company." Mylan smiled broadly, his invitation a sincere one as he gestured toward the tub.

Celiese gripped the door handle tightly as she lifted her chin. "Surely I'm not allowed to share your tub when I'm not permitted to sit at your table, Mylan." She left before he could respond, but she had been serious. She'd not share one part of his life if he excluded her from all others. Her cheeks burned with embarrassment as she rushed out to check the fire that was roasting their supper. It was burning well, so she leaned back against the nearest tree and watched the flames dance and sizzle as fat from the venison dripped into the fire. It was a long while before Mylan appeared, and she could only stare, too surprised to mask the admiration that shone so brightly in her eyes, for he'd gone to as much trouble to prepare for their supper as he had for their wedding. Not only was he clean-shaven, but he'd trimmed his hair and put on one of the handsomely tailored outfits she'd seen in his chest. His tunic and trousers were of a rust-colored suede, the soft lines of the garments defining the power-ful contours of his muscular body with an easy grace. She tried to return his warm smile, but she was so ashamed of her own appearance that she looked away quickly. Her once beautiful gown was no more than rags, her hair a tangled mess, and she hid her hands rather than display her broken and dirty nails. She had never been so unkempt, but she hadn't realized how sorry she must look until the moment he'd come through his front door looking so splendid.

If Mylan noticed Celiese's discomfort he did not mention it. He walked over to look at the meat roasting upon the spit and nodded with satisfaction. "I do believe your cooking has finally begun to improve, Celiese, this is well on its way to being done to perfection."

"My cooking?" Celiese asked coyly. "You killed the deer, hacked up the carcass, put the meat on the spit, built the fire. I'd say you did the major portion of the work yourself and deserve whatever credit is due for the quality of the meal."

Mylan opened his mouth ready to argue, since he'd no intention of doing any cooking when she was there to do it for him, but he was hungry and the venison so savory he saw no reason not to take credit for it. "Yes, perhaps you are right. I am as accomplished a cook as I am. . . ." After pausing to grin slyly he continued, ". . . as I am at most things I attempt."

Celiese walked back into the house without speaking, since she didn't care to comment on his many talents, especially the one he so obviously meant. At least the man had regained the confidence he'd lacked when first they'd met, she'd done that much for him. But she doubted he'd ever stopped to consider how greatly he had changed since the first day they'd met.

It took Celiese almost as long to empty the tepid water

from the tub as it had taken her to fill it, and she had no energy left to begin all over again to heat water for herself. Still, she wanted to be clean, so took the ill-fitting gray wool gown she abhorred with her down to the stream. She peeled off the shreds of the blue silk dress, and, caring little that Mylan was undoubtedly observing her actions closely, bathed and washed her hair in the ice cold water as she had each day since she'd come to his farm. She thought her appearance greatly improved, but when she returned to Mylan's side he shook his head sadly.

"It is unfortunate I had so little time to gather clothing for you before we left my father's house. I have needle and thread; take what you must from my things, but make yourself something that fits tomorrow. That gown is atrocious!"

Celiese held the skirt so she'd not trip as she moved closer. "Yes, I do believe I said this was hideous too, but—"

"Don't tell me you cannot sew!" Mylan exclaimed in disbelief.

"Yes, I do know how to sew very well, but it will not be easy to turn garments made for a man your size into ones that will fit me."

"What is the matter with my size?" Mylan extended his arms, assessing his proportions as though he'd been insulted.

Seeing he'd misunderstood her, Celiese tried to explain, "I did not mean that as a criticism, Mylan. You are tall and well built, a magnificent man in every respect, but I am a slender woman, so my figure is very different."

Although her compliment was a sincere one, Mylan reacted angrily, "I know how I look, you'll gain no favors from me by lying about it."

Exasperated, Celiese followed him as he walked around the fire. It seemed no matter what she said he took exception to it. "All I know is that I seem to be a sorry substitute for the woman you love, and although I have done my best to please you, I have obviously failed. Why don't you go to Estrid now, she is young, no older than Olgrethe, and you shouldn't think badly of her for refusing to marry you after you'd been so badly hurt." Suddenly their problems seemed to have a simple solution—she was never going to win his love and had been a stupid fool to try. "She's the one you want here with you, isn't she? Rather than a slave you despise?"

Mylan lifted his hand, clearly meaning to slap Celiese out of his way, but he regained control of his temper and thought better of such a hostile gesture. "Do not speak that woman's name to me ever again, Celiese, or I swear I will give you a beating you'll never forget!" He had never been so furious with her. She was full of ridiculous ideas, it seemed, but to drag Estrid's name into their conversation was more than he could abide.

With a defiant toss of her damp curls, Celiese continued, "Oh, go ahead and hit me, I don't care! You can have any woman you want, Mylan, but we'd both be far happier if you sent me back to Olgrethe and married the woman you truly love."

"After what I've suffered with you I will never even consider taking another bride!" Seeing that he at last had

162

the feisty blonde's full attention, Mylan yanked the spit off the fire and started to carry the perfectly roasted venison into the house. "Well, come on, this is the first good meal I've had in a week, and I insist you share it!"

Astonished that Mylan would want her company when they were in the middle of such a heated argument, Celiese nevertheless ran after him, tripping and nearly falling as she stepped on the hem of the cumbersome dress. But she caught herself and followed him into the house at a sedate pace, as if he'd issued the most gracious of invitations.

When Mylan made no attempt to begin a conversation as they ate, Celiese brought up a subject she was certain would interest him. "I think we should kill that bear, Mylan. He deserves to die for what he did to you."

Appalled by her suggestion, Mylan took a long drink of ale before he replied. "That bear and I have already had one confrontation, Celiese, with a most discouraging result. I most certainly will not consider going after him again without at least fifty men to assist me. You would be no help at all!"

Celiese had to agree. "I'll need weapons, of course, and time to practice with them. I did not mean that we should go after the beast tomorrow."

"Fully armed you would still be useless, Celiese." Mylan cut another slice of meat as he marveled at her courage, when only that day she'd fainted as he'd drawn his bow to shoot.

"There's more than one way to kill a bear, Mylan. Do they ever dig pits here and lure the animal to it? Once they fall in it is a simple matter to slay them."

Sighing softly, Mylan nodded. "Yes, that can be done, but how do you suggest we distract the bear while we dig? It would take the two of us more than a week to dig a pit of sufficient size to trap that monster."

Since he hadn't scoffed at that suggestion Celiese tried another. "Dogs would be helpful. Why have you no hunting dogs here, Mylan?"

"I had three, beauties I'd raised from pups, but they all died the same day I nearly did."

Celiese swallowed, sorry now that she'd asked, for clearly the loss of the hounds still pained him, but since he seemed to be in a willing mood to talk she asked softly, "You and your dogs were alone when you encountered the bear?"

Mylan looked up from his meal, surprised by her interest in so gruesome a topic. "No, Hagen was with me. We were tramping through the woods, talking about nothing of any importance, when suddenly the dogs went wild. My brother went one way and I the other, thinking we'd circle around to meet and attack whatever quarry the dogs had at bay. Unfortunately, the bear was too clever for such a simple plan, and you've seen the result. Had it not been for the fact that Hagen is so skilled with a spear, my death would have been a swift one."

Since she'd not seen anything to admire in Hagen in the short while they'd been together, she was impressed. "Then you were lucky that he was with you."

Frowning, Mylan could not agree, "I did not think so at the time, but he is a very stubborn individual and refused to let me die in peace."

Celiese knew Vikings believed the best possible death

was one met during battle, but wondered if a fight with a bear would have qualified him for entrance to Valhalla, where brave warriors were thought to spend eternity feasting and fighting where they could never again be defeated by death. That gory image disgusted her completely, and she decided not to ask him about it, as the subject of his death was too painful a one to consider even for the sake of a philosophical argument. "I had little opportunity to get to know Hagen. When next we meet I will try to be more friendly, since you owe your life to him."

"And you owe yours to me?" Mylan finished his ale, then sat regarding her with a cynical stare.

"Don't tease me, Mylan. If you were going to kill me for revenge you'd have done it long ago," Celiese pointed out calmly but she was disturbed by the morbid turn their conversation had taken.

"I do not kill beautiful women for revenge!" the golden-eyed young man scoffed. "I merely meant that as long as I live you will also, so it is to your advantage to see I survive whatever the fates have in store for me, whether it be ferocious animals in the forest, or enemies of the two-legged kind."

Celiese's cool green gaze sharpened to an icy glare. "Is that another threat to toss my body on a funeral pyre? It was to be Raktor's the last time, is it now to be yours?"

Mylan thought the luscious tint of rose that anger gave to her cheeks was most attractive and nodded slightly. "I plan to take you with me wherever I go, Celiese, even into the next world. Do not try and run away from me again, for I will not be so lenient with you the next time."

165

Celiese rose from her chair, backing away from him as she spoke in a defiant whisper. "If you permit other men to speak so rudely to me as that horrible brute did yesterday then I will run away again and again! If it will save your pride to treat me as a slave when others are present then I can do little but try and bear it, but I'll not be pawed by strangers! I swear to you, Mylan, no man is ever going to touch me again unless I want his attentions!"

Mylan was out of his seat in an instant. He dashed across the small distance that separated them and swept Celiese into his arms, holding her captive in a firm embrace as he responded with a livid snarl. "You'll not give me orders. I am the master here!"

Celiese did not struggle or complain, but instead lifted her lips to his, stilling his angry outburst with the sweetest of kisses, her affection for him overflowing her heart in a rush too delicious to contain. Since he understood none of her fears, she hoped only to make him feel the depth of her love, which was his for the asking, but only his.

Mylan was in no mood to ask for the loving he felt was rightfully his, and he carried Celiese swiftly to his bed, allowing her no more than a second to catch her breath before he lay down beside her and drew her into his arms. His kisses were wild, demanding the ready response he knew her lithe body capable of giving, but she placed her hands on his chest in a vain effort to push him away.

"What did you think would happen this afternoon when you bathed in the stream without the slightest display of modesty? Do you think I am devoid of all emotion except anger? What did you hope to catch, if not

166

me?" Giving her no time to respond, Mylan again lowered his mouth to hers, but this time his kiss was teasing, his lips playfully caressing hers until she gradually relaxed and lay calmly in his arms. "Well, why did you make such a show of inviting my affections if you do not want them?"

As Celiese stared up into his golden eyes their bright sheen reflected the glowing embers upon the hearth with a taunting fire, and she could no longer keep her desires hidden. "I do want you, Mylan, desperately, but I still want to be your wife. I want to be your beloved companion, not a slave who must forever bow to her master's will."

Mylan raised his fingertips to her cheek, studying her delicate features with a rapt glance before he replied. "What difference does it make what I call you, when either way you will always be mine?" He'd had enough of her endless defiance and said no more as he leaned down to deepen his kiss. He needed her love too badly to argue over the circumstances that brought them together. She might belong to him, but he was a captive of the passion he could neither deny nor control. He needed all she could give, her lively spirit, her enchanting glance, and best of all her tender affection, which she had given before in such abundance. Wife, mistress, slave, the words rang in his mind with a senseless clatter, she was simply his, and no word could describe the joy the sweetness of her surrender gave him. He gathered up the hem of her oversized dress to slip it gently over her head so he might caress all of her splendid figure without the barrier of the rough fabric to hinder his pleasure as well as hers.

Her skin was glowing with the same deep blush that filled her cheeks, and he let his lips trace her gentle curves with slow kisses that teased the pale pink tips of her full breasts to rosy peaks. He had no gift for poetry, for the beauty of words to make her understand how deeply he'd come to care for her, but his affection was in his every gesture, and he vowed to himself that that would have to be enough.

Celiese laced her fingers in Mylan's soft curls to draw him near to her heart, for she'd not dared hope he would again treat her so sweetly, and she enjoyed the tenderness of his touch greatly. He was again making love to her as he had on the night they were wed, with an irresistible passion that filled her whole being with a deep longing to have more of his enticing affection, and she slipped her hands under his soft suede shirt to help him remove it more swiftly. His scars made his body unique, but no less dear, and she leaned across him, letting her curls tickle the taut muscles of his stomach as her tongue traced the pattern of deep slashes that marred the smooth skin of his chest. She loved all of him so dearly, the scars as well as the perfection of his lean physique, and her lips traveled over his warm bronze skin, gently conveying the adoration she dared not speak.

Mylan's breath quickened to hoarse gasps as he tried to do no more than enjoy Celiese's delightful affection, but she had driven him past the grasp of reason and he felt only the overwhelming need to finish what he'd begun when he'd first placed her upon the deep mound of furs that served as his bed. He tried to catch her, to encircle her narrow waist to hold her still, finally pulling her down upon him to press her slender hips to his as he rolled over, slowly pushing her down among the tangle of lush furs where he could use all his strength to pin her beneath him in a loving embrace. He held her tightly, winding his fingers in her long curls to capture her smiling lips beneath his own. She moved against him, her rhythm far more gentle than his, luring him with a seductive grace ever deeper into the warm, sweet secrets of her vibrant body, until his pleasure was nearly pain and he could wait no longer to bring their passion for each other to the height of ecstasy. He buried his face against the soft curve of her throat, savoring the feel of her lovely body beneath his own until he could feel the rapture that thundered through his own body shudder through hers. He had not counted the times they'd made love, but knew they had been far too few, when it was the most wondrous of pastimes to share. She was like no other beautiful woman he'd ever known, not teasing and flirtatious, nor haughty and aloof, but so giving that he was drunk with the wine of her kisses, and he lay filled with contentment as he pressed her close to enjoy the feel of her silken skin against his own far more rugged flesh.

Celiese's fingertips separated Mylan's golden curls with a lazy caress before her hand moved softly down his throat and over his shoulder. His loving had left her filled with a joy so profound, she knew paradise could offer no greater pleasure than lying with him always did. She had stayed his anger with her first kiss, turning his wrath into playful affection, but he'd not given her the promise she'd wanted so desperately to hear. How could he fail to feel her love and respond in kind? If he still felt nothing for her after she'd given all any woman could, would he never grow to love her? Would she know only the strength of his passion and never the beauty of his love? She knew she should leave his bed, leave him alone to contemplate the necessity for their marriage since only he had the power to choose what their life together would be, but she had no desire even to stir, let alone leave the warmth of his arms so he might see how greatly he'd miss her.

Their many problems forgotten in the dreamy haze of shared pleasure, Mylan propped his head on his elbow and lay watching Celiese as she slept curled against his side. She fascinated him, not only with her beauty, but with her courage, which never seemed to fail her, and he marveled again at the strange twists of fate that had brought her to his bed. Had he not been mauled so savagely he would have been wed to Estrid two years ago, would by now doubtless be the father of at least one son, and yet he never thought of the woman nor missed the child they'd not had. It seemed impossible to him now that he could have come so close to marrying another and might never have known Celiese. The mystery of her past tormented him still. He dared not trust her, and yet he could no longer pretend an indifference to her distracting beauty, when each time he made love to her only made him want her more.

"Celiese." He called to her softly and was pleased by the width of her smile as she opened her sparkling green eyes. He saw only the delight in her gaze and cared little what new deceit might fill her heart when she would again welcome his affection so willingly. A sly grin crossed his lips as he leaned down to kiss her, pulling her back into his arms to again enjoy the gift of her intoxicating loving, and with his last conscious thought he wondered which of them was now the slave.

Chapter Ten

Mylan stood beside his bed, watching Celiese with an admiring glance as she continued to sleep soundly long past the hour she had usually been up to prepare his breakfast. Her flaxen curls were fanned out over the lustrous furs, her creamy skin flushed with a delicate pink, and she was so pretty a sight he could not bring himself to disturb the peace of her dreams. Finally he forced himself away. Wandering outside, he realized that watering the garden was too tedious a chore for so delicate a woman and quickly carried several buckets of water from the stream so Celiese would not have to waste what energy she'd have that day in such strenuous labor. Then turning his attention to his horses, he led them out into the sun, but as he brushed their glossy coats he grew increasingly impatient for Celiese to awaken. He wanted to take her riding with him. He needed to survey the boundaries of his land and gauge the progress of his crops, and, thinking that was excuse enough to wake her, he strode back into his house and shook her shoulder lightly until she opened her eyes.

"The day is half over and still you are lying in my bed! Get up quickly, as I want you to come with me, and if we do not leave now we will not return before nightfall." Pretending anger with her laziness, he placed his hands on his hips and tried to frown convincingly.

Yawning sleepily, Celiese sat up and demurely covered herself with an amply sized pelt. "Where is it we are going with such haste? Is it even dawn?"

"Dawn? It is nearer to noon! Now get up and dress so I'm not kept waiting!"

As he turned away Celiese called to him, "You said I might take something of yours. Would you choose it please, as I'd not want to cut up your favorite garments by mistake."

"There is no time for tailoring now!" Mylan replied crossly, anxious to be on his way.

Glancing out the door he had not bothered to close, Celiese asked curiously, "Is it warm again today?"

"Yes, it is a day that would please Freyr, as well as me. Now get up from that bed without any more delay!"

"Who might this Freyr be that he cares so much for the weather?" Celiese asked sweetly, still making no move to leave his bed.

Laughing at her ignorance, Mylan forgot his impatience as he explained. "He is the god of sunshine, as well as rain, the giver of peace and plenty. Do you know nothing of our gods?"

Celiese licked her lips with an enticing subtlety. "I have heard the name, but you have so many gods, while we have but one, so it is quite natural that I would become confused."

173

"Only one god to aid man with all his troubles?" Mylan was now in a teasing mood as he walked back toward his bed. "He must be very powerful then, to take responsibility for so much."

"Indeed he is, Mylan, but I do not consider his name a matter for jest, and neither should you," Celiese cautioned seriously, for truly she considered the great difference in their faiths not a suitable matter for casual discussion.

"What I will choose to laugh at next is you riding astride your mare nude, for if you do not hasten to dress I will take you with me as you are!" The gleam in his eye turned wicked as he reached for the pelt that covered her slender figure, but at the last instant he did not jerk it away.

For some reason that threat held little to frighten her, but Celiese rose from his bed. Taking the long gray gown that still lay where he'd tossed it the night before, she drew it over her head. "There, does this please you?" She combed her tangled curls with her fingers, giving her hair little thought, since it would blow about in the wind as they rode.

"No!" Disgusted at her pathetic appearance, Mylan pulled his knife from his belt, knelt at her feet, then took hold of her hem. "I can at least shorten this ugly garment so you no longer stumble as you walk, but I'm not happy to see you in it again." Her splendid figure deserved to be clothed as beautifully as possible, and he was sorry he had so few alternatives to offer.

Celiese turned as he worked swiftly to cut several inches from the bottom of the long gown. He was so close

she could not resist reaching out to touch his golden
curls lightly, her caress a fond one, but he looked up so
suddenly she drew her hand away.

"Do not try and distract me. I mean for us to go
riding." Handing her the excess material, Mylan rose to
his feet, then shoved his dagger back under his belt. "I
will saddle our mounts. Use my comb on your hair, as it
needs it badly." Scowling, he turned and left without a
backward glance, and Celiese had no idea why she'd displeased him now when he'd enjoyed her touch so much
the previous evening.

By the time Mylan was ready to depart, Celiese had had
sufficient time to prepare. She'd braided her hair into a
single plait that reached her waist, and had used the scrap
from the bottom of her gown to fashion a belt. She looked
exactly like what she was, the loveliest of young women
clad in a totally unsuitable dress, but she was looking
forward to going riding and smiled warmly as she leapt
upon the gentle mare's back. "Where is it we're bound,
Mylan? Perhaps if there is time I can gather branches for
my weapons."

Laughing at her insistence that she needed weapons
for a sport that sent her into a faint, Mylan teased her
again. "I'll not have you hunting, Celiese, not when you
faint at the sight of a drawn bow."

"It was not the bow but you that frightened me. Must
you be so mean?" Lacing her mare's reins through her
fingers, Celiese pretended to pay him scant attention
while she peeked at him through the veil of her long
lashes. He seemed to grow more handsome each time she
saw him, and she thought that most unfair since she had

175

not the benefit of even one nice gown to help her win his affections.

"You must cease to worry that I'll slay you when you would be so highly profitable to sell." The instant those words left his lips he regretted them, for the pain that filled the pretty woman's eyes was tinged with such furious anger he knew he'd made a grave error in teasing her about being his slave. Striking his mount's flanks lightly with his heels, he set their pace at a brisk canter, giving Celiese no opportunity to make the hostile reply he knew she was about to speak.

The wind stung her eyes, but Celiese forced back her tears. So she was to be reminded constantly that she was his slave! How could she have been so foolish as to have believed their relationship had changed when it so obviously hadn't? He regarded her as a piece of property, no different from the land over which they rode or the mound of furs upon which they'd slept. His jest had sickened her thoroughly, for she'd hoped he would have more consideration for her feelings, but perhaps only his own were important to him. Yet when next he spoke, he seemed so seriously interested in confiding in her that she began to wonder if perhaps she'd only imagined that his comment on her status had been an insult.

Mylan drew his stallion to a halt beneath a stand of linden trees and motioned for Celiese to come close. "The stream provides sufficient water for growing grain, the land is fertile, the crops plentiful, but I find myself too restless here to enjoy the peace this farm should afford. It is a prison without walls, not the pleasant sanctuary a home should be."

Surprised by the sudden change in his mood, Celiese nevertheless responded in as serious a tone as he. "I do not believe it is a home you crave, Mylan, but the freedom to seek your destiny elsewhere." She advised calmly. "Only you know what desires lie hidden in your heart, but you should simply live the life you long to live with no further thought of the drudgery this farm requires to maintain."

"Drudgery, is it?" Mylan smiled at her term. "Torture is nearer the truth, but you do not understand, Celiese." Dismounting, he walked around to her side, placing his hands around her narrow waist to help her down. Taking her hand in his, he led her to the smooth grass beneath the trees and pulled her down beside him in the shade, leaving their mounts to graze undisturbed nearby. "If I were content to sail no further than Kaupang or Birka, or to the other commercial ports my brothers frequent, then I could sail now. But I want to go far beyond the horizon, to a world none has yet seen." Mylan looked away, far into the distance, his expression filling with sorrow as he grew silent.

After waiting a moment Celiese could no longer suppress her curiosity. "If no man has seen this place, how do you know it exists?" She knew Vikings were fond of relating their own adventures, or of listening to heroic tales told by *scalds*, men who were respected for their cleverness with words, but whether the tales they spun were true or not she did not know. "Have you heard a legend perhaps, or some story about this faroff land?"

"No, but there are lands to the north of us, I have been to them. Why should lands not exist in the west, as

177

well?" Mylan pointed out logically. "I have no wish to follow another's lead, I want simply to sail toward the setting sun until I have discovered all the secrets the world has hidden still."

In the clear light of the spring day, Mylan's eyes were a vibrant light brown, filled with the golden flecks that gave them their remarkable topaz shine. Staring into those eyes, which seemed to see wonders beyond imagining, Celiese hoped only that he would realize his dream. Her hand still lay in his, and she clasped his fingers tightly as she spoke. "You are well, Mylan, truly you are, and you must follow your heart wherever it leads you, for it is plain you will never be content living here." Not even with me here to love you, she thought wistfully.

For the briefest of moments Mylan wondered what sane man would sit as calmly as he and seek the advice of his slave. A few tendrils of silvery blond had escaped Celiese's braid to curl softly upon her cheeks, and she was so appealing a young woman he was tempted to accept her recommendations as most sensible regardless of her lowly status. "Strong enough for most things, that is true." A sly smile curved across his lips as he continued. "To grow grain, to hunt deer, to make love to you; but I am not strong enough to begin a voyage of many weeks across the widest of seas. If it were no more than my life I would gladly risk it, but I'll not needlessly endanger the lives of my crew."

That he would mention the intimacy they'd shared so casually pained Celiese greatly, but she'd not let him see that hurt and changed the subject to a far safer one.

"Your brothers sail well, with hands so light their ship nearly flew across the waves. Raktor and his sons are brutish in all things, that their ships do not sink beneath them as soon as they leave their docks amazes me, for they understand neither the winds nor the currents, but only the greed that fills their own hearts."

It was not only the beauty of his slave's appearance that he enjoyed, but the acuteness of her perceptions, which continually amazed Mylan. "I could not have described their failings better, and your compliment for my brothers pleases me, as I am the one who taught them as children. They were clever boys who learned rapidly how to sail our craft expertly."

"It was you who taught them, not your father?" Celiese asked with an enchanting smile, encouraging him to continue.

"The weather is best for sailing in the summer," Mylan explained simply.

That comment shattered Celiese's composure instantly, for she knew exactly where his father had been then—away stealing for himself what other men had earned! Her revulsion showed clearly in her expression as she responded in a vicious whisper, "Traders, your mother swears you all are! Is she so foolish as to believe that preposterous lie!"

Reacting instantly to her insult, Mylan snarled angrily, "No one could tell more preposterous lies than you, Celiese!" As she turned away, ready to spring to her feet, he pulled her back down beside him. "I told you you'd never escape me any time I wanted you, and I find your anger a most powerful aphrodisiac!" Pulling her

179

into his arms, he kissed her with such savage passion that he left his own lips bruised as well as hers, but he did not release her from his confining embrace when he at last lifted his mouth and leaned back to judge her reaction.

Celiese tried to break away but Mylan was much too strong to elude, and he pushed her down upon the grass with only a slight effort. Never one to take such mistreatment without a fight, she continued to struggle, making his task a near impossible one, despite his far greater size and strength. But she knew it would take only one good blow of his fist to end her resistance, and her panic increased tenfold. She could scarcely breathe, let alone scream, but, suddenly remembering the knife he always carried she managed to rip it from his belt and raise it to his throat as she swore, "Damn you, I'll kill you before I'll let you rape me!"

Mylan stared down into the brilliant green of the defiant woman's eyes and in that instant saw the horror she'd suffered as clearly as if it were taking place right before him. He saw a terrified child surrounded by drunken men calling the crudest of encouragement to one another, and, feeling her outrage as well as her pain he drew away, shocked by the clarity of the vision she'd projected to his mind. Releasing her swiftly, he rolled over on his back, stretching out upon the grass as he forced himself to take several deep breaths. Celiese continually drove him to distraction, but he could not believe what he had almost done, for he took great pride in the fact he was a man who could control his emotions so they would not betray him as brutally as they almost had. "I have never raped any woman, and I had not meant to begin with you."

Celiese kept his knife close to her body, suspecting some trick to which she had no wish to fall victim, but as the minutes passed and he did no more than lie quietly by her side she began to relax. "I would rather you killed me than used me so badly, as others have, Mylan. I could not bear that from you." Indeed, it would have broken what little remained of her heart, for she had always given herself willingly to him. The only beautiful memories she had as a woman were of the love they'd shared, and she attempted to make him understand. "Please do not destroy the happiness I've found with you. Please do not do that to me."

"And I'll thank you not to tease me with a knife in your hand, Celiese, that is too dangerous a sport for both of us." Mylan waited quietly for her to make the sudden move he planned to counter with a vicious jab, for he knew she could not stab him without lifting her arm and putting her whole body behind the downward thrust. While he appeared to be resting, all his senses were attuned to the motions of the slender woman by his side. He counted the seconds slowly in his mind, wondering why Celiese was hesitating so long before making her move to try and kill him.

As confused by his words as he had been by hers, Celiese tossed the sharp dagger aside before reaching out to lightly caress Mylan's deeply tanned cheek. "I have never teased you, Mylan, not ever, so why do you persist in teasing me so cruelly?" When he did not immediately begin to argue with her over that question she lay down beside him, placing her head upon his shoulder so they both might rest more comfortably. "I wish . . ." She stopped abruptly then, unable to express the desires which filled her heart. She knew he would scoff at her dream of a marriage between them rather than the relationship of bondage, that held a slave to her master.

Puzzled to find himself in the arms of a woman who'd so recently sworn to kill him, Mylan prompted the reluctant beauty to continue. "Wish what? Since the day is so pretty, and I am in such a pleasant mood, I may just grant your request if you'll make it."

"Just hold me in your arms as you sometimes do, that is all I'll ask of you now," Celiese replied softly, unwilling to ask for more.

Lifting his right hand to her hair, Mylan began to slowly unfasten her braid, letting his fingers slide through the silken tresses with a gentle caress. She fit so naturally against him and he found himself as content as she until she reached up to brush his lips lightly with hers. That subtle invitation was all he needed to recall swiftly what his original purpose had been, but this time he moved far more slowly, holding her gently in his arms as his mouth continued to savor the sweetness of her kiss. He waited until she drew him near, pressing her body closer to his own before he slid his hand down the curve of her thigh and then beneath her dress. The coarse wool had scratched her tender skin, leaving it flushed, but his touch was light, as delicate as the early afternoon breeze, and he caused her no further pain, but gave her instead a warm, soft glow of pleasure that swelled through her loins and then sped along her spine to the lengths of her graceful limbs. Her legs were entwined with his, her whole body eager for his loving, and still he waited, wanting her to feel the ever increasing passion that throbbed within his veins until it was a driving rhythm creating a need he could no longer control. Her gown came off easily in his hands and he lowered his mouth to her breasts, letting his lips slide over their creamy fullness before straying lower still. His tongue flicked across her ribs. She was so slender now he could count them easily, yet he still thought her delicate figure superb. The smooth skin of her stomach was pale, and so soft. He tightened his hands around her waist to hold her close as he began to nuzzle the triangle of blond curls that beckoned to him with an irresistibly enticing promise of delights he meant to savor to the fullest.

Celiese gave no more than the smallest cry of surprise, for the pleasure Mylan gave with his ever more demanding kiss was too great to allow her a moment to either question or protest his methods. Her shock was dulled by the sheer joy of her body's response, and she lay back upon the soft spring grass, unable to do more than wind her fingers in his thick curls so he'd not draw away and leave her on the edge of an unbearably delicious ecstasy rather than plunging with her to its depths. His name escaped her throat in a low, husky moan, the strength of her need matching his own as she lured him beyond his own desire to an awaking awareness of the beautiful woman who longed to be his wife. He felt the exquisite pleasure he gave shudder through her body and wanted only to give more, to command her loyalty with the most splendid gift possible for a man and woman to share. He adored her in that instant, and when he was certain he had pleased her as greatly as any man ever could, his lips sought hers eagerly as he brought an end to his own anguish, conquering her vibrant body without the slightest bit of resistance this time. She welcomed his loving with a tenderness that made his pleasure as great as hers, deepening the bond that had grown between them. But he would not speak of love, and she dared not give voice to her feelings, either.

When at last he could again think clearly, Mylan let his lips trail down the inviting curve of Celiese's throat as he whispered, "I have been alone too long, for it was this wonderful devotion I meant to inspire within your heart, not a knife fight to the death that I wanted."

A devilish gleam lit her green eyes as she reached up to tousle his curls. "Why, Mylan, was that an apology?"

She was teasing him as an equal would, as any beautiful woman would tease her lover, but Mylan was appalled, his blissful mood shattered, and he shoved her away as he snarled, "I seldom apologize to women, and never to slaves, most especially not to you!" Rising quickly to his feet, he yanked his clothing back into place and strode off to get the horses so they might continue their ride without any more of her maddening distractions. Apology indeed! If she did not feel the apology in his kiss and caress, in the way he held her and made love to her, then mere words would never pierce the steel of her heart, and he'd die before he would speak them!

Astonished to have lost the most tender of lovers with a question she'd not thought unreasonable, Celiese made no effort to hurry to follow him. The warmth of his love filled her still, and she was sorry hers had meant so little to him. Finally, she pulled the gray wool gown over her head. Leaving her hair free, she went to join him.

Mylan awoke the next morning to find Celiese sorting through his clothing. She'd laid the garments in neat stacks, but what she'd hoped to find he didn't know. Not wishing to frighten her as he had before, he yawned loudly so she'd realize he was awake before he spoke to her.

"The porridge is ready, Mylan. I thought if I hurried I might be able to fashion something I could wear today. I want to go hunting with you and—"

Mylan swore under his breath. "When it takes all your talent to prepare porridge, I do not think you can spare the time to hunt, Celiese." He turned away as he rose from his bed, grabbing his soft suede trousers but not bothering with his tunic as he went outside to the stream.

Ignoring his taunt, Celiese chose a honey-colored tunic and trousers that appeared to have had considerable wear and laid them aside. She was not at all certain she could make his clothes fit her and did not want to ruin any of his finer garments if she could help it. When he returned, she showed him her choice. "I think you can spare these, Mylan, may I take them?"

"No, the color is faded, and there is no point in your wasting your time on garments that are already worn out." Bending to lift another tunic from those she'd laid out, he made a suggestion. "This green is nearly the color of your eyes; take this and the trousers that match instead."

185

"But these are new, Mylan, they do not look as though they have ever been worn." Celiese looked up, surprised he'd want her to have such nice things. "The green would be handsome on you, too, don't you like it?"

Laughing, Mylan went to fill a bowl with the bubbling porridge. "Yes, I like the color, but I'd rather see it on you. Now stop arguing and make something that fits by the time I return this afternoon."

Putting the other clothing away, Celiese took the things he'd offered. "I will try my best. If I have the outfit completed, may I please go hunting with you tomorrow?"

Mylan watched the pretty young woman's shy smile widen until he could no longer refuse her politely worded request. "I will decide tonight, not before, so cease your begging, as I am hungry and want to eat and leave without having to listen to any more of your chatter."

Celiese saw his smile as he pretended to concentrate on his breakfast and hurried to his side to give him a warm hug. "Thank you! You will not be sorry. As soon as I have weapons of my own I will help you gather all the pelts you want. I will make you rich, Mylan, I promise I will."

"Have you forgotten I am already wealthy? This house may be small, but the farmland is large and fertile. I have many trunks at my father's home filled with riches beyond your imagining and—" Realizing he was bragging shamelessly, Mylan stopped in midsentence, for there was no reason for him to attempt to impress a slave with the extent of his resources. Finishing the rest of his porridge in two hasty gulps, he grabbed his tunic and weapons and started for the door. "You will find needle and thread on the shelf above the chest. Now get to work so you do not neglect your other chores." After striding through the door he ran the short distance to the edge of the woods, then took up a more cautious pace. Celiese was so delightful a companion in bed it was a shame they could not find that harmony after the sun rose—but she had been most agreeable that morning. Perhaps it would not do his cause any harm to take her with him once or twice. She might find his trails too strenuous and ask to remain at the house, or she might actually be of some use, which he doubted, but he decided to tell her that evening that she might accompany him a few times just so he could see if by some stroke of good fortune she did possess the great skill she seemed to think she had.

After washing their breakfast dishes, Celiese studied the cut of Mylan's green tunic closely, trying to decide how best to make a garment tailored for his broad shoulders fit a woman. Since there was a generous amount of the soft deerskin, she decided to simply take out all the seams and begin anew to cut the pieces to her more diminutive size. She worked carefully to fashion a smaller version of the tunic, then sewed the pieces together with a double row of fine stitches before turning her attention to the trousers. Since they had a drawstring waist, she hoped she would have to do no more than adjust the length, but she found the fit so poor that she had to rip them apart as well. She spent the entire day working diligently on her new clothing and was amazed when she looked up to see the sun hanging low in the west before she was finally satisfied with her efforts to expand her wardrobe. She then had to race down to the stream to bathe hastily before slipping on the new garments and hurrying back to the house. She began the preparations for their evening meal as quickly as she could so Mylan would have no cause to criticize her for being idle.

Mylan had again been gone all day, but he'd spent as much time resting while he tried to think of some clever new strategy to use upon Celiese as he had in hunting. When he came through the door he stopped to stare in wonder, for he'd expected the attractive young woman to create a gown from his apparel, not a miniature version of his own attire. She looked at first glance like a handsome boy, but the curvaceous lines of her figure made that mistake readily apparent under more careful scrutiny. Even dressed as a youth she was a beauty, and he tried unsuccessfully to hide his smile. "As a seamstress you're far more clever than I'd imagined. I am glad to see you chose to make a practical suit rather than a merely pretty one."

Insulted, Celiese turned slowly, trying to see what he found so amusing. "I want to go hunting, not attract suitors, Mylan. I thought my work skillful, are you saying that it is not?"

The slight frown that creased her brow as she questioned him brought a momentary stab of remorse to Mylan's heart, but he quickly forced that weakness for her feelings aside in favor of heeding his own. "I just complimented you, do not beg for more flattery until you deserve it." Suitors! The word exploded in his mind with the pain of a thousand knives being turned in his flesh.

That men might make offers for Celiese with marriage in mind was a possibility he'd not even considered, but it was obviously a most likely happening in her view or she'd not have mentioned it. That was all he needed, men coming to court her! He had so little control over her behavior now he could scarcely bear it, but she'd be impossible then. Perhaps the fact that his farm was so remote from any others would finally have some value, at least he hoped it would, for he had no intention of allowing her to entertain male callers. He tossed the small birds he'd shot upon the table, then went to place his bow and arrows in the corner in an effort to gain the time he needed to control his temper. When he turned he spoke far more softly than he had. "Those are tasty when roasted. Pluck them clean and I will build the fire outdoors. Since you are doubtless a fine shot with a bow, I will expect more variety to our meals in the future."

"I may go with you tomorrow, then? You promised to tell me your decision this evening." Celiese held her breath, not daring to hope he wasn't simply teasing her again.

"I have much to do here which I've neglected, but we'll go out for a while at dawn. If you are up when I am ready to leave."

"Oh, you can be certain I will be," Celiese purred coquettishly as she carried the fowl through the door. "I'll be waiting for you—so see you are not the one to oversleep."

Mylan chuckled at her jest, but when he awoke the next morning he found Celiese curled up in a chair at the table. She was already dressed in the green suede outfit

189

she'd made and was eyeing him with a mischievous delight he found most disconcerting. Stretching to flex his muscles, he wondered how long she had been sitting there waiting for him to awaken. Perhaps hours, she was so determined a creature, and he admired that trait greatly, although he doubted he would have left without her regardless of how late she'd slept. She had again made a paradise of his night and therefore deserved some consideration from him, and he would have shown it. Yet, the fact she did not realize that pleased him as well, it was an advantage he would not waste. "Give me a moment, Celiese. Stir the porridge so it isn't filled with lumps for a change, and I will be grateful."

The tall Viking was out the door before Celiese could grab a bowl to hurl at him, but she was certain he'd never found a single lump in the porridge she served him. He never seemed to exhaust his list of complaints, however. He claimed the porridge was either too hot or too cool, too thick or too thin, never properly made, but she noticed he always ate his fill and knew his stomach appreciated her cooking even if his pride would not allow him to admit it.

When Mylan finished his breakfast they left the house, searching for straight branches to make weapons for Celiese as they walked. She went skipping with the enthusiastic gait of a child as she bounded ahead of him, and any game they might have sighted she scared away, but he could not bring himself to call her back. Her joy was infectious that morning, and he counted his pleasure in watching her well worth the cost of a few missed birds. Finally reminding himself he should be instructing her in the proper techniques of skillful hunting, he caught up with her and bent down to whisper softly in her ear. "Let us rest for a few moments, the hour grows late and we need to find something soon or we'll go hungry tonight." He stretched out in the closest patch of shade and patted the grass beside him to invite her to join him. "That you are so at home in the forest is more than I'd dare hope, Celiese, but there is something to be said for approaching prey stealthily rather than dancing over the ground while you sing to yourself. I fear there is no animal nor fowl living nearby who was not warned of our presence long before we could be sighted or our scents perceived."

Sinking down beside him, Celiese realized her delight in his company and the beauty of the day had influenced her to exceed the proper limits of cautious behavior. She brushed the stray curls away from her eyes as she apologized. "I have been very foolish, haven't I? Would it be better if I followed you?"

"Not for me it wouldn't," Mylan admitted slyly. "But you must not make so much noise, or we will have no hope of having a successful hunt."

"I will be so quiet you will forget you brought me along," Celiese promised sincerely. "Shall we continue?" Seeing his frown as he hesitated to rise, she touched his right knee lightly and wondered out loud. "If your leg pains you, I will massage away the tension in the muscles. That will surely help." Before he could offer any protest, she began to run her fingers down his thigh with a slow, easy rhythm, her touch that of an expert as she concentrated upon her task unmindful of the effect she was having upon him.

When the dull ache that seldom left his leg began to subside, Mylan found Celiese's nearness, as well as her tantalizing touch, impossible to ignore and spoke crossly as he pushed her hands away, "If you are as intent upon going hunting as you claim, rather than merely arousing me, I suggest you stop what you're doing so we might continue with our original purpose, which was a quest for game!"

Blushing deeply, Celiese scrambled to her feet and backed away. She'd meant only to soothe away his discomfort, not to create far more for herself. It was ridiculous of her to react with such modesty after she'd lain with him so often, but still she considered herself to be a lady and expected to be treated as such, no matter where they were or what they might be doing.

Mylan threw back his head and howled with laughter, for Celiese's embarrassment was so greatly amusing he forgot why he'd scolded her and could not contain his mirth. "Here, help me up." He extended his hand, but when she took it he pulled her down across his lap, catching her in an affectionate embrace as he nibbled her ears playfully. "You are all the game I want now, Celiese, for you are far more delicious a treat than any prey we might encounter."

Celiese knew better than to pretend an indifference she didn't feel and snuggled against him, the pleasure his nearness brought lighting her smile with an irresistible warmth. She wanted so badly to say she loved him, it was nearly impossible to swallow the words as they leapt to her lips, but she did no more than smile as she reached up to kiss him.

Mylan had never known a more affectionate woman and he planned to enjoy her favors endlessly, but the lazy warmth that enveloped them turned his thoughts to such sweet ones he was content to do no more than hold Celiese in his arms for a moment while he kissed her flushed cheeks lightly. He liked the long sweep of her lashes as she looked up at him, for that dark fringe made her glance all the more inviting, but as he watched her expression the clear green of her eyes darkened noticeably, as if the most disturbing of thoughts had crossed her mind, and he drew back, startled that she did not share his euphoric mood. "What troubles you, my pet, there is still time to hunt, we've not wasted the entire day." Not yet at least, but he now counted no time he spent in her company wasted.

Perhaps it was the gentle nature of his embrace, or the keen interest in his gaze, or merely the freshness of the spring day that overcame her usual reserve, but Celiese responded truthfully with one of her most frequent worries. "If I were to have your son, Mylan, would you set him free?"

Astonished by that totally unexpected query, Mylan grabbed her more securely, nearly shaking her as he asked, "What are you telling me, Celiese? Is this child a reality, or no more than a suspicion?"

Suspicion was scarcely the word, Celiese realized, for she was *terrified* she might already have become pregnant and wanted to know exactly what sort of life her child would have to face. "I am only asking the question because it is so strong a possibility, not because it has already happened."

Relieved, Mylan relaxed his hold upon her slightly. "I see." Chuckling softly to himself he then offered what he thought to be the most sensible reply. "Just bring me the child when he is born and I will decide then."

Infuriated that he'd laugh at a matter that was so important to her, Celiese broke away from him and leapt to her feet. "I know a slave's babe is a thrall too, a slave from the first breath he takes, but I had hoped you would think as much of our child as I will!" The man gave affection in such abundance, but why was it so empty, without the love she craved to inspire it? Searching her mind for a way to gain her own freedom and therefore free all her unborn children, Celiese stood proudly as she asked, "If I kill your bear, will you set me free?"

Getting to his feet and rising to his full height to give himself every advantage in their argument, Mylan continued to scoff at her fury. "Bring me his pelt and I may just do it."

"No! I must have your word now!" Celiese demanded emphatically, not in the least bit intimidated by his height and strength as he towered above her.

That a mere woman, and a slender, pretty one would suggest such an impossible task was so absurd that Mylan felt safe in agreeing. "I'll give my word then, bring me proof the beast is dead and you shall be free."

"It is agreed, then." Celiese turned away to gather up the branches she'd found to make arrows, but her mind was already busily planning strategy. She lacked the strength to shoot arrows with sufficient power to slay a bear, so what weapon could she use?

Confused by the intensity of Celiese's manner, Mylan

shook his head in frustration. He knew he should have simply made love to her again rather than catering to her whims by answering her fanciful questions. Her figure bore no sign of incipient motherhood as yet, but he could not help count back over the days since their farcical wedding had taken place. Had she become pregnant that blasted night she'd know it by now, and he hurried after her, wondering how he could force that truth from her lips when she'd spoken no other credible words in the entire time he'd known her.

Chapter Eleven

The fields of grain were flourishing, the summer was full upon the land, and Mylan paused in his labors to wipe his brow. He'd been chopping the firewood they needed to roast the meat for their supper while Celiese had gone to bathe. She'd have his bath ready when he finished, but she still preferred the fresh running water of the stream to soaking in a warm tub as he did. Her fair hair sparkled in the sun, her skin glowed with the pretty bloom of youth, so obviously her preference for the chill water of the stream harmed neither her health nor her beauty in any way. He'd often invited her, but she would never join him in a hot bath, and the mere thought of their attempting to bathe together brought a mischievous grin to his lips. But in truth, he could not think of the lovely young woman without smiling widely.

Celiese had mastered each lesson he'd presented, and he no longer even considered the prospect of going hunting without her by his side. She had listened carefully to his instructions, then practiced so diligently with her newly made bow and arrows that she had soon proven

196

astonishingly proficient. Were there ever need, he would not hesitate to send her out alone to bring home game for their table, but since that need had not arisen, he preferred that they hunt together. Her lively wit lit his days with laughter, while her delicate beauty continued to fill his nights with the indescribable joy of love. "Love." He whispered the word softly to himself, knowing her love was only an illusion, a spell she wove with no more than a seductive glance as she came to his bed, but it was a magic he'd never tire of sharing. Despite his every attempt at caution, the delightful young woman had simply bewitched him. But too often of late she had been so lost in her own thoughts that she seemed unaware of his existence. He could fault neither her behavior nor her housekeeping, but he worried still that she held secrets in her heart that might again prove disastrous for them both.

"Mylan?" Celiese shook out her damp curls as she called his name. He had split enough logs to last them for many weeks since they no longer needed a fire for warmth in the evenings, and she could not understand his purpose. "Are you preparing for winter already?"

Finally noticing he had greatly exceeded his needs, Mylan turned her question aside with good humor. "It is never too early to begin the preparations for winter, Celiese, for it is long and harsh here, far different from those you've known on the coast."

Coming near, Celiese reached out to touch his forearm gently. As usual, he'd discarded his tunic, and his warm skin felt so pleasant beneath her fingertips she did not lift her hand. "How did you pass the days when you had no one with whom to speak or share your meals?"

"I did not feel well enough to want company, but this winter I will have you to keep me amused." He leaned down to bite her earlobe with a playful growl, sending her backing away with a lilting giggle that amused him all the more.

"Beast!" Celiese called over her shoulder as she ran toward the house, but the prospect of spending the winter in his arms was so thrilling she could not hide her happiness. With luck she would be a free woman by then, his woman still, but by choice rather than command.

Although he did not comment, Mylan considered the supper Celiese served him most delicious. She had a natural talent for cooking, which had developed rapidly once she had an opportunity to practice her skills. As usual, she had steamed the vegetables from his garden, then sprinkled them with herbs he'd found in the forest, so that their flavor was perfection. He'd never tasted better fowl than she prepared, and she'd roasted the wild hen they'd shot to a succulent brown that melted in his mouth. In so many ways she was a treasure.

When he'd eaten his fill, Mylan shoved his plate away and withdrew from his pocket an intricately fashioned silver chain. Holding it up for Celiese to see, he said, "I found this as I was getting dressed this evening. I thought I'd lost it, but it has been a long while since I wore this particular pair of trousers, so the necklace was only mislaid. Have you ever seen one of these?"

Taking the pretty chain in her hands, Celiese found it held a delicate silver charm in the shape of a hammer. For an instant she could not comprehend its significance, then realized what it must be. "Is this a replica of

Thor's hammer?"

"Very good, I see you do know something of value, after all. The god Odin's son, Thor, owns three treasures, a hammer that can shatter rock and is useful to slay giants, a pair of iron gloves to hold the hammer, and a magic belt that doubles his strength."

Celiese nodded slightly. Mylan frequently spun tales for her now, but he had so many gods and goddesses upon whom to report she was certain she'd never be able to remember them all. Knowing Thor was a major god, however, she knew his possessions were worthy of being recalled and whispered the list softly. "Yes, I understand, a magic hammer, gloves, and a belt." Wondering about the necklace, she continued, "Is only Thor's hammer used for charms?"

"Yes." Mylan took the chain from her and walked around the table to stand behind her chair. He lifted her long curls out of the way to slip the attractive necklace over her head, then adjusted it so it lay comfortably around her neck. "There, it will bring you good luck now."

Celiese touched the small charm lightly, uncertain as to why he'd given it to her or how she might refuse to wear it without offending him. "This is so pretty, Mylan, and I am very pleased you want to give it to me, but I cannot accept it."

Forcing himself to hold his tongue, Mylan sat down by her side, trying first to think of some reason for her remark before he gave vent to his anger, but his gaze was too dark for his mood to be mistaken. "This is the only present I have ever given you. Why don't you want it?"

Celiese spoke softly, choosing her words with care, sorry she'd insulted him without meaning to give offense. "I cannot wear this, Mylan, for the charm will have no value on me since my faith is not yours. I do not believe in the power of Thor's hammer to bring me good fortune, and so it will not help me as it would you."

Mylan waited a long moment, considering the wisdom of her words thoughtfully, while he took a deep breath. When he saw the first trace of tears glistening upon Celiese's long lashes he leaned over to kiss them away, all thought of anger gone from his mind. "I don't expect you to accept my faith, all you need ever accept is this." He placed his fingertips under her chin to turn her face to his so he might kiss her lips tenderly, the reassurance in his touch as deep as that in his words.

Never able to resist his caress, Celiese lifted her arms to encircle his neck, hugging him tightly as she welcomed his kiss. When at last he drew away, she was smiling. "I will wear it then, and think only of you."

"That is better." Mylan hugged her in return, grateful she had given in to him so easily. It was not often he won her acceptance for any of his requests without a long and bitter argument, and he'd not meant to begin a fight that night, only to give her something pretty. "Come with me, let us look at the stars for a moment." Taking her hand in his, Mylan lead the way through the door, then stepped behind Celiese and wrapped his arms around her waist to draw her near. "This day was nearly a perfect one, for the crops are thriving without our toil, and we discovered a very beautiful part of the forest I'd never seen."

Placing her hands over his, Celiese relaxed against

200

him. With her loving care and fine meals he had gained a few pounds, his lean physique becoming more sturdy, but his muscular frame was still far from heavy. She found his warmth and nearness so reassuring that she almost purred as she replied. "How can you fault the day we spent? I think it was as perfect in all respects as any day will ever be."

There, she had done it again, chosen to argue rather than agree, but he did not complain of her willfulness. "There is one important thing lacking still, Celiese."

Frowning slightly, she turned to glance up at him. "If there is anything I've forgotten please tell me now, and I will see to it at once."

Mylan did no more than return her steady gaze, holding her in a light but firm embrace so she'd not escape his grasp for any reason. "It is you I want now, Celiese, for only you will make this night as pleasant as the day."

An enchanting smile lit the young woman's features as she turned to tickle his ribs playfully. "Neither your day nor night is complete without my company? Is that what you're saying, Mylan?"

Instantly Mylan grew wary, for he realized he'd said far more than he'd meant to, and her teasing questions demanded the truthful response he was still unwilling to give. Sweeping her up into his arms, he carried her back into his house and dropped her in a careless heap upon his bed. "I've lived too many years without your company to be dependent upon it now. Do not flatter yourself by pretending that I am! Sleep by yourself tonight and we will see just who is dependent upon whom!" Mylan started for the door without any idea of where he wished to go, but he was so intent upon teaching Celiese a lesson that he'd not considered where he would spend the night.

Leaping off the bed, Celiese came after him. "Must you be such an unreasonable bully? If my words displease you, will you not tell me why? I did not mean to make you angry when we were so happy together."

Scowling impatiently, Mylan stopped at the door. "Can you not remember it is your place to do my bidding and not mine to do yours?"

Color flooded the fair young woman's cheeks at that insult and she was suddenly as furious as he. "I am the worst of servants, it seems, but you must recall I was once your wife and forgive me when I treat you as my husband rather than my master!"

Mylan lifted his hand, nearly striking Celiese before he brought his temper under control. "Do not ever make the mistake of reminding me again of our marriage, when we both know you never expected to live for even one day as my wife!"

Celiese stared at the open door, for Mylan had simply vanished he'd fled the house so quickly. There was no point in following him, for he knew the land so well the coming darkness would be no hindrance to him, while she was certain to fall and be injured or at the very least to become lost. She clutched the small silver hammer he'd given her and began to pace distractedly up and down beside the open doorway. "Luck!" She shrieked in frustration, tempted to yank the fine chain from her neck and hurl it as well as the pagan charm out into the yard. How could the evening have ended in such a ridiculous way? Swearing at everything that caught her eye, Celiese cursed at the top of her voice, knowing Mylan was undoubtedly too far away to hear or criticize her language. Finally she noticed the hearth, which occupied the center of the small dwelling. "Damn Vikings, if they are so clever why can they not build a house with a proper fireplace and chimney!" They had roasted the hen outdoors so as not to fill the house with smoke. They often did that. Suddenly, as she considered the discomfort the smoke caused when she cooked indoors, she realized with a burst of insight that smoke could be a powerful weapon to use against a bear and felt foolish for not having thought of using it before that night. Nearly dancing with glee, her anger forgotten, she circled the room, then flopped down upon the large bed to consider the idea more fully. Knowing the bitter scene that had prompted Mylan to flee her presence that night would be repeated endlessly until she won her freedom, Celiese forced herself to consider all her options calmly in order to devise the most clever plan. According to Mylan, the bear roamed the woods near his cave during the day, then returned to it each night and remained there until dawn. If she were to approach his lair while he was sleeping soundly and lay a stack of green wood at the entrance, she could ignite it at sunrise. The beast would stagger from the cave, disoriented, blinded by the dense smoke, and she could kill him before he had a chance to escape or to do her any harm.

Glancing toward their weapons, which were stored in the corner, Celiese tried to make the best possible choice. Her bow and arrows would inflict only insignificant wounds, enrage the bear, and leave her in more danger than he would be. She'd thrown Mylan's spear only half a dozen times and had no confidence in using it as yet. The axe was useful for chopping wood, but she'd have to be far stronger than she was to swing it with sufficient power to kill the beast with one blow, and she'd have no second chance. She sat up then, hugging her knees as she tried to think of what to do. The small silver hammer brushed her hand, and, thinking of Mylan, she glanced toward the carved chest that held his belongings and an additional alternative came to her mind. His possessions included a magnificent sword, double-edged and sharp enough to slay a man with one blow. Could it also be used to kill a bear? She got up quickly, removed his clothing from the trunk, and found the sword where she'd first seen it. It was heavy, difficult for her to hold. But there was a rocky ledge above the bear's cave, and if she were to wait there for the animal to appear and strike him in the neck she just might be able to kill him before he had a chance to kill her. She'd have to leave at dawn, make her way to the other side of the forest, and gather wood near the bear's cave. When she was certain he was asleep, she would make the preparations for the fire, light it at dawn, then climb up upon the ledge. It was possible the plan would work as she imagined it would, but if it did not, she would at least have the satisfaction of knowing she had died fighting rather than spent what remained of her life as a captive. The whole idea terrified her, and yet it was her only chance to gain her freedom. She would have to kill the bear or die trying, and she had simply no other choice. She'd leave at dawn, make her way to the bear's territory, and pray he had had many fine meals that summer and would not be tracking her scent while she planned his death. She'd go in the morning, and if she were successful then the next time she saw Mylan she would be free and he could no longer call her a slave nor reject the love she wanted so desperately to offer him as only a wife could. Her problems solved for the moment, she prepared for bed, knowing she would need strength as well as cunning. She fell asleep promptly, letting the rest she needed wash the fatigue from her muscles as well as her mind.

When his temper cooled Mylan retraced his steps. If anyone were to sleep under the stars that night it should be Celiese, and he vowed that if she was still angry with him when he returned home he'd simply turn her out and sleep alone in his own bed—which was what he should have done in the first place. Finding the door unbarred, he entered the house cautiously, but Celiese was sound asleep, curled up upon his bed with a contented smile upon her face, as if her dreams were most entertaining, and he was disappointed to see that their argument had affected her so slightly. She had simply gone to bed as if nothing were amiss, and it annoyed him tremendously to think she had given so little thought to his comfort that if he had stayed away all night it would not have troubled her sleep.

The night was warm, and Celiese lay uncovered upon the furs, her pose a most attractive one. Mylan found his anger quickly replaced with desire. He was swift to cast off his own clothing, then bent over her, letting his lips slide down her spine to trail light kisses over her moist skin as he joined her upon the bed. Thinking the curve of her slender hip equally inviting, he caressed her lightly, teasing her slowly awake with a tantalizing touch that was sweeter than any dream could ever be.

Celiese snuggled against Mylan, the few hours they'd been apart forgotten as she pulled him into her arms. He gave her no opportunity to speak, but she would never have apologized for she was far too eager for his kiss to waste precious minutes discussing an argument that should never have taken place. Her plans already made, she wanted only to tell him good-bye with affection so lavish he'd never forget her should she be unable to return to his arms.

Mylan wound his fingers in Celiese's silken curls, hoping to hold her fast, but although he'd captured her lips with his own, he felt her hands moving over him with a honey-smooth touch which aroused his passions to an intensity he could scarcely endure. She moved beneath him then, her hands now encircling his waist to press down upon the small of his back, and he could no longer delay the pleasure he knew they would create together. He thought of her as delicate despite her seductive ways, and moved with practiced gentleness to dominate her lissome body with the fierce strength of his own. Agile and sure, he held her enfolded in his embrace, wanting now to conquer her more completely than he ever had. Their bodies joined in an ageless rhythm, the warm, sweet depths of her being welcoming each of his thrusts until the ecstasy she gave washed over him with the shattering power of a cresting wave and he was lost in her embrace. She covered his face with light kisses, then whispered the most flattering of endearments in his ear, but he could think of no words to describe his ever growing need for her, when surely it was a weakness he should fight with all his strength rather than enjoy to the fullest as he did. Savoring the taste of her kiss, he ceased to worry over who had triumphed that night when she gave so generously of her love. This surrender was the only one he needed to make his life complete. Her beauty was superb, her capacity for giving pleasure limitless, and he was sorry he'd wasted so much of the evening walking the forest alone when the joy of being with her was all that made his life worth living.

Chapter Twelve

While Mylan fell into a deep, contented sleep, Celiese lay wide awake in his arms, sadly recalling the weeks she'd spent in his home. If only he had just once spoken of love, or of how much he had come to care for her, she would have some cause to hope their future would be a bright one, but as always he had given unsparingly of his body without voicing a hint of the emotions that filled his heart. Her choice had already been made before he'd returned home that night, but his silence had sealed her fate as surely as she prayed his sword would seal that of the bear.

She left his bed as soon as the first light of dawn lit the small house with a soft golden glow and she could see well enough to gather the things she required. She dressed quickly, then put on the silver necklace Mylan had given her, knowing she'd need every manner of luck she could summon that day. She placed the flint he always carried into her pocket, slipped his dagger under her belt, and took his sword from the chest where it had lain hidden. She was ready to depart. Wishing there were some way to make the proud man realize how dearly she loved him, Celiese hesitated. When she could tarry no longer she bent down to give him a light kiss upon the cheek and whispered softly, "Do not forget me, my darling, for I have loved you well." Turning swiftly before her tears fell upon his face and awakened him, she hurried through the door and ran toward the stream just as she had the day she'd fled the house fearing she'd soon be sold to the rude pair who had come to visit Mylan. Her terror was every bit as real as it had been that day, for her situation was no less desperate. She'd not understood his sullen silence then and still didn't. His touch was always tender, his manner gentle, so why couldn't he return the love she gave to him with words? Was it only the fact that she was a slave that made him so reticent, or something more, a reason far deeper than any she could imagine? She continued to torment herself with unanswerable questions, wanting Mylan's love so badly at the same time she feared she might not survive the day to see him again.

There were many trails through the forest, and since she'd always had Mylan to lead the way when they'd gone hunting she got lost more than once, circling past trees she recognized as landmarks again and again. But still she pushed on, hoping to find her way to the bear's cave before darkness fell. She'd not thought it necessary to bring food, but now she was hungry and sorry she'd been so foolish as to leave the house without any provisions. It was late afternoon when she sighted the uprooted tree where she'd once taken shelter for the night. Knowing the bear's den was nearby, she grew doubly cautious. Scanning the underbrush carefully, she found the trail upon which Mylan had taken her and made her way stealthily to the spot behind the trees where they'd been able to see the cave. She stood perched on the balls of her feet, ready to run at the slightest provocation, but she heard no sounds other than the soft calling of the birds overhead in the trees. The cave was exactly as she had remembered it, set back in the rocks of the hillside, and the ledge that hung over it looked both easy to climb and solid enough to support her slight weight. Seeing no sign of the bear, she approached the lair slowly, finding the animal's scent strong. He had been there the previous night, she was certain of it, and prayed he would return that night as well. Forcing herself to be brave, she scampered up the side of the hill to test the ledge, gauging the angle from which she'd have to strike with the sword before climbing down with all possible haste. She ran then, her destination the meadow where Mylan had shot the deer. Skirting the edge of the wide field, she gathered branches for the fire she'd need, bundling the dry wood with green and carrying it back to the trees close to the bear's den. She was careful to select a spot downwind so as not to attract the bear's notice, and then she began practicing with the flint to be certain she could start a fire in the dim light of dawn. She'd often watched Mylan build fires and understood the process, but she rehearsed it repeatedly, too anxious to leave such an important step to chance. It was nearly dark when she heard the bear returning to his lair, his low growls sending shivers of fright up her spine, but she remained hidden among the trees and her presence went undetected. Huddled in the shadows she waited for the night to pass, blowing on her hands for warmth while she sang softly to herself to stay awake, but most often her mind was filled with thoughts of the handsome man who'd won her heart. She gripped his charm tightly, the coolness of the silver reminding her all too vividly of the differences between them. If she did not live to reach home, then she hoped he would remember the last night they'd spent together as being as beautiful as all the others, for she knew if the bear were to attack her as savagely as he'd mauled Mylan there would be nothing left of her for him to recognize, let alone remember. That gruesome prospect kept her wide awake until dawn lent a faint tint of rose to the eastern sky, and, after stretching to gain confidence that her tired muscles would not fail her, she carried the wood she'd gathered to the entrance of the cave and placed it just inside. Her fingers shook badly as she struck the flint, but the dry wood caught fire instantly and in a moment ignited the green branches, which burned with billows of acrid smoke. The morning breeze carried the evil-smelling fumes well into the dark recess in the hillside and Celiese took up the heavy sword and climbed up to the rocky ledge to await her prey.

Her heartbeat thundered in her ears while the fire crackled and surrounded her with smoke so thick she was nearly blinded. She was afraid she'd outsmarted herself rather than the bear, but at last she heard a low growl and then another. She braced herself carefully against the rocks, and when the enraged beast appeared at the mouth of the cave seeking relief from the dense smoke that had disturbed his slumber he had no chance to escape her forceful downward blow. The sharp edge of the steel blade caught him on the side of the neck, slashing his dark fur and severing the veins in his throat, sending a bright fountain of crimson blood spewing so high into the air that it splashed Celiese, dampening her soft suede clothing with gore.

Terrified, Celiese shrieked more loudly than the wounded bear, but she held on to the shining weapon, ready to strike again. But the bloodied animal staggered back into his smoke-filled lair and was quiet, leaving her no choice but to wait on the ledge as the sun rose. She dared not relax her pose when at any minute the beast might again come lumbering out into the open. He would now surely be able to sense her presence, since the fire had died down to no more than a few wisps of smoke and her scent would fill the air, She heard no sound at all from deep within the cave, but she still shook with the fright of her grisly deed. Her mouth was dry, her breath escaping her throat in hoarse gasps, but she dared not leave the ledge until she was certain the beast was dead. When she'd heard nothing by the time the sun was high overhead she was convinced he could not possibly have survived the vicious blow she'd dealt him. Now her mind focused upon another problem, for even though she'd slain the bear, Mylan had asked for proof, and she could not possibly skin the animal unless she were able to drag the carcass out into the sunshine so she'd have room and light enough to work. The beast had been immense, weighing far too much for her to attempt to move unassisted, so what was she to do? Her only choice would be to summon Mylan to help her, and, after waiting a short while longer simply for safety's sake, she climbed

down from the ledge and ran back through the trees,
hoping she would not become as lost on her way home as
she had on her journey there.

When Mylan had awakened to find Celiese gone he had
not been greatly worried. That she'd left him no breakfast was annoying, but he promptly prepared his own
rather than go without or wait for her return to eat.
When he could not find his dagger he feared it was misplaced and tried to recall if he'd had it with him when
he'd gone out for a walk the previous evening. If he'd lost
it on his walk he would never be able to find it, for he'd
paid no attention as he'd wandered through the woods
and could not recall where he'd been. It was far too warm
a day to require flint to light a fire, and so he did not
notice that it was also missing before he left the house to
begin a series of troublesome chores that could no longer
be ignored.

He worked all day, expecting his ambitious slave to
appear at any moment with game for their supper, but
when he returned to his home in the afternoon he found
her bow and quiver where she'd left them the day before
and was angry with himself for not noticing them earlier.
It was then he began to wonder where she could have
gone and what her purpose might have been if it were not
to hunt. Perplexed by that mystery, he sat down to enjoy
some ale while he considered what her options were.
There was honey, of course, and wild berries, which they
enjoyed, but had she gone to search for those delicacies
she would have returned by now. He grew increasingly
anxious and got up from his chair frequently to go to the
door and survey the path that led to the woods, hoping to

see her approaching. Too late he realized that Celiese was not coming home, and his rage was too fierce to contain, for he'd not thought the young woman would ever dare to run away from him again. He threw himself angrily down upon the furs and attempted to sleep, but could not. At the first light of dawn he set out to look for her.

Celiese had traveled no more than half a mile when she met Mylan upon the path. He was carrying his spear and scowling wickedly as she ran up to him, but she was so excited by what she'd accomplished that she did not stop to consider how greatly her disappearance had angered him. "Mylan, come quickly!" She turned back in the direction from which she'd come, expecting him to follow, but he reached out to take her arm and drew her around to face him with a forceful yank.

"Were you still so angry with me you'd risk running from me again? I thought the matter settled between us." He'd slept no better than she the previous night, and swore bitterly at her before he continued his hostile interrogation. "Did you think me so taken with your charms I'd not beat you as I would any slave for trying to escape me?" Before she could reply he caught a glimpse of the gleaming sword in her hand and lost his temper completely. "That you had the audacity to steal my sword is even worse! Whom did you expect to kill?"

Celiese backed away, repelled by the menacing expression in his amber eyes. She'd been so involved in her own plans to win her freedom that she could offer no other excuse for her actions now. "Your own words tell my

214

story, Mylan. After all we have shared you still think of me as your property, as no more than a slave, and accuse me of theft as well as running away when I'm guilty of neither crime. You gave me only one hope of winning my freedom and I took it. I have slain your bear, he lies dead in his den, and since I must drag him outside to skin him, I will need your help to take the pelt home as the proof you demanded."

"What?" Mylan was shocked to his very marrow by the calmness of Celiese's manner, as well as by her outrageous explanation. He'd thought she'd run off simply to punish him for walking out on her, but that she'd had such an impossible although noble purpose stunned him. "How could you have killed that bear all by yourself? Why would you have attempted such an impossible feat?"

"It was not impossible because I did it, I tell you. Come with me and you will be able to see for yourself." Celiese reached out to take his hand, but he drew back as if her touch disgusted him.

Alarmed, Mylan continued in an accusing tone, "If you have only wounded the beast, no one will be safe in this forest."

Celiese shook her head impatiently. "No, the bear is dead, he has to be." She described what she'd done, but the astonished Viking could only gape as he listened, too amazed to comment upon her outlandish scheme to trick the bear from his lair and attack him before he had an opportunity to harm her.

"Celiese, I was only teasing you when I told you to bring me the hide of that animal. I never expected you really to try to kill the beast single-handedly!" Mylan was horrified to think his playful jest had led her on so perilous a path.

Straightening her shoulders defiantly, Celiese argued her cause. "You said I would be free if I killed the bear and brought you the proof of the deed. Don't think you can go back on your word now, because I insist you honor your promise!" Her green eyes blazed with angry sparks. She'd stop at nothing to win her freedom, and he saw that clearly in her proud posture and furious gaze.

Mylan's expression grew harsh, for no man would dare insult him as she just had. "My word is good, but I do not believe you could have killed that large an animal without help. You probably only wounded him, and he'll be roaming the woods insane with pain and ready to kill anything he sees move. You should never have gone out to hunt that brute alone, but let us see what we can do now to rid the forest of his presence for all time. Let me lead the way while you keep your place behind me where you belong!" Mylan walked slowly, carefully scanning the surrounding brush for places the bear might hide. When they reached the cave he saw the remains of the fire, then the pool of blood drying in the dirt, and turned to stare at his smiling companion. Still unconvinced, he knelt down to study the tracks at the mouth of the cave, then without speaking rose to his feet and pointed, for it was clear the bear had left his den and wandered out toward the clump of bushes to their left.

Celiese shook her head in disbelief, but the tracks were unmistakable. "I was positive he was dead. I struck him before dawn, how can he still be alive?"

Her question ended in an ear-splitting shriek as the ferocious bear rose from behind the underbrush with a terrifying growl. His long, sharp claws flashed in the sunlight with the deadly gleam of highly polished steel, and his teeth gnashed wickedly, slicing through the air as he lunged for them. Mylan's magnificent sword shook in her grasp, but Celiese raised it with both hands, pushing her fear aside as she summoned the strength to swing the weapon.

With a hoarse shout Mylan shoved the frightened woman aside, then hurled his spear with such brutal force that the blade sliced clear through the beast's chest, stilling the beat of his mighty heart instantly. The animal was so close the Viking had to leap out of the way as the beast fell with a thunderous crash that shook the ground and sent every bird within miles soaring into the air screeching a piercing cry of alarm. Satisfied their prey was now thoroughly deceased, Mylan placed his foot upon the bear's chest and withdrew his spear with a contemptuous yank. He forced away the nausea that filled his throat, but had he been alone he would have given in to it gladly, for he was sickened at the sight of the animal that had caused him so much pain, and the beast's death did not begin to even the score between them.

Celiese stared at the fallen bear, devastated to think there was now no way for her to gain her freedom. But perhaps there never had been. Turning to Mylan she said in a threatening whisper, "I thought I had done it. I thought I'd killed that horrible creature so you would set me free, but it was no more than a cruel joke to you, was it? You never meant to give me my freedom! All you thought of was how you were going to punish me for running away, when I cannot believe you would think for a moment I'd ever wish to leave you."

Ignoring her impertinent question, Mylan held out his hand. "That is my knife you have at your belt, and if you will give it to me I will use it. I want my flint, as well, and you are never to touch my sword ever again for any purpose. Now cease your tiresome complaining and help me to skin this beast. It matters not which of us killed him—the job must still be done!" He stuffed the pouch containing the flint into his pocket, then took the dagger and worked swiftly to slit the hide down the length of the bear's underside before he sat back to stare at the deep wound in the animal's neck. "This would have surely killed him, Celiese, he would have bled to death before much longer. I'm certain of it."

Celiese disagreed angrily. "You killed the beast yourself, Mylan, he was your bear all along, and the kill is rightfully yours to claim."

Mylan frowned as he glanced up at her, but did not argue the point as he continued to work rapidly, his task a most distasteful one. When finally he completed the messy job he rolled up the pelt and handed Celiese his spear to carry home. "We'll leave the carcass for the scavengers of the forest to consume. I'd choke if I tried to eat one bite of that wretched animal's flesh." He led the way out of the woods without once becoming lost, but he remained silent as they walked toward his home, his mood no happier than hers. When they crossed the stream near his house they saw Hagen's horse tethered outside, and he called to Celiese to hurry.

Hearing his elder brother's approach, Hagen stepped outside to greet him. That Mylan looked so strong and fit delighted him, and he embraced him with a loud whoop of joy. They hugged and talked excitedly, for it had been many weeks since anyone had seen Mylan, and Hagen had much to relate. Having no wish to intrude upon their happiness, Celiese slipped away unnoticed. She walked slowly back to the stream where she cleaned their blood-stained weapons, but not knowing how long the brothers would spend talking she dared not disrobe to bathe and had to be content to wash only her hands and face for the time being. She strolled slowly back to the house and waited outside, as she felt so utterly defeated and hopeless she knew she would be a poor companion for the two men.

When they at last came outdoors, Mylan drew Celiese aside, placing his hands firmly upon her shoulders as he spoke. "I am a man of my word, and you are free, Celiese. I'm sending you home with my brother. Olgrethe will welcome you, and none will dare to mistreat you now that you are no longer a slave."

Celiese's astonished gaze swept the stern set of Mylan's features as she attempted to comprehend the reason for his sudden decision. "But I failed, Mylan, you killed the bear, I didn't!"

Stepping back, Mylan dropped his hands wearily to his sides. "I did not realize you would gladly risk death rather than remain with me. I've no desire to debate the question of whose blow killed that beast when all that matters is the fact that I've set you free." Calling to his brother to make his point clear, he shouted, "Take her

219

and be gone, Hagen, I want only to enjoy the solitude of the forest as I did before she came!" He stepped quickly into his house, then slammed the door shut with an angry thud to emphasize the finality of his rejection of her.

For a moment Celiese was too stunned to move, but when Hagen came forward, reaching for her waist to drag her away, she fought him so fiercely he could not hold her. Slipping from his grasp, she darted through the door before he could stop her. Without stopping to catch her breath she began to scream at Mylan, "I'll not leave you, I won't go! Why do you want to send me away, why?"

The tall man turned his back on her as he sneered, "I am sick of your lies, Celiese, now leave me be and go!"

"Do not accuse me of lying, for I have never spoken anything but the truth to you!" She hadn't lied to him, truly she hadn't; she'd pretended at first to be someone other than herself, but even then she'd always told him the truth. When she reached out to touch his arm he drew away, then, turning back to face her, he pulled his bloodstained tunic off over his head and threw it at her feet. He ran his thumb down the scars that crossed his lean torso and snarled, "Tell me again you find me handsome, Celiese, when all along you have thought me so hideously scarred you wanted only to be free! To be free of me is what you wanted, isn't it?"

"No!" Celiese shouted, the fury of her temper matching the fire of his. "That is not at all what I wanted! My pride is as great as yours, I know, but I cannot bear for you to believe I don't want to be with you. To me you are the handsomest of men and always will be. Try to understand I could not stand to be any man's slave, and I have never felt like yours, although you've spoken the word to me often enough. I wanted my freedom, so you would finally see me for the woman I am, a woman who would rather die than give birth to babies whose only future would be the degradation of slavery. That is a fate I'll not accept for our children, not for your sons and mine!" Celiese heard the door open and spun around, ready to fight off Hagen again, but it was Mylan who surprised her by coming forward to gather her up into his arms.

"I told you to take this woman and be gone!" Mylan carried Celiese through the door, waited for Hagen to mount his horse, then thrust the disheveled woman into his brother's arms. "Knock her senseless if you must, but take her away!"

"No!" Celiese pounded her fists on Hagen's hands, furious that she was being treated so meanly. "I'll not leave you, Mylan, I won't go!"

Mylan reached out to grip Celiese's knee tightly, inflicting a sharp pain that finally stilled her hoarse shouts. "I wanted only the company of a pretty slave, Celiese, just a young woman who would serve all my needs, but I was foolish to bring you rather than one of the others. You should thank me for being so generous as to set you free, for I'd sell you tomorrow if I hadn't!" He turned then and walked back into his house, leaving her too shocked by the hatred in his insult to struggle or argue as Hagen tightened his hold around her waist. And seeing she had ceased to fight him, he struck his mount sharply with his heels and carried her swiftly away.

Chapter Thirteen

As they sped toward his home, Hagen's grasp was so confining that Celiese made no effort to struggle against him. She was too shocked by Mylan's bitter farewell to notice mere physical discomfort and did not complain at the harshness of his brother's embrace during the long, miserable ride. But as they neared his home she recalled how he'd once thrown her from his horse, rudely tossing her in the dirt at his mother's feet. Wishing to avoid another such clumsy arrival at the Vandahl residence, she wound her fingers in his mount's mane to prevent herself from falling. But when Hagen began to laugh at that precaution she turned to look up at him, wondering what he found so amusing. "When my predicament is such a wretched one, how dare you find humor in it?"

"I'll laugh at whatever I please, Celiese, but you needn't fear me. I will set you down upon your feet very gently if you will let go of my horse." She waited until he drew the spirited stallion to a halt to release her hold upon the animal's mane, and as promised Hagen lowered her carefully to the ground before he dismounted with a quick leap and tossed his reins to a groom who'd come running to meet them. Taking Celiese's arm, he led the way toward the rear of the house as he spoke in a conspiratorial whisper. "There's none here who'll welcome your return, save Olgrethe, but she will be with Andrick now and I'll not disturb their evening." He paused a moment, certain Celiese would know why the newly married couple would not wish to be interrupted. "I have no choice but to take you to my room, where you can bathe and dress, as your present attire will impress no one favorably."

"What is wrong with the way I'm dressed?" Celiese protested heatedly. She'd made the outfit herself and thought it not only practical but comfortable as well. The fact that most women did not spend their days hunting, nor dress for such an activity, did not occur to her.

Hagen stopped walking abruptly and pulled her around to face him. The daylight had barely begun to fade, although the hour was late, and he looked her up and down slowly while he commented truthfully. "There is blood in your hair as well as splattered upon your clothing. Were anyone to see you now, they would no doubt accuse you of Mylan's murder. Do you wish to risk the wrath that mistake would incur? Or the punishment that would be too swift to allow time for you to deny the charge or disprove it?"

Celiese glanced down at the dark stains upon her trousers and suppressed a shudder at the memory of how the bear's blood had showered all around her as she'd struck him. Hagen's disapproving frown was only natural, she supposed, and she had to agree with him.

"You are right, of course. I know I am despised by all who live in this house, and little excuse would be needed for my execution. I have no choice either, it seems, but to do as you say, but is there no other room where I might stay the night?"

Sighing wearily, for he was certain no woman on earth would be safer sleeping in his room than Celiese, Hagen hastened to reassure her. "If you think I find you attractive, you are mistaken, but I had planned to sleep elsewhere, not with you! Now let us hurry, as I am hungry and have no wish to miss whatever was left from supper."

Celiese remained where she was as he turned away. His appearance was too much like Mylan's for her to feel comfortable with him, even had his manner been inviting. He moved with the same confident stride, his muscular build a handsome complement to his even features and unique coloring, but she felt only a deep sense of loss as she watched him walk across the yard. When he turned and came back for her she realized she'd been staring most rudely and took the arm he offered without argument, for she knew it was unfair of her to blame him for his brother's cruelty. When they reached his room she stopped at the door, for his quarters were so littered with clutter she dared not enter for fear of upsetting one of the carefully balanced heaps. "You have no room for me here, Hagen, there's not space to turn about, let alone for me to bathe and dress."

Hagen shoved a bundle of furs aside with a forceful kick, then bent down to push a small trunk from the center of the room to the far wall. "There, does that please you? I have not finished sorting our goods since our last voyage, but I do no more than sleep here and am not bothered by these things, as you so obviously are!" Swearing under his breath, he continued to work, but the stacks were so numerous he cleared little space upon the floor.

Celiese leaned back against the door to rest. She was exhausted and her head ached painfully. "I did not mean to insult you. I am simply so dreadfully tired I want only to sleep if I may."

Hagen frowned as he straightened up, surprised his inadequate housekeeping had not been the real source of her complaint. "Well, you cannot sleep in such filthy clothes. Remove them and I will see you have others when you awaken in the morning."

The delicate woman's eyes widened slightly, but she saw only disgust in Hagen's expression, without the slightest trace of lust in either his manner or words. Perhaps it was her own fault, she realized, for while Andrick had covered her with his cloak at the slave auction, when she'd reached their inn she'd tossed it aside in full view of both brothers before climbing into their bed. "I know you have seen me nude once before, and perhaps you think my modesty misplaced now, but—"

Waving aside her objection, the tall man came forward as he interrupted her. "I have much in common with my elder brother, but his weakness for beautiful women is not among the traits we share! You may take off your clothes, or I will slit the seams and rip them off. Which would you prefer?" Drawing his knife, he made clear his intention to strip her naked.

"I am fully capable of undressing myself without your assistance, Hagen," Celiese replied coldly. If he wanted to humiliate her she'd call his bluff by disrobing in front of him as if he were not even there. After what she'd suffered that day, she considered this small insult insignificant.

Hagen felt little regard for the disheveled young woman, but, as she began to untie the drawstring at her throat with the slow, liquid grace of the most exquisite dancer, he felt ashamed of himself for showing her such a lack of courtesy. Perhaps it was the sorrow in her gaze that touched him, or the pride in her posture as she made no move to turn away, but suddenly he found himself wanting to help her in any way he could. Kneeling quickly at her feet, he unlaced her shoes and found the leather nearly worn through as he slipped them from her tiny feet. Rising, he shook his head sadly. "It is plain my brother has taken very poor care of you. You are dressed in his cast-off clothing, when the soft folds of a woman's gown suit you far better. As soon as Olgrethe wakes in the morning I will tell her you are here and borrow something pretty for you to wear."

Surprised by his sudden change of mood, Celiese smiled shyly. She'd not yet removed her clothing, only loosened the ties, but thought if she waited a moment he might leave her to undress in privacy, and she dropped her hands to her sides. "Why thank you, Hagen, that is most kind of you, but please do not think I was mistreated in Mylan's home. I was very happy there and had no wish ever to leave him," Celiese explained softly, her heartache no less painful for having been voiced.

226

After pausing a moment to make certain his words would carry the meaning he desired, Hagen spoke calmly. "Do not make the mistake of believing you can return to him, Celiese. He has suffered far too much at your hands to forgive you this last insult. He is finished with you for all time, and you would be wise to believe that when he made the decision to send you away he meant it to be forever."

Celiese had no interest in debating that issue, since it certainly didn't concern Hagen. "Your brother made his point most effectively, since I am here rather than with him as I wished to be. It's useless to discuss my situation now when you are anxious to have your supper, and I want only to go to sleep." Turning away, she stepped around his numerous possessions to reach the bed, where she sat down wearily and lifted her hands to cover a wide yawn.

The only hunger Hagen now felt was one that shocked him with a deep, aching need he dared not satisfy, and he started for the door, eager for an excuse to leave the troublesome woman. "Do not wander the house in the morning, stay here until I bring you something to wear that won't cause more comment than your very presence most surely will."

He slammed the door so loudly on his way out that Celiese sat stiffly, waiting for someone to come to investigate the cause of the noise. But when no one appeared after several moments she removed her soiled clothing with a careless toss, stretched out upon Hagen's bed and covered herself with a light blanket. He was a puzzling man, with his mood that was so perpetually foul, but she had too much on her mind to worry over him when it was his elder brother who held her thoughts captive that night.

She had swiftly grown accustomed to having the warmth of Mylan's muscular body by her side when she slept, and she found the large bed uncomfortable without him. She knew her whole life would be empty without his dynamic presence to brighten her days and nights. She wondered if he too was lying awake. She hoped he was as lonely as she, lying alone upon his bed, staring up into the darkness and regretting his haste in sending her away when she had been such a devoted companion. Encouraged by that thought she drifted off to sleep, dreaming of Mylan and hoping someday soon he would realize the great wrong he had done her and at last ask her to be his wife.

The next morning Hagen went to Olgrethe to borrow one of her gowns, but as soon as he'd explained why he needed it she streaked past him, bursting through the door of his room to awaken the still sleeping Celiese with excited squeals of welcome.

"I despaired of ever seeing you again, and here you have been in the house for one whole night and I did not even know it! Wake up! There is so much for us to discuss, how can you lie there sleeping?" She sat down by her friend and shook her shoulders until Celiese finally sat up and pushed her away.

"May I please have a moment or two to open my eyes?" Celiese ran her fingers through her curls to push them away from her face as she realized that marriage had not made Olgrethe any more considerate. She appeared to be as spoiled as ever, expecting to have her own way instantly in all things. As always, Celiese forgave her that fault, but as she tried to respond to her enthusiastic greeting with a warm smile, Olgrethe began to frown.

"You are as tan as a fieldhand, Celiese, just look at you!" Olgrethe peered at her face closely, clearly disapproving, "You even have freckles!"

"I spent most of my time outdoors with Mylan, so it is no wonder I have grown tan, but truly, freckles are the very least of my problems, Olgrethe." Despite the desperate nature of her situation, Celiese found the criticism of her once creamy white complexion so irrelevant that it struck her as being extremely humorous, and she began to giggle uncontrollably. When Olgrethe began to laugh too, they fell into each other's arms, giving way to their delight in being together again.

Hagen leaned back against his still open door and shook his head reproachfully. "For grown women to act like children is unseemly, especially so in this case."

"Oh hush, Hagen!" Olgrethe called over her shoulder, cross that he'd want to spoil their playful mood. She was obviously unconcerned by criticism from her husband's brother and cared little that they had displeased him. "It has been many weeks since I've seen Celiese, and if she and I wish to laugh together you must not let it disturb your sense of propriety."

Celiese drew the soft woolen blanket higher upon her breasts as she looked toward the tall man, startled by the familiar ring in his deep voice. Both his tone and words had reminded her so much of Mylan that for an instant she'd thought it was he who had spoken. "I am sorry if we seem foolish, Hagen, but do you not have close friends whom you enjoy seeing?" He had greeted Mylan with such enthusiasm the previous day, she thought he should be more understanding of the regard she and Olgrethe felt for each other.

Ignoring her question as unworthy of a response, Hagen straightened up abruptly, stepped into the room, and closed the door. "No one else knows you are here yet, Celiese, and I'd rather you weren't discovered in my bed before I've had time to announce your arrival. I will call one of the women to prepare your bath and help you dress, and then I'll take you to my parents."

Celiese was certain she knew all the serving women who might be called and hastened to argue. "I am afraid your household servants will be outraged to see me here again. I'd rather go to Olgrethe's room and dress there by myself than ask for their help, when they will be most reluctant to extend it." Reluctant was too mild a term perhaps; she'd be lucky to escape a bathtub without drowning, if they had their way!

"Your popularity with our slaves need no longer concern you now that my brother has set you free," Hagen commented sarcastically. He had little patience with Celiese's complaint and wanted only to get the ordeal with his parents over with swiftly.

"What do you mean Mylan has set her free?" Olgrethe looked up at Hagen, then back at Celiese. "You were free from the day you married Mylan," she insisted emphatically, then continued, "He took you with him to his home. You are the man's wife, aren't you?"

Before Hagen could respond to make her situation

painfully clear, Celiese tried to explain truthfully. "We were married for no more than one night in his view, Olgrethe. Since then, Mylan has insisted our marriage was not a valid one because he thought he was marrying you, and he regards the ceremony we went through as no more than a trick of your father's to gain entrance to this house."

Blushing with anger, Olgrethe opened her mouth to argue, then thought better of it. "Would he believe me if I told him the truth of what happened that night? You are blameless and—"

Hagen could no longer hold his tongue and stepped forward. "You would only anger him if you mentioned the word marriage to him, Olgrethe. To mention marriage and Celiese's name in the same breath would incite more wrath than I think you'd care to see."

Celiese squeezed her friend's hands tightly, warning her to be silent for the moment. "Would you please leave us, Hagen? I will be in Olgrethe's room after I bathe and dress, as I've no wish to inconvenience you any further."

"Of course, the sooner you are ready to be presented to my mother the sooner I may take care of my own business once again and leave your care to her." With that hostile good-bye he left the room, but this time he did not bother to slam the door on his way out.

"Hagen can be the most impossible bully at times." Olgrethe confided quickly. "You will never know how grateful I am Andrick is the older of the twins and was therefore the one chosen to be my husband."

The mere mention of the word husband was enough to depress Celiese's mood to the point where she felt she and

Hagen might have much in common. "Let's not worry over him, since it is Aldred and Thulyn I'll need to please."

The two young women went quickly to Olgrethe's rooms where the bathwater was already heated. Once she was bathed and dressed Celiese felt far more confident to discuss what her relationship with Mylan had been. As she brushed out her glossy curls she found the truth made increasingly difficult to relate, as Olgrethe kept interrupting excitedly. She was certain Mylan was a great fool if he could not trust the affections of a woman so honest and loving as Celiese and said so repeatedly. When the conversation turned quite naturally to her own recent marriage, she began to smile widely as she revealed her secret.

"Not even Andrick knows yet, Celiese, but I am certain I am already carrying his child. Since Mylan is no less of a man than his brother, is it not possible that you will have a child next spring as well?"

No matter how likely that event might seem to Olgrethe, Celiese hastened to deny it. She had never prayed for a child as most young brides did, and she grew pale at the very thought she might have conceived Mylan's baby. "No, there will be no child for us, I'm certain of it."

Not understanding her friend's suddenly subdued mood, Olgrethe teased her again, whispering softly, "That is a possibility that shouldn't be overlooked, Celiese. If you were to tell Mylan he would soon become a father, wouldn't he be so proud he would forgive you anything?"

"I'll not lie to the man!" Celiese insisted vehemently. That Olgrethe could even suggest such an unprincipled trick appalled her. "Besides, there is no reason for him to forgive me anything—I am the one who has been wronged!" Celiese stood up then, adjusting the fine pleats of her bodice so they fell in a flattering sweep. She thought the linen chemise so pretty she hated to add the soft woolen tunic over it, but she slipped it on quickly and fastened the two bronze brooches that held each shoulder in place. Since her marriage, Olgrethe had adopted more conservative dress, but Celiese thought the borrowed gown a most welcome change from trousers. The beltless dresses were not only attractive but practical as well, for the soft folds would disguise for several months the changes pregnancy would bring to Olgrethe's figure. "I must thank you again for your generosity with your wardrobe. Had you not been willing to share your clothing so readily, I do not know what I would have done." Celiese was sorry she'd spoken so sharply and gave her friend a warm hug, then confided, "I am happy you and Andrick will be parents so soon, but I'll not hope for a child until I'm wed to a man who is proud to call me his wife." Lifting her chin with a defiant tilt, she moved toward the door. "Shall we find Hagen, so he may tell his parents I've come for a visit?"

"A visit is it?" Olgrethe laughed at that term. "When you have nowhere else to go, Celiese, is this not your new home?"

Startled by the truth of that question Celiese did not reply, but how could she ever regard the Vandahl family home as her own when Mylan did not reside there as well?

Just as she had expected, Celiese was given a cool reception by Thulyn, followed by a stern lecture from Aldred. His arm still caused him considerable pain, and, as he saw it, the wound was partly her fault. "I was amazed when Mylan took you home with him, and that he has now sent you back to me is even more appalling. Since you are to be considered a free woman, and the close friend of my son's wife, I will allow you to stay on the one condition that your behavior is as proper as Olgrethe's. I will not allow your presence here to disrupt our home in any way. Is that understood?"

Before replying, Celiese glanced at the others in the room, using the time to control the flame of her temper, which threatened to ignite a bitter refusal of Aldred's invitation. Andrick had come in and stood with his bride, and they looked so happy together, standing close with their arms entwined, that she longed to go to them, if for only a fleeting moment to be part of the love that shone so brightly in their eyes. Erik appeared fascinated, while Hagen's pose was as unconcerned as his expression. He looked thoroughly bored, and she wondered why he'd not gone to attend to the business that had seemed so urgent earlier that morning rather than remaining to listen to his parents' cool welcome. Had she anywhere at all to go she would have left at once, but knowing such an announcement would be foolhardy for the time being, she attempted to smile graciously. "I am grateful you have invited me to share your home, Aldred. I will give you no cause to regret your decision."

Aldred looked toward his wife, waiting to see if she had

any objection, but when she shook her head slightly he said no more. "It is settled then. As my daughter-in-law's friend you are welcome here, but had Olgrethe not wanted you to stay, you would already have been sent upon your way."

Thinking the conversation far too severe in nature, Olgrethe turned the talk to inconsequential matters. She charmed Aldred as well as Thulyn with her warmth and easy praise, but once she was again alone with Celiese she revealed the truth. "I adore Andrick, truly I do, and I know now I was only waiting to meet him when I refused the proposals of other men, but sometimes when I enter the room Aldred will quickly change the subject, or Thulyn will take up her needlework with such great haste that I know they have been talking about me. I hope things will be easier for me after I have given them a grandchild, but just having you here with me again fills me with hope."

Celiese returned Olgrethe's fond embrace, but she had no such optimism for herself, for she had no handsome husband who adored her, nor the hope of bearing his child in the spring. "I have missed you too, Olgrethe." But even as she spoke those sweet words she realized that in Mylan's fascinating company she had not thought even once of her longtime companion.

As one week turned slowly to two, Celiese found the Vandahl home increasingly confining. Much to her relief, the slaves simply ignored her, but she found their silence far easier to abide than their insults had been and simply saw to all of her own needs herself without once calling for their assistance. The early morning weather was perfect for going out on horseback, but Olgrethe did not want to ride, giving the delicate nature of her condition as the reason. Although she longed for the freedom to explore the countryside, Celiese did not try and change Olgrethe's mind, and she dared not go out alone, fearing it would cause unfavorable comment from her hosts. Aldred and Thulyn were civil, but only just barely, and Celiese spent no more time in their company than was required to share a meal. Andrick was so absorbed in his new bride that he saw little that took place in the house. Erik was charming, but Celiese found his youthful exuberance tiresome in the extreme. Hagen's reaction to her was more difficult to describe, still a bit of a mystery. He said little other than a polite greeting, but his glance was no longer disapproving, and when he suggested they join Olgrethe and his brother for a walk after supper one evening she was happy to agree.

"I am glad you suggested this, Hagen, as the evenings have been very long for me here." Celiese held her gown above her feet as they stepped upon the path. The trailing garment was far more practical for wear indoors than out, but she'd had time to complete only one dress for herself, so she had few choices of apparel as yet.

Hagen looked askance, then deciding her compliment had been sincere, he agreed. "Yes, I too have grown bored. Were Andrick not so enchanted with Olgrethe we would be at sea now. As it is, the summer has been almost entirely wasted."

"In your opinion," Celiese offered with a teasing smile.

After a moment's pause, Hagen gave a surprisingly

good-natured chuckle. "Yes, in my opinion only, for Andrick will no doubt recall this as the best summer of his life."

As they strolled along, Celiese was surprised to find her escort in so charming a mood. He led her to the crest of the hill, the best vantage point for a view of the sea, and when Olgrethe and Andrick turned back toward the house he made no move to follow them. "I know things are as difficult for you here as they are for me, Celiese." He scuffed the toe of his boot in the dust, unwilling or perhaps unable to say more.

Noticing a small bench nearby, Celiese asked shyly, "Could we sit down for a moment?" He seemed to be in the mood to talk and she wanted to give him the opportunity to say whatever he wished. "The night is so pretty and—"

"Of course, sit down, I will wait for as long as you wish." Hagen quickly granted her request, but although he walked her to the bench he did not take the place at her side.

That he would stand so stiffly while she rested surprised Celiese, and she patted the place beside her as she invited, "Won't you please join me here, Hagen, there is room for two on this bench, so you needn't stand."

Hagen hesitated for a moment, then sat down beside her and leaned forward to rest his forearms across his knees as he looked out at the sea. "I have been meaning to talk to you about something, Celiese. Andrick and I are partners, but since he is so busy I am considering making a voyage on my own. Our crew is experienced, and I can command our vessel alone."

Sensing that he wanted her opinion, although she couldn't imagine why, Celiese quickly gave it. "I made a voyage with you once; I'd say your skill is equal to that of your brother. Where is it you wish to go?"

Hagen sat up straight then, his light eyes aglow with excitement. "Do not start screaming, as I have no wish to make you hysterical, but there are many Danes who wish to go to your homeland. We are crowded here, you see, and they say France has land aplenty."

Celiese gasped sharply, then closed her eyes tightly to shut out the horror that statement evoked. "Is that the tale, that land is free there for the taking now that the Danes have butchered all my people?"

Insulted by the viciousness of her taunt, Hagen grabbed Celiese by the shoulders and gave her a sound shake. "A province of France has been given to a Dane, to Hrolf, and he has invited other Danes to settle his land. I will be butchering no one if I take farmers there, and neither will they! Save your hatred for Raktor and his clan, for they are the ones who deserve it!"

She needed no permission from him to despise Raktor and his kind, but they were not the issue now. "Mylan told me that same lie, but I refuse to believe it!" Celiese screamed defiantly. She didn't care how angry Hagen got, she'd never accept such an outrageous tale as the truth. She held her breath expecting him to slap her for such insolence, but he shocked her far more as he leaned forward to kiss her lightly, and when she was too stunned to draw away he mistook her reaction for acceptance and drew her into his arms.

Celiese could scarcely breathe as Hagen deepened his

kiss. His lips were soft, his mouth warm, his taste sweet, but she was appalled that he would take her affection for granted and struggled to break free.

"What's the matter? Do I not please you?" Hagen leaned back only slightly, just enough so he could look into her eyes to judge her true reaction no matter what she might tell him now.

"Hagen!" Celiese cried sharply, but no matter how hard she tried to push him away he would not release her. "Let me go!"

"Why? When you complain your evenings are too long, why not let me fill them?"

He was smiling widely now, amused by her display of temper, and Celiese tried to lift her hand to slap his face but he caught her wrist and held it firmly in his grasp. "Hagen, stop it!" She was tempted for an instant to remind him she was Mylan's wife, but that statement was truly ludicrous. She'd heard nothing from Mylan in the last two weeks and with each passing day her hopes that he would come for her had grown more dim. It was clear he planned to live the rest of his life without her, but that prospect filled her with pain. Thoroughly depressed as she was by Mylan's indifference she relaxed in Hagen's embrace, but still managed to avoid his kiss. She laid her head upon his shoulder, hoping he would come to his senses rather than trying to take things any further. "I should not have come out for a walk with you, but I did not understand what you would expect." He had certainly given her no reason to suspect he even liked her, let alone that he imagined she would welcome his kiss.

Hagen caressed Celiese's soft curls lightly, content for the moment to let her rest in his arms. "I am a man, like any other," he explained simply, certain she knew exactly what he wanted from her that night.

"No, you are like no other," Celiese whispered softly. You are my husband's brother she wanted to say, but dared not be so foolish.

"If it is Mylan you want, I'll soon make you forget him." Winding his fingers in her fair tresses, Hagen forced her lips back to his, but his kiss was gentle, soft and subtle with a tenderness that surprised her completely. When he saw tears fill her eyes he kissed her damp lashes sweetly. "You needn't weep, Celiese, not when I want so badly to help you."

"Help me?" Celiese saw only the golden sheen to his gaze and remembered another man entirely, although she was still dazed by Hagen's kiss.

"Yes. If I take Danes to France, there will be room for you to make the journey as well. Does that prospect not interest you, even if I do not?"

Celiese's long sweep of lashes touched her brows as she stared up at him, astonished by his question. "You would take me home? I could return home?" She had not dared hope such a possibility even existed, but she saw clearly in his expression that it did.

Hagen waited a long moment, enjoying the light that filled her sparkling green eyes with hope. It had been a long while since he'd found such an enchanting wench, and he knew if he were simply a little more patient he could have her heart for the asking. Mylan might be a fool, but he wasn't. "Yes, I will take you home, Celiese, but we needn't make our plans tonight. Come, let us walk back to the house before it becomes too dark for you to make the way safely."

Celiese sprang to her feet, nearly dancing with joy as she moved down the path beside him and when he paused at her door she knew he was waiting for a kiss and lifted her lips shyly to his. He drew her into his arms then, his gentle kiss growing passionate, not ending until he'd loosened the ribbon at her throat and slipped his hand beneath her bodice with an insistent caress that left her blushing brightly with embarrassment rather than pleasure. He walked away then, as if he'd given her no more than a light kiss upon the cheek, but she was shocked by the liberties he'd taken and knew exactly what he'd expect were she to travel with him to France. Tears again filled her eyes, but she blinked them away, uncertain now if going home meant more to her than her pride.

Chapter Fourteen

Celiese stretched languidly, pressing her silken skin against Mylan's broad chest as his mouth moved slowly down her throat to nibble the soft curve of her shoulder. His kiss tickled, so she purred with a playful giggle before coming fully awake with a startled gasp, "Mylan?" She sat up then, looking around anxiously, but the pale light that filled the room revealed no trace of the handsome Viking.

Flopping dejectedly across the bed with a frustrated moan, Celiese attempted to go back to sleep but found escape into the oblivion of slumber impossible to achieve. The dream had been much too real, too tantalizing a reminder of Mylan's generous affection for her to force his compelling image from her mind with ease. His memory filled her senses to overflowing, and she rested her cheek upon her arms as she relived in her imagination each moment they'd shared. She had wanted him to love her, to be as proud to call her his wife as she'd been to call him husband, but that had proven to be a hopeless dream. Perhaps her cause had been doomed from the very beginning, but she had no regrets. Even knowing how furious Mylan had been that she'd prized her freedom so highly, she could not have remained his slave forever.

"I am no slave," she whispered hoarsely, her voice sounding hollow in the early morning air. No indeed, she could no longer be called a slave by anyone, but the freedom to love the man she'd chosen had eluded her with a suddenness that left her reeling still with the harshness of his rejection. "Why couldn't you have really been my husband, Mylan?"

Celiese's dark mood had not lightened by the time she joined Olgrethe later that morning. The enthusiastic young woman had tried to interest her in a fine bolt of red silk, but when she made no favorable comment upon the luxurious fabric she was asked pointedly, "Where is your mind today, Celiese? I am trying to help you create the most stunning of gowns, and you act as though we were sorting rags!"

"I beg your pardon?" Celiese leaned forward, forcing herself to pay more attention. "All the fabrics you've shown me are lovely, but red is so ostentatious a color, and I'd prefer not to attract such notice as surely a gown of so bright a hue would."

Tossing the silk aside Olgrethe frowned petulantly. "It isn't the silk at all, is it? I saw you laughing happily with Hagen last night—what happened between you two that your mood is so downcast today?"

Celiese shook her head slowly, uncertain as to how to relate her latest problem, but, hoping Olgrethe might possibly be able to help her, she described her predicament. "Hagen said he is considering a voyage to my homeland, but, while I want so desperately to return to France, I do not think I should make that journey with him."

Olgrethe's honey-colored curls flew about her head as she leapt to her feet, her shock at Celiese's announcement unhidden. Married women were expected to wear their hair covered by a scarf, or at the very least pulled atop their heads in a confining bun, but Andrick considered his bride's glowing tresses too pretty to hide and she had readily agreed to wearing her hair in the carefree style she always had to please him. "You want to leave me now when I will need you the most? How could you abandon me when I'm expecting my first child? Am I to face giving birth all alone?"

Celiese instantly regretted having confided in the self-centered young woman and tried to soothe her injured feelings. "I am not an experienced midwife. It will be no great tragedy if I am not with you." Indeed, other than a cat or two, household pets, she'd not seen any creature give birth, so she did not understand how she could prove helpful.

Her pretty face contorted in an angry pout, Olgrethe continued to fume. "If I mean nothing to you, what of Mylan? How can you leave the man you love without the slightest regret, without even telling him good-bye?"

It was Celiese who tossed her silken curls this time as she scoffed at that question, "Mylan cares little what happens to me, that should be obvious. It has been more than two weeks since I came here and he's not come for me nor given me any hope that he will. He's thrown me away as if I were trash, and if Hagen will give me the opportunity to return to France, why shouldn't I seize it eagerly?"

"Because it is Mylan you love, not Hagen!" Olgrethe proclaimed loudly, the logic that seemed to have escaped Celiese extremely plain to her.

After a long pause, Celiese began to laugh with a delicious giggle that bubbled up from deep within her, for Olgrethe's show of temper was so very amusing. "Yes, I do love him, and most dearly, but of what value is that love if it is not returned?"

Again taking her place beside Celiese, Olgrethe offered more advice, but with a surprising twist. "I've not once heard you mention Erik, but didn't you notice how black his gaze grew last night when Hagen asked you to accompany him on a stroll?"

Confused, Celiese gestured helplessly. "What has Erik to do with this?"

"It is plain you do not appreciate his attempts to impress you with his wit. He is not yet grown, and his feelings are therefore more easily injured, but I thought you were merely being aloof so as not to encourage his infatuation. Are you telling me now you had not even noticed how he adores you?" Olgrethe was puzzled by Celiese's lack of insight when she had always been so perceptive in the past. "Has your rudeness been unintentional?"

"Have I been dreadfully rude?" Celiese asked regretfully. "Erik is so lively and good-humored I did not dream he had grown overly fond of me." Indeed, she had no experience with young men, for she had gone from slave to wife in the space of one day, without ever having been courted.

"Well, he most certainly has," Olgrethe assured her confidently. "If Hagen offers to escort you home, then his feelings for you are just as plain."

Celiese chewed her lower lip nervously, certain Hagen had no feelings for her other than lust, but she'd not reveal that opinion to Olgrethe and risk the questions she'd be sure to ask. No longer able to keep still, she exploded angrily, "Stop it! I've done nothing to encourage the affections of either of Andrick's brothers!"

"How can you be so stupid, they are Mylan's brothers too!" Olgrethe pointed out heatedly.

"So?" Celiese responded curtly, clearly irritated by the pointlessness of their conversation.

"So why don't we think of some compelling reason for Mylan to come home, and he's sure to be driven mad with jealousy in less than one day!"

A sudden chill shot up Celiese's spine, instantly cooling her hot temper and filling her with a dread so deep she could barely find her voice to argue. "Never, Olgrethe, I'll never stoop to such treachery, for Mylan would only despise me all the more were he to think I was using his brothers' devotion to me to inspire his!"

Olgrethe sat back, alarmed by Celiese's dramatic tone. She took a deep breath and let it out slowly, while she tried to rephrase her suggestion in more acceptable terms. "It is not all that easy for me here either, Celiese. I often think of how I was cheated out of having the wedding celebration I deserved. Time for the harvest is nearly here, and since it will be such a fine one this year, I think Aldred might be convinced to host a party that

Mylan can be enticed to attend. There will be no treachery involved, only an opportunity for the two of you to be together again, and once the man is here, who can say what he will see for himself?''

"No!" Celiese insisted, her fists clenched tightly in her lap so she'd not be tempted to slap the triumphant smirk from Olgrethe's face, but she knew the willful girl would do exactly as she pleased no matter how she pleaded with her to do otherwise.

As always Olgrethe was clever, making the most of her feminine wiles. She spoke first with her husband, casually mentioning what little opportunity she'd had to meet his kin at their wedding, revealing that the lack of warmth she'd experienced as she'd joined his family was a slight which still caused her pain. With a downcast expression and a soulful glance she readily convinced him she'd been insulted most rudely and hoped sometime soon she might meet his relatives again, when they would be in a more festive mood and show her the courtesy she deserved. Astonished to find his bride so unhappy, Andrick went quickly to his parents, who listened attentively to his complaint and with only gentle encouragement on his part agreed to invite their relatives and friends for a party as soon as the harvest had been gathered. When at the evening meal Aldred suggested having a harvest celebration the idea seemed to come from him, and Celiese could only stare at Olgrethe, certain the inspiration had come from her, but not knowing any way she could either stop it or avoid it.

Hagen had no objection to a party; he liked them as much as any young man, for there were always races that would provide ample opportunities for him to win praise for his horsemanship. He had often found pretty young women easily impressed by such skill, which made the evenings far more profitable in terms of romance. Turning to note Celiese's reaction to the prospect of such an amusement, he saw her worried glance and realized she had not once looked in his direction that evening, while she had laughed frequently at Erik's jokes. That had only made the young man's humor that much more outrageous, until finally Thulyn had given him the choice of being quiet or leaving the table. Since neither option appealed to Erik, he had grown sullen, and the conversation about the upcoming party continued without any more of his interruptions. Obviously feeling sorry for his younger brother, Andrick suggested his favorite board game as soon as the meal ended, issuing a challenge to which Erik readily responded, leaving Olgrethe talking with Aldred and Thulyn about the harvest festivities while Hagen quickly excused himself and went to Celiese's side.

"I want to speak with you for a moment, come with me into the garden." His request was more of a command than an invitation, but he saw no need for flattery nor flirting where Celiese was concerned.

Having no wish to risk another romantic encounter with the young man, Celiese offered an excuse, "I'm sorry, but I didn't sleep well last night. I'm afraid I'm more tired than usual and would be poor company for you. I think I'll just go on to my room."

Smiling slightly, Hagen reached out to take her arm in a firm grasp as he helped her from her chair. "The garden is not out of your way and the fresh air will help you sleep all the better." Giving her no time to disagree, he propelled her through the open door out into the gathering dusk. As soon as they could no longer be overheard by those still inside he took her hand and drew her around to face him. "I did not realize I'd been too forward with you last night, but I must have been, for you've avoided me all day."

Pulling her hand gently from his, Celiese denied his assumption. "I have not been avoiding you, not at all. It is only that Olgrethe has been helping me to make a new gown. You know how little I brought with me from Mylan's house, so we have been very busy." While she did not want Hagen for a lover, she dared not make an enemy of him either, and hoped he would accept her explanation as the truth.

Hagen shifted his weight, his stance turning from relaxed to militant as he put his hands on his hips. "That is the only reason I've not seen you about, or that you spoke not one word to me while we dined?"

Rather than lie, Celiese changed the subject to the one she wanted to discuss. "I have given a great deal of thought to the voyage you mentioned last night. Have you told Andrick your plans?"

"No," Hagen admitted reluctantly.

"If you two are partners, don't you think you should?"

Though she knew he would not want to leave Olgrethe, were Andrick to go along she would not have to be alone with Hagen, and that thought gave her hope the voyage home might still be possible.

Impatient to resolve the issue, Hagen drew her into his arms, his embrace confining as he explained. "We will be busy with the harvest; by the time it is over I will have all my plans made, our provisions gathered, my crew ready to sail. I will simply tell him I am leaving, and he will not object, for he seems to grow more enamored with his bride each new day."

"Don't you think a man should love his wife?" Celiese asked softly. She made no move to resist his touch. She wanted to push him away and run, but dared not be so rude when it would cause a dreadful scene between them.

Hagen paused a moment too long, then agreed. "Yes, if a man must have a wife, then he should love her."

As he bent down to kiss her, Celiese turned her cheek, then slipped from his grasp before he could stop her. "I must go; it would not be pleasant for either of us if your parents thought your interest in me were other than a friendly one." She hurried away then, passing through the hall where the others were still talking or playing the game that involved moving brightly colored pieces of glass across an ornately carved wooden board.

Thulyn glanced up as Celiese went by. The young woman had been outdoors only briefly with Hagen but when her son joined their group he seemed preoccupied, and she grew worried that the attractive former slave might have set her sights for him now that Mylan no longer had any interest in her. She had not forgotten the innocence in Celiese's gaze when first they'd met, an innocence that was only part of Raktor's evil plot, and her cheeks burned with humiliation still. She had tried to be like a true mother to Celiese, when that was the last thing such a young woman needed. Perhaps the party they were planning would provide an opportunity to repay Celiese for the hurt she'd dealt them. Smiling with thoughts too delicious to suppress, Thulyn agreed to each of Olgrethe's suggestions, then made a few of her own.

By spending as much time as possible in her own company, Celiese managed to survive until the day of the harvest celebration without upsetting the delicate balance she'd created in her relationships within the Vandahl home. Hagen was the most difficult to avoid, but his own demanding schedule worked to her advantage. She'd responded to Erik's flattering attention with sisterly teasing, and since Olgrethe clearly thought she'd had her own way in arranging for a party to which Mylan would surely come, they had avoided further argument on that issue. She tried as before to be pleasant and cheerful with Aldred and Thulyn but the easy rapport they'd shared the day she'd come to marry Mylan had never been restored.

As soon as the guests had begun to arrive, Olgrethe swept into Celiese's room, closed the door hurriedly, and whispered, "Mylan's here. I've just spoken with him and he seems to be in as festive a mood as everyone else. Didn't I tell you he would be here today?"

Celiese turned away from her window, her manner far cooler than her temper. "Yes, you did, and I hope he wins all the races and has a most amusing time, but there is no possible way I will enjoy the day."

Olgrethe circled her friend warily. "You finished your

new gown and the pale green is perfect with your eyes. Your hair has never looked prettier, but there's little we can do to disguise your freckles. Let us pray Mylan is so happy to see you again he'll not notice that flaw."

Lifting her chin proudly, Celiese moved gracefully toward the door. "I would prefer to avoid his notice altogether, Olgrethe, but I'm certain you'll make that impossible."

"You will thank me before this day is over, but I will be gracious and not refuse your praise." With a playful hug Olgrethe walked outside with Celiese where Andrick and Hagen were greeting their guests, but Mylan had gone to prepare for the first race and was nowhere in sight.

"I did not realize your brothers would be here, Olgrethe," Hagen said, nodding toward a boisterous group of men talking amongst themselves as they saddled their mounts for the races. "Apparently my father believes the truce we've enjoyed between our families since your marriage will be a lasting one."

Olgrethe glanced anxiously at Celiese, knowing she would not wish to see any of the Torgvalds on that day or any other. "Yes, it was your father who invited them, I did not even think of it. I hope they will cause no trouble."

Celiese knew it would be miraculous if they didn't and was sorry she'd come outdoors, for she didn't know which would be worse, confronting Mylan or Olgrethe's hateful brothers. Oluf was staring at her now, his beady blue eyes filled with contempt, while he drew his whip across his palm in a menacing gesture she knew was meant to be a threat only for her. She simply turned her back on him, pretending to be amused as Andrick and Hagen exchanged boasts on who would win the most races that day. When Mylan appeared at the edge of the gathering crowd she did not recognize him at first glance, for he'd grown a beard. While it was neatly trimmed and a handsome complement to his classic features, she had expected him to look exactly as he had when they'd parted. She glanced down at her shimmering gown, hoping he would be as pleased by her appearance as she was by his, for, despite her attempts to appear indifferent, she'd spent more than an hour arranging her gleaming curls so she'd look her prettiest. She hoped she could impress him with her beauty and that then she might have the opportunity to make him see reason if his mood was truly as good as Olgrethe had sworn it was. When Olgrethe gripped her arm tightly, her daydream came to an abrupt end and she asked in surprise, "What's wrong?"

"Look who's here, it's that snake Estrid!" Olgrethe nodded to their left as a petite young woman with flaming red hair rushed up to greet Mylan. He returned her charming smile with a wide grin, then leaned down to kiss her lips lightly before leading his stallion toward the starting line of the first race. The whole incident had taken no more than a few seconds, but the affection that existed between the attractive pair was unmistakable even at a distance.

Celiese grew pale, unable to draw a breath or create a coherent thought as the sharpest of pains filled her heart. She was overwhelmed with sorrow, for Mylan had not even seen her, he'd had eyes only for the lovely redhead, whose creamy white skin showed not the faintest trace of freckles. Although diminutive, her proportions were perfect, and Celiese was too devastated to be jealous. "She's very pretty isn't she?" she finally managed to say, too distraught to reveal the depth of her torment, but she'd never met the young woman and had had no idea she would be so enchanting a creature.

"Aye, she is a beauty," Andrick readily agreed, but when Olgrethe poked him in the ribs he realized how tactless he'd been. "I mean, there are some who think she is attractive," he stammered, trying to make amends and failing.

"Well, who invited her?" Olgrethe demanded sharply. "After what she did to Mylan, how dare she show her face here?"

"I would not pursue that question, Olgrethe, for you will insult your own friend as well as yourself if you do." Hagen reached for Celiese's hand, and although she tried to pull away he drew her close to his side as he whispered, "Since Mylan already has someone to cheer for him, I expect you to yell encouragement to me!" With that command he leaned down to kiss her, his mouth bruising her lips before he let her go, leaving her too embarrassed by the stares of those surrounding them to do more than watch as he strode off to get his horse.

Olgrethe gave Andrick an affectionate hug as he left, then put her arm around Celiese's waist and held her tightly, "I'm going to find out why that bitch Estrid is here, but don't you worry, she'll not ruin our plans."

"*Your* plans," Celiese hissed angrily, but it was too late for her to flee to the serenity of the house when all around them the men were mounting horses and issuing loudly voiced challenges. The course that had been laid out was a treacherous one, demanding stamina as well as speed from the horses, but many of the riders were young and therefore unnecessarily reckless. Raktor had loved races, and if a few riders were thrown, perhaps badly injured or maimed, he considered it no tragedy, as skill was as greatly admired as courage in Viking sport. Celiese had never been such a close observer at those races, however, and she found Olgrethe's enthusiasm difficult to emulate. When Erik approached them with a ready grin, she welcomed the distraction he presented. "Aren't you going to ride in the races as your brothers do, Erik?"

The handsome young man laughed as he shook his head. "Just look around you—while the other men ride off to choke on dust, I have my choice of lovely young women to court. I am no fool."

Celiese smiled at his jest, for clearly he was having as much fun milling through the crowd of spectators and talking with his friends as those who had just dashed off on horseback.

"Do you know how Estrid came to be here today, Erik? I know your family and hers were once close but I'd not expected to see her here, since she broke her engagement to Mylan for so foolish a reason." Olgrethe reached out to touch his arm, intent upon knowing who had tried to ruin her well-laid plans to get Mylan and Celiese back together.

"My mother invited her. I went to her home myself," Eric responded casually, not understanding his sister-in-law's concern.

"You did not think such an invitation odd?" Olgrethe inquired suspiciously.

Erik frowned, then shrugged, "Odd? Yes, I suppose so, but no more strange than having your brothers here, which was my father's idea. What is the purpose of this party if it is not to give thanks for the harvest and for new friends as well as old?"

Casting Erik a hostile glance, Olgrethe made no reply, but when he moved on to find more agreeable company she whispered to Celiese, "Do you think we should go over and introduce ourselves to Estrid, since Thulyn has not bothered to do so?"

"Go ahead if you'd like, but I've no wish to meet the woman." Celiese lifted her hand to shade her eyes as a cloud of dust loomed in the distance. The race began and ended in the same spot, near to where they stood, and she tried to move back away from the path, but all around her people were shoving and pushing, trying to gain a better vantage point for the end of the race, and suddenly she was pitched forward. Nearly losing her balance, she would have fallen in the dust of the roadway had Olgrethe not swiftly caught her arm and pulled her back to safety. When the horses streaked by their hooves thundered in her ears with the echo of doom, and she knew she had escaped death by mere inches.

"Celiese!" Olgrethe hung on, dragging her trembling companion away from the race course, but not before she'd looked around quickly to see Estrid standing nearby. "What happened? You were by my side and then you nearly sprawled in the path of the horses!"

"Someone shoved me, Olgrethe, put their hands in the middle of my back and pushed with all their might. Had you not caught me I would have been trampled to death for certain." Celiese was still shaking by the time they reached the house, sick not with fear but with the knowledge that someone hated her enough to wish her dead. "Did you see who was directly behind us?"

"No, I was watching the riders, then you, but I did see Estrid out of the corner of my eye. Perhaps she was the one who did it."

Celiese tried to catch her breath as she sipped the cup of water Olgrethe had brought her. Attempting to think logically, she tried to recall the faces of the guests who had surrounded them. She had met most of them at her wedding and was certain they all remembered her. "I doubt it was she when so many others have a better reason to hate me. I was a fool ever to leave my room today."

Sinking down by her side, Olgrethe explained that her original plan had been far more simple. "I had expected the Vandahls to invite their close relatives, aunts, uncles, cousins, not those and every friend they've ever made. With all the entertainment they have planned it is plain they didn't want anyone to have a moment to even speak with me, let alone become my friend."

Celiese set the small cup aside and gave Olgrethe a sweet hug. "We are both disappointed then, and I am so sorry for I know today meant as much to you as it did to me." They were still sitting together, each lost in her own thoughts, when Andrick found them. When Olgrethe explained what had happened he was as concerned as his bride to think someone had intentionally tried to harm Celiese.

"You must stay with us today. I mean that, for the entire day I want you with us, Celiese. None will dare to insult or harm you when you have my protection."

He looked so genuinely concerned that Celiese readily agreed to his request. "Thank you, I will do as you ask. In all the excitement, we missed seeing who won the race. Who was it?"

"It was close, but I beat Mylan by a good foot," he announced proudly. "He claims now that his stallion had not had the proper rest after his journey here, but I beat him all the same."

"You won and I did not even see it?" Olgrethe complained with real pain. "Oh Andrick, I am sorry I missed your victory."

"It was no more than a horse race, Olgrethe!" But despite his teasing he was pleased to have her praise. He had found her to be the best of wives, and drawing her into his arms gave her a lingering kiss to remind her how dearly she was loved.

Celiese turned away, embarrassed by Andrick's show of affection. She was trembling still, horrified to think that had she fallen it would have been he and Mylan who would have killed her. Their spirited stallions would have flown over her with the swiftness of eagles and she'd have been crushed to bits beneath their hooves. As she looked up she saw a man standing in the doorway. The sun was at his back, his face in shadows, but she knew it was Mylan. If he had overheard their conversation he did not care to comment upon it, or perhaps he simply did not care, for he turned away and was gone without speaking. Celiese stared after him, hoping with all her heart he would come back, if only to say a brief hello, but he was gone and, although the opportunities were many that day, he did not once approach her, nor acknowledge her presence in any way.

Chapter Fifteen

Horse races were not the only thrilling but dangerous sport enjoyed by Viking men. When the fleetest mount had won several races decisively, they turned their attention to a more brutal pastime: pitting the strength of one magnificent stallion against another's. The beasts were high-spirited and naturally antagonistic, so needed little in the way of encouragement to fight as fiercely for the crowd's amusement as they would have fought in the wild over possession of a herd of mares.

Celiese covered her ears, as much to shut out the harsh shouts of the men as the piercing screams of the enraged stallions. She'd not thought anyone could possibly enjoy such a spectacle, but clearly she was the only bystander who didn't. She'd felt the same strained detachment from the Vandahls' guests all day, and when Hagen put his arm around her waist she let him lead her away without argument. She drank the wine he offered, then swiftly regretted that foolishness when she immediately felt its effect upon her senses.

"I can see you are as unused to the amusements we

have provided today as you are to that wine, for clearly you enjoy neither," Hagen remarked with a rakish grin.

Celiese saw the teasing sparkle in his eyes and was not insulted; however, she saw no reason to remind him she'd been a slave in Raktor's home and had never been included in the celebrations he'd hosted. As for the wine, she knew only wealthy families were able to serve it, for Vikings did not make the intoxicating beverage themselves, but brought it home after raiding France. The source of the wine was not a subject she'd approach, as she assumed the Vandahls, being traders, had bargained for it rather than stolen it from a winery in her homeland. Since Hagen had obviously enjoyed himself that afternoon, she thought he'd prefer to talk about the stallions they'd been watching. "Are the horses not badly injured? I know I would never risk a pet of mine in so ridiculous a sport."

"Neither would my brothers and I. Our mounts are in their stalls in our stable where they have been brushed and fed, their sleek coats marked by neither bite nor kick."

Smiling with genuine delight, as well as the lazy warmth with which the wine had filled her, Celiese complimented him graciously. "I should have known the Vandahls would value their animals too highly to risk their lives needlessly simply to provide entertainment."

"The stallions do not battle to the death, Celiese—it is as much sport to them as it is to us," Hagen explained good-naturedly, for her ignorance greatly amused him.

"It can't be!" Celiese glanced back toward the pen where a chestnut animal's mane shone in the sun with golden highlights, while his jet-black opponent glowed with the sparkle of the midnight sky. The proud beasts circled each other warily, then one gave chase, trying to bite his adversary while avoiding being kicked. The advantage passed back and forth frequently, for the two horses appeared to be a match of equal strength and bravery, and their antics brought delighted cheers from the enthusiastic crowd of spectators. "Those stallions are magnificent beasts and are clearly true enemies. Their teeth and hooves are sharp; they are not simply playing, but each is trying his best to do the other harm. That fight is no mere sport to them—they are most serious."

Hagen laughed at her fears, then took her arm again, "And so am I." He led her around the house to the flower-filled garden where they would enjoy more privacy while they talked. Once Celiese was comfortably seated upon a bench he put his hands behind his back and began to pace slowly up and down in front of her. "We have seen little of each other the last few days, Celiese, and I cannot speak of the things I must when others are present."

"Do you anticipate problems with the voyage? I know the spring is the best time to sail, and it is nearly autumn." Celiese thought this the safest subject to discuss and hoped it was what he was referring to. "The weather will turn cool soon, is that your worry?"

Sighing sadly, Hagen assured her that while weather was a factor, it was not his only concern. "The days are still long and warm enough if we make haste, but I find myself becoming increasingly reluctant to depart when I know the journey will have to be made swiftly and I will be returning home alone."

Celiese waited for him to continue, hoping he would say something to let her know how futile he knew such thoughts to be. She had done all she could in both her manner and actions to discourage his affections, and she prayed he would not persist in trying to show them. Had she never known Mylan she would have thought Hagen most handsome, rather than merely a slightly less perfect replica of the man she loved. He was intelligent, but he lacked his older brother's ready wit and keen sense of humor. His dark moods were now less frequent, and if his disposition was not truly pleasant, it had at least greatly improved. But she dared not encourage him in any way. As tactfully as she could, she tried to explain her feelings. "The world into which I was born was such a gentle place, and I long to return home even if none I loved will be there to greet me. If you cannot or will not take me, then I shall have to wait for someone else who will."

"I have not refused to take you," Hagen responded angrily, "only said I do not want to let you go!" That declaration appeared to be a most painful admission, for his cheeks flooded with a vivid blush his deep tan did not hide, and he turned away for a moment to try and compose himself once again.

Touched by the obvious depth of his emotion, Celiese tried once again to make him understand her true feelings, "I am flattered that you have grown fond of me, but—"

"Flattered?" Hagen threw up his hands in disgust, exasperated by her lack of response. "I want you to stay here. Are you saying you will not?"

Celiese rose slowly to face him, her expression as serious as her tone as she replied softly, "I am saying that I cannot stay."

Swearing loudly with the vilest oath he knew, Hagen left the garden without looking back. Pits had been dug to roast sides of beef over coals, and if not properly supervised the servants might uncover the meat before it was fully cooked and spoil its flavor. He doubted he'd taste a bite, but he went to take charge of the final supper preparations himself rather than argue another minute with Celiese when she was so determined to go her own way. In an instant his mind was made up: With one excuse or another, he would delay the voyage to France until it would have to wait until spring. He was determined to have the delectable beauty, for he'd spent the entire day comparing all their attractive female guests to the enchanting Celiese and had found each of them wanting.

For a long while after Hagen left her Celiese wandered the garden alone. It depressed her greatly to realize she'd hurt him, but clearly she had, although it had most certainly not been her fault. Why had he been the one to want her to remain in his home when it was Mylan she longed to hear speak those same sweet words? She was so terribly confused, but knew she'd been right to tell Hagen the truth. She'd not thought him capable of love; indeed he had not even mentioned the word in their many conversations, but still, regardless of his motives, she had not responded as he'd hoped she would and he had been deeply hurt and angered. She could think of no way to make amends with him without compromising her own ideals, and she walked toward the house, intent upon returning to the party, for she did not want Hagen to think he had upset her so badly she could not bear the company of his many friends.

After stopping by her room to brush her hair and wash the dust kicked up by the day's sports from her face and hands, Celiese rejoined the gathering of guests where she found to her relief that the stallions who'd been battling so fiercely were being led away. Neither appeared to be any the worse for the fight, but she was happy to see the party turning toward more lighthearted pursuits. Musicians had begun to play lilting melodies to lure the guests inside, and Thulyn invited everyone to begin dinner while the food was at its best. There would be plenty of ale, so she had little difficulty enticing the hungry crowd to enter the hall where the tables were fully laden with the most delicious of repasts. The harvest had been as splendid as predicted. The oats and barley were stored for the winter, while the apples, nuts, and honey were being sampled liberally that day. As always there was fish, but there were game birds too, in addition to the beef, which, thanks to Hagen's watchful eye, was done to perfection. Over the summer the goats had produced a generous supply of milk, which had been made into delectable cheeses, so there was something to please each and every guest as they took their places to dine.

Celiese joined Olgrethe and Andrick but had little appetite, although the sumptuous food was well prepared and attractively served. She found it difficult to eat when people were staring at her still, as they had been all day. They were so curious they made not the slightest effort to be discreet, but simply gawked openly as if she were one of Aldred's and Thulyn's many entertainments. And as if that rudeness were not enough to make her uneasy, she could hear Mylan's deep voice as he stood nearby. He was laughing with keen enjoyment, while Estrid's sparkling giggle floated across the crowded room. Had he intentionally wished to hurt her, he could have found no better method than courting another woman in front of her, but Celiese had too much pride to let her pain show.

Pretending an interest in Erik, who sat opposite her, Celiese found that he and two friends were attempting to compose a poem to commemorate the day, but could not agree upon the first line and therefore found their task impossible, much to their amusement. Their high spirits only made her isolation all the more complete, for she was but a year older than the smiling trio of handsome young men, but a barrier far more insurmountable than age separated them. When Olgrethe and Andrick became involved in a friendly conversation with one of their guests, Celiese found the cheerful part she'd attempted to play all day impossible to continue, and, hoping to avoid further anguish, she slipped away unnoticed.

The twilight lent a softness to the coastal scene, which made the outdoors enormously inviting, compared to the raucous gathering in the crowded hall. After wandering aimlessly for a while, Celiese followed the trail she'd once taken with Hagen, up to the top of the hill, but rather than stopping at the bench to rest she continued along the path hoping to discover where it came to an end. When she reached an impressive stone, a monument covered with runes, she ran her fingertips over the deeply incised carvings and wondered what event the stone had been raised to commemorate. She could not read the Viking symbols with any fluency, and these were old, worn away by the sea breeze and salt air, which made her task doubly difficult. So intent was she upon making out the faint inscription, she did not hear the footsteps upon the path until the large man stepped upon a dry twig, snapping it with a crisp retort that warned her of his presence.

Oluf Torgvald gave an evil chuckle as Celiese spun around to face him. He leered at her as he said, "It has been far too long since we were alone together. I have been waiting all day for just such an opportunity, and I do not plan to waste it."

With her back to the massive boulder the agile young woman found her choices for escape few, so she attempted a show of bravado. "We are not alone—all I need do is call for help and dozens of people will come running. I warn you, do not make such a summons for assistance necessary, for you will suffer far more than embarrassment if you do."

"Your tongue is as sharp as your wits, girl, but you'll call no one." Oluf took a step closer, reeling slightly on unsteady legs, for the day had been a hot one and he'd had more than his share of ale to quench his thirst. While his clothing was well tailored from fine fabrics, it did not disguise his ample girth, and the aroma of stale sweat made him even less appealing. He had been well built in his teens, but now, nearing thirty, his features as well as his physique had grown coarse. The ends of his moustache shone with the grease from the beef he'd consumed. He taunted her cruelly again, "Mylan has cast you aside. What other Vandahl would want a woman he's discarded?"

Not about to reply to that insult, Celiese glanced over her shoulder. A sharp ravine veered off to her left, and the brush at her right was too thick to traverse. She could not leap over the stone behind her, and Oluf stood squarely in the narrow path. As her panic continued to mount, she again attempted to reason with the rude man. "The Vandahls are generous people who invited you here today as a courtesy to Olgrethe. If you have no respect for me, then have some for your sister!"

Oluf was drunk, and he was not a clear thinker even when sober. He failed to respond to her logic. He saw only a young woman of astonishing beauty and moved closer still, hoping to catch her off guard. "You will dishonor only yourself if you reveal what we've done here. There will be no scandal to touch Olgrethe."

"We will do nothing more than speak, Oluf, and I have said all that I wish to. Please stand aside, for I wanted no more than a few moments of fresh air, and I've enjoyed them." Celiese stood with a confident pose, as if unconcerned by the threat the bully presented to her safety.

Oluf shook his head slowly. "We are staying right here, and if you do not return to the house for hours none will notice or care."

Celiese dug her fingernails into her palms, forcing herself not to shriek uncontrollably. Andrick had told her not to leave his side and she'd been a fool to disregard his warning. It could have been Oluf who'd shoved her that morning, for if any man were capable of murder, surely it was he. She saw him shift his weight and knew he would spring at her in the next second if she did not take some quick action to stop him. The prospect of death was preferable to again being raped by such an unspeakable fiend. He had been the worst of the Torgvald brothers, his beatings as savage as his passion, and her decision to attack was made swiftly. In the next instant the knife that had been tucked under his belt was in her hand, gleaming wickedly as she lunged forward. Seeking only to flee, not to kill, she slashed through the fabric of his shirt sleeve, and when the startled man bellowed with pain she dropped the knife and darted past him, running down the path toward the safety of the brightly illuminated home.

Mylan glanced over Estrid's head, scanning the party crowd for the only face he thought worth viewing, but Celiese had disappeared again. He cursed to himself, wondering where she might have gone and with whom. During the day he had seen her far too frequently at Hagen's side, but his brother sat at their mother's table, surrounded by attractive young women who appeared to hang on his every word. He could not recall Hagen's ever enjoying feminine company so greatly, and wondered what had gotten into him of late.

Estrid saw the intense gaze in Mylan's amber eyes and reached out to touch his sleeve with a possessive caress. "You are not even listening to me, shall I begin all over again at the beginning?"

"Of course I am listening," Mylan replied curtly. He'd not thought any woman could bore him as completely as Estrid did, but he had not meant to be rude. "Please continue, your plans for the autumn are fascinating." He forced himself to look at her for a moment. He had once

269

thought her sweet as well as pretty, but she was no more than a selfish child, and he longed for the company of a real woman. When he saw Oluf leave the crowded hall he waited a moment, thinking the man might swiftly return, but when he did not he excused himself quickly. "Forgive me, Estrid, I fear there is a situation that needs my immediate attention." Leaving the astonished redhead staring after him, he sprinted through the open door and out into the night, but there was no sign of either Oluf or Celiese, and his throat tightened into a painful knot as he forced back the scream that filled his whole body with a lust for blood. If that brute had so much as touched her he would see him dead, but as he stood in the yard, trying to decide in which direction to search, he heard the unmistakable sound of a woman's light step flying across the dirt toward him.

Celiese ran straight into Mylan's arms. Gasping for breath she looked back over her shoulder, certain Oluf was no more than two paces behind, but when she saw they were alone she stepped back quickly. "I am sorry, I did not see you standing there and—"

"Sorry? You are running as though you fear for your life, and you apologize as if we'd simply bumped elbows in a crowd?" Mylan kept a firm grip upon her slender arms and waited for a more sensible comment than she'd made.

Swallowing nervously, Celiese tried to pull free rather than involve Mylan in her plight. "I am no longer your responsibility. Please let me go, I said I was sorry!"

Mylan looked toward the path from which she'd just appeared as he released her. "I saw Oluf follow you out of the house, and if he bothered you in any way he will suffer for it now. If you didn't kill the bastard, then I will!"

"No, wait!" Celiese grabbed his arm and held on tightly. "Oluf will never change, and you needn't fight him!" That he'd noticed her presence in a room filled with people having such wonderful fun surprised her, but that he wanted to avenge her honor was truly amazing, considering the way they had last parted.

Mylan brushed her aside as he drew his knife from his belt. He knew Oluf to be a despicable sort who deserved exactly what he intended to give him. He ran up the path but stopped as he heard the overweight man breathing heavily as he approached.

Oluf was muttering obscenities to himself as he walked along. He clutched his arm to stem the flow of blood from the gash Celiese had inflicted and vowed not to let the spirited woman escape him again. His shirt sleeve was soaked with the crimson liquid that continued to ooze from the wound, but he gave that discomfort scant notice as he considered what pain he would cause her in return.

Mylan stood on the path, his feet braced, his whole body tensed for action, but had he not been looking for a fight Oluf's crudely worded insults would have swiftly inspired one. "Are you lost? We expect our guests to enjoy our hospitality indoors, not to wander the fields unattended."

Oluf sneered a hostile reply. "Get out of my way, it's the woman I'm after. That slut might once have been your wife, but she'll be my whore again before the night's over!" He had no interest in arguing with any man about the matter; he wanted Celiese and nothing less than her

271

blood would satisfy him.

Celiese knew better than to fling herself between the two men, for Oluf would surely use her as a shield and then probably slit her throat while Mylan watched in horror. She dared not run to summon help either, for she did not want to leave Mylan alone to face a man who not only fought with every dirty trick imaginable but who outweighed him by at least forty pounds, as well. They were equals in height, their reach the same, but should Mylan slip on the rocky path she knew Oluf would fall upon him, using his considerable bulk as well as his knife to every advantage. Stepping back, she searched the ground for something to use as a weapon to help Mylan should he need it. Picking up a jagged stone, she gripped it tightly in her hands and waited for the first opportunity to use it.

Mylan knew Oluf's skill with a knife from bitter experience and moved out of his reach as he slowly circled to the left. "That you are drunk is no surprise, but you are also stupid or you would know better than to insult Celiese in front of me, for neither she nor I will accept an apology!" Despite that warning Oluf continued to describe the young woman in the vilest of terms, but Mylan ceased to listen. He heard only the roar of his own heartbeat pounding in his ears and planned his strategy swiftly. With a savage lunge he struck at Oluf's thigh, then yanked his blade free and jumped clear when the outraged man swung his knife at his throat. Escaping that slash, Mylan darted away from another, then, moving in close, made a vicious jab at Oluf's sagging belly, again drawing blood if not injuring the man severely. The fight continued to grow in intensity as each man warily circled the other, but every time Mylan drew near he managed to inflict another deep gash in Oluf's flesh while cleanly escaping each of the brute's wild, swinging thrusts.

Mylan knew that against such a brutal opponent he would have to depend upon his wits rather than on the endurance he'd once had but still had not completely regained. His right leg was already growing weak, the pain that shot up the muscles causing him to stumble so he missed a clear strike at Oluf's throat. He recovered his balance in time to avoid falling in the dirt, but not before he'd seen Celiese spring forward ready to assist him. He shouted at her to get away, for that was all he needed, a slender woman to fight his battles for him! Disgusted by that prospect, he fought on with renewed vigor, his desire for vengeance undiminished by his own lack of strength until he no longer felt the pain but only a deep rage that drove him past his own limits and beyond.

Oluf grinned when he saw Mylan slip, for he knew he'd need no more than one well-placed kick to disable him. Waiting for the proper moment, he raised his knife high to draw Mylan's gaze away as he struck with his foot, hitting him sharply in the right knee. Knocked off balance, Mylan tried to scramble back to his feet, but Oluf was upon him instantly, rolling over the rock-strewn path as he tried to bring his knife clear to plunge the blade deep into Mylan's heart.

Celiese screamed again and again while the dust flew all about her obscuring her vision as well as that of the two men as they wrestled at her feet. She lifted the rock but dared not strike a skull-crushing blow when it might be Mylan she killed rather than Oluf. The men were cursing each other loudly now, using their fists as well as their knives, and she feared Mylan would die while she watched helpless to save him. Suddenly a huge hand closed around her ankle, knocking her off her feet, and she went sprawling into the midst of the struggle. No longer able to tell friend from foe, she tried only to protect herself as she saw a blade flash in the moonlight as it tore through the air toward her heart. She heard a shriek and then a strangled cry as a warm rush of blood covered her hands, and then for one horrible moment all was still until one of the men got slowly to his feet while the other lay in a growing puddle of his own blood.

Celiese leapt to her feet, ready to run, before she realized it was Mylan who stood before her. Throwing her arms around his neck, she wept for joy, but he did no more than pat her back gently before he drew away and said, "I did not plan this tragedy, but I will take all the blame. Be silent while I explain, and do not try and help me again, for I shall not need it." Taking her firmly by the hand, Mylan led her down the path toward a confrontation he knew would bring the worst of consequences. They stopped momentarily to rinse the grim evidence of his deed from their hands, but their clothing was still streaked with Oluf's blood, and as they entered the crowded hall a sudden hush fell upon the room bringing an unnatural quiet, until a hysterical Thulyn began to scream and could not stop.

Chapter Sixteen

While Aldred attempted to calm Thulyn, Mylan
walked swiftly to his father's side and whispered a terse
explanation of what had transpired. Stunned by the
announcement of Oluf's death, Aldred gave his wife a
withering glance, which immediately hushed her tears.
The day had been going well in his estimation—the
Torgvald brothers were as crude a lot as he'd expected
them to be, but they had not caused any trouble and he
had thought his efforts to include them in his family
gathering a success. It *had* been one, he knew it had, until
someone had lured Oluf to his death. He stared straight at
Celiese then, his eyes widening as he realized she might
well be the one who had killed Oluf, while Mylan might
be lying to protect her. Furious that so innocent-
appearing a young woman had again been the cause of
tragedy in his home, he cleared his throat and announced
loudly to his guests, "My friends, I beg you not to let the
frightening nature of Mylan's appearance upset you as
greatly as it did his mother. He has suffered only a small
mishap, so there is no reason to interrupt our celebra-

275

tion," He lifted his ornately decorated drinking horn in a toast to the crowd, then sat down and hugged Thulyn warmly as though nothing were amiss.

Celiese looked up at Mylan, unable to comprehend why his father had told such a preposterous lie. Surely someone would notice Oluf was missing before long. It would take only a brief search to locate his body, and there would be no mystery as to how he had died. "Mylan!" she whispered a desperate plea, praying that he would be more sensible than his father, and to her great relief, he was.

Mylan understood Celiese's concern at once, for he had not expected his father to pretend nothing had happened when he'd just admitted killing a man. He knew his parent's excuse would soon be recognized for the transparent fabrication it was, and then there would be chaos for certain. Seeking to be well prepared for that unfortunate eventuality, he went to Hagen's side and confided in a low voice, "Keep the Torgvalds amused for as long as you can. I will be back as soon as I have changed my clothes and I will need all the help you can give me."

"You shall have it," Hagen agreed, for he was not nearly so gullible as their guests and knew from Mylan's tone that he had been involved in something dreadful indeed. Since it seemed to involve the Torgvalds, he looked quickly in their direction. Noting Oluf's absence, he was afraid he already knew what had happened. That Celiese was with his older brother alarmed him too, for her gown was as soiled as Mylan's linen tunic, and he could not understand how she could have become so disheveled unless she'd been thrown in the dirt. His imagination filled in all the missing details in so lurid a fashion that he was tempted to follow Mylan and find out just exactly what had happened, but he'd promised to keep the Torgvalds occupied and got up to do so. He moved down the long table, encouraging his relatives and friends to have more to eat or another horn of ale. In a few moments' time conversation began again, but as Mylan and Celiese left the large room, all eyes were still upon them.

"What are we going to do?" Celiese asked breathlessly as Mylan whisked her up the stairs to his room. She had wanted to speak with him, had hoped they would have some time together that day, but never had she dreamed they would share in so grim a deed as they had.

Mylan tore off his tunic and used the water left after his bath to wet the end of a towel and wash off the blood and grime he'd not been able to remove outside. "We are going to clean up as best we can, then I will seek some way to speak with Jens alone and tell him what has happened to Oluf. I do not want him to challenge me in the hall, or we're sure to have a brutal brawl in which others might be killed."

Celiese went back to the door and threw the bolt, insuring their security for the moment. "What can you possibly say to Jens that won't enrage him? How would you react if he were to casually draw you aside and say he'd just slain Hagen?"

Mylan tossed his now filthy towel aside and turned to face her. "I have two other brothers, why did Hagen's name come so quickly to your lips?"

Startled that he would pick such an inopportune time to be jealous, Celiese ignored the implication of his question and replied, "Do not tease me now, Mylan, for we will never be in more danger than we are at this very moment, and we must not fight between ourselves!"

Mylan stared at his fascinating companion, enjoying the beauty a bit of dirt did not diminish in the slightest as he considered her words. Then, since her point was well taken, he agreed. "I have no desire to argue with you, so if you will not answer my question I will not pursue it. Now you asked me what I would do if the situation were reversed, I would not leave the Torgvald house without taking revenge, and I fully expect Jens to respond with the same blind anger I would feel. That is why I want to speak with him alone, so no one else need suffer his rage."

"You have the advantage here, use it!" Celiese cautioned him immediately. "Jens is not alone, he is merely the eldest now, so don't think Ansgar, Sorgen, and Korsor won't be looking for blood as well. The four of them are every bit as violent as Oluf ever was—the only quality those men respect is strength, and you have enough kinsmen here tonight to make an attack upon you impossible. Do not face Jens alone, surround yourself with the biggest brutes you can muster to provide an unbeatable defense."

Mylan felt he had no need for her advice and said so bluntly. "I had forgotten how much you like to plan strategy for a battle. Well, here you are again, right in the thick of it!"

"How dare you!" Celiese had taken enough of his

indifference and responded angrily. "Oluf brought this upon himself with his own insatiable lust and endless stupidity. I refuse to take the blame for his death and I will not allow you to, either!"

For a moment, Mylan did not know whether to turn Celiese across his knee or simply to turn his back on her, as both alternatives had a certain appeal. Finally he chose the latter and went to his trunk for a clean tunic. "Have you another gown? Put it on and meet me downstairs. I should have sent you around to the back entrance, so none would think you involved in this gruesome business, but it is too late now to consider your reputation."

"My reputation? Surely you jest, for I have none!" Celiese ran to the door but found her hands shaking so badly she had difficulty sliding the bolt out of the way so she could leave. When Mylan came up behind her she stood aside, thinking he meant to help her open the door, but he put out his arms to block her way. He smelled of the soap he'd just used, a rich blend of exotic spices he'd gathered on his travels, and his mere closeness made it almost impossible for her to concentrate upon his words. She had always found him irresistibly appealing, and neither her anger nor the desperate nature of their situation made any difference in the longing that filled her heart. It was as though they had never been apart, she loved him so deeply.

"We have no time now for one of your temper tantrums, Celiese. You must do exactly what I tell you to do. Keep out of any argument that might occur, offer no comments of any kind, and remain by my mother's side as if you were the fine lady you claim to be. I may just be able to save both our necks tonight, and if I do, I promise to give the quality of your reputation my full attention first thing tomorrow morning." Mylan's voice was low, a seductive whisper as his warm breath caressed her cheek, but he was deadly serious and wanted her to know it.

"You needn't bother!" Celiese tugged at the bolt, finally freeing it so she could fling open the door herself, but when she ran down the corridor to her own room Mylan followed right behind her. Pausing at her door she said flippantly, "I thought you wanted me to meet you downstairs."

"I have decided that would be foolhardy when you have so little inclination to obey my commands." When she opened her door he followed her inside and was immediately displeased by the size of her quarters. "Why were you given this room? It is no larger than a closet." Scowling angrily, he surveyed the cramped space and knew instantly that she had been shown little in the way of hospitality in his home, and, for a reason he could barely name, that thought pained him greatly.

"It's close to Olgrethe's, and I have little to store and do not require larger lodgings." She felt fortunate not to have been assigned a stall in the stable, but thought better of reminding him how she had come to be living in his home. She hesitated to disrobe in front of him, but he leaned back against her door, clearly meaning to observe while she changed her gown. "Would you please be so kind as to turn your back so I might have some privacy here? As you said, the room is a small one, and I am not used to having company when I dress."

Mylan gave an exasperated chuckle, then realized to

his dismay that Celiese was serious. "I am in no mood to admire your figure, so you needn't fear displaying it will distract me. Just hurry, as every minute we spend here lessens our advantage in dealing with the Torgvalds."

Blushing deeply in spite of his assurances, Celiese hastened to remove her new gown and lay it aside. It could be washed to remove all traces of the evening, but she knew she'd never wish to wear it again so made no plans to rinse it clean before the stains set. She washed as hurriedly as Mylan had, then slipped on the gown Olgrethe had loaned her since she thought it was so pretty.

Mylan took a deep breath and then another, but Celiese's effect upon him was as profoundly erotic as it had always been. She was a woman like no other. He had not allowed himself to dwell upon how greatly he had missed her until that very moment, but the longings that flooded his senses now were impossible to ignore. He straightened up abruptly and opened the door rather than remain in the small room where the sweet perfume of her lithe young body overpowered his reasoning so completely that he had nearly forgotten what had to be done. He wanted to send someone out to wrap Oluf's body and carry it down to the docks for the voyage to the other side of the fjord. "Hurry, there is no time to lose!"

"I need but a moment more," Celiese called softly, but her fingers were trembling so she dropped her hairbrush and then inadvertently kicked it as she bent down to pick it up. It clattered across the floor, landing beside Mylan's foot as if she'd deliberately tried to catch his attention, and she was horribly embarrassed that he would think that was exactly what she had done.

"Here." Mylan picked up the brush and placed it in her outstretched hand, but she seemed so flustered he could not resist giving her a light kiss upon the cheek before he drew away. He then felt foolish for having been so sweet when he saw by her deep blush that he had made her all the more nervous. "Your appearance can not be faulted, Celiese, put the brush away and let us go." Taking her hand again, he led the way down the back stairs through the kitchen, where they found several fieldhands talking to the girls who had worked all day to prepare the food for the guests. They were all slaves and flirting among them was commonplace, but tonight he had no time for such nonsense. Taking the men aside, he explained they were to get a blanket from his room, locate Oluf's body on the path to the bluff, wrap it well so it would be easy to carry, and then take it down to the docks. They were so terrified by that prospect that they lost all interest in the young women and dashed off to complete the errand before the death had been discovered and they had to pay for it with their own lives.

That chore under way, Mylan and Celiese turned toward the hall. They could hear laughter and music; all the sounds of a joyful gathering echoed around them while they were each lost in their own dark thoughts. When Mylan stopped again to caution her to be silent, Celiese interrupted him quickly. "I will cause no further trouble, Mylan. All I can think of is how devastated Olgrethe will be to learn of her brother's death. She had such high hopes that today's party would draw us all closer together, and I am afraid she will blame herself for this unexpected tragedy."

Gazing down into Celiese's tear-filled eyes, Mylan understood exactly what Olgrethe's hopes had been and how great a part he'd played in ruining them. He had come home for only one reason: to show Celiese how little he needed her company to live a contented life. He had tolerated Estrid's clinging affections merely to hurt his willful wife, and the results of her sorrow had proven to be disastrous for them all. "Why did you leave the hall? What possessed you to go wandering so far from the house when you must have known it wouldn't be safe for you to do so?"

Celiese looked away shyly. The answer seemed so obvious she could not bring herself to reveal the truth if he did not see it for himself. "It matters little why I left, the problem was that Oluf followed me."

Mylan did not press her for the truth when he realized she was unwilling to speak it. Frustrated, he hesitated at the entrance to the large room, angry with himself that he had been unable to formulate a clear plan for dealing with Oluf's unfortunate demise. He could see that Celiese was barely able to maintain her composure after what had happened, and he had no hope that Olgrethe would be able to do so either. "Would you like to take Olgrethe to her room and give her the news of her brother's death yourself? I know how devoted you are to her, and this is not something she should hear from a stranger."

"You are no stranger to her, Mylan." Celiese was puzzled by his remark but appreciated his thoughtfulness. "I know I should be the one to tell her, but I doubt she will leave Andrick's side, for they were both enjoying

283

themselves greatly when I left them." She fidgeted nervously with the soft folds of her borrowed gown. She dreaded telling her friend what had happened, but was even more terrified that Mylan might be seriously hurt if he persisted in his plan to speak with Jens alone. She longed for him to take her into his arms, to pretend if for only a moment that together they could overcome any problem, but he stood with his hands at his sides, staring impatiently, and clearly in no mood to be loving. Forcing herself to be brave for his sake, she stepped forward. "I will tell her as gently as I possibly can. Now let us hurry and get this frightful ordeal over with swiftly."

Astonished by her courage, but admiring her all the more, Mylan took Celiese's arm and escorted her into the noisy gathering. Suddenly the memory of their wedding night came back to him with the eerie tingle of the most frightening premonition, and he realized that was the last time he'd spoken with most of those present. The Vandahls were a large family, and he knew that night he'd need all the cunning and strength he'd inherited to avoid further tragedy. No matter how difficult Jens and his brothers proved to be, he knew Raktor would not rest until he'd extracted the most gruesome revenge possible for the death of his eldest son. The feud that had separated the Torgvalds and Vandahls for more than a generation would seem like a small squabble compared to the anger that would be generated over Oluf's death. Not wishing Celiese to witness any further bloodshed, he gave her a stern command: "Go at once to Olgrethe and tell her any story you can to make her leave the hall with you. Now go, take her away!" With a wide grin he entered the

284

hall and scanned the crowd for Hagen. Seeing him on the
opposite side of the room, he made his way through the
boisterous gathering, stopping frequently to return a jest
with a teasing response and deep laugh.

Estrid sat pouting angrily, surrounded by young men
she thought impossibly silly, and having no intention of
forgiving Mylan for leaving her alone for so long. When
he walked by without even looking her way, she nearly
screamed with indignation. How dare the man ignore her
as if she did not exist? He had spent the entire day with
her, never once mentioning how foolish she'd been to
break their engagement, and she had expected to leave
the Vandahl home the next day engaged to him again. He
was as handsome as ever, so dashing in his appearance
and charming in his manner. She had thought Thulyn
had invited her simply to give Mylan the opportunity to
court her again without the formality of going to her
home to do so. Now she did not know what to think,
except that the Frenchwoman who had been his slave was
far more attractive than she'd been led to believe, and she
was worried that he might have grown fond of the slender
blonde. That was only natural, she supposed, for an
unmarried man had needs that had to be satisfied somehow, but she would not be content until Mylan was
finally her husband, and then she'd make certain he
never saw the pretty young woman ever again. What they
could have been doing together to have gotten so dirty
she couldn't imagine. Mylan was fond of his horses;
perhaps they'd been in the stable. But that mystery didn't
really concern her now since he had returned to the party.
All that mattered was that he was again handsomely

groomed, and she wanted him to return to her side where he belonged.

Celiese watched Mylan walk away and prayed it would not be the last time she saw him alive. She felt chilled clear to her marrow, despite the warmth of the room, and she knew Olgrethe would see her mood and completely misunderstand its cause.

Andrick noticed Celiese approaching and whispered to his bride, "Something is wrong, I have never seen Celiese so pale. Perhaps you should convince her to go to her room if she is ill."

Olgrethe turned to greet her longtime companion and had to agree. "Whatever have you and Mylan been doing? I care not what the secret might be, I insist you tell me all that happened between you two just now." Eager for that confidence, Olgrethe drew near and waited for Celiese to respond.

"Will you please excuse us, Andrick?" Celiese smiled sweetly, hoping he would think she had some tantalizing bit of gossip to impart and allow his wife to leave. "I want to speak privately with Olgrethe, if I may."

Seeing the merry sparkle in his bride's eyes, Andrick could not resist the charms of two such pretty young women and readily agreed. "Of course, she will not be content until you have satisfied her curiosity, but do not be gone long, my love."

"We will be no more than a moment," Celiese assured him. "I believe Mylan wants to speak with you, why don't you join him and Hagen while we are gone?" When the young man gave his wife a light kiss and walked away to join his brothers, Celiese took Olgrethe's arm and led her toward the door. "I want no one to overhear my words, let us go to your room to talk."

Olgrethe could barely contain her curiosity and followed willingly. Mylan had looked more than merely pleased with himself when he'd escorted Celiese into the room, and she was certain he'd asked her to again be his wife.

Mylan wasted no time in explaining to Hagen how he'd become involved in a fight to the death with Oluf, and when Andrick joined them he enlisted his aid as well. With a few well-placed suggestions to several close relatives, they managed to draw the Torgvalds away from the center of the room, isolating them in one corner where they kept them amused and drinking steadily until most of the other guests had retired for the night. A few of those living close by had left for home, while others and those having to travel to more distant locations had been given lodgings for the night.

Aldred saw what his sons were doing and approved. As usual, Mylan had taken charge of a difficult situation and appeared to have it well in hand. He was speaking to the Torgvalds of nothing more serious than hunting, but watching their reactions closely in order to be better able to predict them. He was proud of all four of his sons, but Mylan had been his firstborn and had enjoyed that privilege all his life. That he was again looking so well and fit pleased the older man immensely, but he knew they all still had that night to survive before they could make any plans for the future.

When Aldred joined their small group, Mylan looked up in surprise to see the hall nearly empty and knew he could no longer delay in reporting Oluf's death, and he proceeded to do so. As he saw it, Olgrethe's brothers had gotten the better of him once, while he had outfought them in their own home in return. Things had stood even between them, but he knew he was about to tip the scales, and the delicate balance they'd held that day would be destroyed for all time if he was not careful. "We have never before met together as friends, and I deeply regret what I must tell you now."

Ansgar did not bother to cover a wide yawn, then finished the last of his ale before he interrupted rudely. "I want only to find a bed, as Oluf must have done." With a sly wink he continued, "Knowing him, it is a bed with a wench in it!"

Mylan looked toward his father for assistance when he saw the Torgvalds' jovial mood had not been dampened by his somber statement, but Aldred shook his head and encouraged him to continue on his own. Clearing his throat, Mylan tried again to explain. "That is precisely the problem. Oluf did indeed try to bed a wench, who happened to be most unwilling."

Frowning now, Ansgar leaned forward. "So what? That is not the first time some girl has refused him. Didn't he change her mind?"

Mylan rose slowly to his feet, flanked by Andrick and Hagen who stood ready to help their older brother make his point clear. "No, he did not. When I came to her defense we fought and I won. You will find his body ready to be taken home in the morning."

Jens leapt to his feet, not so surprised he couldn't insult an old enemy. "That's a bloody lie! You never saw the day you could beat my brother at anything!"

Sorgen was so drunk he could scarcely follow the conversation, but when he turned to ask Korsor what had happened he found him asleep where he sat and so demanded an explanation from Mylan. "What's happened to Oluf?"

Mylan spoke distinctly to make certain he was understood. "I killed him." He had no opportunity to say more as Jens lunged for his throat, knocking him into the wall where he grabbed ahold of the enraged man to ward off his punishing blows. Now that the fight had begun in earnest, he was filled with the same furious anger he'd turned upon Oluf. In his mind he saw only Celiese, and how defenseless so delicate a beauty would have been against brutes such as these. He would have swiftly killed Jens too, had his father and Andrick not pulled them apart. Hagen had drawn his knife so rapidly that Ansgar and Sorgen had had no opportunity to leave their seats before they were surrounded with Vandahls, each brandishing a dagger they clearly intended to use at the slightest provocation.

With the help of his kin to enforce his words, Aldred now took charge of the situation. "Enough!" he shouted, and when Jens had been forced back into his place beside his three brothers, he demanded their attention. "You have every right to be angry. Oluf's death was a senseless tragedy, but it needn't be the excuse to begin the feud between our families all over again. We have all had too much to drink and are too tired to make any rational decisions tonight. In the morning we will talk again when our tempers have cooled and our alternatives will be more readily apparent."

"What difference will the morning make when Oluf will still be dead!" Jens snarled fiercely. He leaned over to shove Korsor off his stool, finally arousing him from a sleep so deep he'd not heard the shouts of the fight right beside him. "We came here in peace, and we'll not go home without having satisfaction for our brother's murder!"

Mylan looked up then to see Celiese standing in the doorway. How long she'd been there he did not know, but he motioned for her to approach them. "Did you tell Olgrethe of her brother's death?"

"Yes, I stayed with her until she had cried herself to sleep, but she knew her brother's vices well and does not blame us for his death." Celiese came close enough to be understood without shouting, but not so near that the Torgvalds could touch her.

Jens's pale blue eyes narrowed menacingly as he looked back at Celiese. "It was you, wasn't it? Oluf is dead because of you!" Clearly he was astonished to realize she had been the cause of the tragedy.

Celiese made no attempt to reply, for she knew Jens would never accept her explanation of what had occurred between her and his brother. She simply returned his icy stare with the same bitter hatred reflected in her eyes that shone in his. They were despicable villains all of them, and she was sorry no more than one had died that night.

Mylan watched closely as Celiese stood calmly returning the murderous glances the Torgvald brothers turned upon her. The hatred in the air was so thick he felt as though he were suffocating, yet she appeared to be impervious to their evil gaze, and he marveled at the strength of character that had allowed her to survive their brutality to become the loveliest of young women. He could not bear to have her in the same room with such filth as they represented, and he tried to send her away. "Olgrethe may awaken and need you, Celiese, please go back to her now and leave this to us to settle."

"No!" Jens shouted hoarsely, "Give her to us—my brother's life is high enough price to have paid for her!"

"She is a free woman, not for sale at any price," Mylan replied promptly, somewhat surprised by how easily that truth came to his lips, but he did not like the hostile expression in his father's eyes and hastened to enforce his words, "My father was right, this matter is too important to be settled tonight. You will be shown to a room, and do not try and leave it before dawn, as the door will be well guarded." Signaling to his cousins, he ignored the loud curses sent his way as the Torgvalds were escorted from the hall.

Estrid was among the few ladies remaining in the room, and she had drawn close in order to hear what was being said. Clearly Celiese was the cause of all the mischief, and in her opinion the young woman should have been given to the Torgvalds in appeasement for Oluf's death. She licked her lips slowly, and prayed Aldred would soon come to the same conclusion, for she had seen his reaction to Jens's demand and thought it a strong possibility she might soon be rid of Celiese for good. Surely Mylan had defended her because he was a gentleman, but he would soon forget her charms when he had an equal for his wife. She would go to him as soon as his father bid them all a good night. He had fought bravely and deserved the generous reward she planned to give him. A wicked smile lifted the corner of her mouth. Yes indeed, she would bed Mylan that very night, and he would call her wife in the morning, or her family would demand that he did.

Without the Torgvalds present to argue Aldred was free to speak his mind. "Leave us, Celiese; this discussion no longer concerns you."

Since there were still a dozen or so guests looking on, Celiese had no intention of leaving the hall when it seemed obvious Aldred had something important to say. "I prefer to stay," she announced calmly, her tone not argumentative, but confident and proud.

Drawing himself up to his full height, Aldred dealt with her defiance swiftly. "You have brought disgrace upon the name of Vandahl not once but twice, Celiese. I am tempted to hand you over to Jens right now, but that seems too cruel a fate even for you to suffer. I will send the Torgvalds on their way at first light, but you must leave here as well. You are no longer welcome in my home, and I want you gone for good by noon."

"No!" Hagen shouted instantly. "You'll not send Celiese away, for I want her as my wife!" His knife still drawn, he was determined to fight if there were no other means to get his way.

"What! That woman is no fit bride for you!" Aldred was appalled. He looked for Thulyn, but she had turned and hurried away, leaving the matter entirely in his hands to settle. He saw Erik pushing his way closer and feared his youngest son would speak for the former slave too, but it was Mylan who ended the controversy abruptly.

"If Celiese is any man's wife she is mine!" he declared emphatically, challenging Hagen as well as his father to dispute him. His defiant glare and proud stance made them both back away, for neither cared to be his second victim that night.

Large tears welled up in Estrid's eyes as she saw the man she wanted so badly for herself state openly that he wanted another. Furious that he preferred a pretty slave to her, she ran from the room, all her hopes dashed for a secure future as the wife of the enormously wealthy Mylan Vandahl. She felt the same terror she'd known two years before when she'd broken her engagement to him when she'd thought he would not live to see their wedding day. Her delicate features contorted in a vicious mask, she fled from the people she was certain would be laughing at her, but none noticed her sudden departure, nor cared.

When she realized all eyes were upon her, Celiese tried to respond in the most tactful and gracious manner possible. First she approached Hagen, and seeing his confusion finally understood that he truly did care for her, even if he had never been able to state his feelings in words. She did not want to hurt him now, but knew she must. "I am greatly honored that you want me to be your wife, Hagen, but I cannot marry you when your father has banished me from his home. I will not be the cause of such unbearable strife in your family, and I beg you to accept my refusal and understand its cause." When he nodded slightly, his cheeks burning with a bright blush, she stood on her tiptoes to give him a kiss upon the cheek before turning to look up at Mylan. She had prayed that he would come for her, take her back to his home and make her his wife, but he had ignored her and clearly he had no wish to include her in his life. All day she had watched him laugh and flirt with Estrid, so obviously he had not missed her, and only his pride had prompted him to challenge Hagen for her hand. She could not hide her tears then, and they slid down her flushed cheeks, glimmering brightly in the soft light that still filled the large room. "When I wished with all my heart to be your bride, you refused to accept my love. It is too late now for us to find happiness together, so if that was a proposal you made just now I must refuse it. I ask only that you help me return to France, so that my presence here will no longer create such a painful embarrassment to you all."

For a long moment Mylan could not find his voice, for he knew Celiese had loved him once and could not understand why she did not love him still. He had not thought her as empty-headed and fickle as Estrid, but perhaps all women were the same and he was better off without them. No matter what he thought of the fleeting nature of her affections, he knew she could not simply be shoved out the front door and left to wander Denmark with neither friend nor kin to take her in. She had been miserable in his homeland, and he quickly agreed to her request, but his amber eyes glowed with hatred as he did. "If that is what you want, you shall have it. We will depart as soon as my ship can be made ready to sail."

"You cannot make such a long voyage now!" Aldred protested heatedly, "Winter will arrive before you can return, and the trip will be needlessly dangerous. I forbid it, you may not take this woman anywhere but to the crossroads where she might find someone willing to take her where they are going."

Mylan took a deep breath and let it out slowly. "I know the perils of making a voyage in the autumn, but I have given my word and will not go back upon it unless you have changed your mind about sending Celiese away."

Aldred was seething with rage, for he knew Mylan was trying to force him to change his decision and he'd not do it. He wanted Celiese out of his home before Raktor and his sons returned looking for her and one of his own sons might be killed protecting her. He could see the deaths multiplying; like ripples in a stream the killings would continue unless he put a stop to them now. Suddenly the obvious solution came to him, and he regretted he'd not pursued it when Jens had first presented it. When the Torgvalds left the next morning he'd send Celiese with them, at dawn before any of his sons were up to stop him. The fact that she was no longer a slave would not trouble the Torgvalds in the least, and he knew they would kill her at Oluf's funeral and let him deal with her in the next world as he had failed to do in this one. Sighing sadly as if he had no hope of solving so difficult a problem, Aldred lied convincingly. "Mylan, it is too late for us to argue this point further. I am going to bed and will speak with you again tomorrow, for I am certain we can come to a solution that will please us both." He walked from the room then, hoping to find Thulyn still awake, for he was positive she would welcome his idea with enthusiasm, for she had no love for Celiese either.

Chapter Seventeen

Pacing the close confines of her cramped quarters, Celiese could not forget the rage that had filled Mylan's golden gaze as she'd declined his offer of marriage. Actually, she was not even certain he had proposed to her, he had spoken so quickly, responding angrily to Hagen's proposal rather than making one of his own. All they had done that evening was fight, but at least he had not carried out his original plan to face Jens alone, and whether that was because of her advising him to do otherwise or mere happenstance did not matter, since the result had been the same.

As the hour grew late, Celiese still could not rest. Her mind as well as her supple body were filled with torment, but she'd had no choice in her actions that night. After she had been ordered to leave the Vandahl home, she could scarcely marry into the family. She had done no wrong, yet they constantly blamed her for the evil deeds of the Torgvalds. It was all so unfair! She could not stop her restless pacing, her rage growing more deep with each passing step. Why did her life continually run to tragedy, when to win Mylan's heart was all she'd ever wanted? Was the love of that proud man so unattainable a prize that she would never be his no matter how greatly she longed to call him husband? He had not understood why she'd refused him, that had been plain in the darkness of his glance, but he had understood none of her dreams when they'd been together either, so she'd been a fool to hope he would be sympathetic now.

Her hand tightened around the small silver hammer she still wore suspended upon its pretty chain, her fingertips caressing the cool metal in a vain effort to affect a calm as icy as the delicate charm. She had never removed the pagan symbol, although Olgrethe teased her constantly for wearing it, but it was the only thing she had of Mylan's and it provided the sweetest of memories for her. Knowing his room was nearby, she could not help but wonder if he had been able to fall into his usual untroubled sleep, when she could not even bear to lie down long enough to close her eyes. Finally deciding to seize the initiative, Celiese slipped silently out of her room and tiptoed down the hall. Finding the door unbarred she entered Mylan's room quietly and slowly slid the bolt into place so they would not be disturbed while she was with him. She waited a moment, wanting to be certain he was alone in the comfortable bed, and when she heard the easy rhythm of his breathing she knew the dilemma that had plagued her mind that night had not troubled his. She approached the bed cautiously, not wanting to startle him by waking him suddenly. Finding room on the bed, she sat down upon the edge. Mylan lay upon his stomach, his cheek resting upon his arm, and she leaned down to kiss his shoulder lightly, letting her lips caress his warm skin while he continued to sleep, unaware of her gentle touch. Enjoying herself too greatly to stop, Celiese slid her fingertips down his back, then over his narrow hips. His skin was smooth, taut over the powerful muscles of his shoulders, and she savored his warmth as she cast off her light shift and stretched out beside him to cuddle close. Winding her fingers in his soft curls she bit his earlobe playfully, and hoped he would awaken in an affectionate mood regardless of how little he liked or trusted her.

Mylan was exhausted. Oluf had hurt him more badly than he'd let anyone see, and his whole body ached from the punishing blows the brute had inflicted. As if that were not enough, Jens had struck a glancing blow to his left cheek. His eye was swollen and would be black by morning, but that was so minor a discomfort he had simply ignored it. He had fallen across his bed, wanting to sleep for days rather than contemplate for another agonizing moment what he was to do with Celiese. When his father wanted her gone and she wanted to leave, why was he filled with such terrible dread at that prospect? He had to keep his promise, however, and escort her safely to France, even though she would then be lost to him forever. He knew he would never be able to forget her astonishing beauty nor the exquisite rapture they had shared far too briefly, but she was a liar, who possessed a heart made of a substance more unyielding than the finest steel, and those were faults he could not forgive.

When Celiese's light kiss moved across the back of his neck Mylan stretched slightly, his sleep lightening by degrees until he came fully awake and realized the enchanting creature who so often filled his dreams was once again in his bed. He rolled over slowly upon his back, staring into the darkness as he reached up to touch her curls. She had such beautiful hair, such silken strands that tickled his bare chest as she leaned down to kiss him, her lips brushing his only lightly until he pulled her down into a far more erotic embrace. He swore to himself he would never let her go; she had slipped into his bed of her own accord, but she was a captive now, a prisoner of passion too strong to deny, and he felt her relax, her lithe body melting into his own, her mouth opening eagerly to accept his deep kiss, and all thought save one left his mind.

To have hoped for affection and be welcomed with such delicious ardor was more than Celiese had dared expect. Mylan was so alive, his strength and tenderness so finely meshed she could not seem to hold him tightly enough to enjoy all he wished to give. His hands moved slowly down her soft curves as if memorizing her every contour, gently fanning the glowing embers of her passion until they leapt into flames. She slipped from his grasp then as she trailed sweet kisses down the scars that ran across his broad chest, wanting only to give him the deepest of pleasures, the same glorious thrill he gave to her. She knew the pattern left by the bear's claws—the long sweep of the animal's paw had slashed his bronze skin ruthlessly, yet the deep scars were as unique a part of him as his golden curls or his amber eyes, and she whispered softly, "You are the most splendid of men, Mylan, truly you are, and I have always thought you far more attractive than merely handsome." Before he could argue with her sweet compliment, she slid her fingertips up the inside of his thigh, her tantalizing touch a promise of the love she longed to give him. As she moved alongside his lean body her tongue sent a flickering flame through the muscles of his flat stomach, teasing his senses until she felt him shiver. Driven on by the untamed desire his mere presence kindled within her heart, she moved lower still, longing to bestow a gift of love so magnificent that the memory of her would fill his heart forever. Her lips burned his flesh with a fiery kiss, which flooded his powerful body with a torrent of ecstasy so wild that he wound his fingers in her shining curls to make her finish what she had begun. He drew her close, savoring each delicious ripple of the joy that shuddered through him, exploding at last in a shower of such brilliant rapture that he could no longer keep silent and called her name in a low, slurred moan, his pleasure so close to madness that he could not keep that delectable insanity from resounding in his deep voice.

Knowing she had succeeded in pleasing Mylan as greatly as she had hoped to, Celiese laid her head upon his chest, content to listen to the wildly thundering beat of his heart until it grew steady once more. His fingers moved slowly through her tangled curls, sharing the bliss with her still, and she was filled with the same marvelous peace he enjoyed and had no desire ever to leave his warm embrace. She wanted to make the night last forever, extending each precious moment to the fullest so her memories would all be sweet when they parted.

Still astonished by Celiese's lavish display of affection,

Mylan hesitated to inquire as to its cause. He had no desire to provoke her, which he knew was all too easy a feat, for her temperament was a tumultuous blend of passion and fury he had never been able successfully to predict, but he could imagine no more splendid female creature ever having been born, and he remained silent until his need for her overpowered his reason once again.

Moving with exaggerated slowness, Mylan pulled Celiese's lissome body against the length of his own. His injuries were no more than dull aches now, the sharpness of their pain blurred by the enchantment of her marvelous affection. She had moved over him with the fluid grace of the most entrancing of dancers, her every motion giving so rich a pleasure that he longed to repay her sensual gifts with a magic of his own. His lips caressed the soft curve of her throat and he felt the silver chain he'd given her and smiled, for the charm had brought them both good luck that night. His mouth lingered at the hollow of her shoulder before seeking the flushed pink tip of her breast. Savoring the sweetness of her silken skin, he drew her near, turning her tenderly in his arms so he might run his fingertips down her spine. His touch was deliberate, yet honey-smooth, as his hands slid over her hips, drawing her closer still. She came to him readily, a perfect mate whose voluptuous body seemed designed solely to pleasure his, but again he moved with such loving devotion that he made their union last until he felt the heat of her body's response and knew the depth of her hunger for him had been satisfied. He lost himself then in his own sparkling dreams of her. Swift and sure, his power still tender, he let his own need build to a rapturous conclusion, and, hearing the softness of Celiese's contented sigh, he drifted back to sleep with her cradled in his arms. He was not altogether certain he had ever been awake, for making love had never been more splendid, and he would not have been surprised to discover it had all been simply a magnificent dream.

While Celiese lay sleeping peacefully in his arms, Mylan was awakened by the distinctively metallic sound of iron scraping against stone. Someone had just walked by his door and had carelessly let his weapon strike the wall. Instantly alert to possible danger, he sat up, easing the delicate beauty from his arms before he left his bed and went to the door. Opening it no more than a crack, he waited, and, again hearing the sound that had shattered his dreams, he grew more bold and peered out into the corridor to discover what was amiss. Two men stood at Celiese's door, and while he was certain one was his father he could not make out the identity of the other until he heard him speak. He recognized the man instantly then, and knowing Jens would have no good purpose visiting Celiese at that hour, he stepped out into the shadows and pressed his body against the wall, moving close enough to overhear the rest of their conversation.

His voice stern even at a whisper, Aldred insisted forcefully, "You must slip into her room without making another sound, or you will awaken the entire household! Shove the gag into her mouth so she cannot cry out as you tie her hands and feet, then carry her from my house as swiftly as you can. What you choose to do with her then I will not question, but the night is coming to an end, and you must be on your way before this abduction is discovered!"

"I am no fool!" Jens responded with a hostile sneer. "My brothers are already on board our ship, and we will take Celiese without mishap. Now let us cease talking and I will finish the deed!"

Mylan watched as Jens entered Celiese's room with stealth a cat would envy, but he was inside no more than the few seconds it took him to realize her small chamber was empty. Gesturing angrily as he returned to the corridor, he accused Aldred of some further piece of treachery, but the older man took him firmly by the arm and led him down the hall toward the stairs so they might discuss this unexpected predicament without fear of arousing those who still slept.

Mylan stepped back into his room, closed the door silently, then threw the bolt. His heart was pounding so loudly in his ears that he could scarcely hear his own thoughts. Never had he ever thought his father capable of stooping to such an evil plot as the one he'd just discovered. Seeking to create harmony between two warring families was a noble quest, but not when it was accomplished at the cost of an innocent life, and he'd not forgive the man for betraying Celiese to further his own goals. Furious, he tried to catch his breath, but the thought that Celiese had escaped being kidnapped and murdered by so narrow a margin appalled him and he could not force himself to affect a calm he did not feel.

Forcing himself to think clearly in order to devise the most devious plan for eluding her pursuers, Mylan could not help but contemplate what Celiese's fate would have been had she not come to him that night. He remembered his grandfather's funeral vividly. A handsome man, his posture had still been proud despite his years. After his death his body had been burned with that of his favorite female slave. She was a young woman whom Mylan recalled fondly, for she had often looked after him when his mother was busy with his twin brothers. On the day of the funeral the attractive slave had been brought to the spot on the beach where his grandfather's ship had been towed and surrounded with firewood. His body was already on board, inside a tent so none might see what transpired before the pyre was lit. A curious child, he had watched the pretty young woman drink deeply, dulling her senses with the intoxicating beverage she had been given. She had sung a song, a soft, sweet ballad that had touched him even then with its sadness. After telling her friends good-bye, she had been led into the tent, but his mother had taken him away then, not wanting him to witness what was to come. But he had pestered an uncle to tell him the truth, and the man had explained that his grandfather's sons had all lain with the woman. Next the old woman known as the Angel of Death, the same one who had prepared his grandfather's body for the funeral, had entered the tent. She had placed a rope around the slave's neck and given the ends to two men to pull, strangling her so she could not cry out as the Angel plunged a dagger into her heart. To a child the ritual murder had seemed strange and awful, but now as a grown man he was thoroughly sickened by the memory of what had taken place that day. A beautiful young woman had been sacrificed along with horses and cows to serve a dead man, and he was certain now that she must have been Christian, as was Celiese. Her place in paradise would therefore have been far different than that occupied by his grandfather's spirit, so what had been the purpose of such a senseless death? None; and he was ashamed to think that on more than one occasion he had threatened Celiese with such a ceremonial slaughter. He shuddered as though chilled. Her death would have served no useful purpose whatsoever, and he swallowed hard to force back the nausea that filled his throat as he realized what a gruesome fate awaited her should she fall into the hands of the Torgvalds.

They were brutal butchers, all of them. They would send Celiese to her death at Oluf's funeral after raping her so often she would welcome the Angel's blade, and he was so outraged at his father's duplicity that it was all he could do not to take up his sword and challenge him as he would any other man who tried to harm Celiese. Had she been afraid, perhaps terrified that she would be given to the Torgvalds at dawn and had come to seek his protection? She was clever, perhaps she had seen what he had not and knew her hours in his home were numbered. He had been warned now too, though, and if it had been protection she'd sought she would have it.

Dressing hastily, Mylan stopped to gather extra clothing, which he quickly shoved into a suede bag before he went to the bed to awaken Celiese. He shook her shoulder as he spoke. "You must come with me now, Celiese, there is no time to lose!"

Since she had had no more than the briefest of rests, Celiese yawned sleepily, not understanding Mylan's words until he repeated them. "Where are we going with such haste at this hour?" she asked in a puzzled tone.

"To France; we will sail with the rising sun. Now get up, for there is no point in my leaving without you!" Still frightened for her safety, Mylan coaxed her out of the bed and tossed her the shift he'd found upon the floor. "Get dressed, we must go!"

Celiese had never seen Mylan in so anxious a mood and reached out to catch his hand. "What is wrong, tell me first so I will know what danger to expect." She sat down on the bed, ready to listen.

"There is no time to discuss that now. We must gather your clothing and enlist my brothers' help. Well, put on that shift or I shall drag you down the hall naked!"

Her green eyes widening at the harshness of his tone, Celiese nonetheless rose from his bed and slipped the short linen garment over her head. She shook out her curls to keep them away from her eyes, then walked to his side. "I did not realize you wished to sail with the morning tide or I would have packed what few belongings I have last night."

His emotions still in turmoil, Mylan could do no more than frown as he reached for her hand. "Do not ever remove that silver charm, Celiese, for surely Thor saved your life tonight, and his emblem should be regarded as your greatest treasure."

Surprised by his serious comment, Celiese replied truthfully, "I prize it because it was a gift from you. Thor has no reason to protect me, but what danger existed tonight when I lay in your arms?"

Mylan took the gleaming sword that was never far from

his side, and after opening his door he looked up and down the hall to be certain Jens and his brothers were not lurking nearby. When he saw the way was clear he replied distractedly, "That I will not reveal, but whether it was your passion for me or Thor's intervention that saved you we needn't debate. Now, how much do you have to bring?" Leading her the short distance to her room he ushered her inside and lit the oil lamp by her bed. He then stood impatiently, looking about the room for what she might think necessary.

"I have little once I am dressed." Celiese picked up the gown she'd removed several hours earlier and explained, "Olgrethe has always lent me her clothing, will there be time for me to borrow something more and bid her farewell?"

"No more than a moment." Mylan began to pace nervously, too preoccupied to notice then how lovely Celiese looked as she dressed. Her cheeks were filled with a delicate blush and her eyes sparkled with excitement as she gave him her full attention when he spoke. "The ship Hagen and Andrick command is a *knarr*, a merchant vessel, as is mine. Since theirs is ready to sail and mine is not, I will simply make them a trade. I should have returned long before they wish to set sail in the spring, so that they will again have their own vessel when next they wish to trade goods."

"Yes, I understand. I have my cloak, but I would like to have an extra dress and another pair of slippers. I will speak with Olgrethe about that while you talk with Andrick." Ready to leave, Celiese preceded him to the door, but he put out his hand to stop her and looked out again to see if the corridor was unoccupied.

"Mylan, this is your own house, but you act as though we were trespassing," Celiese said, puzzled.

"Just stay behind me, Celiese, my caution is not foolish no matter what you might think. Now the way is clear, and we must go." He took her hand again as they walked to the quarters Andrick shared with his bride. At the door he knocked softly, and his brother soon came to see who might wish to see him at that early hour.

"I have little time, Andrick, you must lend me your ship and permit Olgrethe to give Celiese a few articles of clothing. We are leaving for her homeland now and have no time to search for apparel to supplement her wardrobe," Mylan told his brother urgently.

Andrick wore no more than a towel knotted low upon his hips. Having been awakened from his dreams, he was clearly astonished by both of Mylan's requests. "You may have the ship, of course, and anything Olgrethe can spare, but is this not a peculiar time to depart?" He yawned loudly then, and rubbed his hand over his eyes to keep them open.

"I will explain when I return. Please keep Celiese here with you while I talk to Hagen." Giving her a stern glance, he insisted, "Do not leave these rooms, Celiese, for it is far too dangerous for you to be walking about the house without me."

He was so serious in his demand that for once Celiese did not question his motives, but nodded agreeably. "I will wait here, you needn't worry I will wander off and become lost."

"See that you don't!" With that spirited parting

remark Mylan left them alone and walking with a long stride disappeared down the hall in the direction of Hagen's room.

Embarrassed to have disturbed Andrick, Celiese apologized as best she could. "Mylan seems determined to depart swiftly; I am sorry that I cannot provide a lucid explanation for what he is doing, but he did not give one to me." She held her few belongings wrapped in a silk scarf and was afraid she presented so pathetic a picture that Andrick would simply pity her rather than being curious about her unexpected appearance in his rooms.

Andrick had spent little time with Celiese, but he knew his wife valued her friendship greatly and offered to awaken her. "Olgrethe did not spend the best of nights, but she will want to get up to help you find whatever you need. Please wait here while I call her, for I don't want to face Mylan in the mood he is in if he should return in a moment and find you gone."

Seeing his teasing smile, Celiese reached up to kiss his cheek lightly. "Thank you, Andrick. Olgrethe is fortunate to have so understanding a husband as you."

"Rather than Mylan, you mean?" the handsome man teased playfully.

"No, that wasn't what I meant at all!" Celiese denied quickly, her face flooding with color, her embarrassment was so acute. "Will none of you ever forget that deception? Am I never to be forgiven for it?"

Andrick watched the sudden rush of tears fill her eyes and realized his joke had been in very poor taste. "I am sorry, Celiese, all I meant was that Olgrethe and I are a far better match than she and Mylan would have been. I did not even think that remark would insult you, and I am sorry that it did."

Celiese turned away, ashamed she had been so ill-tempered when Andrick had been so nice to her. "I do not think you should tease me about something so important as marriage, nor Olgrethe either, as she might as easily misunderstand as I did."

Perplexed to have caused such a disastrous scene when he had only meant to make Celiese smile, Andrick apologized again, hoping he would be able to soothe the distracted young woman's feelings, since he had hurt her unintentionally. When he heard his wife approaching he grew silent, not wanting her to know he had insulted her friend, but she could tell by his sheepish expression that something was wrong.

Awakened by the sounds of their voices, Olgrethe walked slowly into the room. She was dressed in a robe of yellow silk, her eyes red and swollen from the tears she'd shed for her brother. "Why Andrick, were you and Celiese fighting? Has the entire house gone mad?"

Andrick went quickly to her side and gave Olgrethe a reassuring hug. "Of course not, beloved, we were merely talking, and I was just coming to wake you. Mylan and Celiese are leaving, she wanted to bid you farewell, that is all we were discussing." Looking over her head at Celiese, he was pleased to see she understood the cause of that lie and would not dispute him.

"You are leaving me now?" Olgrethe's already pained expression grew even more woebegone as she pleaded, "Oh Celiese, how can you leave me now?"

Mylan slipped through the door in time to respond to

that question. "If she is not gone before sunrise your grief will be compounded tenfold, Olgrethe. Do not try and influence her to stay, for such a choice is impossible." Mylan leaned back against the door to catch his breath; he'd run all the way back from Hagen's room and felt dizzy, his strength impaired by pain.

"Mylan?" Celiese regarded him closely, surprised she'd not noticed the deep purple bruise that marred the lid of his left eye. It looked very painful, but she'd not call attention to it when she knew how little he enjoyed sympathy. "Is everything all right? What did Hagen say?"

"Why didn't you tell me he had offered to take you home? He is not at all pleased I am to be the one to do it."

Celiese knew he had a good point, for she had let Hagen think she would make the voyage with him when she'd not known what else to say. "The situation is a confusing one, I agree, but you and I have had no time to talk, Mylan, so there was really no opportunity for me to tell you of Hagen's plans."

His glance suspicious, Mylan continued, "Of course, you would have told me, you are always so prompt to tell the truth that I don't doubt your sincerity one bit!"

Not understanding why his brother was behaving so badly, Andrick was quick to send his wife from the room so he might question him. "Olgrethe, Celiese needs a gown or two, have you anything to offer?" Since he frequently teased her about the extensive size of her wardrobe, he was certain she did.

"Of course, you may take whatever you wish, Celiese. Come, let us look to see what we can find." Apparently resigned to losing her, Olgrethe led Celiese into her bedroom where her clothing was kept.

Waiting to be certain they could not be overheard, Andrick spoke in a low whisper. "What is wrong that you must flee with such haste? Do you expect the Torgvalds to give pursuit? Their warships are far more fleet than our *knarrs*, so it may be impossible to escape them."

Mylan closed his eyes as he sighed deeply. Never had he spent such an exciting night, and it was not yet over. "Our father made some kind of a bargain with Jens; he meant to hand over Celiese, and I think Jens must have promised his family would not attack us again to avenge Oluf's death."

Aghast, Andrick shouted hoarsely, "That cannot be true!" He was appalled at that bit of treachery and found it unthinkable. "It simply cannot be the truth, Mylan. Where did you hear of this bargain, from Jens himself?"

Straightening up to his full height, Mylan was surprised to realize Andrick was now nearly his equal in size. He was still slightly taller and considered that an advantage when he wished to make a point. "I saw Father lead Jens to her room and instruct him to hurry with the abduction. Is that evidence enough for you?"

"Does she know?" Andrick looked hurriedly toward the room where the two women had gone, fearing they might return in the middle of Mylan's explanation.

"No." Mylan's expression gave no encouragement to that question. "She is not to know, either. It is a betrayal I cannot disclose, for she would hate us all for it."

"Mylan, her love for you is painfully obvious. She saw nothing all day but you. She would not hate you for our father's treachery." That Estrid had been on his brother's arm all day was not a subject he wished to mention, for he was certain Mylan had only used the attractive young woman to make Celiese jealous and he thought such a trick incredibly foolish.

Swearing under his breath, Mylan replied in a hostile whisper, "The woman loves me so dearly she refused to be my wife in front of more than a dozen witnesses! You heard her yourself, Andrick, she'll not have any of us for a husband!"

Laughing, Andrick reached out to touch Mylan's shoulder with a good-natured slap. "You have not courted the woman with anything other than neglect. How can you expect her to want you when you have given her no evidence of your love?"

"I do not love her!" Mylan vowed hoarsely, incensed by his brother's teasing, but as he turned he saw Celiese and Olgrethe at the doorway, and, knowing they had overheard that bitter remark, he was filled with remorse. Thinking his best option simply to ignore the comment rather than trying to explain it, he spoke quickly, "Have you all you need? The journey is a long one."

Olgrethe had just finished reciting a nearly endless tale of woe. Her sorrow was deep at losing the company of her dearest friend when her brother had just died so tragically. If that had not depressed Celiese most thoroughly, here was Mylan screaming for all to hear that he did not love her. Trying to make the best of an extremely embarrassing situation, Celiese came forward with a smooth, graceful stride. "Yes, Olgrethe has always been most generous, and I will never forget her." She kissed the young woman's cheek sweetly, then gave Andrick a warm hug before carrying the things she had gathered through the door. She did not wait this time for Mylan to look for whatever danger he seemed to suspect awaited, for it mattered little to her what her fate might be if she did not have even the hope of winning his love. And from the fury of his denial, she knew she never would.

As she slipped past him, Mylan turned to look at Andrick, knowing he should have prepared some more formal farewell when—if luck were not with him—they might never meet again. "You will be the eldest, if—"

"I will be the eldest only after you die of old age, now go before Celiese takes command of our ship and leaves you behind!" Andrick drew Olgrethe into his arms with a joyful hug, grateful he was not the fool his brother was. Mylan was too proud by far, but he hoped his favorite brother would lose neither his life nor his love on a voyage that was sure to be filled with adventure.

Chapter Eighteen

Hagen met Celiese and Mylan on the path to the docks.
He was out of breath and frowning apprehensively as he
greeted them. "The Torgvalds have gone, but they were
arguing so heatedly amongst themselves I do not see how
they could give enough attention to sailing to reach their
home."

"Let us pray they do not, then," Celiese remarked
softly, the bitterness of her comment surprising the two
men.

"We will not be rid of them so easily as a few rats we
might toss into the sea, but should they sink from the
weight of their own evil deeds, I shall not miss them."
Hagen turned to join the attractive couple on their way to
the beach, his stride long and sure. "Most of our crew
were near enough to summon. I had spoken with them of
the possibility of this voyage, but they had not expected it
to begin so soon."

Mylan cast Celiese a sidelong glance, but she did not
seem embarrassed by Hagen's admission that he'd
planned a voyage to France. That she would have sailed

316

with his brother, simply gone away without once thinking of telling him they were making so dangerous a journey or bidding him farewell, pained Mylan greatly. Apparently she lived entirely for herself, without ever considering how her actions affected others. Why he could never seem to remember how faithless she was he did not know, but she knew how to bewitch him as no other woman ever had, and he found himself hurrying her along the path, still anxious to depart before any further danger overtook them.

"You found adequate provisions so quickly?" Mylan turned his attention from the distracting young woman at his side in an attempt to concentrate on the details of the voyage.

"I had gathered our stores, since I had not expected to spend the entire summer at home," Hagen replied crossly. "We had other plans until Andrick found he could not bear to be away from his bride for more than half a day!"

Rather than remark upon his cynical view of marriage, since Mylan apparently felt the same way, Celiese kept still but she envied Olgrethe greatly for having married a man with so devoted a nature as Andrick had proved to have. She turned back to look at the Vandahl home then, knowing she would never return. She had been terrified when she'd arrived to become Mylan's bride, and she felt no more confident now. The imposing stone structure was silhouetted against the rising sun. Although she could not see any of the inhabitants watching their departure, she was certain many were.

"Did you forget something?" Mylan had noticed

Celiese's pensive mood and backward glance and thought perhaps she had just recalled something important she'd not thought to bring. He'd not let her return for it, however, no matter what it was.

"No, I've left nothing behind." Celiese lifted her skirt carefully so as not to step upon the hem as she continued down the path. "I wish I had had the time to make another suit from one of yours, that would have been ever so much more practical than this gown will be for a voyage."

"Your clothes are the least of our worries, Celiese!" Mylan chuckled at her comment, then assured her he'd not put her to work. "You will have no more to do than sit and enjoy the view, your gowns will be adequate for that pastime."

Celiese smiled at his teasing. He'd been so stern with her that morning she was glad to see his mood was improving as the sky brightened with the light of the new day. As long as the view aboard his ship included him, she knew she would be content. "I will be glad to assist with whatever duties there might be. I do not mind doing my share to make the voyage a smooth one."

Mylan glanced over her head at Hagen and saw him wince. It would be a difficult voyage in all respects, but he doubted he'd need to call upon a pretty young woman to help him complete it. "I will be content if you will but follow my orders, Celiese, that will be service enough for me."

Her green eyes sparkling with the mischief she made no effort to hide, Celiese agreed. "As you wish, captain." She moved aside as they reached the ship and the two brothers began to confer with the crew. Unlike the Dragon, which Raktor was fond of sailing, this vessel was broader and deep enough to carry a sizable cargo or livestock in the center. That area was now rapidly filling up, as about a dozen men tossed in the provisions they'd require and their own belongings to keep the deck clear for working the large sail. A *knarr* was too heavy a craft to row, so there were no holes cut below the rail for oars. When Vikings went raiding, they preferred the slender warships that could navigate the shallowest river, while the sturdier *knarr* was used for the coastal trade routes Andrick and Hagen favored, or the long voyages of discovery Mylan loved to make. This *knarr* had a surprising beauty, however. She'd been so distraught on the voyage home from Kaupang that Celiese had noticed little about the ship, but now it seemed most attractive to her. The graceful prow as well as the stern were decorated with intricate carving of an ornate swirling design, while the large white sail was trimmed with red to make a diamond pattern that was very handsome. She thought the vessel a beauty and wondered if Mylan's was so sleek and impressive a ship.

When Mylan was satisfied he had all he needed to complete a successful voyage, he went to where Celiese stood watching them prepare for departure. "It is time we left. Come, I will help you aboard." He extended his hand and she placed her small hand in his. She had very beautiful hands, he thought suddenly, her fingers long and slim, and so delicate that her slightest gesture was filled with grace. That once in France he might be able to discover her true identity intrigued him enormously, for her background provided no end of puzzlement to him. She was certainly not of peasant stock, but was she really a member of the French nobility? He was so curious he could scarcely wait to find out the truth, and he vowed to himself that he would not leave her homeland before he did.

"What is the name of your brothers' ship, Mylan? It is very handsome and I have been wondering what it is called." Celiese smiled shyly, not daring to hope his more agreeable mood would last for the entire voyage.

"This is the Surf Falcon, and while mine, the Raven of the Sea, is her twin, the two ships handle differently, and I wish I had not been so foolish as to let my own vessel go unattended." That he would not have his own ship to sail pained him greatly, for he knew the Raven as thoroughly as he knew himself and trusted her to do his bidding no matter how rough the weather. That he would have to push to its limits a ship he did not know well was only another problem with which he would sooner not deal.

"I have sailed aboard this vessel once, Mylan, and Andrick and Hagen seemed to make her fly. I am confident you can make her even more swift, if that is your desire." Celiese was sincere in her compliment, but she saw Mylan stiffen, ready to argue. Then Hagen came to his side, and he did not speak whatever thought he had intended to impart.

"I want to come with you, Mylan." Hagen stood in a relaxed pose, not demanding or hostile, but determined in his request.

Mylan looked back toward his home, hoping the flurry of activity upon the docks had not yet been noted.

"There is no time for argument; you must stay behind. If I do not return, divide what is mine among you and Andrick with a smaller share for Erik. Since Andrick will then inherit our father's house, my farm should go to you." When Hagen backed away, not willing to discuss the division of his property while Mylan was still so very much alive, Mylan spoke crossly. "I mean what I say, Hagen. I should return before winter, but if the summer comes again and I have not come home, then you will know what is to be done with my possessions."

"Your chance of survival will be more than doubled if I am with you!" Hagen interjected hoarsely. He had expected to have to plead his cause and was ready, but he was not encouraged by the fierce gleam of Mylan's gaze. It was a glance he'd learned to fear as a boy, and he'd not meant to provoke that response ever again.

"No." Mylan shook his head, his decision firm. "Busy yourself with refitting the Raven. If you still wish to ferry your farmers to Hrolf's land in the spring, then go. This voyage is mine alone to take."

Scowling fiercely, Hagen saw there was no point in wasting any more time in talking with his brother when he was in so obstinate a mood. Mylan had always been the leader, his commands obeyed, and he would not disregard this one now. "If you have not returned by the time I sail for France, I shall scout the entire country for you, and you better have a ready explanation for your failure to return!"

Mylan laughed at his brother's anger, but he knew what it was like to watch another sail and feel the pain of being left behind. That was a sorrow he had endured for two long years but could never bear again. "You will only have to visit Celiese, and I am certain she will be able to tell you what has become of me."

Hagen turned toward the young woman he'd wanted so badly and realized perhaps his cause was not thoroughly lost. "I will do that gladly. Where is your home so that I might find you, Celiese?"

Her golden tan paling noticeably, Celiese responded in a voice filled with unshed tears, her memories all unbearably sad. "My home is gone, destroyed, burned to the ground. There is nothing left for me except the land upon which it stood."

Startled by the tragic tone of her response, Mylan spoke in a sympathetic tone, "Yes, that might be true, but surely whatever home you now establish will be in the same location. Where might that be? I will need this information too so that I may see you there safely."

Celiese looked up at the two tall men. She knew them to be honest, but they were Vikings still, and she had no intention of leading them to her home. She was no traitor to her people and would not be used as such. "Mylan, if you take me as far as the mouth of the Seine I can find my own way home, and it would be far better for both of us if you did not try and find me next spring, Hagen."

Mylan took a deep breath. He'd not simply put Celiese ashore on French soil. He planned to see that she was left with a roof above her head and food for the winter, at the very least. "Is your home near the Seine, with a view of the sea, or was that just part of your story and not the truth?" Mylan had not forgotten what she'd told him on their wedding night and wondered if she remembered what she'd said.

Blushing, Celiese nodded shyly, for she recalled exactly when she'd told him that. "Yes, my home was bordered by both the Seine and the sea. That is the truth." As was everything else she'd ever told him, but she didn't add that spiteful comment, since it would only have served to anger him all the more.

Growing more curious, Mylan persisted, "On which side of the Seine, near Bayeux or Rouen?"

Appalled that he knew her homeland so well, Celiese could not decide which would be worse, to lie or to tell the truth. Mylan's glance was so insistent, however, that she dared not lie. "Rouen is nearest my home. If you were to ask for me there, Hagen, someone would be able to give you directions to the home of the d'Loganvilles."

"Rouen, is that not where—" Hagen's surprised question was interrupted by a hearty slap upon the back from Mylan, and he knew enough not to complete it.

Laughing, Mylan gave his brother a warm hug and bid him good-bye. "We cannot stand upon the dock discussing geography all day! Come, Celiese, we must be gone, and if Hagen cares to seek you out in Rouen next spring he may do so!" With a warning glance to his brother, Mylan led the slender beauty up the gangplank of the Surf Falcon and gave the order to cast off the lines that secured the graceful ship to the dock. It was all done so quickly that neither Celiese nor Hagen had the opportunity to say another word to each other.

"Are your parents not coming to bid you farewell, Mylan?" Celiese thought his sudden haste extraordinary and wondered as to the cause, but figured as usual his motives would be beyond comprehension.

Since his parents had no idea he was sailing, Mylan thought it unlikely they would appear. His father had forbidden the voyage, so he'd certainly not come to offer advice and encouragement. As for his mother, he was uncertain what to think of that good woman. If she had known Celiese was to be kidnapped and had not warned her then he'd not forgive her, either. No indeed, he had no desire to see either of his parents that morning and shook his head. "You heard my father last night, he wanted you gone but do you really think he would come to tell you good-bye?"

Celiese looked down, sorry now that she had asked about his family when their dislike of her had been so unhidden. Perhaps that dislike was what had prompted Mylan to hurry, but she thought it likely that had been to spare himself trouble rather than out of any regard for her feelings. Since it would be a long voyage, she did not want to be in the way. She had enjoyed standing at Andrick's side as he'd held the tiller, but she did not think Mylan would welcome such informality. "Where would you like me to stay?" she asked. "I do not want to interfere in any way with your work or that of your men."

Mylan laughed out loud at that sweet offer. "It will be the first time you haven't!" When he saw by her expression that she was not amused by that remark, he softened his tone, but only slightly. "I have told the men to drape a tent over the stern so you will have some shade in which to rest. Sleep as long as you like. I will try and command the Falcon as best I can without your advice."

Hurt by his scorn, Celiese turned away and walked toward the rear of the ship, stopping to wave at Hagen as she passed by. He looked no more pleased than Mylan, and she wondered how a voyage begun with such haste and bitterness could possibly end well. She was going home again, however, and that prospect would have to sustain her. She found that not only had a tent been raised, but fruit and bread had been left for her, as well as the softest of blankets. After eating a light breakfast, she was too tired to feel the hardness of the deck beneath her as she stretched out and, planning to rest only a moment, was soon sound asleep.

The wind was strong and Mylan made swift time, not once looking back toward his home but constantly glancing over his shoulder to be certain no ships came in pursuit. He'd taken the best of Hagen's crew, but knew if his father really wanted to he could find men among their houseguests to man a ship. That thought presented a painful possibility, for he did not want to fight any sort of battle against his own father, but the man had brought it upon himself by betraying Celiese so cruelly. As little as he relished the thought of facing his father, the Torgvalds presented a far more dangerous threat. They would need time to bury Oluf, but once he'd been laid to rest, what would their next thought be? Revenge, he knew without question, but would they attack his home or come after him when they found he had taken Celiese out of their reach? A warship could easily overtake a *knarr*, but he had the advantage still, for he'd had a vessel ready to make a long voyage, and as far as he knew the Torgvalds did not. By the time they assembled their supplies

325

and made ready to sail, he thought he would be so far ahead they could not overtake him. The days were still long and hot, autumn barely begun, but those cowards would think twice about sailing now, when winter might overtake them with unexpected swiftness. Plotting strategy as he held the ship to a steady course, Mylan went over each possibility, and how he might best counter an attack. His crew were not the experienced warriors Raktor could summon with a snap of his fingers, but mariners whose only talent lay in making long voyages with both skill and daring. If he so chose, Raktor could pursue him in a ship with fifty armed men, each a worse cutthroat than the next. It was not a pleasant prospect to consider, and since his only weapon was time, he prayed he would not lose that advantage.

So far north the autumn days are long, night fleeting, and Mylan did not look for shelter until visibility became so poor he was forced to do so. While he had sailed his own country's coast himself, he had memorized the rest of the route in the few minutes it had taken Hagen to explain it. He knew if he followed the coastline, France could be reached easily enough, and with a river so wide as the Seine for a landmark, they would have no trouble finding Celiese's home, or what was left of it. That it was near Rouen disturbed him as greatly as it had Hagen, though, for he knew Hrolf was living there, and the sur-rounding lands were now his.

After a long nap, Celiese had spent the afternoon standing at the rail, watching the coast of Denmark pass by. The country was a remarkably flat one, with only a few rolling hills, rather than the beautiful countryside backed by mountains shrouded by a lavender haze she had known at home. She watched Mylan as he spoke with his crew. He worked them all hard, but spent long hours himself at the tiller, which she knew had to be the most strenuous job, and she was tempted to go up to him and ask if he was not being foolish to waste what strength he had when the other men could have helped him keep the ship upon a true course. Since he had taunted her about giving him advice she kept still, but continued to worry about him all the same. They kept sailing long past the time she'd expected him to put in to shore for the night, and she was yawning sleepily by the time he did look for shelter.

Mylan was tired and dirty, and the last thing he wanted was Celiese's company, but he dared not assign one of the young men of his crew the duty of seeing to her needs. He'd noticed that the men's curious stares had constantly drifted in her direction, and he had no intention of allowing any of them to befriend her, or worse. That would be all he'd need, he thought bitterly, to have the members of his crew falling all over themselves to impress her! To make her situation clear, he would gather the men together after dinner and explain she was not on board to provide an amusement. She was a passenger and no more; that she was so pretty to look at was a distracting nuisance they'd just have to ignore. He would be blunt with them. If they could not stop regarding her as the lovely female creature she was, then he would simply have to make the fact she was his woman abundantly clear. He laughed to himself as he realized how simple a fact that would be to prove.

Hagen had given him charts as well as verbal directions and, while he didn't know how reliable those drawings would prove to be, he hoped the harbors listed as safe would still be tranquil. Often what one man discovered on a voyage did not hold true for the next to follow the same route. The land did not change, but the mood of the inhabitants frequently did, and he hoped to find deserted inlets in which to sleep each night and fresh water to replenish their supply. That the weather was fair was a good omen, for that made navigation a simple matter, but if the temperatures turned cool, or if there was a fog that made the sky and sea one immense gray sphere, their progress would be slow, and the Torgvalds' chances of overtaking them all the better.

Celiese sat on the edge of the circle of men gathered around the fire. They had eaten well and enjoyed the ale Mylan had provided in generous amounts, but she could tell from their frequent glances that her presence among them was causing undue stress. She had expected Mylan to speak with her at least, if not to spend all his time with her that evening, but he had taken a place on the far side of the circle and had not looked in her direction once. The men all had bags made of hides as he did, which they used to store their clothing in and to sleep upon at night, but while they appeared to be getting more comfortable as they lounged around the fire she felt increasingly out of place and wished there were some discreet way for her to ask Mylan where she was supposed to sleep. Finally, too tired to care about risking his disapproval, she rose to her feet, and carrying the blanket she'd found aboard the Surf Falcon went to look for a secluded spot to rest.

As soon as Mylan saw Celiese disappear into the shadows, he cleared his throat and spoke convincingly. "Our passenger is always to be treated with the same respect you have shown her today. You may answer her questions should she approach you directly, and being the inquisitive sort, she just may, but do not take it upon yourselves to keep her entertained. I will take care of that responsibility myself." With a sly grin he knew they would readily understand, he followed Celiese into the darkness, wondering why it had taken her so very long to seek some privacy in which to sleep when he could not have kept his eyes open much longer.

"Celiese?" He called to her softly, not wanting to frighten her unnecessarily.

Celiese turned quickly, afraid she had offended Mylan by leaving those at the fire. "I do not belong with your men, Mylan, they seem uncomfortable with me nearby. I hope you will not object to my sleeping here by myself."

"Oh, but I most definitely do." When he saw she did not understand he reached out to encircle her narrow waist and drew her into his arms. "I have no intention of allowing you to sleep alone, Celiese. I am positive I told you once you'd not escape me any time I wanted you. I probably said that more than once, didn't I?"

Surprised by his sudden interest after he'd ignored her all day, Celiese was quick to disagree. "I will never forget the beauty of last night, Mylan, but please, let us end what was between us, for to continue it will only make our inevitable parting that much more painful."

Mylan stood silent for a long moment, confused by her request when her nearness overwhelmed him as always

329

with an unquenchable desire. Filled with that intoxicating warmth, he lowered his mouth to hers, softly ending any hope she might have had of eluding him. She had always responded to tenderness, to a sweet caress or a gentle kiss, and he was pleased when she let the blanket slip from her fingers so she might wrap her arms around his neck. He deepened his kiss then, savoring the luscious curves of her body with no more than the slightest pressure from his fingertips, until he felt the need he'd created shudder through her slender body with a wave of cresting passion. He tried to undress her swiftly, but was so clumsy in the darkness that she pushed his hands away and slipped her gown off over her head without bothering to unfasten the brooches at her shoulders that had caused his predicament. Her pale skin glowed in the moonlight with an iridescent sheen, and he sank to his knees, covering the soft curve of her stomach with light kisses that made her giggle so she begged him to stop. When he would not, she sank down upon the blanket beside him, as lost as he was in the delicious enjoyment they always shared.

Her touch was far more demanding than his as she helped him out of his clothing. He had bathed and put on a fresh tunic but he now tossed it into the bushes with little regard for the garment when he had such a delightful purpose in mind. He wanted Celiese too desperately to play with her emotions now, and he gathered her into a confining embrace, pinning her body beneath his own as her passionate kiss demanded all he could give, her invitation irresistible, and not in the least bit subtle. It was then he paused, his voice hoarse even in his own ears, as he asked the question he'd not dared to ask the previous night. "When you want me as badly as I want you, why did you refuse to be my wife?"

Celiese could barely hear his question, let alone make a coherent response. The sounds of the night surrounded them with a rhythmic purr as steady as that of a complacent cat. She wanted the splendor of her loving to make such a ridiculous question unnecessary, and she wound her fingers in his curls, pulling his mouth down to hers so he could not speak in any language save that of love.

With a low moan of surrender, Mylan gave up all pretense of caring what Celiese's answer might be. He knew only that no matter what she thought, she was the only wife he would ever want or have. His mind was filled with her smiling image, her grace as she'd moved through the forest at his side, the sparkling light of the sun reflected upon her gently flowing silver hair. No adventure he'd ever had compared with the excitement she'd brought to his life, and he vowed to himself he would do all in his power to recapture the love she had once felt for him and he had so foolishly thrown away.

Exhausted by pleasure, Celiese lay dreaming in Mylan's arms, a blissful smile lighting her pretty features even in the darkness. The only true peace she had ever known she'd found in his embrace, and she loved him more dearly with each passing day. His intelligence and ready wit had always delighted her, but it was the beauty of his affection that captivated her anew. She knew he had asked an unanswerable question, but through the veil of her dreams she could not even recall what it had been.

At dawn Mylan dressed hastily, fearing one of his men might come looking for them, but when he walked back to the place where they'd built the fire and cooked their supper he found them all still asleep. Criticizing them sharply for such sloth, he woke them up. He then returned to the secluded spot he'd shared with Celiese and bent down to kiss her cheek sweetly. "Wake up, my pet. If the sun finds us here lazily enjoying our leisure, someone far less tolerant may discover us as well."

Holding the blanket modestly to her breast, Celiese greeted him warmly. "It is another fine day for sailing isn't it, Mylan? I will dress quickly so as not to delay our departure."

"First I want an answer to that question you would not answer last night. There is no reason for this voyage to continue if you will but agree to be my wife now."

Swallowing hard to force back the wave of dread that swept through her, Celiese shook her head. "What of Estrid, I thought perhaps you were again engaged to her? Was there time for you to tell her good-bye?"

Mylan was tempted to describe Estrid in such precise terms that Celiese would never again question his dislike for the haughty redhead. He had only used the woman as she'd used him, but he felt not the least bit of guilt now that they were even. "Estrid is not the issue here. You are. I want to hear your reasons for refusing me, if you have any."

Celiese had never felt so uncomfortable. Mylan was demanding the truth of something she thought too obvious to bear comment. "You do not love me, Mylan.

You did not want me when I was your bride, so do not tell me you want me now simply to save yourself the trouble of this voyage. I am sorry I asked you to take me home when Hagen was more than willing to do it."

His face filling with rage, Mylan got to his feet and backed away. "We will have to continue this discussion tonight, Celiese. Dress and join us for breakfast as soon as you can." With that terse command he was gone, disappearing from view as he made his way back to the beach, but Celiese sat staring after him, completely bewildered by his anger when she had done no more than repeat his own words to him.

As Mylan pushed the Surf Falcon to a speed his brothers would have envied, he wished the hours of the day would pass with the swiftness of the wind. Still keeping a watchful eye, he hoped the entire journey would go as well as the first day had. He had not forgotten, as he had feared he had, how to make a wooden craft follow his command, but the Falcon responded to almost as light a touch upon the tiller as his own Raven did, and he was pleased with her, after all. The sail was stretched taut, filled with wind, pushing them toward their destination, and he felt the same ageless thrill his ancestors had known when they'd first taken to the sea in search of adventure. This was an adventure, indeed, he reminded himself. Seeing Celiese again standing at the opposite rail, he wondered what could be the cause of her pensive expression. She had every reason to sing the entire way, but he could readily tell her mood did not lend itself to expression in song. More confident of his ship on this second day, Mylan called another man to take the tiller and then crossed the deck to her side.

"When we are making this voyage simply to please you, why do you appear so downcast?" He shouted in order to be heard above the noise of the brisk wind.

Turning to face him, Celiese was surprised to see his left eye looked no better that day. The deep purple bruise now had a decidedly greenish cast, making it look all the more painful. "I am sorry about your eye," she offered shyly.

"It is nothing compared to all the other bruises I have, but you did not answer my question. Do you intend to evade them all?" Mylan took ahold of the rail to brace himself. Every muscle in his body was painfully protesting the long hours of strenuous labor he'd done since the voyage began. He'd not thought himself so out of condition, nor would he admit such weakness to her. His deep tan and lean build gave the appearance of strength, and he had no intention of letting either her or his crew suspect the truth. He had already begun to rotate the duty at the tiller, since the men seemed to be a capable lot, but he planned to continue to do his fair share of the work no matter how much he suffered for it. The anguish Celiese continually caused him was an entirely different, but no less painful sort, and he waited impatiently for her to respond.

"No," Celiese admitted with a slight smile, realizing she'd given him no real reply.

Taking her hand firmly in his, Mylan led the impossibly perverse young woman back to the stern where they could sit beneath the tent and be sheltered from both the sun and wind while they talked. "It is important that I know the precise location of your home, Celiese, for I don't want to risk your life nor the lives of my crew by trespassing upon land belonging to others. I am a trader, but there was no time to gather goods to trade at the end of this voyage, so any of your countrymen we chance to meet will think us raiders and put up a fierce resistance even though we make no threatening advance."

Celiese sat down beside him, understanding his concern was justified but not wanting to be the cause of it. "I told you all I know, Mylan. Our home was visible from both the sea and the river Seine. I was a child, however, not an adult skilled in drawing maps, so I can tell you no more than I have."

"You mentioned the city of Rouen, though; was it close by?" Mylan pressed her to continue, for each piece of information she still remembered would be useful.

Celiese shook her head. "No, I went there so seldom I do not know the exact distance. It was perhaps half a day's ride on horseback, maybe a little more."

Mylan took a deep breath, weighing the benefits of explaining his worry, and, deciding she had a right to know what to expect when she reached home, spoke deliberately. "Hrolf is in Rouen. If he was given a sizable amount of land, his holdings may include what was once the estate of the d'Loganvilles."

Appalled by that conjecture, Celiese hastened to argue. "That can't be true, Mylan, it simply can't. Perhaps as you and Hagen insist, the man was given some property by King Charles, but I refuse to believe it is so extensive as you say, or that he could possibly be occupying what rightfully belongs to me!"

The fury that filled her deep green glance was not one he'd care to see directed at him, and Mylan offered the only encouragement he could. "Cease to worry then, for nothing can be known for certain until we arrive, and you must not torture yourself with doubt."

"Doubt?" Celiese scoffed. "The man has no right to my land, Mylan, and if he should be so stupid as to think he does, he will soon learn I mean to avenge all the wrongs done to the d'Loganvilles and I will be happy to begin with him!"

Mylan sat back, stunned by the depth of her anger. She had already risked death once in a desperate bid to win her freedom, and he knew without asking she'd do it again to restore to her family what was rightfully theirs. "I think you have answered my question after all, Celiese. It seems revenge is a far more powerful emotion in your heart than love. I cannot expect you to choose to stay with me when clearly that would mean you'd have to give up your lust for blood—which seems to be your destiny."

Furious that he would taunt her so cruelly, Celiese wound her arms around his neck and sought his mouth with a kiss so desperate in its intensity that he was shocked by her passion. Her hands moved over him with so tantalizing a touch that he gave no thought to resisting the force of her affection and enfolded her in a ready embrace, forcing her down upon the blanket he'd provided for that exact purpose. The gentle loving they often shared was replaced by an urgency too great to delay with soft kisses or the sweetness of a tender caress. They were lovers consumed in the fires of desire, all restraint burned away in an instant as they sought the immediate satisfaction of the most glorious of shared pleasures. That the tent provided less than complete privacy did not disturb Mylan in the slightest, for Celiese had told him herself she had no reputation left to maintain, and he knew his own would scarcely suffer for what he was doing. But he would not have cared one bit if it had.

Chapter Nineteen

The autumn weather continued to be fair, the skies blue and cloudless, the Surf Falcon's progress swift. While Mylan had taken care to insure there would be no repetition of the erotic scene they'd played on deck that one afternoon, Celiese seemed completely unconcerned by it. He realized with chagrin that he was no closer to understanding the complexities of her nature than he had been the morning they'd set sail for France. They had established an agreeable routine, that he had to admit. She kept to herself during the day, but sat beside him while they ate supper, and when he walked her to a secluded spot for the night she came into his arms with a playful eagerness he found enchanting. That did not mean their problems had been solved, however; if anything they had been compounded as the journey drew to its end. He wanted to keep Celiese as his wife. That desire had grown within him until he could accept no other possibility, but she seemed so totally absorbed in her dreams of returning home that she had no interest in discussing what future they might share as man and wife. He had no doubt he could force his parents to accept her, and as they wouldn't reside in his father's house he would not have to worry about her safety whenever they were apart. But while he could deal with his parents, it was Celiese he had failed to convince. Andrick's words rang often in his mind, for he knew he had never courted the lovely young woman with the charm and courtesy to which she was entitled. She had simply become his bride, then his enemy, all in the space of one night. Fate had continually separated then reunited them, but their lives were now so entwined he had lost all thought of her as a separate being independent from himself. Celiese was simply his; whether he called her wife or mistress did not matter when she was too great a part of his life ever to let go. That she did not realize that fact for the truth it was caused him far more anxiety than the complexities of the voyage had ever presented.

"We have come a great distance, Mylan. I have not counted the days, have you?" Celiese stretched out their blanket upon the soft moss that covered the forest floor. They'd seen several small settlements along the shores in recent days, but they had skirted them all, searching out the most desolate stretch of coast each night to make their camp. At sunrise they would be gone, leaving no trace of evidence they had ever tarried there. If they were being followed, they left no trail of clues by which they could be found.

Tugging his tunic off over his head, Mylan teased her sweetly. "I have counted only the nights." In truth he knew exactly how far they'd come and how many hours it had taken them. A skilled captain, he remembered each nuance of a journey, the force of the wind, the contours of the shore, landmarks that would guide him should he travel that way again. He missed nothing, and thought it unlikely she had either, for she seemed to be observing all with the same intensity she gave to everything she attempted to master.

Turning to cast a seductive glance over her right shoulder, Celiese responded skeptically. "You are too precise in your calculations for me to believe that, Mylan. Are we not nearly there?"

Mylan placed his hands on his hips, bracing himself for an argument he hoped wouldn't come. "Do you find my company so objectionable you cannot wait for our journey to end?"

Saddened that he still did not appreciate the depth of her regard for him, Celiese stepped close. "You are the best of all possible companions, Mylan, as dear to me as anyone will ever be."

Mylan racked his brain for a suitably complimentary response but could think of none, so he changed the subject with the first thought that entered his mind. "I wonder if Andrick has gotten over his fascination with Olgrethe."

Startled that he would think of his brother at such a time, Celiese did not realize how much Mylan had revealed about his own emotions with that question. "I certainly hope he never does!" she replied with a lilting laugh. "He loves her; with all her faults I believe he truly loves her, and I know she adores him." That Mylan would soon be an uncle was not a secret she thought she should reveal, however, so she kept silent about that bit of news.

"What faults does Olgrethe have that my brother seems to find so easy to overlook?" Mylan sat down upon the blanket and patted the place beside him to invite her company.

Not ready to join him, Celiese slowly began to disrobe, hanging the layers of her clothing upon the nearby bushes until only her light shift remained. "I did not mean to be critical of her, but she has always been pampered and that is what she expects."

"Is a man not supposed to pamper his bride, whether she deserves it or not?" Mylan asked, his confusion plain in his puzzled expression.

Kneeling down to face him, Celiese reached out to touch the curls at his temple. The sun had bleached his golden hair with streaks of silver, while his beard was still a dark golden shade. He was so very tan and handsome, his light eyes shining with an inquisitive gleam, and for a moment she could not recall what it was they were discussing. "I think love should be shared equally, Mylan, each spouse wanting only what is best for the other."

As she waited patiently for his response, Mylan knew if he said he loved her now she would never believe him but think only that he had saved that weapon for the last in hopes of taking her back home with him. A painful knot filled his throat and he knew he would be unable to speak any words and retain what slight hold he still had upon his sanity where she was concerned.

Mylan's emotional turmoil was so plain upon his even features that Celiese did not insult him with questions about his mood. As always, he seemed to find the mere mention of the word love revolting in the extreme, and she had not meant to cause him such sorrow. She placed her hands upon his broad shoulders and leaned forward to kiss the pulse that throbbed steadily in his tan throat, her love unspoken but lavish in its expression.

Knowing she would stop at nothing less than the most passionate response from him, Mylan lay back upon the blanket, drawing Celiese down into his arms where he held her in a tender embrace. Surely words were unnecessary between them when they had shared so much in the few months since they'd met. With her he had known the joy of acceptance, which he had no longer thought possible, the bitter anguish of betrayal, the warmth of a friendship as deep as any he had ever known, and now this quiet pleasure he could not begin to describe adequately. From the depth of his soul he knew he loved Celiese and, praying it was not too late, he moved to prove with his strong, sleek body what he had never been able to speak in words.

Celiese welcomed him with a provocative purr, accepting his forceful affection with a grace all her own. She felt the exquisite joy swell within him until it flooded through her as well, a bliss so delicious that her dreams were always sweet, filled with the memory of his rakish smile and magical caress. No matter what fate awaited her in her homeland, she knew Mylan's image would fill her heart until the last of her days and prayed her face would light his dreams for half as long.

The next morning Mylan summoned Celiese to his side as soon as he had guided their ship through the surf to the open sea. "Stay with me today. We are close, and I will keep the Falcon near to shore. You may recognize something that I would not."

Taking hold of the rail so she could stand slightly in front of him, Celiese gave the coastline a long, careful glance. "I was never out in a boat, Mylan, not until Raktor tossed me in the bottom of his to begin the long voyage to your country. I know the other view, from the land to the sea, not this one."

Suddenly realizing Raktor could come for Celiese whenever he chose, Mylan's expression grew stern. Perhaps that fiend would wait for the summer, or the next, but he could come for Celiese and she'd have no way to defend herself if he were not there. "All I ask is that you try. We'll surely see the river when we come upon it, but perhaps there will be something more."

"I understand. I will try to help." Celiese turned to smile warmly, but Mylan's gaze was locked upon the shore, searching for something she could only imagine. She watched the coastline with strict concentration, and it was early afternoon when she saw a cliff that seemed strangely familiar. There was a path visible through the rocks and a stretch of white sand where an old man sat fishing. Seeing the Surf Falcon, he threw down his pole and ran as though the devil himself were pursuing him. He scampered up the cliff with the agility of a mountain goat and was gone, the entire incident lasting no more than a few seconds. But Celiese was certain she had recognized the place, although she could not name it.

"Mylan!" She turned to touch his arm, excitement lighting her eyes with a bright sparkle. "I know that place, Mylan, I'm certain I do! My mother liked to walk down to the sand when the day was warm, and I'm positive it was in that very spot."

Not discounting her enthusiasm, Mylan knew they were within a day's sail from the Seine. If they were that close to her home, then perhaps she did recognize the area as she said she did. It would do no harm to stop for a moment, but he wished they had not been seen, for surely the old man would give a cry of alarm, and whatever men there were to defend this small piece of land would come running. "I will not take the ship all the way in to the sand. Let us just go in part way, so you can have a closer look."

"You don't believe me?" Celiese asked sharply. "Why did you ask me to watch for landmarks if you are going to disregard my reports?"

Mylan gave the necessary orders to bring the ship about, shoving the tiller hard to starboard to turn toward the shore. "It is not your memory I am questioning, Celiese, but the mood of the crowd that old man may have summoned. You know yourself you would launch every arrow you owned before you'd ask questions as to why we've come."

"I am not afraid to go ashore alone, Mylan. That way I can look around and allay whatever fears the residents might have. They would not attack a lone woman, not when I can greet them in a language they will understand."

Mylan shook his head slowly. "Never. Now take another look, does the place still look like the one you remember?"

Exasperated with his domineering manner, Celiese

turned away. The afternoon sun struck the cliff with a golden glow, making the scene all the more appealing, but she was more convinced than ever that her home lay just over the rise. "Yes. The pattern of the rocks is what I recall. Our land reached to the sea, and this is the very spot. I'm sure of it."

By the time André arrived at the small village he was gasping for breath, his description of what he'd seen nearly incoherent, but he had to do no more than wheeze the word "Viking" for his frantic message to be understood. Women went screaming to hide their children in the woods while the young men, armed with no more than pitchforks and knives, ran toward the beach, hoping to stop the murdering northern bandits before they could reach their homes. André loped along behind them. No coward in his youth, he planned to be in on whatever action there might be. When the small group reached the cliff they stood at the edge looking down on the tranquil scene below while they tried to plan how to mount an attack. The Viking ship André had seen lay at anchor offshore, while a tall, fair-haired man and a slender blond woman walked across the sand. Their clothes were wet from the short distance they'd walked through the surf, but to the Frenchmen's delight they saw the man was unarmed. He wore no helmet nor suit of mail, carried no sword or shield, but instead offered his arm to the woman to lead her across the beach. Puzzled, they waited for André to reach them, then stood aside to provide him with the best view, hoping he might have some explanation for the unusual landing party.

Still breathing heavily from the pain of his exertion, André watched closely as the young couple moved toward the path at the bottom of the cliff. The man was well built but had an uneven gait, a slight limp that was no doubt the result of some brutal raid, but the beauty by his side seemed to float across the sand, her grace and bearing so regal that André was reminded at once of the noble family he'd spent most of his life serving. He knew it was not possible, but as the young woman drew near tears filled his eyes, and when she reached the summit of the hill he threw himself at her feet, kissing the damp and sandy hem of her gown as he whispered her name. His companions heard no more than the name d'Loganville, and they moved back to a more respectful distance in order to observe what might transpire between André and the young woman whose fair beauty seemed to glow with a light from within, as they had been told the angels did. Indeed, in her flowing gown she was the closest being to an angel any of the men had ever seen, and their awe was as great as the old fisherman's.

While Mylan gaped in astonishment, Celiese bent slightly to pull André to his feet and began speaking in a tongue he did not understand. "André, is that you? My dear friend, I had not expected to see any face I'd recognize, but such devotion is unnecessary." The French words rolled off her tongue with a lilting accent, the result of her years in Denmark, but that her speech was somewhat unusual did not occur to her. She kissed the old man's weathered cheek sweetly before turning to look up at Mylan. "He was a groom in my father's stable, a dear friend I had not dared hope would still be alive."

Backing away, André continued to regard Mylan with a terror-filled gaze, then said, "That you have returned when we need the d'Loganvilles most is a great blessing, but who is this barbarian at your side?"

Knowing Mylan could not follow their conversation, Celiese spoke to him first, carefully choosing her words so he would not be insulted. "He is happy to see me, as there seems to be some trouble, but he is puzzled as to who you might be."

Mylan gave the most charming smile he could manage, hoping to put the assembled group at ease since Celiese seemed to have found a countryman who knew her. "Say I am your husband, for they seem to admire you greatly, and to describe our relationship as anything less than a lawful one would destroy that esteem."

Celiese gave the Viking a withering glance, but knew he was right. She was now home, where she had little other than her good name, and she had no desire to sully it. Lacing her fingers in his, she introduced him to her old friend. "May I present my husband, Mylan Vandahl. He rescued me from the villains who destroyed my home, and wanting only to please me has brought me back to France. You are in no danger from him, for he is a good man, unlike the other Danes you have known."

Mylan thought Celiese's native tongue very pretty to the ear, but did not trust her to say what he'd asked until he saw by the men's curious appraisal that she must indeed have introduced him as her husband. That they had planned to attack him with pitchforks brought a smile to his lips, but he had to admire their courage.

Small in stature, with dark hair and brown eyes, they were exactly the type of men he'd expected to see in France, but that still didn't explain why Celiese was so different in appearance from them.

Turning to lead the way, André spoke excitedly. "You must come with us, for there is much to discuss. I have a little wine, not much, perhaps you would honor me by coming to my home."

"Will that be all right, Mylan? André has invited us to his home, and I would like to go," Celiese translated quickly.

After waving to the men on board the Falcon, Mylan took Celiese's hand. "Yes, but please tell him again that I am your husband, for I do not want to walk unarmed into a trap."

Shocked that he would accuse André and his friends of such treachery, Celiese whispered softly. "My countrymen are nothing like yours! These are peaceful men who will do you no harm, so you have no need to worry." Then, just in case his suspicion should prove true, Celiese reached up to kiss him lightly. Turning to André, she praised her "husband's" virtues for the entire walk into the village.

The homes of the farmers were litle more than crude huts. Deserted now, they lined the muddy path with a sorrowful, vacant silence. "Where is everyone, André?" Celiese looked around, wondering where the women and children might be at that hour of the day, since she'd seen no one working in the adjacent fields.

"Forgive me, but I did not know it would be you aboard the Viking ship, and all our loved ones are hidden." With an embarrassed gesture, he showed them to the small house he called his own.

"How clever of you, André. Have there been many attacks?" Celiese stopped to warn Mylan to be careful, but he had had years of practice in entering homes through doors not made to accommodate men of his size and had already slipped through without mishap. There was a small table, two rickety benches, and a bed alongside the wall. The fire on the hearth was cold, but the smell of fish still pervaded the one-room structure, and Celiese thought André must catch most of his food and hoped he did not often have to go without, but the village did look like a very poor one. She took a place upon one of the benches, and Mylan sat down beside her ready to leap up should his weight prove to be too great, but the old wood held together with only a slight moan.

André produced a flask of the promised wine and three wooden cups. Taking a place opposite his guests, he poured them a small sip of the beverage and apologized for having no more. "It was a great tragedy we lost the vines, but they are all gone, burned beyond recovery, and no one has been able to travel inland in search of cuttings we might cultivate to begin our vineyards anew."

Mylan thought the tragedy a slight one after he tasted the deep red wine, for it had a most unpleasant aroma and taste, but he saw Celiese smile sweetly as though it were delicious and attempted to do the same. As always, she seemed to have the finest of manners. He could well imagine Olgrethe refusing to enter such a humble abode let alone sample the wine, but Celiese appeared quite at home, the most gracious of guests no matter what her surroundings.

"I have lost count of how many times our land was ravaged, our possessions stolen, our women raped, our sons murdered. Now King Charles has handed over to that rascal Hrolf what little we have left. It seems we cannot escape the greed of the Danes, except in death." Glancing toward Mylan to be certain his words were not understood, André continued. "There are many who would fight the king's decree, many who recall the proud name of d'Loganville and would rally to your side should you wish to lead them."

Taking a deep breath, Celiese asked pointedly, "How much belongs to Hrolf now, exactly how much does the man have the audacity to call his own?"

"All of Neustria, dear lady. The lands on both sides of the Seine are his."

Worried by the frantic troubled glances passing between his companions Mylan interrupted. "What are you two discussing so earnestly that you have no time to describe it to me?"

Celiese brushed away the tears that filled her eyes and spoke proudly. "It seems the king is the coward you thought he was, for he has given Hrolf the entire province, not only my estate but dozens of others, as well. André thinks many would fight, however, were there someone to lead them."

Knowing only too well who that someone would have to be, Mylan shook his head as he issued a stern warning. "Raktor is a playful child compared to Hrolf, Celiese. Do not encourage this man in his belief the thief can be defeated by peasants wielding pitchforks!"

Celiese had seen as much as Mylan. This village was not simply poor, but destitute, and despite her own rage she would not risk the lives of the few surviving inhabitants on a quest to regain what was hers. She would have to reclaim it by means other than a fight, but what that could be she did not yet know. Finding the close confines of the small home suffocating, Celiese thanked their host warmly for his wine and asked to be excused, explaining, "I would like to see what is left of the house. There is still light, and the way cannot be far."

"I will come with you." André rose to his feet, pausing to shut the door as they left his home, more to keep out the chill should he not return before nightfall than to protect any valuable possessions.

As they left the house they were surrounded by a strangely silent crowd, the women holding their small children aloft so they might see the pretty lady who had arrived from the sea. Celiese smiled and waved, but she had never expected to be greeted with such awe and was terribly embarrassed. Mylan, on the other hand, was simply worried. He knew how little it would take to set Celiese on a trail of revenge that would lead all too swiftly to her own death, and he took her hand to draw her near as he whispered, "It is always far wiser to listen than to speak, Celiese. Do not make any promises to these people you cannot keep."

"I want only to see what is left of my house. It was all in flames when I was carried away, and I am curious, that is all. Besides, what can I promise these people that would have any value?"

"Sometimes a name is all that is required to start a war,

and I do not want it to be d'Loganville, dear wife." Clasping her hand all the more tightly, Mylan walked with care down the edge of the muddy road. The peasants were still following along, and that he had not thought to bring someone to guard his back pained him greatly, for he did not want to meet his death on French soil, either.

The walk was farther than Celiese had remembered it, but at last they reached the top of the gently sloping hill where her family home had stood. Little remained of the once elegant structure. The stone walls had not been completely destroyed by the fire that had swept through it, but many of the carefully gathered stones had been carried off by the peasants who had used them to rebuild their own homes. Celiese did not think such vandalism a crime, for the stones would probably have lain upon the ground for decades had they not been put to a more useful purpose. She was glad to see the house had been serving someone, at least, since she'd had no use for it.

Mylan surveyed the ruins of the house, roughly gauging the proportions from the walls that remained standing. "It is clear you cannot live here until some reconstruction has been done, but what Hrolf will have to say to that prospect I don't care to speculate."

"You think I should ask the man for permission to rebuild my own home?" Celiese asked indignantly. "I plan to speak to him, all right, but I'll not beg for what is rightfully mine, including the right to construct a home upon my own land!"

Smiling at the assembled crowd, who still regarded them with rapt interest, Mylan whispered a stern warning. "Do not involve these wretched souls in your battles, Celiese. If you care so little for your own life, then think of these people and how diligently they have obviously struggled simply to survive."

"As if my survival were a small matter?" Celiese responded defiantly, taking only a moment to enumerate a few of the wrongs she'd suffered. "My parents were slaughtered, my home destroyed, my lands stolen, I was raped and kidnapped, and you think I should calmly walk away?"

"Yes!" Mylan responded, trying to keep his voice low so it would not be obvious they were arguing, but he could tell André was greatly amused by their animated conversation. "Let us go back to the Falcon, and decide what we want to do from there."

"Couldn't we sleep here tonight, Mylan? What is left of my house provides more in the way of shelter than we've ever had on this journey. Couldn't we please stay here?"

Mylan was certain the screams of ghosts would keep him awake all night, but if so small a concession would please her he'd agree. "If that is what you want. The ground is dry, the nights still warm."

"Thank you." Celiese hugged him tightly, her display of affection for the Viking startling the crowd, but she had no reason to hide the love she felt for a man she'd introduced as her husband. What she'd tell everyone when he returned to his homeland without her she didn't know, however. Turning to André she explained in a few simple sentences, "We will rest here for the night, for my memories of my parents are so dear here, far outweighing the nightmare of their murders."

Raising his hands to the heavens, André exclaimed excitedly, "But you do not know! I buried your father's body myself, but your mother is alive, living in the convent at Yvetot! Forgive me for not telling you that immediately, but I am an old man and sometimes forgetful."

Mylan saw Celiese grow pale and stepped forward to catch her before she fainted in a heap upon the ground. "Celiese, what has happened, tell me!"

Celiese looked up into Mylan's eyes. The golden flecks seemed to be spinning among the brown, and she wondered how he managed to do that, but his rapt gaze was so intense she came to her senses swiftly and struggled to stand without his help. "I am sorry, Mylan, but André has just given me a great shock. My mother is alive, it seems, and living in a convent nearby."

Not recognizing the word, Mylan asked her to explain. "What is a convent?"

"You have heard of monasteries, have you not? They were a favorite target for Viking raids, for the monks had the most marvelous of treasures."

Exasperated by that bit of unwanted news, Mylan urged her to continue. "Yes, I know what a monastery is, a place where men live to study your god."

"A convent is a similar place, only it is women who live there, they devote themselves to prayer and the religious life, as monks do." Seeing he understood, she continued excitedly, "My mother is alive, Mylan, she's alive! I want to visit her tomorrow, as it is too late to go today. Will you come with me?"

Mylan looked around at the curious faces of the

peasants and nodded. "Yes, but we will need more than we have with us now. Let us go back to the ship for the night. I am afraid if we stay here these good people will only offer to share food they cannot spare."

Pleased that he would be so considerate, Celiese laced her fingers in his before turning to André to explain. "We are going back to our ship, but at first light I will come for you if you will show us the way to Yvetot."

"With pleasure. I will find a horse for you to ride, but I fear your husband, like Hrolf, is too tall to ride one of our ponies."

"A small problem, André, if there is no horse for him then I will walk too, for I want to hold his hand in mine." Smiling happily, Celiese nearly skipped alongside Mylan as they went back down the path from the ruins of her home, for her joy at finding her mother alive was too great for her to contain.

Being adventuresome by nature but cautious from experience, Mylan insisted all remain on board the Surf Falcon that night. He'd seen no boats and doubted enough of the Frenchmen could swim to mount an attack through the waves, but he posted a guard to keep watch, nonetheless. As for Celiese, she was still so thrilled by the discovery of her mother's survival she could scarcely sit still, and he knew better than to ask her to try and sleep when she was in so talkative a mood. Instead he sat up with her, listening attentively to all her fond memories.

"Don't you see, Mylan, she was the best of mothers, but I was only twelve when I was kidnapped, I'd no opportunity to ask her the most important questions of all. I had no knowledge of life's secrets, and suddenly I was thrust out into the world to fend for myself and I had nothing to sustain me. I had absolutely no hope I would survive one day to the next, no hope any of those I loved were living still, no hope I would set foot in my beloved homeland ever again."

"Yet you are the most charming and confident of young women, Celiese, so if you had no more than the determination that makes up such a large portion of your nature it must have been enough," Mylan replied with a rakish grin.

Celiese studied Mylan's teasing glance for a long while. It was an expression she knew well but had never enjoyed. "Do you think I am being foolish, Mylan, to remember my home and childhood so fondly?"

"No, every child should be so happy as you obviously were." Mylan had tried his best not to yawn, but he could not hide his next one, although he raised his hand quickly to cover his mouth. His stamina had increased measurably during the voyage, but still had its limit.

"I'm sorry, I'll be quiet so you can rest." Celiese put out the small oil lamp and moved to his side to snuggle close, but she was too restless to sleep and lay wide awake trying to imagine her mother's excitement when they met the next day. Despite her promise to be still, she continued to talk. "My mother is a very beautiful woman, Mylan. I know they will not allow you to enter the convent grounds, but perhaps she can come to the gate to meet you."

Surprised by her enthusiasm for that event, Mylan pulled her close, tousling her soft curls playfully. "You saw André's expression and the townspeople's when they saw me. I was amazed they summoned their women so swiftly. Do you want to subject your mother to that same fright?"

Celiese sat up, not pleased by his question, for who he was was ever so much more important to her than what he was. "I am not ashamed of you. Not in the least. I would be proud to introduce you to my mother—why shouldn't I be?"

"I am flattered, of course, but do you plan to tell her the truth? That I am your husband?"

Celiese hardly knew how to respond. In the darkness she could not see his expression, but she was positive he was simply teasing her again and she did not appreciate his humor in the least. "When I really was your bride, the last thing you wanted was for me to call you husband. You were ashamed of me then, don't bother to deny it!" Had they been on shore she would have grabbed the blanket and run off to find a place to sleep by herself, but now she had no choice but to stay under the makeshift tent with him, since she had no desire to cuddle up with his crew or to leap over the side into the sea.

Mylan hadn't meant to begin an argument, but since she had he decided to finish it. "I was never ashamed of you! That's ridiculous. I was furious with you for pretending to be Olgrethe, but I was never ashamed!"

Suddenly Celiese knew better and kept silent. Too angry to cry or scream, she clamped her mouth shut and moved to the edge of the blanket, her posture as rigid and unyielding as her anger. She had finally discovered the truth. Raktor himself had told her she was no fit bride for any Viking. Why had she never realized before that was why Mylan would never love her? By pretending to be Olgrethe, she had pretended to be the innocent young woman she most certainly was not, and that was what he had never forgiven, nor would he.

Swearing to himself, Mylan tried to pull the defiant Celiese back into his arms, but he failed. She had been ecstatically happy, happier than he had ever seen her, and somehow he had ruined everything without meaning to. He tried to apologize, "Celiese, I am as happy as you are to learn your mother is alive, and I will be proud to meet her no matter how you wish to introduce me." Since he would be unable to understand what she said to her mother, he knew he could scarcely specify what words she was to use.

Her nervous energy finally exhausted, Celiese answered calmly, "I know why you did not want me for a wife, Mylan. Raktor told me what your reason would be before I ever left his house."

His temper flaring anew, Mylan responded heatedly, "I would prefer you did not mention that villain's name in the same breath as mine. I cannot even imagine that man's having the brains to attempt to analyze my thinking. Whatever he told you was a damn lie, so put it out of your mind and don't think of it ever again, as it is undoubtedly unworthy of contemplation!"

What he asked was impossible, and Celiese explained why. "Were it not for that evil man we would never have met, for I would not have set foot in your country nor you in mine. My life seems to be becoming increasingly complicated, like some ancient riddle that can never be solved, but I have learned that once a woman is taken, by one man or many, she is never again thought worthy of love."

Mylan took a deep breath. He'd have much preferred to scream every vile curse he knew, but, knowing that would relieve only his own tensions without soothing hers, he restrained himself with a mighty effort to be civil. "I am a great fool, I know that. I should have killed every last one of the Torgvalds when I had the chance; then maybe you would finally be content!"

Celiese did not move. She lay upon her side as tears began to roll slowly down her cheeks, dampening the soft woolen blanket where she lay. It was not the Torgvalds who mattered, but only Mylan. Why was he talking about vengeance and death when she'd just asked for his love?

Exasperated beyond all endurance, Mylan knew he would never be able to sleep when Celiese was so miserable. His words seemed futile, and he could think of nothing else to do but try again to slip his arm under her neck so she would have to rest her head upon his shoulder. When this time she made no objection to that move he drew her closer still, covering her damp cheeks with light kisses. He then wiped away her tears with his fingertips, knowing somehow he had caused them. He held her cradled in his arms and in no more than a minute she was sound asleep, nestled in his embrace as if they'd made love. Yet somehow he knew it was important to her that they hadn't.

When Mylan awoke, Celiese was already awake and dressed. Her gown was freshly washed, the pleats of the bodice falling in an elegant sweep, but she looked exactly like a Viking woman, and he wondered what her mother would think when she saw her. Knowing such a question would not be appreciated, he hastened to get ready to leave, choosing his most handsomely tailored clothing, as well. They were sure to make a lasting impression upon Lady d'Loganville, but he was afraid to imagine just what kind.

Celiese had not recovered from her bout of tears the previous night. She felt sad through and through, but when André produced not one horse but three, her spirits rose considerably. The mounts were not young, but sturdy of build, and the stallion was large enough to carry Mylan with ease. "Why André," she asked, "have you a stable hidden nearby? These horses seem well fed and they are most handsomely groomed, are they yours?"

After stammering a moment, André confided his secret. "They are the last of your father's, my lady, the few I managed to hide the night the others were stolen. That they have survived so long is due more to their own perverse nature, which leads them to frequently run off into the forest, than it is to my care."

When Celiese explained his words, Mylan knew exactly what the elderly man meant, for if the lovely young woman thrived on anything, surely it was perversity, but he was not so foolish as to speak what was on his mind. He was grateful to have a mount, even a half wild one, and after a few tense moments he had the beast under sufficient control to begin the journey to Yvetot.

The Convent of Saint Valery at Yvetot was surrounded by thick underbrush. Set amidst a dense forest, it had escaped the notice of more than one raiding band of

Vikings because of its remote location. That threat never forgotten, however, the treasures it contained were all well hidden beneath the floor of the deepest cellar. The surrounding stone walls were high, the few windows narrow, a forbidding place even on a sun-drenched day. Celiese drew her horse to a halt so she might view it for a few moments before knocking at the small wooden door that faced the seldom-traveled path. She had only a child's concept of a loving God, and she could scarcely imagine that magnificent being wanting to bless such a dismal place. That the vibrant woman her mother had been would seek refuge there puzzled her immensely. She looked toward Mylan as she wondered aloud, "It does not look as though they expect many visitors here. Had André not led us to the door I would never have found it."

"Surely the interior is far more pleasant," Mylan offered in hopes of giving encouragement. He had no real hope, however, that beyond the small weathered door there existed a dwelling more attractive than the gloomy one it appeared to be. He did not like the austere looks of the institution no matter how lofty its purpose, but he dismounted without further comment and led the stallion he'd ridden to the edge of the overgrown path where the animal could graze while they waited. "You might as well knock upon the door, I don't think anyone will come out to invite you to go inside unless you do."

"Probably not." Celiese was still anxious to see her mother, but now the moment had arrived she was overcome with nervousness. She had expected to find a tranquil estate surrounded by lush gardens, not so cold a place as this, and she shivered despite the pleasant warmth of the sun. When André took her mount's reins, she gathered her courage and went to the small door. Finding a brass bell, she pulled the cord and hoped someone would be near enough to hear her summons, but it was a long while before a tiny window in the door swung open. Although she could not see anyone on the other side, Celiese spoke a friendly greeting. "Good day, I am Lady Celiese d'Loganville. I believe my mother, Marie, is a member of your order, and I should like to speak with her, if I may."

Two bright eyes came closer to the opening and observed a young woman whose likeness to Marie was so extraordinary that she did not question the veracity of the caller. "Are you alone?" the nun whispered cautiously.

Waving to warn the two men to stand out of sight, Celiese replied that she was, but the door swung open only widely enough to admit her.

When the wooden door slammed shut the ominous ring of the old hinges made Mylan step forward, for Celiese had disappeared so suddenly inside the imposing structure that he'd had no time to ask her how long she wished to remain, and now he feared she might never reappear. Seeing his pained expression, André stepped forward and tried to offer some philosophical words of encouragement, but he understood little other than the old gentleman's sympathetic tone. Deciding the wait would most likely be a considerable one, he walked to a nearby tree and sat down, leaning back to rest while he passed the time. But he vowed that if Celiese had not come out by sundown, he would go in after her.

Marie was working upon a small tapestry, the silken threads depicting scenes from the life of the Virgin, when she was told she had a visitor. The messenger had no wish to alarm her unnecessarily, and bid her only to come speak with a young woman who had asked for her by name. It had been so long since she'd been addressed as Lady d'Loganville that she was intrigued, and leaving her loom quickly went to see who had come to call. Visitors there were infrequent. As she entered the small parlor she recognized her daughter instantly and rushed to embrace her tightly, crying, "Celiese, my dearest, I have prayed for your soul all these many years, but I never dared hope you were still alive!"

"Nor did I dream you were either, Mama." Celiese stepped back, overjoyed at their reunion. Her mother had aged, but only slightly. The dark gray robe of her order covered her from head to toe, but she was obviously still as trim as a young girl and nearly as pretty. Her clear skin was unlined, her bright green eyes filled with happiness, and Celiese gave her another warm hug before leading her over to the small bench across from the hearth. Although the day was a warm one, the sunlight did not reach all the convent's many small chambers, and a fire had been lit to insure their visitor's comfort.

"How were you able to find me?" Marie had not dreamed there would be anyone to search, and was afraid it might have taken Celiese a long while to locate her.

"Do you remember André? He was a groom in our stables and now lives in the village nearest the sea. He knew where you were living."

A curious blank stare came into Marie's eyes as she tried to remember the man. "So few of us survived, Celiese, but I think I do recall André. He is an old man now, isn't he?"

"Yes, that is he." Sorry she had prompted what she knew were the most horrible of memories, Celiese tried to continue her tale. "He is a very agreeable fellow and was kind enough to bring Mylan and me here today."

"Who is Mylan?" Marie inquired softly. "Was that someone else who worked for us? There were so many, I've forgotten most of their names, but I pray for them still." She tried to remember, but through the mist of the years she could recall no one by that unusual name.

She had not meant to confuse her mother, but Celiese knew there was no simple way to explain who Mylan was, and what he meant to her. Sparing her the lurid details of the summer she'd spent with the Torgvalds, she emphasized instead the most pleasant aspects of the years she'd lived as a companion to Olgrethe. She told the truth about her marriage, though, and the numerous problems she and Mylan had encountered since then. It was a spellbinding tale, but when she finished her mother recoiled in horror, responding in a way she never would have anticipated.

"This man is here, you have led him to our doorstep when you know what he is?" Marie cried accusingly, "How could you have led him here when to do so is to

364

jeopardize the lives of all who reside in this sacred sanctuary!"

"Please, Mama, he is a fine man, truly he is, and I wanted you to meet him, as he is the only husband I will ever have." Celiese was sorry her mother was so badly frightened when there was no cause for such great alarm as she clearly felt.

Rising to her feet, Marie paced the small chamber distractedly before she wheeled to face Celiese with an impassioned plea. "You have forgotten all I taught you, all memory of your dear father, as well, if you can call one of those murdering Danes, one of those unspeakably vile butchers, your husband! Have you no shame that you have brought this terrible disgrace to the name of d'Loganville?"

Deeply hurt by her mother's cruel insults, Celiese rose to face her. "I thought you would understand. I love Mylan, as dearly as you loved my father."

Marie drew back her hand and slapped Celiese across the face with all her strength, nearly knocking the young woman to the floor. "Never, never, are you to speak your father's name to me again until you have repented every one of your many sins!"

Stunned by the force of that unexpected and undeserved blow, Celiese nevertheless made another attempt to explain her true situation. "Mylan is my husband, Mama, and a dear one, but he will soon leave for his homeland while I will remain here. I hope to restore to our family what is rightfully ours, but I have no need to beg God for forgiveness when I've done no wrong."

Gripping her daughter's shoulders in a firm grasp, Marie hissed sharply, "No, you must come here to me, to God. This is your rightful home, and you need never leave it! Pray with me now for forgiveness for the life you've led since we parted, and surely God will grant you his blessing if you promise to devote the rest of your life to serving him."

Celiese shook her head. "That is a prayer I will never speak, for I am blameless for all that has happened to me, and I will never deny I love Mylan or say that I am ashamed to be his."

Seeing the small chain around her daughter's neck, Marie withdrew it carefully, fascinated by the delicate silver charm. "What manner of magic is this?"

"It is the hammer of their god, Thor. I have not adopted Mylan's religion, but I wear it still." Taking the charm from her mother's grasp, Celiese dropped it down again inside her neckline where it would be safe from harm. She had no desire to have it yanked from around her throat, as she was afraid her mother was about to do.

Horrified that her daughter had embraced such evil pagan ways, Marie shrank back. "I wish you had died with your father, for you were the dearest of daughters but now you are a traitor to his memory, no more than some despicable Dane's whore! Leave this sacred ground and do not return until you are ready to make peace with God by begging Him to forgive your sins, as you must know in your heart you should!"

Backing slowly toward the door, Celiese knew the woman before her was a total stranger, her mother no more. "I thought you would understand everything I wished so badly to confide in you, but you have understood nothing. You are consumed with hatred, while you dwell in a house you call holy. Your heart is as cold as these ancient stone walls, and I am truly sorry I have come here today if you would have preferred I remained dead!" Celiese ran from the room, sobbing as though her heart were broken, for indeed it was. Raktor had called her unfit to be a Viking's bride, while now it seemed she was unfit to be her own mother's daughter, as well.

Chapter Twenty

Celiese dried her eyes hastily on her sleeve before she rushed through the convent door but she did not realize the bright red print of her mother's hand was still plainly visible upon her left cheek. She walked to where her mount, a pretty bay mare, stood grazing and picked up the reins. Swinging herself upon the animal's back, she turned toward the path and called to her companions, "There is no need to linger here, let us be gone."

Mylan scrambled to his feet, leapt upon the stallion's back, and with only gentle urging the animal drew alongside Celiese's mare. "Well, have you nothing to report? I expected you to spend the whole day talking with your mother; what happened?" He saw the trace of tears gleaming upon her long lashes and thought perhaps she had been happy enough to cry until he noticed the telltale mark upon her cheek and realized instantly what sort of reception she must have received. His heart fell then, for he knew how high her hopes had been and how truly devastated she must feel.

"My mother appears to be well." Celiese lifted her chin

proudly, trying to think of some other comment she might make that would be the truth without inflicting the agony she'd just suffered upon Mylan as well.

Confused by that less than revealing remark, Mylan encouraged her to say more. "She was not too shocked by your sudden appearance, I hope."

Taking a deep breath in an attempt to calm her ravaged emotions, Celiese responded softly, "Naturally she was as astonished to find I am alive as I was to learn she had survived Raktor's assault upon our home." Celiese turned to see if André was following, using the time to wipe her eyes again while Mylan could not see her gesture.

"You had little time for a serious conversation, Celiese, but did your mother not have some words of advice for you?" He sincerely hoped the woman would have cautioned her daughter, if not forbidden her entirely, to pursue the cause of reclaiming her estate from Hrolf. He would welcome help from any quarter in making the headstrong young woman see reason and hoped her mother had foreseen the danger Celiese did not.

Celiese bit her lip, forcing back a fresh flood of tears, her concern far different from his. "Yes, she is content and tried to influence me to enter the convent, too."

"What does that mean?" Mylan pressed her to explain, since the complexities of the Christian religion were beyond the scope of his knowledge.

"Young women, as well as widows, are accepted by the Order of Saint Valery." Celiese hesitated a moment, attempting to make her mother's hysterical demand

369

sound more reasonable than it had been. "She invited me to join with her in the service of God."

Mylan reached out to catch her mare's bridle, jerking the startled horse to an abrupt halt. "Women do not come and go as they please there do they?"

"Well, no." Then, seeing he did not understand, she explained more fully. "Once a woman enters a religious order, she remains there until her death." Surprised by the bright flash of anger that burned in his amber eyes, she inquired as to its cause. "Why are you so concerned with our religious customs, Mylan?"

Furious that she did not even seem to realize what she was saying, Mylan sneered menacingly, "Your mother simply said, 'Good day, how are you, dear, and why don't you leave your husband to take up residence here?' Is that what she said to you?"

"Mylan, please, we need not discuss this in the middle of the road!" André had been following closely but had pulled his mount to a halt also so he might remain at a discreet distance, but she was embarrassed to have him see them arguing again.

"Our surroundings hardly matter! Did your mother demand you leave me without giving me the slightest opportunity to impress her favorably? I expected to speak with her, for a few minutes, at least." He could not believe any woman could be so unreasonable, even a French one. He thought she would have been consumed with curiosity about her daughter's husband.

Celiese sighed sadly, sorry that he had not accepted her presence as proof of what her response had been. Reaching out to touch his sleeve lightly, she tried again to shield him from her mother's wrath. "Please forgive my mother's rudeness, but her memories are such that she cannot accept my description of your fine character as the truth. I did not remain with her, but am here with you, is that not proof enough of what my response to her invitation must have been?" Smiling bravely, Celiese continued, "Please let us return to the village. André was kind enough to lend us these mounts, but I am certain our journey has tired them." When she attempted to turn her mare away, he released the reins and gave no further comment on any subject until the small settlement came into view.

As they had the previous day, the peasants came forward, quietly observing Celiese and her tall companion as they dismounted in front of André's cottage. Not pleased by that unwanted attention, Mylan sought a way to avoid it. "Where are these animals stabled? I do not mind taking them there and seeing to their care."

Celiese conveyed his offer to André, but the man refused to consider accepting the Viking's help. He'd not reveal where the village hid their livestock for fear their animals would swiftly be stolen or slaughtered. He gave another excuse, however, but Celiese understood the true reason for his reluctance and thought his thinking as illogical as her mother's. "I am sorry, Mylan, he says he enjoys working with animals as he has since his youth and requires no assistance. He hopes you will not be offended."

Mylan handed over the stallion's reins without comment, but his gaze had grown dark. "I will pay him then, for the use of the horses."

Celiese did not bother to translate that offer since she knew it would be refused. "I think you might leave some gift when you sail, he'd not accept pay for helping us. He was a part of our family."

Disappointed he could not reward André immediately for his help, Mylan reached out to take Celiese by the hand. "Well, at least thank him for his help. Then I want to look at your house again, without being followed by the entire village this time. Is that possible?" Mylan knew he sounded angry, and he was, but he did not want Celiese to think she was the cause of his foul mood.

Celiese smiled at the people who had begun to gather. "I can think of no polite way to refuse their company if they wish to give it, but I am certain you are the only good-natured Dane they have had an opportunity to observe and you can understand their curiosity." Good-natured was perhaps not the way to state it; he was the only one without a blood-drenched sword in his hand was a more likely description, but she kept the horror of that thought to herself.

"It is not me they are watching with such awe, Celiese, but you, and I do not like it." He drew her close as they started up the path that led to the ruins of her home. She could not be expected to bring prosperity to the impoverished village simply by her presence, but he could readily see from the peasants' adoring glances that she had inspired a hope that had been absent from their hearts only the previous afternoon. "Your family was so rich they could afford to feed all these people?" he asked incredulously.

"There were several villages similar in size to this one,

although I do not recall any being in such a sad state when my father was alive. The peasants farmed our land and gave us a share of what they produced as payment for the use of our property. We did not prosper unless they did, it was not the other way around. My father was always generous, however, if a man were ill, or some tragedy befell his family, he would wait until the man could pay what he owed. No one was ever put out of his home on our estate as they would have been on many others."

"The peasants did not take advantage of your father's kindness?" Mylan asked skeptically.

"How could they have done that?" Celiese inquired innocently.

"By being lazy, doing only what was the minimum to insure their survival." He knew slaves were always lazy, and he could not believe peasants would have any more ambition.

"The rent was a flat fee, Mylan, not based upon how much a man produced. It was to his own advantage to cultivate all he could, for only a tiny portion went to us and the rest he kept for himself and his family." Thinking she understood his confusion, she continued, "Free men are not like slaves, they have a reason to work, a purpose for their labors other than serving a tyrannical master."

Laughing, Mylan asked, "Are you calling me a tyrant? I have owned slaves from time to time." She had been the most difficult to manage, but he thought better of offering an opinion such as that.

Celiese did not reply, for she couldn't. She had never been his slave, but that was an argument she'd not begin again, either.

Seeing by her expression that he was on dangerous ground, Mylan returned to the far safer subject of agriculture. "Well, was this system effective? The crops were cultivated, the people fed?"

"Some years were better than others, for the weather plays a great role in production, as you well know, but the fields were lush when I was a child, the peasants happy. You have seen the respect the name d'Loganville inspires in these people. It is not without cause, but well deserved."

Mylan turned to be certain they were not being followed. Apparently, since André had not accompanied them today, the villagers had gone about their own business also. Relieved to find they would have some privacy for a short while at least, he lengthened his stride to hurry Celiese along. "I cannot rebuild your entire house in the short time we have remaining, but if you want to stay here, I can at least see part of it is made livable again."

Celiese wandered about as Mylan studied what was left of the once magnificent structure. She could see it so clearly in her mind; to consider rebuilding anything less than the perfection it had been saddened her greatly. When he sat down by her side, she tried to refuse his offer as tactfully as she could. "The house was so pretty, Mylan, filled with sunlight and good cheer, surrounded by fragrant gardens. I know you want to help me, but I'd rather leave my home in ruins than build anything less than the splendid residence it was."

"Celiese," Mylan began sternly, then, realizing the day

had gone no better for her than it had for him, he softened his tone. "I want you to come home with me." He reached for her hand and laced her fingers tightly in his, bringing them to his lips. "I won't leave you here amidst this rubble."

"But you must!" Celiese insisted. "This is where I belong. And I know how desperate my situation appears, but I can make everything right again in time, I know I can."

Gesturing toward the few remaining walls of her home, Mylan asked sarcastically, "How? You have not even so much as André to call your own! You are no more than one fragile young woman, how do you expect to accomplish any of your dreams?"

Attempting to hold her temper, Celiese tried to win his sympathy. "If you were to return home and find Raktor had leveled your house, killed your family, slaughtered your livestock, and sold off all your slaves, would you not try to restore all you could to its proper place?"

"I am a man, Celiese, and a strong one. I would never rest until I had repaid Raktor for each wrong he'd done, but you are little more than a girl. While you do have some skill with weapons, you do not even own any!"

"I would say I have a great deal of skill! I almost killed your bear, have you forgotten that?" Her patience at an end, Celiese responded angrily, "I can use weapons, but I may not need to. If I can see the king, I can make him understand that what he has done in making a bargain with Hrolf is wrong."

"The king?" Mylan was appalled. "You plan to visit the king and demand he restore your lands to you?"

"Why not? The spineless weasel needs someone to tell him how to rule the country with the pride it deserves!"

Mylan rested his head in his hands, "I should wring your neck now and save King Charles the trouble!"

"He would not dare to harm me!" Celiese replied instantly, shocked by his threats. She was as angry as he, her cheeks flushed with color, her green eyes bright with unshed tears.

"Because you are Lady d'Loganville, your name as proud as his?" Mylan scoffed disparagingly.

"Yes!" Celiese rose as a final gesture, ready to end their argument. "Sail with the morning tide. You have brought me home, which was all I asked, and I am grateful for the favor. I will follow the bank of the river Seine to Paris and seek an audience with the king. Were my father alive he would do no less!"

"Your father is dead!" Mylan sprang to his feet to confront her, "All are dead who tried to resist the invading Danes; Hrolf is only the last and the most fierce. Don't you understand no king gives away part of his realm if he has any other choice? That one pretty young woman objects will matter not at all to him. He is buying peace for the rest of his lands by giving away yours, and nothing you say will sway him from the course of action he has already chosen!"

Turning her back on him, Celiese took several steps away, trying to fight the overwhelming sense of frustration that confronted her at every turn. Their marriage had not survived their wedding night despite her best efforts to make Mylan accept her love, and to return to Denmark as his wife now was impossible. And to enter the convent as her mother had insisted she do was unthinkable when there was no one else to rectify the terrible injustice her family had suffered. Her plan might be naive, it might even be ridiculous in the king's view, but she knew she had to try in every way she could to reclaim what was rightfully hers. Bending down to pick up a handful of earth, Celiese sifted the rich soil through her fingers. "Perhaps I do have more courage than sense, Mylan, but I have not survived this long for no purpose. There are more ways to fight than with a sword, and I'll not rest until I've exhausted every possibility to return my home to the grandeur it had in my father's lifetime."

Walking around to face her, Mylan took her soiled hand in his. "This is no more than dirt! If that is all you want, I own plenty! Give up this cause, come home with me and be my wife. Do not refuse what can be the best of all possible lives for both of us."

Celiese shook her head sadly. "No, Mylan, this is my home, right here where we stand. This is where I belong, and I must stay." It was not just that she felt a responsibility to the peasants who farmed her land, but a firm conviction that this was a duty she could not shirk.

Livid with her continual refusal to be his wife, which he was certain she knew damn well she was, Mylan simply swept Celiese up into his arms and carried her behind the shelter of the nearest wall. The stones of the floor were overgrown with thick grass, but he wished the spot were a more comfortable one. Laying her down gently, he dropped down beside her. Not bothering to remove the garments she wore, he simply pushed them aside, slipping the layers of silk out of his way before he grabbed her wrists to stop any protest she might have considered before she attempted to make it. His mouth covered hers with a deep kiss, silencing any verbal argument as well. Consumed by the need he could neither fight nor deny, he saw only her vibrant beauty in his mind and, seeking to win her acceptance of a marriage already consummated by countless passionate encounters, he waited for some small sign that she would accept his affection as she always had.

Loving Mylan as deeply as she did, Celiese felt the same anguish that pierced his heart. To think they would soon be parted was an agony too great to bear, and although she could scarcely move in his confining grasp her mood was clear. Her body was soft and pliant beneath his, hungry for the rapture he offered so insistently, and when he realized from her relaxed pose that she had made no move to fight him, he raised his head, a puzzled gleam lighting his golden eyes.

An amused smile played across Celiese's pretty mouth. Knowing she was going to start giggling at the ardor she continually inspired in him that he could not control, Mylan released her wrists to draw her into his arms with a playful growl. "I'll teach you to laugh at me!" After kissing her lips soundly with a fervent passion, he nibbled her earlobe, then lowered his mouth to the creamy expanse of breast he'd exposed to view in the first frantic moments of his embrace. Her physical beauty bewitched him anew, and he never tired of caressing the gentle swells of her superb body. But he had a far more serious purpose than mere pleasure in mind. He wanted her spirit to blend with his in a bond she'd no longer seek to sever.

He slid his hand over her slender hip as his mouth moved slowly down the elegant contours of her shapely form. Her legs were perfection, long and slim, the ankles delicate and lightly tanned. After sampling the firm muscle of her calf, he found the smooth skin of her inner thigh delicious, and he let his tongue move up with deliberate slowness toward his goal until he heard her breath quicken to soft gasps, all thought of laughter fleeing her agile mind as her desire grew to a fevered intensity that matched his own. The warm inner recesses of her supple young body lured him now to explore their depths, and he began to savor her honey-sweet taste with a hunger he could no longer disguise with teasing nibbles. He held her fast so she'd not escape him as he drank deeply of the rich, creamy essence her body had created especially to please him. It was far more intoxicating than mead, and he was drunk with desire, lured on by the same exquisite joy that shuddered through her, inspiring him to give more and more of himself in return.

Celiese felt as though she were floating above the warm, fragrant earth, carried aloft so gently she might never reach a plane where she would wish to stop and rest. Surrounded by the lush pleasure of Mylan's irresistible affection, she could scarcely lift her fingertips to caress his curls, her shy touch holding him near until the ecstasy of his loving kiss flooded her veins with a contentment so superb she found making even that small gesture impossible.

Lost in the same exotic dream of love he'd created for her, Mylan at last enfolded Celiese in a tender embrace, his mouth seeking reassurance from hers before he buried his face in her bright haze of silver curls and let the rapture he'd given her wash over him, as well. Pleasure this rich was meant to be shared for a lifetime, and he knew that without her by his side the best part of himself would already be dead.

When he started to draw away, Celiese held Mylan more tightly, the softness of her deep green gaze giving no hint of the turmoil that still raged within her heart. "Will you not hold me for just a while longer? I do not want the beauty of this moment to ever pass," she whispered.

"I want only to hold you forever," Mylan responded hoarsely, uncertain what he had proven by his latest demonstration of the unbridled passion she kindled within him. He could no more control the fires of his own emotions than he could control her, and yet he had seldom known a more exhilarating challenge than the effort to conquer her elusive spirit. He could not separate her willfulness from her intoxicating beauty, and he wondered if she had any idea what a fool he'd become in his quest for her love. He lay still, cradling her head gently upon his broad chest until at last she was ready to leave him.

"There was a stream that ran through the trees at the bottom of the hill. I wonder if the water still tastes as sweet." Without waiting for Mylan to follow, Celiese scampered off, her tiny feet flying over the autumn grass as she went to seek the answer to that question.

Startled by her sudden departure, Mylan sat up slowly, a rakish grin lifting the corner of his well-shaped mouth. He was thirsty too, for something far stronger than water. But remembering the foul taste of André's wine, he thought it better not to inquire as to what else the village might have to offer. Pulling his clothes back into place, he stood up and brushed the grass from his knees. He knew he must have taken leave of his senses to have made love in such a tempestuous fashion when their privacy was hardly assured. He looked around to be certain no one had observed them, then started off after Celiese, whistling happily to himself as he went.

Not only was the stream flowing with the pure spring water she had recalled so fondly, but it collected in a wide pool that looked too inviting in the afternoon sun to be resisted. Removing her clothing and shaking it out briskly to remove the wrinkles Mylan had just so thoughtlessly put in the fine fabric, Celiese draped her gown over a tree limb and waded into the sun-drenched pond. The chill water provided a heady rush of excitement, and with renewed vigor she washed quickly, removing all trace of Mylan's distinctive masculine scent from her body. When he called to her she invited him to join her, as she thought the pool a far more pleasant place than either the small village or his ship were likely to be.

"Since I was never successful at luring you into my tub, I have no choice but to accept your invitation, but I fear the result will be far less erotic than what I always had in mind." With a sly chuckle Mylan sat down to unlace his boots, then tossed the rest of his apparel aside. He watched Celiese's face for a hint that she found the sight his body presented less than an appealing one, but her smile never wavered, and forgetting his scars he stepped into the cool water, then swam toward her.

Celiese put her hands upon his shoulders, treading water to stay where he stood. "The two of us would not have even fit in your tub, Mylan. That is not an erotic idea, but a ridiculous one!" Sparkling droplets of water dripped from his curls and clung to his thick lashes, giving him the appearance of a pagan god from the ocean's depths. She was tempted to ask him which of his many gods ruled the sea, but the memory of her mother's disapproval of his beliefs discouraged that thought so completely she did not voice it. Instead, she leaned forward to kiss his smiling lips lightly. "Have you not had enough, Mylan, does my affection never satisfy you completely?"

She looked so young with her damp curls clinging to her shoulders, so innocent and dear, that he wrapped his arms around her waist and drew her close, suddenly afraid she would disappear even as he watched her smile shimmer in the sunlight's reflection off the spring water. "Is it compliments you are after?"

Surprised, Celiese pulled away. "No, I have no wish to be compared with other women you have known."

Grabbing her wrist, Mylan pulled her back into his arms. "Good, for there is no comparison between you and any other woman who has ever lived." He knew at that exact moment that he would never be able to leave her. If she insisted upon remaining in her homeland to pursue a noble though foolish cause, then he would have to stay, too. That weight off his mind, he released her and swam with a long, graceful stroke back toward the shore.

Confused by his flattery, Celiese followed. "At least my loving puts you in a far more agreeable mood. I will

382

consider that the only compliment I deserve." Having no towel upon which to dry herself, she turned slowly so that Mylan could pat her flushed skin dry with his tunic. "Thank you, but now your tunic is wet. It will dry quickly if you place it in the sun."

"I would sooner go without a shirt than have you appear in the village without your gown," Mylan teased playfully, his mood positively euphoric.

Celiese knew better than to reply in kind and dressed quickly, for it was possible children might still come there to play as she once had, and she did not want to be discovered cavorting in the nude with Mylan by anyone of any age. They seemed to have settled nothing, yet she felt close to him once again and was content with that happiness for the moment.

While they sat in the late afternoon sun waiting for his linen tunic to dry, Mylan explained an idea he'd just had. "Celiese, let us not anger the king by consulting him upon the matter of your property, since he has already given it away. We should go directly to Hrolf instead."

"We?" Celiese asked with a wonderous gaze, "Why, Mylan, do you mean you will stay and help me?" She was astonished by the offer he'd just made so casually.

Not wishing to reveal how foolish he'd become in his pursuit of her, Mylan replied flippantly, "I will stay for a short while longer, since I am curious as to the outcome of your cause. If Hrolf is inviting Danes to establish homes here, perhaps our simplest approach would be to tell him you are my wife and we have grown fond of this particular piece of property. He may just give it to us for our own."

"You cannot be serious!" Celiese argued immediately. "You cannot expect me to keep still about who I am and the fact this land is rightfully mine!"

"Which would you prefer, to own the land again or not?" Rising to his feet, Mylan extended his hand to Celiese. "Give the matter some thought, and we will leave for Rouen at first light."

"Tomorrow we will go?" Celiese accepted his help, straightening the soft pleats of her bodice as she questioned him. "I have not thought, well, I mean I have had no time to prepare what I want to say."

Before Mylan could tell her she should just be still and let him handle the matter, André appeared upon the path. He hesitated to come forward until he saw Celiese wave, but the sight of the Viking's hideously scarred chest repelled him so greatly he could not keep the revulsion from showing in his expression.

Knowing what had caused the Frenchman's fright-filled glance, Mylan took his tunic from the branch where it had hung to dry and pulled it over his head. It was slightly damp still, but that discomfort was easier to bear than the fear André could not hide. "Tell him I am the worst of warriors, and that's why I'm so badly scarred. That tale may give him the courage he needs to walk with us back to the village."

"Anyone would be surprised by your appearance, Mylan, don't fault him for it. It isn't necessary that we lie, either." Walking up to greet him, Celiese smiled warmly as she began to explain that Mylan was a fearless hunter who had slain the most ferocious of bears with one mighty toss of his spear. The old man's eyes widened in awe, his respect for the Viking growing immeasurably as he realized the tale must be true, for the man had the scars to prove it.

André was so taken by Celiese's charming conversation that he almost forgot his original purpose in having come to look for her. "Lady d'Loganville, we would like to provide a more appropriate welcome than we were able to give you yesterday. If you and your husband would join us for supper, we would all be greatly honored."

"We are delighted by your invitation, of course, but we do not want to be a burden, to deplete the provisions you've saved for the winter." Celiese took the old gentleman's arm, confiding in him since she thought he would appreciate her honesty rather than being offended by it.

"Everyone has offered to bring something. A burden shared is a light one." André's eyes sparkled with mischief, seeing he had pleased her.

Turning to include Mylan in their conversation, Celiese explained André had come to extend an invitation. When the handsome Dane winked slyly, she knew he was as grateful as she was that the friendly man had not arrived any sooner.

"I will be happy to attend any celebration he has planned, but only if he will allow me to contribute something too," Mylan remarked with a pleasant grin.

"What did you have in mind?" Celiese inquired hesitantly, hoping he would not insult the peasants by his request.

"We've ale aplenty, and if they have no more wine perhaps they would welcome something to drink." Mentally, Mylan began to add up what stores they had remaining in sufficient amounts to donate, since these people, while friendly, appeared to be living near starvation.

Once it was explained, Andre accepted Mylan's generous offer of liquid refreshment, and he went back to his ship to fetch a couple of kegs of ale while Celiese stayed with André. There was a small grass-covered square at the end of the row of cottages, and a few long tables had already been set up and were soon laden with freshly baked loaves of bread, buckets of wild berries, vegetables steamed with herbs after having been freshly picked from gardens Celiese had still not seen, and from somewhere, a succulent ham. What the feast lacked in elegance it soon made up in enthusiasm. When a sudden hush fell over the assembled crowd, Celiese turned and saw Mylan approaching with two of his men carrying the casks of ale he'd promised to provide. A wave of tension swept through the peasants and she knew they were badly frightened. Expecting some trick, they were ready to bolt and flee into the nearby woods, but she ran to meet Mylan, smiling happily as she led him back to the party.

Seeing the love that radiated from her eyes, the people felt Celiese's confidence, and after no more than a moment's awkwardness welcomed Mylan into their midst. The two crew members hung back, polite young men who had no wish to intrude where they were unwanted, but they were soon escorted to the tables and encouraged to take whatever they wished and handed cups filled to overflowing with ale.

Although the food was delicious, Celiese ate only a small portion, then moved to the edge of the happy gathering, uncomfortable at being the center of all the attention. She could not help but overhear the excited whispers, and knowing these dear people truly expected her presence to improve their lot considerably, she grew increasingly apprehensive. Soon the memory of another such party on a day long past filled her mind. She'd been with her parents, out enjoying the beauty of a summer afternoon, when they'd chanced upon a celebration of some sort. She could no longer even recall the occasion, but there had been wine and someone had played tunes upon a lute, plucking out the lilting melodies while her parents had laughed and sung with the same joy as the peasants. The memories flooded through her then, bittersweet images of a striking couple, both tall and slender, their coloring fair and their voices soft, filled with words of love for each other and for her.

Mylan watched Celiese's pretty smile fade, her expression now impossible to read, and he stepped close to whisper, "Shall we leave them? I think the party will last all night, even without our company. If you are tired we need not stay, unless you wish to remain."

Celiese looked up at him, thinking as always how handsome a man he was. His expression was so sincere that she wanted to share her thoughts. "My parents were first cousins, Mylan, I had forgotten that. My relatives were fair-skinned and blond, but they were all of one family, all d'Loganville."

"Celiese?" Mylan signaled to his men to start back for the ship before he took her hand to follow them into the shadows. "I know I did not believe you once, but it no longer matters to me why your parents were blond. This is clearly your home." That he had once thought so enchanting a creature as Celiese could have been one of Raktor's undoubtedly many bastards embarrassed him greatly. He had said so many really stupid things to her, and he was sorry she remembered he'd not believed her story of her lineage when she'd first told him. She was clearly Lady Celiese d'Loganville, without the slightest doubt he knew it now, but unfortunately, so did she. He had been able to understand none of the peasants' excited conversation that evening, but their hopes had been in their adoring glances, and he wanted Celiese to belong only to him, not to them, as they so clearly thought she did. The gentle rocking motion of the Surf Falcon would lull them to sleep, but he was not ready for the world of dreams, and, lifting Celiese into his arms with a playful toss, he carried her aboard the ship and into her tent for what he hoped would not be the last night they'd share the magical splendor of love.

Chapter Twenty-One

Despite Mylan's loving attentions, Celiese slept poorly. Her mind was far too preoccupied with what they might find in Rouen for her to relax enough for the peace of slumber to overtake her as it usually did while she still lay in his arms. She was deeply worried about what sort of man Hrolf would prove to be. Mylan had described him as being worse in all respects than Raktor, but she thought that appraisal an impossibility. There could be no more despicable villain abroad in the world than the head of the Torgvald family. The mere thought of that hateful man turned her stomach, and, thoroughly miserable, she tossed and turned, unable to find any comfortable position in which to rest.

After he'd slept a few hours, Mylan was sufficiently refreshed to feel the constant motions of the restless young woman by his side. Knowing she'd not be so active simply to annoy him, he sat up to ask what the matter might be. "Are you ill? If you will tell me what your problem is, I will try to solve it so we both may get the sleep we deserve."

"Forgive me, I am simply too anxious to rest, but I did not mean to disturb you. Were we sleeping on land as we usually do I would get up and go for a walk, but that is impossible tonight."

As the deck of the Surf Falcon was littered with sleeping men stretched out upon their soft suede bags, Mylan could think of no way for Celiese even to pace successfully. Wide awake now, he tried to think of some alternative. "Here, sit up and move in front of me."

Not knowing what to expect, Celiese sat up slowly. "Just what is it you have in mind, Mylan?"

Exasperated by her curiosity, Mylan issued a firm order this time. "Come here!" When Celiese put her fingertips upon his lips to silence him before he woke the entire crew, he pushed her hand away and whispered gruffly, "You should have worried about whether or not I'd be discreet before you woke me!"

"I have already apologized for it, and it was unintentional," Celiese responded demurely. She was certain the men of his crew knew they were lovers, but still she did not want to flaunt their relationship. The fact that he had insisted of late that she refer to him as her husband was not a matter they had ever really discussed or decided. She was simply confused by that demand, but thought this a poor time to mention her apprehensions, so she crawled over his leg and sat down with her back toward him. "Is this what you had in mind?"

"Precisely." Placing his hands lightly upon her shoulders, Mylan began to massage the smooth skin of her back with slow, easy circles. "You know how to do this, at least you swore it would help my leg once. Do you remember that day?"

Celiese relaxed against him. His hands were warm, his touch very pleasant, and she closed her eyes to enjoy the delightful sensation more fully. "I didn't think you appreciated my efforts then; are you saying now that you did?"

Mylan leaned forward to kiss the elegant curve of her shoulder before he replied tersely, "I'll admit it was relaxing, no more." He knew were he to begin revealing the depth of his weakness for her he'd never stop, so he chose to remain silent and hoped she would simply wonder.

Since he'd brought up the subject of his health, Celiese felt safe in commenting, "At least we did not have to walk all the way to Yvetot today, that would have been difficult for André and me, as well as you." While his limp was a slight one, she knew he'd never admit the walk was causing him pain, but she was glad they'd all avoided such a tiring ordeal.

Mylan increased the pressure of his fingertips until he was certain Celiese would beg him to stop, but she did not even squirm to get away. Disgusted with himself for being so brutal, he dropped his hands to his sides. "Do you truly think I lack the stamina of an elderly man or have less than you?"

Shocked he'd be so deeply offended, Celiese replied with far more care, "No, of course not, but I know walking a great distance is difficult for you, and your comfort is important to me, even though mine obviously matters little to you." She did not move to escape him though, but sat quietly holding her breath, unable to predict what his reaction would be to that comment.

Again lifting his hands to her shoulders, Mylan continued with the gentle massage he'd meant to give. He let his fingertips move down her spine, attempting to ease the tension he'd just created while he tried to apologize. "I was not always so ill-tempered." He had no idea if she found his touch soothing, but he could not keep his mind upon his task when her nearness distracted him so. The sweet fragrance of her soft curls was too entrancing for him to concentrate on anything other than the desire that had begun to tease his senses with a maddening intensity. Giving up all pretense of maintaining the detachment with which he'd begun, he wrapped his arms around her tightly and drew her near. "I want you to keep your sympathy to yourself no matter what we are called upon to do. You must give Hrolf no reason to suspect I am not as good a man as any other Dane."

Smiling to herself, Celiese put her hands over his. "That will not be difficult, Mylan, for you are far better."

That she would tease him now appalled Mylan, and he was tempted to shake her soundly. "Promise me!"

Still not understanding quite what it was he wanted, Celiese rephrased her reply. "Should the subject of your health ever come up in a conversation between Hrolf and me, I will swear you are as strong as an ox. Is that what you want to hear?"

"Yes!" Knowing he must have sounded like an idiot, Mylan pulled Celiese across his lap and kissed her sweetly. "The man may recognize my name, but I doubt he will have heard I was injured so badly I barely cheated death. That is a secret you must keep, Celiese, for Vikings abhor weakness of any kind, and I need to win Hrolf's respect, not his pity."

"You are still far too sensitive if you think anyone could possibly pity you, Mylan; I never have and no one else does, either." Snuggled in his embrace, she felt very safe and secure, but she knew her presence did not provide the same marvelous sense of acceptance to him and was saddened by it.

Celiese seemed so comfortable in his arms, Mylan wondered if perhaps his backrub had relaxed her enough for her to sleep, but he was not at all sleepy now and hoped she wasn't either. Lifting her cascade of bright curls out of his way, he trailed light kisses slowly up her throat, but when his lips reached hers her reaction was so spontaneously loving that he pulled her down upon the soft woolen blanket that served as their bed. Being wide awake with her was better than any dream, but, curious, there was one question he had to ask, "Do you really think of me as an ox, Celiese? Is there not some other animal who has such strength, but is also blessed with intelligence and grace?"

"Is it compliments you want?" Celiese lifted her fingertips to his nape, slowly combing his soft curls. "I said you were as strong as an ox, not that you possessed that beast's wits or disposition."

"I misunderstood then," Mylan admitted reluctantly, fascinated by the bright shine of her eyes when the moonlight that filled the small tent was so very pale.

"You are more of a stallion, smooth and sleek, bright and so very proud. Does that comparison please you more?"

"This is what pleases me, Celiese, only this." Mylan tightened his embrace as he deepened his kiss. Smooth, sleek, bright, proud, all those same adjectives described her as well, but it was her affection he found too delectable to resist, and that was one thing he'd never let Hrolf even suspect. The less that man saw and heard of Celiese, the better it would be for all three of them. Pushing thoughts of Hrolf aside, he let his mind dwell only upon giving pleasure in new and ever more exciting ways. His touch light but knowing, his kisses generous, he was in a playful mood, and when Celiese at last fell asleep, she did not stir until well after dawn.

After he'd used such imaginative methods to insure Celiese enjoyed a restful night, Mylan decided he would be foolish to awaken her the next morning. He strode into the village alone, using the time to practice what he hoped would be a near normal walk. The torn muscles of his right thigh no longer caused him excruciating pain with each step he took; he limped simply because favoring that leg had become habit. With concentration, he could manage two even steps, and he did so as he approached André's small cottage. Since the hour was so early, he did not disturb the man but left a bag of silver coins tied to his door latch and returned to the Surf Falcon to give the order to sail.

Since the merchant vessel was so lightly laden, Mylan was certain he could navigate the Seine to Rouen without mishap. He knew the river curved with a slow, rhythmic pattern, like the undulating motions of a serpent. Danes had used the river to reach Paris in warships, and the route was one frequently discussed and well known.

Mylan stood with his hands on the rail. There was only a short stretch of coast to clear before they entered the mouth of the river, and since the territory they'd traverse was under Hrolf's rule he anticipated no resistance to their passage, but was alert to danger all the same. The French countryside had been ravaged so often by marauding bands of Vikings that he doubted there was still a man alive who could hurl a spear, but it was foolhardy to think such a man might not exist somewhere, and he had no intention of allowing anyone aboard a vessel under his command to be easy prey.

When Celiese finally awoke from the most pleasant of dreams, she realized instantly that the Falcon was under sail. Greatly alarmed, she drew on her gown and ran to find Mylan without so much as bothering to brush her hair. Her bright curls flew about her head, caught by the wind as she grabbed his arm. "Where are we bound?"

Surprised by her agitated mood, Mylan reached out to caress her cheek lightly. "To Rouen, as I promised. Where did you think?"

"But it would be far easier to ride on horseback to Rouen. The path is straight, but the river course is not."

In a tolerant mood, Mylan replied calmly, "I am confident I can find the city even without your assistance. Why don't you complete your preparations for the day?" He stood back to survey her disheveled appearance with a sly grin as he enumerated a few of the tasks she'd obviously overlooked in her haste to speak with him. "There's fresh water, should you care to bathe. Borrow my comb if you've misplaced your own, and I'm certain your slippers can be found if you search for them a little more diligently."

Embarrassed now that she'd not thought to take more care with her appearance before she'd rushed out upon the deck, Celiese turned away and with a light running step returned to her tent to begin anew to greet the day with more decorum.

After he'd given Celiese's question some thought, Mylan considered it strange she would not have understood their destination. When his curiosity got the better of him, he went to ask her to explain.

Celiese was brushing out her hair, curling the long tresses over her hand to make the waves fall neatly, but when Mylan joined her she handed him her brush without thinking and he continued the task.

"When I say I am on my way to Rouen, that is where I intend to go. Why did you doubt me?"

"I was merely surprised you wished to sail, Mylan." Celiese hoped he'd believe that explanation, but truly she had been terrified he had begun the return voyage to his homeland. "I did not expect you to leave before I had an opportunity to bid André and the others farewell. I wanted to see them all again and thank them for their hospitality."

"We will return soon enough and you can talk with everyone until your heart is content." Mylan thought her shining curls far too lovely to merit further effort at grooming and laid her brush aside. "Now come with me so we can enjoy the beauty of the morning without further strife."

Taking his hand Celiese walked with him to the port rail, and with rapt attention gazed at the passing scene. "I did not mean to fill your day with strife, but André had horses, and the ride to Rouen is not much farther than Yvetot was from my home."

From the ruins of your home, he was tempted to say, but restrained himself. "Since we had a choice, need I explain why I decided to arrive at Hrolf's doorstep in this magnificent ship, rather than upon a less than impressive stallion?" The fact that he'd also have a dozen men to assist him should the need arise was a consideration too obvious to merit comment.

Knowing he was serious, Celiese responded in kind. "I understand it is important that we impress the man favorably. André's horses are well into their prime if not past it, but still—"

"But nothing!" Mylan interjected harshly. "You must let me decide how best to deal with Hrolf, and we'll not argue the matter in front of him either!" Mylan had no intention of riding overland to Rouen when he knew Celiese would attract a large following of devoted peasants. That would impress Hrolf most definitely, but certainly not favorably, as he hoped to do.

"This is my fight, Mylan, and while I am grateful for your help, I cannot allow you to pursue the cause of the d'Loganvilles alone."

Looking down at the determined tilt of her chin, Mylan thought only how dangerous a mission they had undertaken and how little was the likelihood for their success. He was tempted to tie her up and leave her on board the Falcon under heavy guard when they reached Rouen. Should she prove unreasonable when they arrived, he might just do it. "I am not alone, I have the most devoted of wives to assist me!"

Frowning petulantly, Celiese turned away. "Do not tease me with that fantasy again, Mylan."

Seeing a way to avoid an argument that might have unfortunate ramifications when they reached Rouen, Mylan reached out to turn Celiese back toward him. "What Hrolf understands is strength. A penniless French noblewoman will never impress him, whereas the wife of a wealthy Dane will have considerable bargaining power. If you are truly as devoted to the cause of restoring to the d'Loganvilles what is rightfully theirs, then you will follow my lead."

Celiese stared up into Mylan's fierce amber gaze and knew that while his plan might succeed she was extremely uneasy with it. Were they truly husband and wife, equals who shared in all things, she would trust his word without question, but that was not the truth of their situation, and it pained her to pretend that it was. It was to her advantage to be reasonable however, and she knew it. "It will do no harm to observe the situation for a day or two, that I will admit. But if Hrolf is anything like Raktor, then I know I will never be able to trust him, let alone be civil."

"You need do neither. I will tell him you are an intensely shy and virtuous young woman who prefers privacy to the company of others. The less he sees of you, the better I will like it."

"Why, Mylan, are you jealous?" Celiese laughed at the absurdity of that prospect and her eyes sparkled with a merry twinkle as she teased him. "Hrolf is the last man in France I would find attractive, don't you know that?"

Appalled by the mischievous gleam in her eye, Mylan took hold of her shoulders and gave her a firm shake. There were undoubtedly many French noblemen still dwelling in the country whom she'd find acceptable as mates, but he'd no intention of giving her her freedom. "Jealousy is an emotion we can do without. See you give me no cause for it."

When he released her, Celiese backed away slowly, sorry he could believe her capable of deliberately provoking his anger with such frivolous behavior. "I don't even know *how* to flirt, Mylan. I never had an occasion to practice the feminine wiles young ladies are supposed to affect to impress men."

She looked so crushed by his warning that Mylan regretted it immediately. "Oh Celiese, you are so very lovely, you need do no more than smile at a man to capture his heart."

Preferring the view of the river to his taunting grin, Celiese turned away. She had often smiled at him, but if he had a heart, it most definitely did not belong to her. Thinking he had won her silence at last, Mylan left her to see to his other duties, wishing she were as easy to command as the Falcon.

The city of Rouen was surrounded by a high walled fortress, the stone walls topped with lookout towers that commanded an unobstructed view of the surrounding countryside as well as a considerable distance of the river Seine. The approach of the Surf Falcon was noted when first the red and white sail could be seen, and a runner sent to inquire as to what sort of reception should be extended. Since Hrolf had no such *knarr* himself, nor did he expect one to arrive, he was exceedingly curious and told the captain of his guard to ascertain whose ship it was and what the owner's purpose might be, but to do no more than allow the ship to dock. Its passengers were not to be welcomed to the city until he was positive no mischief was afoot. Being the fiercest of raiders himself, he trusted no one, and he suspected everyone of attempting to take from him the prize he had been awarded. He guarded Rouen and all his lands well, as he planned to keep every inch of his territory by whatever ruthless tactics were necessary to hold them.

The docks were filled with *dreki*, the Danish warships, their graceful lines masking their deadly purpose, and Celiese turned away, sickened by the sight of what the once pretty city had become. A center of commerce in her father's time, it was now an armed citadel, ringed by ships of the Danes who had decimated the countryside with raids that had, over the years, become repeatedly more barbaric, until nothing remained to be seized but the land itself. Growing pale, she gripped the rail, uncertain that she could meet Hrolf without becoming physically ill. Disgusted by that weakness, she looked up at Mylan, but his expression was both proud and determined, without a trace of the fear that had nearly paralyzed her.

"Do you expect to be welcomed here without challenge, Mylan?"

"No, not immediately I don't." He had also noted the guards upon the battlements and was certain their presence had been noted and reported to Hrolf. "Whenever I have sailed into a new port, whether it was to trade goods or merely to explore, I found the best approach was to be patient. If we were to leap off the Falcon with swords in our hands, our purpose would immediately be misunderstood. However, if we wait for Hrolf to send an emissary, the advantage will already be ours."

"I have always thought you clever, Mylan, but if, like Raktor, Hrolf says one thing while plotting another, none of us will be safe."

Mylan chuckled at her keen observation. "Are we not planning the very same sort of deception, Celiese? I will introduce myself to the duke as merely a prosperous merchant searching for new markets, when, in fact, it is your land we are really after."

"That the king has made him a duke is ludicrous!" Celiese exploded angrily, livid at the very thought of such a travesty.

"Did I ever mention he also gave him his daughter, Gisela, as a bride? Does that not anger you more?" Since they had met as the result of such an arranged marriage, he expected her to see his point readily.

Celiese's thick lashes swept her delicate brows as she recalled the princess. "Mylan, I met Gisela, more than once, I think. I was no more than six or seven years old, but it is possible she may recognize me!"

Mylan swore angrily, as that was an unwanted complication. "I had not even considered that might be a problem. Let us hope the woman has so much on her mind she will not recall a pretty child she met ten years ago. Dressed as you are and by my side, she will think you a Danish princess, not a French one."

"I am not a princess, Mylan." Celiese blushed at the

word, but she was pleased by his compliment all the same, for there was a great difference between a princess and the lowly slave he'd once sworn her to be.

"If you speak French to no one, not even to the servants, the truth of your nationality will not be guessed. You must give Hrolf no cause to be suspicious of us, Celiese, or we will never succeed in wrenching your estate from his grasp."

"I will try your way first, I have agreed to that," Celiese reassured him with far more confidence than she felt.

"Do not doubt that it will work, for it will." Mylan gave the order to drop anchor in the center of the river and leaned back against the rail to wait for whatever welcome they might receive. Celiese wore his silver charm still, and the hope that Thor might be willing to assist him in so dangerous a cause as he'd chosen amused him greatly. "Hrolf has taken your religion, Celiese. Perhaps you should give that necklace back to me now."

"You cannot be serious!" she exclaimed.

"Oh, but I am. It was part of his bargain with your king that he accept the religion of the French people."

"How could the man embrace Christianity with the sins he must have upon his soul? Surely his conversion was no more than an expedient one."

"Since you are supposed to know nothing of Christ's teachings, perhaps you would like to invite him to instruct you. Then you could judge for yourself whether or not his beliefs are sincere," Mylan suggested slyly.

"That is not a subject I'd care to discuss with that rogue, Mylan." It would be difficult not to blurt out the purpose of her visit when first she saw the man; she'd never be able to calmly discuss religious doctrine as if she were no more than curious.

"If luck is with us, you will have no need to discuss any topic with him." Sighting a small boat headed their way, Mylan nodded confidently. "You see, curiosity is a powerful weapon, and someone has been sent to investigate the nature of our visit, just as I knew they would. You must rely upon me to make the first contact with Hrolf, for as captain of this vessel that is my duty."

Those were the last words Celiese was to hear Mylan speak for many an hour. He went ashore accompanied by two of his crew, but she did not argue with his decision to leave her behind for the moment. As far as she knew, no Viking sailed with his wife at his side, so her presence was a distinct oddity. His arrival would be regarded as remarkable enough without her to cause a distraction.

She found the wait interminable. She shared the crew's rations at suppertime, then paced the deck until it had grown dark, but Mylan had still not returned.

Mylan found Hrolf to be exactly what he'd expected, an arrogant brute who dominated every conversation no matter what the subject. Immense in size, he was nevertheless fit, his looks pleasant if not handsome, but his appetite for meat and drink was extraordinary, and by the time Mylan staggered aboard the Surf Falcon he was exhausted by the duke's hospitality and more than a little drunk.

Celiese had been unable to close her eyes, fearing

Mylan had come to some terrible harm and that she and his crew would all be taken prisoners at dawn and promptly slain, but when he lurched across the deck and stumbled into her dimly lit tent she knew immediately what his activities had been. "When I have been so dreadfully worried I might never see you alive again, how could you have been drinking yourself into a stupor!" she demanded angrily.

"I am not in a stupor." Mylan replied with difficulty. "Hrolf is as generous a host as my father and insisted I did not suffer from thirst while I dined at his table."

"How thoughtful of him!" Celiese responded through clenched teeth, but when Mylan sprawled across their blanket she began to unlace his boots without being asked for assistance. "I have never seen you drunk, Mylan, not ever. How the Danes can pass so many evenings swilling ale I will never know, and I have always been grateful you did not have such slothful habits, but perhaps you only lacked the opportunity!" She yanked off his suede boots and tossed them aside but remained seated at his feet, unwilling to do more to make him comfortable.

After rolling over upon his back, Mylan raised his right arm to cover his eyes as he yawned sleepily. "He believed all I told him about wishing to establish a profitable trade agreement, and if he wants a drinking companion I will be one. Now hush your complaints and come here to me. I told him I would bring my bride with me tomorrow when we take his falcons out to hunt."

"You expect me to go hunting with that fiend?" Celiese asked in disbelief.

"No, with me. Now come here as I asked you," Mylan

called in a far softer tone.

Celiese had been frightfully worried, terrified he had been met with the very worst of receptions, but the fact that Mylan had been enjoying himself so fully at Hrolf's table was more than she could tolerate or forgive. "No! I'll not sleep with a drunk!"

Mylan opened his eyes long enough to fix Celiese with a sullen stare that would have turned a lesser woman to stone. Thoroughly disgusted that she did not appreciate his efforts on her behalf, he answered sarcastically, "If what you see is a drunk, then sleep elsewhere!"

"I intend to!" Grabbing her cloak, Celiese moved to the edge of the tent and sat huddled in the shadows, so furious with the handsome young man who was her husband only when it suited him that she did not close her eyes until more than one cock had crowed to welcome the day.

When the small boat Hrolf had sent arrived alongside the Surf Falcon the next morning, Mylan helped Celiese into the vessel and held her hand tightly for the short trip to the docks. Thinking the best approach simply to ignore the argument that had spoiled his plans to enjoy her company the previous night, he began to explain, "The duke, Robert, as he now calls himself—he told me it is the custom of his adopted religion to choose a new name at the time of baptism—lives in a magnificent residence that faces the town square. It is difficult to go from one room to the next with the great number of treasures he has stored there."

Whispering defiantly, Celiese contradicted him, "Booty!"

"Yes, of course, I know the goods are the spoils of his raids." Mylan tightened his grip upon the delicate bones of her hand, sorry now he'd been so foolish as to bring her along when her temper was so quick. "Should you by some strange twist of fate chance to see something that belonged to your family or to their friends, please pretend you see nothing more than straw being stored to feed the livestock in the winter!"

"Don't you understand what you are asking of me?" Celiese asked indignantly.

"Yes," Mylan hissed crossly, "I am asking you to be as fine an actress today as you were the night we were wed!"

Devastated by that insult, Celiese clamped her mouth shut and turned away. She had been a fool to come to Rouen with Mylan when clearly he found Hrolf, or Robert, whatever he wished to call himself, a most interesting and doubtless admirable man! She already knew he'd own nothing from her home, for Raktor had burned whatever he'd not stolen, but all his possessions would have belonged at one time to families as dear as hers, and that thought was tragic enough. At the dock they found horses waiting, beautifully groomed and spirited mounts, which she knew were stolen, and, thoroughly sickened by the day that lay ahead, she ceased to think of anything other than how she might regain possession of her land.

Rouen was so changed in character that Celiese would not have recognized the city had Mylan not sworn that was where they were. There were Danes everywhere, robust men whose fair hair and blue eyes shone brightly above their wide smiles. These men had stopped their raiding to take up permanent residence in France, and yet she knew there was land for them only because her countrymen had not been able to defend their homes and so had lost them, as well as their lives. Because she was fair-haired and green-eyed, she could pass among them unrecognized for what she was by birth, and was seen as only what she appeared to be. If it was an actress Mylan wanted, then that was what she'd be, but only while it served her purpose.

Bored as the summer drew to an end, Hrolf was pleased to have the benefit of the company of a young man as intelligent and charming as Mylan Vandahl. While he had spent his own years pillaging France, Mylan had sailed to the edges of the known world and far beyond, yet he related the most astounding of adventures with a disarming modesty. He was exactly the type of man Hrolf wished to befriend, and he looked forward to a day of hunting with eager anticipation.

The duke and his party had already reached the open fields outside the city walls and were ready to begin the hunt when Mylan and Celiese arrived to join them. They were greeted warmly, since Mylan had impressed all those he'd met the previous day, and Celiese's fair beauty brought her instant acceptance.

"Your husband is far too modest a man, Celiese, for you are a wife who should be cherished, and he told us little of your virtues. We were not prepared to meet a woman of such extraordinary loveliness." Hrolf flashed what he hoped would be a charming smile, expecting to see a pretty blush rise in the young woman's cheeks, but she regarded him with a cool gaze he found most disconcerting. The power of his position made women eager to please him, but he realized his flattery had failed to win so much as a smile from this beauty.

Ignoring his compliment, Celiese inquired instead about the hunt. "How have you found the time to train falcons for sport, sir? I should think you would have been far too busy." Busy with murder and thievery, she was tempted to say, but she was too discreet to insult him so openly.

Surprised that she should be interested in the sport, Hrolf explained proudly, "I have not raised these birds from the nest, but they are mine as is all you see in every direction. I have not known a woman to enjoy falconry, but perhaps you would care to join us rather than merely observe?" He extended his left arm, upon which sat a magnificent peregrine falcon whose sharp talons were firmly embedded in the padded gauntlet he wore. Thinking Celiese would be foolish enough to reach out and pet the bird, he waited patiently to see how badly she would be injured when it bit her.

"Had I a bird of my own I would be happy to participate, but alas, we own none." Celiese remained upon her horse, her hands holding the reins lightly as she admired the falcon he was showing off so proudly. Clearly he thought her a fool where falcons were concerned, but she knew exactly what would happen were she to make a move toward this one. "This is a hawk of passage then, one captured from the wild and tamed, not an eyas, one taken from the nest and raised for sport?"

Impressed that she knew the difference, Hrolf realized Celiese did indeed know something of his favorite sport. "We have several birds; do you object to your wife joining in the hunt, Mylan?" Hrolf's booming voice attracted the notice of all who were nearby. There were several other women, but they appeared to be content to be spectators.

"Celiese has many talents; if she wishes to hunt, I have no objection." Yet Mylan gave her a warning glance. He knew she had nerve aplenty, but falconry involved skill, as well, and he doubted she had any experience with the powerful birds of prey. Moving close, he whispered so only she could hear, "Have you ever done this before?"

"Of course, my father raised hawks as a diversion." Celiese was surprised by his question until she saw by his worried expression that he was concerned for her safety.

Seeing something pass between the attractive couple that he did not fully comprehend, Hrolf inquired curiously, "What is your father's name, Celiese, perhaps I know him."

"He is long dead, sir, and I'm certain you would not recognize his name. Now, shall we begin? Your other guests look most impatient."

Distracted by the warmth of her smile, Hrolf signaled to one of his men to bring the bird he'd selected for Mylan. "The glove will be too large, I know, but you need only see if you can bear the weight of the hawk upon your wrist."

"Yes, I understand the secret is a steady hand." Celiese and Mylan dismounted quickly and handed their reins to a waiting groom. She then pulled on the thickly padded gauntlet and extended her left arm to invite the hawk to come to her. Another peregrine falcon, she was also a beauty, her breast a soft beige tinged with pink, her back and wings brown with black markings. Celiese held the jesses, the two strips of leather tied to the bird's legs so she might be carried more easily, but unfastened the leash to be ready to send the bird aloft. Small silver bells had been attached to the bird's legs so she could be found were she to become lost. When Celiese turned into the morning breeze so the bird would be most comfortable while being carried, they rang with a pleasant sound, making music with every step.

Smiling happily, Celiese waited for Mylan to step to her right side. "You see, I do know how to do this, but I know enough also to let the duke send his falcon up for the first kill."

Mylan nodded slightly, impressed that she had stopped to consider the man's feelings when to disregard them would have been disastrous. Hrolf's falcon took a pheasant out of the sky with all the grace and agility that made falconry so favored a sport. Then, at his signal, Celiese slipped the leather hood from off her bird's head and sent her up soaring far above them. Well trained, she took another pheasant with astonishing speed and returned to land upon Celiese's outstretched arm. Knowing she had proved her ability, Celiese passed the beautiful bird back to the waiting falconer but stayed with Mylan and the other men for the rest of the hunt.

"The hour grows late, but this was the best of days. I insist you return with me to my home so you may both join me this evening." Hrolf smiled widely, charmed by the handsome young couple's grace and quiet manner.

"Thank you, sir, but I would prefer to return to my husband's ship where I might dress more appropriately for the evening." Celiese could not look at the Duke without imagining his clothing splattered with the blood of his innocent victims, but she managed to sound genuinely pleased by his invitation.

"We have clothing in all sizes for our guests; you will lack for nothing. Now come with us." While Hrolf's voice was still pleasant, his command was not to be ignored.

"It will be our pleasure," Mylan responded through clenched teeth. What Celiese's purpose had been he could not imagine, but clearly she had captivated the arrogant man with an attitude he could only describe as nonchalant. She had turned all the duke's compliments aside coldly, apparently too absorbed in the excitement of the hunt to notice his growing admiration. He held his temper until they were shown to a suite of rooms in their host's mansion, where he questioned her angrily.

"Falcons, Celiese? Is there no end to the lengths you will go to accept a dare?"

Celiese walked slowly around the well-appointed room, admiring the elegant furnishings and wondering from where they had come. "Was that a dare? I'd say Hrolf wanted to take advantage of what he imagined would be my inexperience, and I simply turned his trick aside. Had I no skill with hawks, I would not have accepted his invitation to hunt, but merely watched you, as the other ladies did."

Astonished by her reasoning, Mylan asked incredulously, "Why would he wish to see you hurt?"

"Perhaps he is the one who is jealous; he seems very taken with *you*."

Mylan sank down into the closest chair, completely dismayed by her observation. "He is no different from any other man, Celiese. He likes male companions with whom to exchange stories, but he has no need to be jealous of our wives!"

"I was mistaken then." She'd confused Mylan, so he did not criticize her further. After they had bathed she found none of the many lavishly trimmed gowns in the wardrobe attractive. Since they were all doubtlessly stolen, as was everything else under the duke's roof, she was loath to wear one.

Mylan, on the other hand, could not decide which garment was supposed to be put on first and called to her to assist him. "All these were laid out—I am to wear them in layers?"

Laughing at his confusion, Celiese helped him to dress. "The *chainse* is worn first; see it is lightweight, the sleeves are close-fitted and extend to the wrist. The *bliaud* is a heavier fabric, worn like a tunic over it, the sleeves are three-quarter length and full so you will not get the two garments confused. *Braies* are just like your trousers, *chausses* are made to fit your legs and you wrap the garters around your legs to make them fit more snugly. That is not so different from the way you wrap the laces on your boots."

Following her directions, Mylan managed to dress in a reasonable facsimile of a French gentleman, but he was unused to wearing such bright colors as he'd been given and felt uncomfortable. "I am far happier in my own clothing, Celiese, but since the other men here have chosen to dress as the Frenchmen do I will not argue with

412

their taste." When her expression grew solemn he looked down at his borrowed garb. "Is something wrong?"

"No, you look very handsome, but you are still obviously a Dane in some Frenchman's clothes. That is not a masquerade of which I approve."

"You misunderstand Hrolf, he plans to be a Frenchman now, truly he does. That he lends his guests French attire is understandable. Now what have you chosen to wear over that lace-trimmed chemise?"

"You must select something, for I cannot." Turning away, Celiese left the matter up to him, and he quickly handed her a gown of deep emerald green, the neckline and sleeves banded with wide silk embroidery.

"This will match your eyes, but let us hurry, we have kept the others waiting too long as it is." He kissed her nape sweetly as he helped her smooth the gown over her glossy curls. "There, let us go."

Celiese hesitated to give him her hand when she was so worried as to how the evening would end. "Please do not drink so much tonight, Mylan, we will never succeed in our purpose if we do not keep our wits about us."

His gaze darkening, Mylan shook his head. "I can take care of myself, Celiese, despite your worries. Cease your nagging and let us join in the fun." He swept her along beside him to the hall, where the merriment had already begun. Hrolf made room for them at his side, but although he made numerous toasts Celiese drank no more than a drop of the wine that flowed so generously. Gisela had not been present for the hunt, nor did she appear that night, and Celiese wondered if her husband's amusements did not appeal to her, either. When the hour

413

grew late and the conversation turned to boisterous singing she could bear no more, and slipping away from Mylan's side unnoticed she made her way through the imposing home. Thinking that if Hrolf had become a Christian the chapel of the house would be in use, she wandered along the front hall until she came upon the candlelit room. The fragrance of incense was sweet, but she felt a strange detachment, the same inexplicable feeling of uneasiness she'd experienced since they'd arrived upon French soil. Once the prayers had come to her lips without effort, but now she could remember only random verses, none complete, and after sitting quietly by herself for a while she was overcome with sadness for the lost world of her childhood, and she made her way slowly to the room she and Mylan had been given. She undressed in the darkness and climbed into the comfortable bed without bothering to wait for Mylan to appear. When he did finally return to their room he decided not to awaken her, since it would only cause another bitter argument. His head ached badly, but he knew he was not half as drunk as Hrolf had been, and laughing at the absurdity of that comparison he tossed his borrowed clothing aside and fell into bed beside his lovely bride.

After nearly a week filled with daily rides to enjoy the sights of the countryside, or hunting parties that netted generous amounts of game, followed by long nights of boisterous merrymaking, Celiese had had more than enough of Hrolf's hospitality, while Mylan had become the duke's closest confidant. He was obviously enjoying the easy life Hrolf provided in exchange for his company, but she was disgusted and was ready to leave.

Irritated that Mylan had apparently forgotten the real purpose of their visit, she drew him aside when he returned from yet another day in the duke's company. The men had gone hunting for wild boar, but considering the beast too vicious to risk inviting ladies along to watch, they had left them behind in the city. The garden of the duke's mansion was well tended, but the pleasant surroundings were in sharp contrast to Celiese's dark mood. "We are no closer to our goal than the day we arrived, Mylan. You may enjoy the leisure that Hrolf provides, but I do not. Winter will soon be here and I cannot bear the thought of spending it under the villain's roof!"

Mylan sighed sadly, sorry she had misunderstood his motives. "We have had little time to walk, and none to make love as we used to, and I am as dissatisfied as you are, but we will gain nothing until we have Hrolf's full confidence. You have waited years for this opportunity to come home, and a week is not long to invest in your future." Drawing her near, he tried to end her criticism with a sweet kiss, but she shoved him away rudely.

"Stop it! A few kisses will not still my complaints! I want to go home now, to rebuild my house where I can finally live in peace! Can't you understand how desperately I want to go home? I despise this place and everyone in it!"

As Mylan glanced up he saw Hrolf observing their argument from a balcony overhead, but how much the man had heard he could only guess. He tried to smile as though the mysteries of love were beyond him, but the duke strode down the stairs and crossed the path to join them, his expression showing he was clearly not amused.

"What is all this? Mylan is content as my guest, but it seems you most certainly are not. Why have we failed to make you happy as well?" He planted his feet firmly upon the path, daring Celiese to try and avoid his question by flight.

Tossing her curls as she turned to face him, Celiese spoke the truth she could no longer conceal. "Although I am here with Mylan, I am French by birth. My estate, the home of the d'Loganvilles for generations, is now under your control. I came here to ask you to return it to me, since I am the rightful owner and you are not!"

Stunned by the willful young woman's hostile demand, Hrolf folded his arms across his expansive chest and stared down at her coldly. "Just where might this estate be?"

"Between the Seine and the sea, south of Yvetot and east of Rouen. The house lies in ruins, and the uncultivated fields are of no use to you, but it is my home and I want to return it to the prosperity it knew before France was overrun with Danish vermin!"

The back of Hrolf's hand smacked Celiese's jaw with the speed and force of lightning, knocking her to the path, where she lay barely conscious until he'd summoned two men to carry her away. Through the bright haze of pain that blurred her vision she saw Mylan still standing by the Duke's side. He'd not come to her aid, nor spoken one word in her defense, and she could readily tell by his murderous glance that he had made his choice and never would.

Chapter Twenty-Two

Celiese heard the men talking but lay perfectly still, sprawled in an uncomfortable heap where they'd tossed her, hoping they would think her unconscious. The room was small, unlike the one she and Mylan had been sharing, and the echo of their deep voices reverberated around her with a hollow ring. They were whispering excitedly, but she understood all that they said.

"He had dozens of men out searching the countryside for this woman, and all the while she was within his own walls!"

"Women! Who can understand them, but she'll gather no resistance around her now. She is as good as dead, but perhaps before—" The man jabbed his friend in the ribs as he winked knowingly.

"You'll not have this wench, Jaret, so cease your daydreaming. Have you not seen how her husband watches her every move?"

"Aye, that I have, but how is it possible a Dane has such a wife as this? Did he not understand who she was and the trouble she would cause before he brought her here?"

Shrugging, since the matter troubled him little, the heavier of the two men moved toward the door. "All wives bring trouble, this French one simply more than most."

Still reticent to leave, Jaret bent down to stroke Celiese's tangled curls with a fond touch. "She is a rare beauty, it is a shame we cannot stay with her a while longer."

"Your appetites are insatiable in all things. A few minutes would soon turn to an hour! Leave the woman before we find ourselves in as much trouble as she is!"

With a slow, shuffling step, Jaret left with his companion. Then, after locking the heavy oak door, they returned to Hrolf to report that the elusive Lady d'Loganville would trouble him no more that day.

Attempting to rise, Celiese slipped back to the rough wooden floor, too dizzy to do more than try and focus her eyes for the moment. Hrolf had hit her such a forceful blow that she was grateful her neck had not snapped, but finally having the opportunity to speak her mind as she'd longed to do since the moment of their arrival had been worth the pain. He was no more than a rat, living upon the garbage heap of a once proud people, and she'd never think otherwise. She despised him and all he stood for. Then, recalling his men's words, she wondered how he had been alerted to her presence in France and why he'd sent men to ascertain her whereabouts. One woman hardly constituted a threat of such proportions as to merit a search. Of what had he been so afraid? Did he honestly think she could assemble enough half-starved peasants to storm his stronghold at Rouen? She would have laughed had she not been in so much pain, but as she blacked out again Mylan's hate-filled stare flooded her dreams with a terror far worse than any Hrolf could imagine or inflict.

The small tower room had only one high, narrow window, which faced the north. The reflected sunlight cast long shadows across the floor only at noon, the rest of the day an eerie twilight veiled the room in semidarkness. A small cot sat against the southern wall, the straw-filled mattress none too clean, but Celiese managed to crawl upon it when she awakened. Uncertain as to the day, let alone the hour, she lay quietly trying to imagine what fate Hrolf might be planning for her. Prisoners had been kept locked away in towers for years, so the fact the man had not slit her throat instantly proved nothing. Perhaps he might seek to trade her for further concessions from King Charles; that was a possibility whose details might take many a month, if not years, to arrange. In the week she'd spent in Hrolf's house, she'd not once seen Gisela and had not dared ask where she might be, but it was not presumptuous to think the princess might intercede in her behalf. In truth they had much in common, and she hoped the young woman would be inclined to help her. A ransom was also a possibility, it was a popular Viking tactic, but who other than the king would be inclined, or able, to pay one for her?

Unable to foresee what the future would hold, Celiese sat up slowly, being careful not to bring back the intense pain to her head by too sudden a move. From her place on the edge of the cot she could see the whole room: There was a small table, one low stool, a pail in the far corner, but nothing else. Hardly fit quarters for a woman, even one being held prisoner, and she wondered how long she'd have to endure the discomforts of such humble surroundings. Using her right thumbnail she made a light scratch beside the bed, marking the wall for day one as she wondered how she was expected to survive with neither food nor water. She had no idea how many days a person could exist with neither and had no desire to find out from experience. When Raktor had first taken her from her home she'd gone hungry many a night, spent days with a thirst so great she could think of nothing but the cool, refreshing trickle of the stream upon the rocks near her home, but even in those dire times she'd known food and drink would not be withheld indefinitely. Now, she was not at all certain Hrolf hadn't decided just to let her starve. He might do it, he was ruthless enough; but if she had to avenge the wrongs he'd done her countrymen as a ghost, then her spirit would haunt him till the last of his days. Determined to outlast the villain regardless of what cruelty he'd chosen to inflict, Celiese lay down again and went back to sleep, deciding she would need all the rest she could get to give her strength to face whatever lay ahead.

Marcela carried the tray through the door and placed it upon the table, but rather than leaving immediately as she'd been told to do she went to the cot and after a moment's hesitation reached out to touch Celiese's shoulder. "Madame, please awaken. I have brought your supper and it will grow cold."

Celiese sat up slowly, then smiled as she recognized the

petite maid as one who'd frequently been assigned to her quarters. There was no harm in responding to her in French now, and she did so. "*Merci*, thank you. Do you know how long I have been here? I have lost all track of the time."

Marcela looked toward the door and seeing they were not being observed by the guard spoke rapidly. "Since yesterday. I am to bring your supper each evening beginning today. I know nothing more, my lady."

"I am grateful for the food as well as for your company. What is your name?" Celiese smiled warmly, delighted to see a friendly face.

"Marcela, but all here now know who you really are, Lady d'Loganville, and there is talk of little else among us."

Certain she had failed in the purpose that had brought her to Rouen, Celiese shook her head sadly. "I have no wish to be an object of gossip, but is there no word of how long I am to be kept here?"

"I have said too much!" Marcela hurried to the door, but stopped to whisper farewell. "Until tomorrow, dear lady, until then do not despair, for we will see you do not suffer!"

The young woman was gone before Celiese could respond. Was there some plan afoot among the servants to see she came to no harm? What had Marcela meant by suffering? Merely the pain of hunger and thirst, or something far worse? Rather than being reassured, the maid's vow terrified her. She had no appetite whatsoever now, but knew she'd be foolish not to eat something now her supper had arrived. Pulling the stool up to the table, she sat down and removed the cover from the meal. She'd been given roast pork in a succulent gravy, boiled peas, a slice of freshly baked bread with butter, a wedge of cheese, and a glossy red apple. There was a carafe of wine, a napkin, a cup and spoon, but no knife to cut the pork into bite-sized pieces. Since that was more food than she could possibly eat, she wrapped the apple and cheese in the linen napkin and set them aside for the morning, then ate what she wanted of the rest. She had never been fond of wine and knowing its effect she took only a sip and decided to ask Marcela when next she saw her to bring water instead. A candle would be useful too, as the chamber was so poorly illuminated by the sun. Perhaps if she were to be held in that wretched room for some time, they would bring all her belongings, and other personal items. Hrolf would never grant her request if she asked for everything at once, but perhaps Marcela could remove the things she needed one at a time from their room. From Mylan's room, she corrected herself angrily. He was the sole occupant of that elegant chamber now. Too restless to remain seated, Celiese got up and began to pace the narrow space between the cot and the table. When the sun set she could make out nothing of her grim surroundings, but she continued to pace with slow, even steps while she let her mind wander to far happier times.

When she was a child the walls of her room had been decorated with bright tapestries, and a thick carpet whose intricate design depicted a hunter chasing a stag through the forest had covered the floor. She had walked around the edges of that fanciful scene knowing the stag would always escape the hunter's arrow. The man had been a handsome fellow, his mount a spirited while stallion, but the forest belonged to the deer, and he'd used speed as well as cunning to elude his pursuers. Sinking down upon the lumpy cot, Celiese attempted to devise some clever plan to survive the duke's wrath, but she could not even think of Hrolf as a duke, for that title implied all the virtues of nobility, and from what she'd observed those were attributes he lacked. A deer was at home in the forest, and she was at home in France. She'd been an idiot to confront Hrolf as she had when an oblique approach would have been far more effective. Depressed by her own foolishness, she lay down upon the cot and tried to sleep so her mind would be clear at dawn.

The hours of the next day passed slowly with nothing but the wretchedness of her situation to occupy her mind, but Celiese knew that was precisely why she was being confined: to break her spirit and subdue all her resistance to Hrolf's will. Determined that he would die an old man before she gave him the satisfaction of shedding one tear over her predicament, she paced her cell with a long, easy stride, waiting for Marcela to again appear so that she might question her more fully.

Unfortunately, when the door swung open that evening it was not the pretty Frenchwoman who brought in the supper tray but a burly Dane. Celiese backed away, putting as much space between herself and the tall, grinning man as possible.

Eyeing the remains of her supper from the previous night, the brute laughed heartily, "I did not think the duke's commands were taken so lightly, but you are to have bread and water now that I am bringing your meals, nothing more." Placing the tray he'd brought upon the table, he picked up the other one and turned toward the door.

"What else do you know about the details of my confinement? Am I expected to merely die of boredom in here?" Celiese asked defiantly.

"If it is amusement you want, I will have to return later," the man teased her as his glance hungrily swept the curves of her shapely figure.

"Do not bother!" Celiese replied instantly, having no wish to encourage his attentions. Laughing again, he slammed the door shut and locked it, but she had not felt nearly as brave as she'd sounded. She'd recognized his voice as that of one of the men who'd brought her there, obviously the more amorous of the two, and that thought sickened her thoroughly. She'd been a fool not to hide the spoon Marcela had brought with her supper. She could have sharpened the edges against the stone walls of her cell and made a passable weapon, but since no utensils were required to eat bread she'd been given none that night. The small loaf was fresh, the crust crisp, the inside soft and tasty; perhaps the friendly guard did not know the bread given to prisoners was supposed to be stale, but she'd not offer instructions for her treatment if he'd been given none. Not wanting his or any other guard's company, she struggled to move the cot across the door. It would not serve as much of a barricade, but at least the room could not be entered while she slept. The door would slam into the wooden frame of the cot and jostle her awake, and then she'd have the advantage of being alert should she have an unexpected and unwanted visitor. She'd saved half the cheese from breakfast and ate that with some of the little loaf. The water was fresh and cool, readily quenching her thirst, and after dining upon what little she'd been served she made another line upon the wall to mark her second whole day in the small chamber. When the room was completely dark she lay down and went to sleep, hoping to break the monotony of the dreary hours with the sweet peace of dreams, but they were as wild as the night before, for asleep she could not suppress Mylan's taunting sneer from her mind. His presence pervaded her thoughts with the most sensuous of memories, filling her heart with an anguish too great to bear without the relief of tears.

In the morning, Celiese replaced the cot against the southern wall. Moving the table, she stood upon it but still could not reach the narrow window. Since neither the table nor the stool were sturdy, she decided against stacking them together but tossed some crumbs of bread upon the sill, hoping a bird would come to eat them. She would welcome any company except that of a Dane, for other than pacing restlessly or lying down to nap she could think of nothing to fill her time. Active by nature, she found the enforced leisure in itself torture, but she told herself to count the fact she was being left alone a blessing while it lasted.

Jaret was back at dusk. Hoping to win a smile if not much more from the defiant beauty in his care, he'd stuffed his pockets with apples and nuts, which he placed upon her tray beside the bread and water he'd brought. "The duke is generous with his men; I do not mind sharing my rations with you."

Although she was surprised by his kindness, Celiese had no intention of sharing anything with him. "If there is something you expect in return, then take it all back to the kitchen." She stood on the opposite side of the table, ready to hurl the stool at his head should he move toward her.

Giving an unconcerned shrug, Jaret picked up the largest of the apples and took a bite. The fruit was crisp and juicy and he wiped his chin as he savored its marvelous taste. "It is a pity you have no manners, but perhaps by tomorrow you'll be more agreeable, or next week, or next year. I am a patient man."

"Get out of here!" Celiese whispered a command in so threatening a manner that the burly man had left the room and locked the door securely before he realized she had no means to enforce her words.

After making another line upon the wall, Celiese sat down and ate some of the nuts and an apple with bites so tiny she made the meager meal last a long while. In the morning she'd eat the bread as slowly, and that would provide the only excitement to which she could look forward. She stretched out upon the cot, but sleep, no matter how troubled, would not come, and she lay wide awake, finally letting her thoughts focus upon Mylan. He was undoubtedly getting quite drunk with Hrolf at that very minute, having completely forgotten her and the dire predicament in which she found herself. "Snake!" she cried out bitterly, for had he been the one to be locked away in a forgotten tower she would have done all she could to set him free within the hour. He had not lifted a hand to help her when she'd been struck so

426

brutally and carried from tne garden. He had not even spoken in her behalf. No, he had simply severed what tenuous ties there had been between them and had chosen to serve Hrolf rather than save her.

As her depression deepened she recalled their first meeting with a rush of emotion that brought a flood of bitter tears to her eyes. She'd thought Mylan so attractive, his golden gaze haunting, his touch as well as his kiss enchanting. His heart had been open to her then, his hopes unhidden, and yet the love that had flared so brightly between them that first night had left only smoldering embers of hatred by the time dawn had lit the sky. Mylan would be glad to see her banished from his life forever, for the marriage she'd longed to share had existed only in the beauty of her dreams and never in the stark reality of his perceptions.

Olgrethe was the lucky one, Celiese thought with a faint smile, she'd found the best of husbands in Andrick, not due to well-laid plan but purely as the unexpected result of her father's treachery. The afternoons she'd spent with the pampered young woman making plans for the future seemed years in the past now. They'd been so foolish, thinking the choice of mates was theirs to make, when fate held the course of their lives forever hidden from their view. Her fingertips closed around Thor's silver hammer and she recalled that Mylan had asked her to return his charm, but she had refused. The silver necklace was a symbol of all her dashed hopes, and he'd have to remove it from her body to ever take it back. Hurt, confused, desperately lonely, she lay still knowing she had fallen in love with Mylan with a childlike faith that her kindness would be appreciated, that her affection would be returned, but the only happiness they'd found had been in the passion they'd enjoyed to the fullest. But while she had sought love in his embrace, he'd longed only for the pleasure he could have found with any woman. From the moment they'd met he had been her husband, while she had never truly been his wife.

Growing increasingly more desolate as the hours passed, Celiese began to envy the haven from the trials of the world her mother had found. Perhaps the love of God was the only true affection and she'd been far too hasty in leaving the convent of Saint Valery with so much of her life in confusion. The once bright hope of regaining her estate was no more than a faint glimmer now, while the rapture of Mylan's embrace was a joy forever lost. Perhaps she would live no longer than the seventeen years she'd managed to survive in the world. That was a feat of some kind, she supposed, but her existence seemed pointless now, totally without reason or reward.

When Jaret entered the dimly lit chamber to bring Celiese her meal the next evening he found her sitting upon the cot as though in a trance, her gaze blank, her posture rigid. Suspecting some sort of trick, he placed her meager meal upon the table and waited for her to speak, but when she didn't he moved close. "There is talk in Rouen of little but your plight, Lady d'Loganville. I expected more than this complacent mood from a woman of your breeding. Have you no more courage than the rest of your countrymen whose faint hearts we've stilled with our swords?"

Celiese looked up at the stocky guard, barely aware of

his insult. As her lips curled into a vicious smile, her green eyes glowed with so menacing a light that he backed away, certain she'd gone mad. Not wanting to incite a hysteria he might be unable to contain, he dashed through the still open door and after locking it hastily fled for the security of the guard room. Knowing he'd been a fool to taunt her, Jaret vowed to follow his orders to the letter and not make any attempt to speak with the lovely young woman ever again.

After that slight interruption disturbed her thoughts, time ceased to exist for Celiese. She saw neither the changing pattern of sunlight moving across the bare wooden floor nor the trays of food that appeared upon the table each evening. She had wrapped herself in the cloak of numbness that dulled all pain, as she had done years before to escape Raktor's brutality. She was alive only in her mind, preferring to relive the time she'd spent alone with Mylan on his farm. During the days they'd found the challenge of the hunt exciting, for the game had always been plentiful and the nights had been filled with love's most blissful expression, regardless of Mylan's insisting that she was his slave and no more. Those memories brought a peace that soothed her ravaged heart as the troubled contemplation of her future never had. Her thoughts took on an absorbing rhythm, and she ceased to struggle against the bitter reality fate had presented and floated instead upon a bright cloud of remembered love. That brief happiness was all consuming, burning away the need for anything more.

At the week's end, Marcela scurried through the door

ahead of Jaret. She rushed to Celiese and knelt by her side. "My lady, come, it is time. You must come with me now." Patting her hands, she found the pretty woman as cold as death, and seeing the uneaten food upon the table she turned to look up at the powerfully built guard. "Fool! The master wants this woman alive, not dead from the chill of this room or starvation! How long would you have continued to bring meals she did not eat before you had summoned someone with more sense than you possess!"

Understanding few of the Frenchwoman's words, Jaret nonetheless found her critical tone and fierce expression easy to comprehend. It was plain his prisoner had suffered far more from her confinement than had been intended, but she had brought her troubles upon herself and he had no sympathy for her now.

Marcela persisted in her efforts to awaken Celiese, and at last she opened her eyes and regarded her two visitors with a curious glance. Yawning sleepily, she apologized, "I'm sorry, I must have dozed off, is it time for supper?"

"You have missed several, dear lady, but it is near dawn and we must hurry, as the duke will not be kept waiting," Marcela warned sternly. She was overjoyed to find Celiese coherent at last, but they still had much to accomplish and little time.

When Celiese got unsteadily to her feet it was obvious she'd never be able to manage the stairs, and Jaret scooped her up into his arms, then nodded for the troublesome maid to precede them. "If she cannot walk I will carry her. Let us be gone."

Startled to find herself in the obnoxious guard's arms, Celiese had no choice but to lift her arms to encircle his

430

neck. For all his strength, his touch was surprisingly light, but she was too tense to relax in his arms. The hallway was long and dark, followed by a narrow flight of stairs that led to still another gloomy passageway before they entered the corridor she recognized as the one where the room she'd shared with Mylan was located. He did not take her there, however, but to the room at the far end of the hall.

Once inside the opulently decorated bedchamber, Marcela gestured toward the bed while she poured a generous amount of wine into a silver goblet. "Please place her carefully upon the bed, and I will do my best to help her." Once she was certain Celiese was comfortably seated, she lifted the wine to her lips. "Drink this, it will restore your strength."

Celiese thought Marcela's concern sincere but misplaced, and she took only a small sip of the rich red wine. "What is the cause for this sudden attention? Hrolf has kept me waiting for so long, why should I hurry to please him?"

Marcela set the goblet aside and gripped both of Celiese's hands tightly. "You must not even think such a thing! There is no time for even the smallest delay!"

Celiese looked closely at the little woman, alarmed by the urgency in her voice. "Did Hrolf tell you why he wishes to see me at so early an hour?"

"His reason is unimportant, he is the duke and his order must be obeyed!" As if to emphasize her point, Marcela pulled Celiese off the high bed and pushed her toward a tub of steaming water. "I will help you bathe and dress, but there is no time to waste in conversation!"

Looking over her shoulder at Jaret, Celiese refused to move. "You must wait outside, as I've no wish to bathe in front of you." The very idea disgusted her, and her expression clearly showed her mood.

"I do not trust either of you out of my sight. I will stand right here while you bathe, so be quick about it," Jaret replied forcefully.

Realizing she was too weak and dizzy to argue any further, Celiese turned her back on the guard and slipped off her rumpled clothes, too grateful for the opportunity to bathe to create a scene over his presence. She stepped into the tub and sank down into the warm water, lathering the bar of perfumed soap Marcela had provided. The bubbles were so soothing that she washed her hair twice before the diminutive maid brought a towel and insisted she climb out of the water immediately.

"I have your clothing laid out, the most beautiful gown ever fashioned, but you must put it on quickly, as we are late as it is."

As Celiese patted herself dry she noticed that the Danish guard had gone to the door where he was speaking in hoarse whispers to another man who was apparently stationed in the hall. Hrolf certainly had her well guarded—but why, was an escape attempt expected? She whispered to Marcela in French in a voice too low to be overheard, "What is the truth, where am I being taken?"

As she helped Celiese don a lace-trimmed chemise of the softest silk, then an exquisitely embroidered brocade gown, Marcela responded softly, "The priest is waiting for you in the chapel. Then you are to be taken to the duke before the light of dawn fills the skies; those were his orders to me, and I know of no others."

"The priest?" In her first week in Hrolf's home she had not even met the man, and she could not imagine why he wished to see her now. Had he had some interest in her, why had he not come to the cell where she had been held to speak with her or to pray? "I do not understand why the priest wishes to see me." Celiese fluffed out her damp curls with her fingertips, then stepped into the velvet slippers Marcela had placed at her feet.

"To hear your confession, I suppose." Proud she had accomplished what had seemed the impossible, Marcel stood back to admire the beautifully groomed young woman.

Celiese gasped sharply, stunned that the smiling maid seemed to have no idea what she was saying. Prisoners were executed at dawn, and surely that was what her fate was to be after she'd been extended the courtesy of making her peace with God. She was being prepared for only one thing, for the most gruesome of deaths, but it was not a prospect to which she would submit meekly. "The priest is a Frenchman, is he not?"

"Of course, a most sympathetic man he is, too. Father Bernard is his name," Marcela explained calmly.

Although she could scarcely think for the violent pounding of her heart, Celiese hoped only that the good priest had a back door to his chapel, or would offer sanctuary so she could escape the hangman's noose or the executioner's blade that she was certain Hrolf would swing himself. Sitting down upon the edge of the bed, she removed her right slipper, as if it were ill-fitting, in hopes of gaining a moment or two more to devise some plan.

Clearly Marcela had no idea of what was to happen, but as she glanced around the pretty bedroom she saw no way to escape the guard, for other than the door to the hall at which he stood, there was no exit.

Thinking she had perhaps brought the wrong pair, Marcela knelt down to help Celiese with her slippers. "These seem to be perfect for you; Gisela has many but these were new and she said you might have them."

"Is this room near hers? If so, I would like to speak to her, to thank her for her generosity." Celiese smiled warmly, as if she were making only a small request. She had no idea what sort of relationship the princess had with her Danish husband, but she prayed it was a good one. If Gisela would take her side, then surely Hrolf would not execute her without further thought. Perhaps she would pay a ransom herself rather than let her countrywoman be put to death so unjustly.

Puzzled, Marcela shook her head. "No, Gisela's room is in the other wing, but I am certain you will see her later; when you speak with the duke she will probably be there. Now come, we must hurry." Taking Celiese's elbow, she helped her from the bed and escorted her to the door.

Jaret tried to appear bored, but he'd found the lovely young woman's slender body too erotic a sight to be ignored. Now he could hardly recall what his orders had been, but with a forced calm he took her arm and led her down the flight of stairs that were closest to the chapel. There was no sign of the priest, but he escorted his prisoner to the front pew and thinking she would like to be alone with her prayers went back to the door to stand guard.

Celiese clenched her fists tightly in her lap, trying only not to scream hysterically, but if the priest did not arrive in the next few seconds she knew she would lose the thin grip she still had upon her composure. Just as a shriek formed in her throat, the brown-robed priest slid into the pew beside her. His features were hidden by the shadows cast by his hood, but she cared little what his appearance might be as she begged him to help her. "Father Bernard, I have been told you are a good man, and I trust you are a fair one as well." Giving him no opportunity to respond, she continued in a frantic whisper. The guard did not seem to understand French, but she wanted to take no chances on his overhearing her remarks. "Perhaps you have heard my name, I am Lady Celiese d' Loganville and I was raised on an estate not far from this city. When the Danes overran our home my father was murdered and I was taken prisoner and spent more than five years in the home of a villain every bit as despicable as the man who now calls himself Robert and resides here as the duke." She hesitated no more than a moment, then plunged on with her tale, revealing the love she'd felt for Mylan from the moment they met. Swiftly she recounted their adventures, ending with the voyage that had brought her again to the shores of France. "I was a fool to challenge Hrolf so openly, I know that now, but my home means everything to me. He means to kill me in only a few moments' time, I am certain he does, but is there not some way you can help me to escape him? If only you will help me leave this accursed house, I can make my way out of Rouen and go to Yvetot where I can join my mother at the convent of Saint Valery. I will stay there forever if I must, but I will not die like this, not when all I wished to accomplish is still left undone. Please say you will help me, for you are my only hope.''

As she reached out to take his hands, the man moved toward her, his hood slipping back upon his shoulders as he turned. She saw only the bright gleam of the candles' glow upon his golden curls and the menacing shine of his amber gaze, and she knew Mylan had betrayed her trust again, and this time most cruelly. All hope of saving herself gone, she could not catch her breath, and with a small strangled sigh she fainted in a languid heap, falling into his outstretched arms.

Chapter Twenty-Three

Having no idea what Celiese's long frantic speech was even about, Mylan was completely bewildered when she collapsed in his arms. He sat for a moment, simply holding her tenderly in his embrace while he tried to decide what was the most logical course of action. Realizing he could accomplish nothing until he revived her, he promptly turned his attention to that task first. When gentle coaxing had no effect he picked her up in his arms, carried her back to the sacristy, and laid her upon the priest's small red velvet couch. He lit two more candles from the small one that had been burning upon the chest containing the vestments, then stood looking down at the unconscious beauty with a bemused stare. It had been a week since he'd seen her, the longest seven days of his life, and as his perceptive gaze swept her delicate features he was surprised by the change in her appearance. She had been slender, but now she was thin, her high cheekbones clearly evident beneath her translucent skin. Her long, thick lashes seemed too heavy for her fragile eyelids to support, and he knelt down to brush her pale lips with a light kiss, hoping she would awaken and be pleased to see him this time, but she did not stir, and he knew he would have to find a more effective method.

After a brief search, Mylan found a flagon of wine he was certain had not been blessed for use in the Mass that was soon to be said, and he poured a small amount into a cup for Celiese. Kneeling by her side, he propped her head upon his arm, brought the stimulating drink to her lips, and forced her to take several sips. "There, now open your eyes, you have nothing to fear from me." Rising to his feet again, he placed the cup upon the chest, pulled the monk's robe off over his head, and replaced it upon the peg where it belonged.

Celiese opened her eyes slowly, uncertain what to expect from Mylan now. He was dressed in the most splendid of apparel, looking very much like the favorite of the duke that he clearly was. His *bliaud*, or tunic, was a deep blue wool with embroidered borders of silver silk at the neck, sleeves, and hem, girded by a jeweled belt. He wore dark blue *chausses*, gartered with silken ribbons woven of the same precious thread that decorated his tunic. His black leather boots were new, as well. The fit of his clothing was superb, it had obviously been tailored for his sleek build rather than being merely borrowed. It was only his blond hair and light eyes that made him look less than the French nobleman he appeared to be at first glance.

She found her tongue at last. "I suppose I should be flattered that you have bothered to dress in so handsome a fashion, but perhaps it is not simply for my benefit that you have done so."

Confused by her remark, since it seemed to hold more of an insult than a compliment, Mylan pushed her feet to one side and sat down beside her. "I did not mean to startle you so badly by wearing Father Bernard's cloak, but it afforded me an opportunity to speak with you before you see Robert, and I did not want you to go to him without being warned of what he will ask. I am certain you understand why I do not trust you to give him a reasonable answer on your own."

Sitting up so she might face him squarely, Celiese allowed herself to take a cautious breath before she dared hope the answer to her question might make a difference in her fate. "He means to kill me at dawn, doesn't he?" she whispered softly, terrified that the duke had such a ghastly plan.

Mylan frowned, surprised by her question, and yet he would not lie to save her from a prospect that clearly already had her badly frightened. "This has been a very long week, Celiese, and a most tiring one, but you are safe for the moment, and this day will not be your last unless you behave as foolishly as you did when last you saw the duke."

Her cheeks burning with embarrassment, Celiese responded bitterly, "At least I have never turned my back on my friends!" Friend was too soft a word, she knew, but she'd not call him lover, for it implied too little, nor could she say husband, for that term implied far too much. There was no word to describe their relationship, but she knew when she had needed his help most desperately he had failed her in every way possible.

Disgusted by her anger when he considered it

completely misplaced, Mylan began to swear, then caught himself. "Is that what you think I did, turned my back on you? You are an even greater fool than I thought then, for the only reason you are alive today is because of me!" Rising to his feet, he began to pace the small room with the seething power of a caged beast. His steps were even now; after much practice he no longer had to make a conscious effort to walk without limping and his stride was graceful and sure. Unable to contain his fiery temper any longer, he released it in a torrent of frustration. "I obviously wasted my time, too! You have so little sense I should simply make you take the punishment you deserve!"

He was tempted just to walk out on her, simply to leave her on her own to face whatever Hrolf's whims might be, but when he turned to give her a murderous glance her expression was so innocent, so devoid of guile that he was suddenly ashamed of himself for being so cross with her. She had provoked his anger with her insult, but knowing now that she had misunderstood his motives so completely he sat down again by her feet and attempted to explain his actions in so calm a tone she could not fail to comprehend what his true feelings had been. "I was more shocked than Hrolf, than Robert." He corrected himself quickly, trying to remember to use the man's Christian name. "I was appalled by the outrageous manner in which you chose to insult Robert when I had warned you repeatedly that we had to behave with the utmost discretion, but you just blurted out your grievances as if he would be powerless to retaliate."

Lifting her chin, Celiese returned Mylan's accusing

stare with a steady glance. "I know that was lunacy, but we seemed to be making no progress whatsoever in our true reason for coming here, and I had had more than enough of that hateful man's company!"

Taken aback by that burst of unexpected anger, Mylan asked softly, "And my company as well?"

For a moment Celiese could not find her voice to respond; a painful knot filled her throat and she had a difficult time forcing it away. "I have had very little of your company since we came here, Mylan, for you seemed to prefer Hrolf's to mine."

Mylan sighed sadly, beginning to feel his cause was truly hopeless. "Well, as usual, you were wrong!" Exasperated that she did not seem to see the justification for the most obvious of his actions, he had to force himself to continue. "What choice did I have when Robert struck you? Had I jumped him at least ten of his men would have come running to join the fight, and I'd have been thrown in the cell next to yours, and neither of us would have had anyone to help us regain our freedom. At least that is what would have happened if I'd been lucky enough to survive what would surely have been a most brutal beating if not a ready sword thrust through my back. If you think I wanted to see you lying in the dirt or dragged off to the tower you are mistaken, but I have to consider my actions fully before I take them, since you continually fail to see the consequences of yours until it is too late to undo them!"

When Celiese did not interrupt, but instead sat staring at him wide-eyed, Mylan was encouraged to go on. "So, rather than commit suicide by attacking Robert, I waited until his temper had cooled and proposed the most reasonable solution to the problem he faced with you."

"Oh, I see, I am regarded as no more than a temporary problem that must be solved in the most efficient manner?" Celiese's temper flared anew at that remark. "And just what was this wonderful solution you proposed?"

Mylan clenched his fists, tempted to try Robert's method of silencing her himself. "Have you learned nothing in this past week? I had hoped you'd spent your time thinking about what a terrible mistake you'd made in revealing your identity and resolved to control your willfulness, which could easily cost both of us our lives."

Intrigued by his remark, Celiese leaned forward. "But he knew I was here in France and had men out searching for me, Mylan; I heard Jaret and the other man who took me to the tower say so."

Surprised she knew so much, Mylan decided after a moment's hesitation to share the information he had. "Robert guards his lands jealously, but you've seen for yourself that what peasants remain to work the farms are desperately poor. Perhaps it was no more than one man passing the word of your arrival to another, giving him hope their lot would improve; then that man told someone else from the next village and so on until the news reached Robert's ears. By then we had left your home to come here, but the peasants knew only that the beautiful Lady d'Loganville had been there to remind them of far better times and then had vanished. I had no idea men were searching for you until Robert told me after you'd been so stupid as to reveal your identity yourself. By then it was too late for me to work on anything more clever than a plan to save your life."

"I am grateful you were at least able to do that, then!" Celiese replied with bitterness. Her head ached with a painful throb, and she still felt dreadful, weak and sick to her stomach. Perhaps it was only fright, but she'd not thought herself such a coward. "I am sorry to be so spiteful, but I'm afraid I'm going to be ill. I should not have drunk that wine."

Alarmed, Mylan leaned forward to take her hands in his. Her skin was cool to his touch, but he could do no more than rub her fingers lightly to provide warmth. "Celiese, listen to me, this is no time to give in to such weakness. You must do as I say while Robert is of a mind to let me handle your defiance myself. I have no idea what ghastly alternative may occur to him tomorrow, but I'll not risk any delay now that the advantage is mine."

"Is this no more than a game to you, with the advantage belonging to Hrolf's side or to yours?" Celiese asked softly, certain her fate meant little to him other than the challenge avoiding it seemed to present.

"Ours!" Mylan corrected her sharply. "I have done little this week but try and persuade Robert that despite occasional fits of uncontrollable temper you are usually the most reasonable of young women. Now you must behave that way for both our sakes!"

His bright golden eyes shone with a demanding gleam, but Celiese knew his request was not a frivolous one and readily agreed. "I would never do anything to harm you, don't you know that?" She seemed to continually anger him, and she had not meant to do so when it was Hrolf who was her enemy, not him.

Taking advantage of her more sensible tone, Mylan hastened to enlist her support for his plan. "All right then, now listen carefully while I explain what we must do." Taking a deep breath, he hoped he could be concise as well as persuasive in his explanation. "The time I have not spent with Robert this last week I have been with Father Bernard, for the only way I can remain here in France is to swear my allegiance to King Charles and to accept your religion as my own."

"What?" Celiese gasped sharply, astonished that he would even consider making such enormous sacrifices, "But you—"

"Just be still and listen as I told you," Mylan cautioned sternly. Hoping she would be silent for another moment or two at least, he continued, "I managed to satisfy the good priest that my conversion to Christianity is a sincere one. I was baptized yesterday and have taken the name Michael, since it is a Christian name and closest to my own. Now we are going to be married again, in a Catholic ceremony this time, so that there will be no question as to whether or not you are truly my wife."

"You would do all this for me, Mylan?" Celiese was near tears, she was so touched by his gesture. It was so completely unexpected and so dear that she was deeply moved, and yet she did not dare hope his actions had been motivated by love alone.

With a rueful smile, Mylan warned her again to be still. "You have not heard all of this yet, Celiese. Robert needs men he can trust to be loyal to him in order to make his claim to this portion of French soil he has been given a lasting one. That I have a French bride as he does is all the better, for it ties his new rule to the old in a way even the most ignorant peasant can understand. He will give me land to call my own in return for my promise to remain here and serve him loyally. Naturally, I asked for the estate of the d'Loganvilles, since that is your home."

When he paused to judge her reaction, Celiese could barely speak she was so outraged. Color flooded her cheeks as she demanded he explain more fully. "My land will be yours, is that what you're saying? That no matter what I do, my home will always belong to a Dane? If not to Raktor, or to Hrolf, it will belong to you?"

Insulted that she would group him with two such ruthless men, Mylan got to his feet and moved away. "I convinced Robert that you would do nothing to undermine his rule in this province, that you would be as loyal to him as I am willing to be. After we are married he wishes to speak with you. What you say to him will be your choice, but I can do no more than warn you in the strongest terms possible that what you are truly choosing is to live as my wife or to cease to live at all."

Confused by his insistence upon marriage, Celiese inquired with open hostility, "Why are you bothering to marry me? You will have my land whether or not I am alive, so what is the difference?" The advantage was indeed his as he had said, but she could see no reason for him to marry her when he already had everything he wanted without the unnecessary aggravation of taking her as his wife.

Mylan was ready to shout the vilest of insults when he recalled where they were and had no choice but to lower his voice and speak calmly. "I am bothering to marry you, Celiese, if that is the way you wish to look at it, because it will save your life. When you are usually so bright, why does my reason escape your comprehension so completely?" He raked his fingers through his curls in a vain attempt to control his temper rather than turning her over his knee and spanking her as he would a naughty child. That was all she was, he realized with a start, a beautiful, headstrong child. "You are no more than seventeen, Celiese; you need a responsible adult to care for you, and I am willing to do it. Just be grateful for that."

"Somehow, I did not think it was gratitude you wanted in a wife, Mylan," Celiese taunted him with a toss of her curls, but she did not expect his reaction to be so immediate nor so hostile.

Mylan swept Celiese up into his arms, then sat down upon the couch to place her across his lap. Winding his fingers in her curls, he ravaged her mouth with a brutal kiss, demonstrating forcefully exactly what he did expect from his wife. "There, does that satisfy your curiosity? I want you for my bride because you arouse my passions as no other woman ever has, and I am certain my touch weaves the same magical spell upon your senses."

Celiese found the effort to struggle against him exhausting and soon had to sit still, despite her determination to break free of his confining grasp. Since she had no way to fight him except with words, she did so. "That is a remarkable story, Michael. You will leave your country to take up residence in another, swear your allegiance to a king you've never met, change your religion, indeed, exchange all that you have known as a Dane for the life of a Frenchman simply because you cannot control your lust for me? Since you will not tell me the truth, I wonder what preposterous lie you told the duke to whom you've become so loyal!"

Mylan's eyes filled with an evil light, the darkness of his thoughts shockingly plain. Were they not in a church he would have shown her just how difficult the desire she inspired was to control by taking it to its limit. Knowing that would result in the worst of reactions from Celiese, however, he restrained himself from being so foolhardy. "The priest will join us in a moment. I must have your answer now, do you want to be my wife, or not?"

He had not proposed to her the first time they were wed, she had simply been sent to him to be his bride, but she knew he was capable of thoughts of the sweetest sort and was heartbroken that he had not at least attempted to win her consent in a loving manner. She raised her hand to her temple, her pain now so intense she could no longer see clearly, and she knew she could neither accept nor refuse no matter how his proposal might have been worded. "Please take me out of here, Mylan, I'm going to be sick, and there's no way I can avoid it."

She had gone limp in his arms, her color fading to a deathly pale, and he did not doubt her word. Rising with her still in his arms he carried her out of the sacristy by way of the small passageway that led directly to the stairs. He knew the guard would still be at the main door of the chapel, believing Celiese was confiding in the priest, but stepping into the shadows he carried her up the stairs and into his room unnoticed.

After placing her gently upon the bed Mylan went back to shut the door, not wishing to be disturbed when he'd still not managed to win a promise of cooperation from Celiese. She was so strong-willed an individual he could not understand why she'd fallen ill at the worst of times, but he brought a small copper basin and placed it at her bedside should she need it.

"Would you send Marcela to help me remove my gown? It is so pretty, and I do not want it to be ruined," Celiese called to him, her voice barely above a whisper.

'I've no time to search for a maid, I will provide all the help you'll need." Totally out of patience with her, Mylan sat down upon the edge of the bed and turned Celiese upon her side so he could reach the back of her gown. He began to slip it off, taking care not to disturb her rest unnecessarily. The brocade was stiff, an opulent fabric but not one intended for wear while sleeping, and he laid the gown over the back of a chair rather than leaving it upon the bed.

Celiese curled up then, wanting only to sleep until the pain in her head stopped hurting so badly. "I am sorry to cause you such trouble, Mylan."

That she would apologize after being so obnoxious made no sense at all to him, but he'd not take exception to her words to begin another argument. "It is Michael now, try and remember so you will say the correct name when we are married. I will go and find Father Bernard to tell him your health is too delicate to permit you to participate in a wedding ceremony at this early hour. I am certain we can delay the marriage for an hour or two, but no longer, Celiese, as I want to be out of this house

448

before nightfall."

Mylan's voice seemed to come from a long way off, and Celiese was not certain she had understood him, but she was positive she had not agreed to marry him even though he seemed to be behaving as if she had. Too tired to argue the point, she remained silent, but decided to let him think what he liked until she had gathered sufficient strength to speak in her own behalf.

Celiese slept deeply for more than an hour, pushing all worry aside while she restored a pleasant sense of equilibrium to her slender body. When she awoke the house was very quiet, unnaturally still, and she saw no reason to behave as if she were still a prisoner if that was no longer the case. She rolled off the high bed and hurried to the wardrobe, hoping her own clothing might still be stored there, and to her immense relief she found it was. She slipped on the soft silk dress she'd borrowed from Olgrethe, then knelt down to fasten the ties on her slippers before she wrapped her cloak around herself and put up the hood. With luck she'd be out of Rouen before anyone discovered she'd awakened from her nap, but as she took a step toward the door Mylan came through it. He was carrying a silver tray upon which he'd balanced a large bowl of steaming soup, but he stopped so suddenly when he saw her that the hot liquid splashed upon his hands. With a loud oath he nearly threw the tray upon the small table that sat next to the door.

"Go ahead, I want to hear your explanation for where you're going, since what I'm tempted to believe cannot possibly be the truth!" he shouted hoarsely.

Stalling in hopes some plausible explanation would

come to her, Celiese began slowly, "Well, I just awakened and I felt so much better that I—"

When she hesitated, Mylan came forward, his expression still menacing. "Go on, I am listening."

Celiese saw only a tall and exceedingly strong man, a very angry one, not a friend in whom she wished to confide, but she had little choice in the matter. "You said I never consider my actions, well I have been thinking of little other than escape for several days. I never should have come here feeling the way that I do. Turn your back and let me go, I will cause neither you nor your friend the duke any further trouble. I will vanish as if I never existed, you have my word on that."

Mylan shook his head in disbelief. "You have this well thought out, do you? Just whom do you think Robert would send after you should he discover you have suddenly turned up missing only minutes before our wedding? Since you think you have made such careful plans, just whom do you think he'd charge with the responsibility of bringing you back?"

Seeing his point, Celiese replied promptly, "You?"

"Of course. If I succeeded in bringing about your return, then you would suffer the most severe of punishments. If I failed to find you, however, then I would be the one to be punished. I don't suppose that matters much to you, though, does it? Even though you swore only this morning that you did not want to see me come to any harm, as usual you have thought only of yourself." Mylan was beyond anger now. "I thought you were really ill; that was one of your finest performances, by the way, you had me completely fooled, again."

When Celiese drew back her hand to slap him Mylan stepped forward quickly to block her blow. He grabbed her wrist, then twisted her arm behind her back to propel her across the room. "You will first sit down and eat every drop of that soup, as I'll not have you fainting upon me again. Then you will remove that gown and put on the other. I expect my wife to dress like the Frenchwoman she is, is that clear?"

"I don't deserve that insult, Mylan, I don't deserve any of your abuse!" Celiese knew her denial was futile, for he heard only lies no matter what truth she spoke, but she would not take his scorn in silence.

"Abuse!" Mylan scoffed at that term. "I am merely trying to provide some nourishment for my bride, who seemed to be so weak she might not survive our wedding ceremony. Now enough of your senseless chatter—sit down and eat!"

When he drew a chair to the table Celiese sat down without having to be pushed. The aroma of the hot broth was most tantalizing, and despite her anger with him she was glad he had provided something to eat, for now she was ravenously hungry. She picked up the spoon, and taking care to sample only the cooler broth at the edges of the bowl began to eat with such obvious appetite that Mylan could only stand back and stare.

"Were you given no food all week?" Mylan placed his hands upon his slender hips, fascinated by her keen appreciation of a soup he'd tasted and thought quite ordinary.

Stopping only briefly to glance up at him, Celiese responded truthfully, "Marcela brought me one meal,

451

then Jaret provided some apples and nuts once. I think he usually brought only bread and water when he came each night, but I wasn't hungry by then."

Shocked that she had been treated so badly, Mylan now thought her hunger only natural, and forgetting his anger inquired in a solicitous tone, "Is that enough? I will find something else if you'd like it."

"No, this is fine, thank you, it is plenty." Celiese tried to eat more slowly, but Mylan's expression did not change. He continued to stare at her with rapt interest until she had finished the last drop.

"Now if you'll but remove your cloak and dress, I will help you with the other." Helping her from her chair, Mylan attempted to untie the ribbon at her throat but found himself too clumsy and stepped back.

"I know you think I behave childishly, but I am at least able to dress myself, Mylan." Celiese found herself smiling at him for the first time that day, but the tension between them had eased considerably, although she was uncertain just why.

"Michael, you must remember to call me Michael now." When she had unfastened the ties to her cloak he took it from her and replaced it in the wardrobe. "Now give me your dress." He tried not to look at her, to focus his attention at something else in the room, but she was far too pretty a sight not to enjoy, and he could not turn away. She was wearing a chemise, at least, but its silken folds hid none of her beauty, and he knew they would never reach the chapel on time if she did not hurry.

"Michael is a very nice name, but what will it matter if I call you Mylan?" Celiese tossed him the silk dress, then

452

lifted the brocade gown from the chair and struggled to put it on by herself. It was a deep rose in hue, making her pale skin glow with a soft tinge of peach that was most becoming, but only Mylan could appreciate that subtle effect. "This gown is not nearly so comfortable nor so practical as Olgrethe's. Must I wear it?"

"Yes! Now hurry and brush your hair. We have kept Father Bernard waiting all morning, and his patience should not be abused so badly." Mylan began to pace near the door, wanting only to take Celiese to bed and knowing that was the last place he could afford to be that morning. She was the most seductive of creatures, her every pose impossibly alluring, and she was doing no more than brushing her hair! Mylan cursed his own weakness, which had led him into one of the most dangerous situations he'd ever faced, and for what? For a young woman who would leave him at her first opportunity, leave him with no regard for how greatly he might suffer in her absence. When she laid the brush aside and turned to face him with a sad, sweet smile brightening the confusion in her gaze, he wanted only to take her in his arms and hold her so tightly she would never escape him. Instead he reached out and took her hand in a firm grasp. "Finally! Now let us hope the priest has not been called away, so that we may get this over with quickly."

"Surely this is the most ill-advised match ever made, Mylan, for neither of us is happy with it." Celiese implored him to wait just a moment, to seek other solutions to their dilemma, but he was in no mood to converse. Sweeping her along beside him, he hurried down the stairs to again enter the chapel from the small door in the sacristy.

Father Bernard was kneeling, deep in prayer. He was badly startled when Mylan and Celiese appeared so suddenly at his side. Leaping to his feet, he tried to regain his composure, but he was a nervous individual, still fearful his existence in a house filled with Danes was a precarious one, and he stuttered as he greeted them. "This, this young woman is to be your bride, Michael?" He knew his Danish was poor, but all his converts were learning French so slowly he hardly dared hope any would ever be able to converse with him in that tongue. When Celiese replied in flawless French he was not only astonished but delighted. "My dear, I hope you are again feeling your best, for marriage is one of life's most important events, and today will always live in your memory as a most blessed one."

Celiese glanced up at Mylan, wondering just what he'd told Father Bernard, for she had no wish to shock him. Since the priest spoke his language, she had no way to inquire without his knowing what her question was. It seemed apparent the priest did not realize this was not to be their first wedding, and while she considered that an important point it was clear that Mylan had not. Not wishing to create another bitter scene with him that morning, however, she kept still. "I am so pleased to meet you, Father Bernard."

"Well come then, let us enter the church so the ceremony can begin at once. Michael told me of his desire to marry a Christian woman, but it did not occur to me that you would be French. From what city do you come?"

The priest turned to smile as he led the way into the chapel.

"I am Lady Celiese d'Loganville, Father. If Rouen is your home then you will have heard the name," Celiese responded proudly.

"Oh, indeed I have." Startled, the man wondered why a young woman from so fine a family had chosen to marry a Dane, even one as handsome as Michael, then thought he would be smart to avoid such a question. He was doing his best to bring the word of God to men who in his opinion could only be described as the most barbaric of pagans and, finding little pleasure or success in his task, he thought himself fortunate to have so intelligent a convert as Michael and hoped he would attract more. "I will summon two witnesses and then we will begin. I will be only a moment."

The priest returned all too quickly, and when he began the ceremony in a soft, low voice Celiese found it easier to focus her attention upon the candles' bright flame, or upon the sweet fragrance of incense or upon any distraction the chapel contained other than the taunting smile of the handsome man who knelt by her side. He seemed to regard her consent to their marriage as a victory of some sort, when she could not even recall agreeing to it. She wondered how much of his new religion Mylan understood, for as one of the sacraments marriage was considered a lasting bond, one that could be severed only by death. That thought sent a chill up her spine that she could not suppress, for perhaps he realized only too well that her life was unlikely to be a long one and so had no qualms about going through a ceremony that was supposed to form a permanent tie. She repeated her vows in a steady, soft tone, but her heart was heavy, filled with none of the joy the priest had alluded to as creating lasting memories.

Mylan simply wanted the ceremony to be finished, but the priest seemed to continue speaking for hours, each successive prayer growing longer until he despaired of ever leaving the chapel before sundown. As the wife of a man who'd pledged his loyalty to Robert, Celiese would have a measure of safety she'd lacked before, and he hoped it would be enough to protect her for the time being. He'd found the duke to be a volatile man, fond of pleasure but swift to anger, a man who demanded his way in all things, and most definitely not a man who would tolerate the interference in his affairs by a young woman so high-spirited and defiant as Celiese had become. With a touch of sadness Mylan recalled the first time he'd taken her for his wife, surrounded by family and friends. She had seemed the dearest of young women. Softspoken and sweet, she had changed his outlook on life from despair to optimism with no more than the brightness of her smile. That day was months in the past now, but he remembered it clearly, and looking down at the pretty woman he was surprised as always by the innocence of her expression, as if she shared the purity of heart of the angels. But he had learned through far too many bitter lessons just what treachery the astonishing beauty of her delicate features concealed.

Chapter Twenty-Four

Mylan thanked Father Bernard graciously for performing so beautiful a wedding ceremony, but he had sensed from the moment he'd first broached the subject with the French cleric that the man would not dare to refuse him. He had spoken no threats, but the balding priest had been apprehensive throughout all their conversations, his brown eyes darting nervously about as he'd pleated the fabric of his woolen robe with long, bony fingers that were never still.

"May God bless you both," Father Bernard responded with an anxious smile, relieved that he had apparently pleased the tall blond man. He did not know what else to say as the striking couple moved down the aisle toward the door of his chapel. He wanted to wish them an abundance of earthly blessings, yet they both seemed preoccupied, and, unlike most newly married couples, not with each other. Shaking his head with puzzlement he watched them depart, a most unusual pair in every respect, but still he hoped he might see them again, for he sensed a depth to their characters that he found most intriguing.

Once they had left the sanctity of the duke's chapel Mylan drew Celiese aside. "We must find Robert now and I'll caution you to remember just one thing."

That those were the first words her husband wished to speak to her did not surprise Celiese, but she would have much preferred some sweet compliment and a tender kiss. Looking up at his intense expression, she saw the ceremony in which they'd just participated had made little difference in his mood. They had gone through the formality of exchanging vows, but clearly his only emotion was still an anger he could barely control. "And what might that be?" she asked softly, certain she already knew what he was about to say.

"Whatever you wish to accomplish for yourself and your people, you must be alive to do it. Give Robert no cause to think the benefits of your death outweigh those of giving you your freedom. No matter how he might insult you, do not give him the satisfaction of making you lose your temper, for you'll forfeit your life, as well," he warned her sternly.

Celiese nodded, her expression as serious as his. "He already knows what I think of him, Mylan, how can I make him forget that?"

"You need do no more than smile to make him forget the sound of his own name!" Mylan whispered fiercely. "Now come, dear wife, let us do our best to win his blessing for our marriage, and then we'll depart Rouen with all possible haste."

Appalled by the prospect of receiving any sort of good wishes from Robert, Celiese opened her mouth to remind

him just what she thought of the scoundrel and how little
he valued his blessing, but then, knowing Mylan would
not appreciate a repetition of her opinion, she kept still.
"Why was he so insistent that I speak with him before
dawn?"

"Merely to frighten you out of your wits, and I'd say
he ploy was a success," Mylan commented tersely as he
led the way through the large manor, finally locating the
duke at the rear of the garden. He was practicing his skill
with the broad sword, using several of his men as sparring
partners. When he saw Mylan approaching he tossed him
a weapon and invited him to join in their sport, giving
Celiese no more than a stilted nod.

Knowing a request from the duke was never refused,
Mylan gripped the hilt of the finely balanced steel sword
with a confident grasp. Turning to direct Celiese to a
nearby bench, he gave her a warning glance to insure her
silence, and she sat down to observe as if they were about
to provide a spectacle solely for her amusement. After
unbuckling his belt and pulling his *bliaud* off over his
head, Mylan laid them upon the bench next to his bride.
He did not discard his *chainse*, however, for the lightweight linen shirt covered the scars he had no wish to
display. Turning to Robert he responded readily, "I am
not dressed for games, but I will accept your challenge."

Robert's ample mouth curved into a slow smile, as if he
were a spoiled and lazy tomcat who had just managed to
corner a tasty mouse. He nodded slightly, indicating he
was ready to begin, then raised his sword and leaped
forward, his eagerness for the warm, sweet smell of blood
shockingly clear.

When the duke came after him immediately, as though they were embattled in a duel to the death, Mylan had no illusions as to who was the more skilled with a sword, but he had no intention of quitting without putting forth his best effort. The older man was much heavier, but agile still, a veteran of many years of armed combat. But Mylan outthought his every move and escaped his brutal blows with a grace that made his evasive actions seem effortless, when indeed they required every ounce of his newly regained strength to accomplish.

Celiese sat upon the edge of the wooden bench, her heart beating wildly as she saw Robert swing his sword again and again in a powerful downward arc. When the had first entered the garden he had seemed in a playful mood, but when he had realized that Mylan was going to be so wily an opponent his face had contorted in a vicious snarl, all thought of sport gone as the battle became a real one in his mind.

Mylan had little choice, he knew. He could not wound Robert and escape his wrath, neither could he throw down his weapon and risk being branded a coward. He had simply to continue to defend himself as best he could and hope the man had already been practicing for a sufficient length of time to become quickly exhausted and call off the match himself. At least the sword he had been given was a fine one, for he could block Robert's blow without fear the steel blade would snap under the intensity of the man's assault.

Celiese was ready to scream, for she could see what Mylan could not—that Robert had expected an easy victory over his young friend, and each second the match continued he was growing more irate at the unexpected difficulty he'd encountered. Surely the rest of his men let him win easily, so he was unused to having to apply his skill in so vigorous a manner and did not enjoy in the slightest having to do so now. The staged battle took on so vicious a tone that both men were soon drenched with sweat. She could hardly bear to watch, and yet she could not turn away while Mylan's life was so clearly in jeopardy. A keen observer, she noticed the moment he began to favor his right leg and knew if Robert sensed his opponent had any weakness he'd play on it unmercifully. Hoping she might stop the fight before such a disaster occurred, she called out in a cheerful tone, "I beg you, sir, to remember this is our wedding day, and I'd like Mylan to save most of his energy for me."

At that teasing comment Robert let out a roar of laughter. Grateful for the excuse to end a match he sorely regretted beginning, he stepped back and lowered his sword to his side. "I had forgotten the significance of the day, Michael, but I will leave you with whatever stamina you have remaining."

Bowing slightly, Mylan handed the weapon he'd used to one of the bystanders and joined in the laughter as if he were greatly amused by his bride's request. "Thank you, sir, as I do not want to disappoint the lady."

"Have you ever?" Robert asked in his usual booming tone, his blue eyes alight with mischief.

"You will have to ask Celiese that question, for I'll not speak for her." Mylan knew he had disappointed Celiese in several ways the duke had not even considered, but he kept those failures to himself.

Wiping the beads of sweat from his brow, Robert turned his attention to Celiese. She was smiling still, the delight in her expression far different from the usual cool disdain she turned upon him. Her fair curls fell about her shoulders in a soft blond cascade, framing her exquisite features with a glorious silver haze. Perhaps the ice she had appeared to have running through her veins could be warmed with a little effort, and he regretted his haste in setting her free before he'd bothered to sample her favors to the fullest. Since she was in no position to refuse him any request, he still might have the time to enjoy the charms of her shapely figure if he delayed the meeting he'd demanded she attend to a more opportune time. With that thought in mind he gestured at his soiled clothing and said, "I had planned to talk with you earlier in the day, and as you can readily see my appearance is now unsuited for a discussion with a lady on any topic. You will be here for supper, of course, as we all want to celebrate your marriage, so I will talk with you before we dine."

Celiese looked up at Mylan, knowing he wanted to leave immediately, but he did no more than narrow his eyes in the slightest of frowns, and she saw he expected her to agree. "Thank you, I will look forward to speaking with you then." Picking up Mylan's cast-off clothing, she walked ahead of him up the path toward the imposing home. "What shall we do? I thought he knew you wished to leave immediately," she whispered anxiously.

"I said only that I wanted to leave as soon as you were free to go. Perhaps he did not think we'd wish to spend our wedding night on board the Falcon."

Celiese frowned impatiently. "This is not our wedding night, Mylan. Why didn't you tell Father Bernard this was our second wedding?" She was tempted to ask if he was ashamed to admit it, but his mood was obviously a dark one and she dared not push him with such a provocative inquiry.

Mylan did not understand her question, "That we were married in what he considers a pagan rite would not have mattered to him. In his view we were not married, but now we are. Did you not feel the same way?" They had reached their room and he held the door open for her to enter.

Celiese walked to the bed and folded his *bliaud* neatly upon it before she turned to face him. "I had spent five years in your country, and while I did not fully understand your beliefs, I thought the fact that you held them to be true gave them value. I have always considered us to be married, it was only you who continually said we were not."

Mylan could do no more than stare at the bewitching creature who stood so proudly before him. He could detect not the slightest bit of hope or happiness in her emerald gaze. She was regarding him as though they were strangers discussing a topic of only slight interest between them, and he found her cool detachment impossible to return. "Well, Lady d'Loganville, you are now truly my wife in the opinion of those who matter most to you, your beloved countrymen. Regardless of what I now call myself, or to whom I choose to pray, they will forever see me as a Dane and distrust me, but at least whatever sons I give you will be legitimate and free. That was your greatest worry at one time, or at least that was what you said." His amber gaze had a mocking shine, taunting her again with the unspoken accusation that her words had been lies.

Startled by the unexpected turn of his conversation, Celiese swallowed nervously. "I not only said that, but I meant it. Perhaps you do not prize your freedom as highly as I do, because you have never lost it."

"Oh, but I have, At least I have been too badly injured to exercise most of life's privileges that freedom affords. That must be the same desperate feeling of helpless rage you felt at being my slave."

"Your slave?" Celiese responded bitterly, "I was never your slave, never! In every way I was a wife to you!"

Mylan shrugged, as if the truth of what their relationship had been did not interest him. "Whatever. Since we now share the same faith and have been married by a priest there should be no further need for discussion of the subject." He began to walk away, then turned back as an afterthought. "I want to bathe, can I trust you to remain here while I do?"

"Of course!" Celiese answered as though insulted, but she'd not forgotten how desperate she'd been to escape the house that morning, and obviously neither had he.

"Take another nap, if you wish, or send Marcela to bring you something to eat. We have hours to wait until Robert will be ready to see you." Mylan hesitated to leave her when she seemed so unsettled, but he wanted to change his clothes and go out to the Falcon to alert his crew to their unexpected change in plans.

"I will be all right," Celiese answered quickly, too

independent to let him see how greatly she needed his courage to face what still lay ahead. Even when things did not go in Mylan's way he had a quiet confidence she envied, for none of her dreams were coming true as she'd hoped they would, and she was simply worn out by her continuous series of problems. Since the bed had been a comfortable one, she decided to lie down again rather than simply pass the hours pacing up and down trying to think of some way to outwit the villainous duke when none existed. "I think I will take a nap. You'll find me here later."

"Just see that I do." Mylan strode into the adjoining room so as not to disturb her rest. He bathed quickly, then dressed in his own clothing for a change and went down to the docks to speak with his men, since he wanted them to be ready to sail at a moment's notice. The river would be difficult to navigate at night, but if they had to flee under cover of darkness he wanted the ship ready.

When Mylan returned from his errand Celiese was still sleeping soundly, but the two damp trails her tears had made showed clearly upon her flushed cheeks, and he stood beside the bed trying to think what more he could possibly do to insure the delicate beauty's happiness. He seemed to have succeeded only in depressing her thoroughly, when he'd thought the fact he'd married her in a Christian ceremony would finally make her content. She seemed not in the least bit grateful that he'd saved her life with his wits alone and with promises to Robert that would take him his entire lifetime to fulfill. Despite his best efforts, it seemed they could not converse without arguing no matter what the subject, and he felt the same sense of hopelessness he'd battled all week. He'd missed her terribly, but she had apparently dismissed him from her mind, undoubtedly blaming him for the misfortune she had caused herself. Even after he had explained how hard he had labored to save her she had tried to run away from him at her first opportunity. Nothing he did pleased her, not one single thing!

As Mylan watched Celiese sleep he realized there was one time they enjoyed the harmony that was supposed to exist between a man and his wife, but the tender peace they found in each other's arms eluded them with astonishing frequency during the rest of their waking hours. Seeing no reason to wait any longer to capture what pleasure he could from his willful young bride, he hurriedly cast off his clothing and then slipped beneath the light blanket. He drew Celiese into his arms, covering her face with sweet kisses until she opened her eyes and began to smile.

Snuggling against him to get more comfortable, the pretty young woman's expression took on a seductive glow as she greeted him. "Mylan, I—"

"Michael," he corrected her softly, then lowered his mouth to her throat where he nuzzled her silken skin with playful nibbles. He enjoyed the sweet, warm softness of her skin so greatly that his play swiftly turned to passion.

"Michael, then," Celiese replied as she lifted her arms to encircle his neck. She loved his strength, which he held in check to enfold her in the fondest of embraces. She slid her fingertips across the taut muscles of his broad shoulders to enjoy the fiery warmth of his deeply tanned skin. At least he had not been furious with her for the manner in which she'd stopped his mock battle with Robert, but she had not wanted to see him hurt, no matter how slightly, and the possibility he'd suffer a severe injury had been too great. "I want to leave here as swiftly as possible, for I fear your life is in grave danger as well as mine."

"Am I the reason for your fears?" Although he could not believe he was, Mylan leaned back, watching her expression closely as he lifted his fingertips to wipe away the last drop of moisture from her cheek.

Celiese felt no need to reply to so obvious a question and pulled his mouth down to hers, her loving kiss the only response she'd give. She had missed the closeness they'd shared during the voyage, when their entire world had existed of no more than the deck of the Surf Falcon and the small stretch of beach where they'd made their camp each night. She wanted to return to that joy, to a far simpler time before their lives had become so unbearably complicated.

Mylan sensed the same urgency in Celiese's enticing affection that throbbed within his own heart and tightened his embrace, pulling her supple form firmly against his own to savor each marvelous curve of her lithe figure. He spread her shining curls out upon the pillow and kissed her eyelids gently before he found her eager lips again brushing his. His mind filled with dreams of her then, and he lost himself in the web of her desire, drawn closer and closer until they were no longer two separate souls but one vibrant being whose heart beat in time with love's most ancient melody. A thousand pretty verses came to his mind and yet he gave voice to none, afraid to speak for fear of breaking her captivating spell.

Celiese hugged Mylan even more tightly, wanting the pleasure that swelled within her to sweep them both away. His touch teased her senses, drawing the joy he'd begun with his gentle kisses to the blissful peak of rapture. This was the reason they'd been born, to become as one, and she spoke his name in a deliriously happy sigh, remembering this time to call him Michael.

Mylan could not bear to release his bride when the love they'd shared had again been perfection. It had been the same tantalizing ecstasy for them both from the beginning. He'd promised to teach a woman he'd thought little more than a beautiful child the wonders of love, but she'd known far more than he of the gentle art of romance. That was her secret, he realized with a sly grin, her touch was tender, yet it seared his flesh with the heat of flames. But he could think of no way to inspire the same devotion in her heart, if the depth of his emotions were not returned in kind.

"That is a marvelous smile, are you at last content?" Celiese purred softly as she lifted her fingertips to his lips, outlining their perfect shape gently.

"It is you who must be content enough to give Robert the answers he seeks. I wanted only to put you in so blissful a mood, if such a thing is even possible, that you will please him." Mylan meant to tease her, but had to grab her wrists to avoid being slapped for that jest.

"I want your affection to be for me, not for his benefit!" Celiese cried out indignantly, crushed that he'd be so underhanded in his purpose.

"Why do my words always confuse you so when my kiss never does?" Mylan inquired thoughtfully. He lowered his mouth to hers, stilling her complaints with a slow, sweet kiss that left her again languidly relaxing in his arms.

Celiese's luminous green eyes swept his tender expression, hoping for some sign of agreement as she asked, "Must I see that horrible man again? Couldn't we simply leave Rouen now?"

"Yes," Mylan responded agreeably, but then he explained the conditions. "If you've changed your mind about wishing to remain here in France, then we can walk out of his house now and be gone before he has sense enough to realize what we've done. We would have to make haste for Denmark and never return to these shores. Are you now prepared to abandon the cause that brought you home in the first place?" Mylan held his breath, praying she wanted only to return to his farm and be his wife, as if no other consideration would ever occupy her heart or thoughts. She still wore Thor's small silver hammer and he brought it to his lips, kissing the charm for good luck, despite his recent conversion to her faith. He would gladly seek help from whatever sympathetic source he found available, if he could win her for his own.

Celiese gave his words careful thought, then shook her head. "That would be a cowardly thing to do, and neither of us lacks the courage to follow through on our convictions." She saw his gaze darken as he moved away and knew her answer had displeased him, but it had been the truth and she could not avoid speaking it.

Their loving mood shattered by the response she'd given to her own question, Mylan spoke gruffly as he gathered up the clothing he'd scattered about the floor in his haste to join her in the high bed. "When you are dressed we will seek out Robert, and then I hope your common sense rather than your courage will prevail."

Recalling the way the duke had looked at her that day with a lust he'd made little effort to conceal, Celiese grew even more apprehensive about their meeting. "Michael?" She sat up, clutching the lightweight blanket to her breast as she called to him. "You will stay with me, won't you? I won't have to face him alone?"

Not understanding the reason for her concern, Mylan returned to sit down upon the edge of their bed. "It matters little whether I'm there or not when you must speak for yourself, Celiese. He will not accept my answers as yours."

"But you can't leave me alone with him!" Celiese implored him frantically, making no effort to be brave now.

Suddenly understanding her worry, Mylan had little patience with her fears. "Don't be ridiculous. He knows you are my wife and he'd not take advantage of your situation to satisfy his own desires." Mylan thought her idea ludicrous until he realized Robert had undoubtedly raped dozens of women in the years he and his men had spent pillaging the French countryside. They'd gloried in the thrill of their own violence, striking terror into the hearts of all those not fortunate enough to escape their thirst for blood in their relentless pursuit of the treasures gained honestly by others. He knew exactly what sort of man

Robert was, and he had no reason to believe he'd moderated his behavior in the slightest simply to satisfy the edict of King Charles that he adopt the French culture as his own. All he'd done was accept the thin veneer of the French civilization; surely his heart was no less filled with greed and lust than it had ever been. He'd not trust Raktor to speak alone with Celiese and not abuse her, why had he forgotten in his efforts to win her freedom just how vicious Robert could be? Without explaining his reason, Mylan agreed to her request with one condition. "I will remain at your side only if you promise to give the replies Robert wants to hear. Is that a bargain?" He felt a slight twinge of guilt in asking for her word upon something he'd already decided in his mind, but he was at his wit's end as to how to make her present a moderate viewpoint to the duke.

"That's cruel!" Celiese objected sharply. She was tempted to refuse his offer, but then she realized it was in her best interests to accept, no matter what terms he might present. When he got up to leave she reached out to touch his arm. "Yes, it is a bargain. I promise to be so agreeable the beast will think me the most pleasant woman he has ever met!"

Seeing the fire of anger blazing brightly in her eyes, Mylan leaned down to kiss her cheek lightly, his gesture a sweet one simply for spite. "Wear your hair in a modest style, and see if Marcela can find a suitable veil. If your appearance is more circumspect he will expect your answers to be also."

"Whatever you wish," Celiese replied through clenched teeth, yet she did not trust Mylan not to hand her over to the overbearing duke should the man have the audacity to demand he do so. Her heart fell at that prospect, for that would be a betrayal of an unimaginably evil sort, and more than her heart could bear to consider.

Mylan was soon attired in the magnificent blue apparel he'd worn for their wedding, and Celiese had again bathed and dressed in the new brocade gown. Mylan thought better of repeating any of the instructions he'd given her earlier. If she did not understand what it was she was to do by now, then he had no hope at all that she would leave the duke's palace alive. He had his dagger at his belt, but could see no way to wear his sword in the man's home, although he would have preferred to have that deadly weapon at his side as well. "Are you ready?" His glance swept over her quickly; she'd coiled her hair atop her head and covered it with a light veil as he'd asked, but the only result was that the elegant line of her slender throat was doubly appealing. He extended his hand and she took it, her fingertips trembling slightly as they met his, and he tried to smile, but his expression seemed to do little to give her courage.

Robert was waiting for Celiese in a small chamber off the main hall. He had wine ready to serve and looked forward to winning several concessions from the striking beauty before he released her from his protection. Mylan would be traveling most of the time, so Celiese might prove an amusing mistress if he warned her sufficiently of what she'd suffer if she did not please him. That thought filled him with a heady anticipation, and when the elegantly clad young woman arrived upon her husband's arm he dismissed the young man immediately.

"Michael, I have many things locked away in store-rooms, items I neither want nor need. Have Jaret unlock one of the rooms for you now, and set aside those items you think would bring the best return in trade. I am anxious to see how skilled a trader you really are."

Celiese recalled Andrick's saying that he and Hagen were far more interested in profitable trade than their older brother, who sailed for adventure alone, but if Mylan had convinced the duke that trade was his interest she'd not dispute his word. She only hoped he would now find some tactful way to refuse the duke's offer; he had not been able to avoid becoming his sparring partner earlier in the day, and she feared he might again have to give in.

"That is not an assignment I care to begin tonight, sir," Mylan replied forcefully, his tone polite but firm. "I must see Celiese safely to her home where I will have to make extensive repairs to her house before I can devote myself to the ventures we have discussed."

Anxious to be alone with the attractive young woman, Robert frowned impatiently. "Need I remind you I have not given my permission for her to leave Rouen? It is pointless for you to worry over where she will live as long as I insist she reside here!"

Mylan straightened to his full height, his posture proud as well as assertive, "Celiese is my wife, sir. Our reason for marrying today in your chapel was so there would be no argument as to my responsibility for her happiness. I plan to be the most protective, as well as loving of husbands." He waited a moment to be certain the threat in his words had been understood, and he could readily see from Robert's furious glance that it had been. "Now what is it you wish to ask her, so we might have your permission to leave Rouen as freely as we entered it?"

Fuming with frustration at his missed opportunity to have such a ravishing beauty, Robert could see no way to send Mylan out of the room when he'd refused to go. He needed the young man's skill to make the wealth he'd accumulated grow in value through clever trading, and he'd not jeopardize what could be an extremely profitable arrangement over a woman, not even one as lovely as Celiese. He poured himself a full goblet of wine and tossed it down his throat without bothering to invite his guests to have any. Wiping his mouth on his sleeve, he enumerated his demands as he strode up and down in front of them.

"This province is mine to rule, as I see fit. I want no interference in the matter whatsoever. The peasants must not shirk the work of cultivating crops, for until sufficient Danes arrive to establish farms we are dependent upon their labor for our food."

Making a valiant attempt to hold her temper, Celiese inquired softly, "And what is to become of these hard-working peasants when their land has been given away to strangers?"

"I have no plan to put them to the sword!" Robert exploded angrily, then seeing her startled reaction he took a more moderate tone. "There is room here for us all to dwell in harmony, if you and others of your class make no effort to subvert my will!"

"The king has made you the duke, sir. My family was

loyal to Charles, and I shall continue to be so as well." Celiese hoped her answer would satisfy him although she had not replied directly to his angry demand. He was a tyrant of the worst sort, in her view, and she'd never lift one finger to help him.

Mylan could barely suppress a smile. He knew Celiese to be a clever young woman with the most facile of minds when it came to getting her own way, and he could see she had confused Robert completely and prayed she would continue to do so.

"I have your word, then?" Robert demanded harshly.

"I beg you to ask King Charles himself if the d'Logan-villes have not always been loyal to the Crown," Celiese responded demurely. "As for those residing upon my land," she continued smoothly, "I know they will follow my example, but if I have no home I will be unable to provide any sort of influence upon anyone."

Knowing her point was well taken, Robert stopped to regard her with a fixed stare. "The d'Loganville estate shall be yours then, for as long as I can depend upon you to serve me as faithfully as I know Michael will."

"I have taken him again for my husband, sir, is that not proof enough that my loyalty lies with the Danes?" Celiese attempted to smile in the most charming fashion possible, dazzling the arrogant man completely with her radiant beauty.

"The matter is settled, then." Stopping now to fill two more goblets with wine, the duke proposed a toast. "To our new home in France!"

"To France," Celiese responded readily, but she knew the thought behind her toast was far different than his.

Mylan raised his goblet without speaking, but his gaze was upon her, and she understood his unspoken salute clearly.

Escorting them into the main hall where the many others who resided in the sumptuous home had already begun to gather for the evening meal, Robert found himself in a surprisingly good mood, despite his failure to seduce Celiese as he'd planned. Power was an intoxicating substance and he was again drunk with it, proud he had gotten his way with the willful young woman, since he knew he could not hold the province without the support of the French residents, no matter how grudgingly they gave it.

Mylan drank nothing that night, and he was not surprised when Celiese did not either. They would not think clearly on empty stomachs though, so he insisted they dine with the others. That they had chosen to remarry sparked gentle teasing, but he responded in kind, and at their first opportunity he gave the excuse of wanting to enjoy their wedding night, and taking Celiese by the arm led her upstairs to their suite of rooms. His mind, however, was not upon romance. "Gather your belongings quickly, and we will go. I want to reach the sea before dawn, for the promises you gave Robert were transparent ones, and I don't want him to remember them in the morning and reconsider his decision to let us depart."

Having no wish to remain even one moment longer under the despicable duke's roof, Celiese took the garments she'd brought with her from the wardrobe and folded them into a neat bundle without argument. That she had managed to fool the villain with such vague statements had surprised her too, but she'd given Mylan her word she'd try to please him and was glad she had. "Will he do that, change his mind after he has given us his word?"

"Not if you behave as he believes you promised to do." Wasting no more time, Mylan carried his own possessions as well as hers as they slipped out of the mansion and made their way down to the docks. He had come and gone so frequently in the last week that he was recognized and not challenged by the guards they met, but he'd taken the precaution of wearing his sword at his side, just in case such an unlikely event occurred. When they were safely on board the Surf Falcon he gave the order to weigh anchor, and catching the evening breeze they followed the winding moonlit path of the river Seine all the way to the sea.

Too excited to rest, Celiese stood at the rail for the entire journey, waiting anxiously for a glimpse of the shore near her home. When she sighted the cliff she knew she begged Mylan to take her ashore, even though the dawn had not yet begun to light the eastern sky. Wanting to rest as much as he wanted to please her, Mylan readily agreed, taking the ship in close to the beach so they did not get thoroughly drenched making their way to the dry sand. Taking their blanket with him, he held her hand as they skirted the small village and made their way to the ruins of her once magnificent home.

Deliriously happy, Celiese skipped up the gentle hill. "Everything will be as it was before, Mylan; I know it will take time, but we can make it happen, I know we can!"

He didn't bother this time to again insist she use his Christian name, but her childlike enthusiasm saddened him greatly. She seemed to see nothing in the shadows that surrounded them but the happiness of her past, and he knew he'd failed in his efforts to make her focus on a future she'd want to share with him. What he needed and wanted mattered so little to her she could not even remember to use the name he'd taken when he'd accepted her God as his own. He had done so much, and all willingly, not only in hopes he'd be able to save her life but to win her respect and trust, as well. Yet as he watched the joy sparkle in her eyes he knew the walls of the half-destroyed mansion meant more to her than he ever would. "I would be content if instead of constantly swearing that you are my wife, you would *be* one!" Mylan shouted suddenly, the sound of his deep voice echoing against the few stone walls that remained standing.

Startled by his outburst, Celiese approached him warily. "What is wrong? I did as you asked, I did not anger that swine who dares to call himself a duke. He did not forbid me to rebuild my house, but said we may live here as the d'Loganvilles always have. Why are you so angry with me?"

"It was my first name I changed, Celiese, not my last, and this ruin is now the home of the Vandahls! You may lie to everyone around you, but you're a fool to lie to yourself, and if I ever find you lying to me again I will finally give you the beating you have always deserved!"

Appalled by his threats, Celiese responded wearily, "It always comes back to the day we met, doesn't it? You saw me for what I truly am for so few hours, and I've never

478

had that same sweet, unconditional acceptance from you ever again. That was better than any paradise could ever be, but I had your love for so short a time I can scarcely remember its beauty now."

"How can you speak to me of love when I have never had yours?" Mylan responded bitterly. "You betrayed me on our wedding night, risked your life gladly to escape what you described as the agony of being my slave, accepted the hospitality of my family while you used my brother's affection simply to gain passage to France, and then, when I brought you here to save you from certain death at the hands of the Torgvalds, you let your passion for revenge lead you to insult a man who could have ended both our lives with the snap of his fingers! You are the most selfish woman ever born, and you have not once stopped to think of me!"

Her senses reeling under his barrage of vicious insults, Celiese nevertheless sprang to her own defense. "Why is it you constantly twist each action I take to make it appear the worst possible choice? As if I spend all my time thinking of new ways to hurt you, when you mean the world to me. I have never betrayed your trust nor told you a single lie, but you despise me all the same!"

Mylan took two steps away, then turned back to face her, "I will help you as best I can to rebuild your home, and I will work often enough for Robert to satisfy his requirements so that you may keep your land. But unless you give me your promise now that you will lead the most circumspect of lives so that he will never have any cause to suspect you are working to undermine his authority, I have no intention of being your husband."

Confused by his demand, Celiese could do little more than stare up at the handsome man. "What do you mean?"

"You know exactly what I mean. If you plan to spend your time plotting schemes to drive the Danes from France after we have the king's invitation to remain and establish this province for our own, you will do it alone! I gave my word to Robert that I would be loyal to him so you could keep your precious land, to say nothing of your life, but if you're going to continue to lie to me as well as to him, then you will live in whatever splendid dwelling we can erect by yourself, as I will never set foot inside it!"

Her happiness of only moments before vanished in the face of his rage, but Celiese saw no way she could promise to mend her ways when she had not committed any of the crimes he'd imagined. "I see; but when I say that I have never lied to you, you consider that a lie in itself, don't you?"

"Which you know it is!" Mylan shouted fiercely. "What I want is a wife who will consider my feelings for a change. A woman I can trust not to leave me again and again without the slightest provocation!"

"I have never left you," Celiese replied indignantly. "You threw me off your farm yourself when I begged to stay, and it was Hrolf, or Robert if you will, from whom I was running yesterday, not you." Celiese was miserable, desperately sorry he had not accepted the reason she'd given him the day before as the truth.

"Why are you bothering to argue with me? The past is a dead issue, I want only your promise that you'll bring no more pain to either of us with any more thoughtless actions in the future. Will you give it or not?" He'd lost his patience entirely with her now and voiced his demand in a hostile sneer.

"How can I give you my word on any subject when you don't trust me? And there's no point in my promising that my behavior will be above reproach when you accept none of my actions as good." Celiese was near tears, for she could think of no way to please him when no matter what she attempted to do she failed.

The sun's rays had just broken over the horizon behind her, illuminating her shimmering curls with the bright glow of a halo, but Mylan saw only a young woman so defiant she'd never be tamed. Pushed beyond all reasonable limits by her refusal to accept terms he thought most generous, he drew her into his arms, crushing her in an embrace from which she could not hope to escape. Not bothering to spread out their blanket, he lowered her to the dew-covered grass, for once letting the passion she aroused in him rage without restraint through the tensed muscles of his powerful body. His blood aflame with an all-consuming desire, he sought only to break the power of her enchantment, to take all she could give in one last act of love that would for all time satisfy his compelling need to possess her.

Although shocked by the speed with which he'd moved, Celiese wound her fingers in Mylan's golden curls, wanting only to capture his mouth in a kiss whose affection would inspire the tenderness he'd always shown her. Barely aware of her gesture, Mylan was lost in a glorious quest, seeking only to end the agony of the insatiable desire her slightest touch created within his heart. But the heat of his passion ignited her own, and she drew him close, her need expressed in a far more subtle manner, but her hunger for love no less deep. She found his affection intoxicating, no matter how he chose to give it, the pleasure undiminished by the wildness of his mood, and she accepted his strength with the same eager surrender she had always given to invite his tenderness. She wanted to bring a smile to his lips and laughter to his amber eyes, to please him in the only way she knew she ever had.

Mylan had expected Celiese to fight him, to scream and call him vile names when he'd first lowered her to the grass, but instead she had astonished him by enfolding him in a loving embrace, her sweetness encouraging the passion he could not hope to control as if it were the most tender caress. His conscious mind refused to consider her purpose; he knew only that he would never have enough of her smooth, graceful body and honey-sweet kiss, for the more he wished to give the more eagerly she responded, until the brightness of the new day went unnoticed through the haze of their passion's flames. If it was magical spells she cast he could not fight their power, and once again he became her willing slave.

Chapter Twenty-Five

Celiese awakened slowly, the subtle aroma of the warm earth and tangled grass upon which she'd slept surrounding her with the most pleasant of fragrances. She was wrapped snugly in the blanket, the soft folds that gently caressed her bare skin still holding a haunting trace of Mylan's presence, an exotic blend with the freshness of the sea breeze mixed with his purely masculine scent. She inhaled deeply, bringing back the memory of his passionate embrace with a slow, satisfied smile. He was the most surprising of lovers, slow and sweet upon one occasion, then driven by the fires of passion the next, and yet he was always tender, his loving so splendid she would never tire of his affection. He was as fascinating an individual to her now as he had been from the moment she'd first entered the darkened room in his home where he'd stood waiting to meet her, his voice filled with anguish as well as anger.

Missing his warm presence by her side, she rose up on one elbow to look around for him, but was disappointed to find she was all alone upon the hill. The brocade gown she'd worn for their wedding lay folded nearby, her slippers tucked neatly beneath the long skirt. She could not even remember removing the lavishly embroidered garment, and yet there it was as clear evidence that she had. That was precisely the effect Mylan always had upon her. When he wanted her she had no wish to refuse his attentions, and the constraints clothing presented to their ardor were always swiftly cast aside. Their bodies were so attuned to each other that their flesh longed to merge from the moment their fingertips brushed lightly together, and she could not wait to see him again, certain his mood would be as fine as hers for a change.

The day looked to be a glorious one. The sun was already high overhead, but as she sat up a sudden wave of nausea made her dizzy and she lay back down, hoping it would soon subside. But it worsened, until she finally gave in to it. Feeling faint then, she rested for a long while before she felt physically able to stand. Wrapping herself in the blanket, she decided a bath in the stream would be refreshing. She hoped such an indulgence would restore her health as well as the euphoric mood with which she'd awakened. She'd not tell Mylan she'd been ill again, as it would only worry him needlessly, for surely it was no more than a reaction to lack of sleep and the excitement of finally escaping the clutches in which Robert had held her ensnared.

She knew they had settled nothing by their bitter argument before dawn, but wondered if perhaps she shouldn't tell her husband she'd felt unwell if it would help her avoid another such ghastly scene in the future. She did not want to risk his anger on the chance he might consider her keeping a secret as being the same as telling a lie. She felt uneasy with that decision, though, and thought her first impulse the best, for it was certainly a wife's duty to save her husband from needless worry, and that was all she hoped to do.

Reaching the place where the brook widened into a pool, she looked about to be certain she'd be unobserved, then dropped the blanket to her feet. It was then she noticed the silver charm she'd worn so proudly was gone. Had the delicate chain broken and slipped to the grass as they'd made love, or had Mylan finally taken it back while she slept too soundly to refuse his request? Angered that he would treat her so unfairly, she splashed the cold water upon her body with vigorous strokes, wanting only to finish her bath and find him to demand he return what was rightfully hers. But as she returned to the spot where they'd slept she thought first she should make certain the necklace was not lying hidden in the tall grass. Getting down on her hands and knees she searched diligently, traversing a larger section than what they had occupied, but she saw little other than an assortment of industrious ants and a few tiny beetles. "Is this what I am supposed to do, Mylan, to search for the answer to each and every problem that confronts me with the thoroughness I've given to finding my necklace?" she muttered softly to herself as she dressed in the rose-colored gown, hoping he had taken Thor's tiny hammer for safekeeping. She would feel dreadful if it were lost.

Satisfied her appearance was presentable, after she'd spent the most reckless of nights, Celiese suppressed her laughter at that tantalizing memory, slipped on her shoes, and started down the hill. She chose the path upon which they'd come, bypassing the village as she scanned the ground for the flash of sunlight upon silver, but she reached the edge of the cliff without finding her necklace. She raised her hand to shade her eyes as she looked out upon the sea's bright sparkle, but she could do no more than stare, unable to catch her breath, for where she'd expected to see the Surf Falcon lying at anchor there was only an endless expanse of gray-green water. The sleek ship was gone, but was Mylan gone as well? Or had he only sent his men out to fish, or to sail up the coast in search of timber to rebuild their house? More than a dozen possibilities came to her mind as she ran down the path to the beach. His crew had not expressed any desire to remain in France, as far as she knew. Perhaps he had sent them home to return the Surf Falcon to Hagen and Andrick. Hagen had planned to come to France in the spring, but there was little time left to sail now before winter's chill gripped the land and turbulent seas made voyages too dangerous to consider. Why had he not awakened her to tell her what he'd planned so she'd not be so dreadfully frightened when she found him gone?

Celiese paced up and down the damp sand with an anxious step, hoping at any moment the red and white sail of the Falcon would come into view, but she could not contain her growing apprehension, and large tears welled up in her eyes as she wondered if perhaps she'd been deserted and her hopes of seeing her husband again soon would prove futile. She remained on the beach, waiting and hoping Mylan would appear at any moment to laugh at her foolishness, but her heart was filled with dread. When she heard André calling her name she wheeled about suddenly, desperate for some news of her husband's whereabouts. She ran to meet the elderly man as he came down the path, but his pleasant smile told her nothing.

"Have you seen my husband today? We arrived very early this morning and slept near our house, but when I awakened he was gone." Her long lashes were damp with tears, her anxiety readily conveyed to the friendly Frenchman.

"Alas, Lady d'Loganville, as I do not speak his tongue and he does not speak mine we have little means to communicate," André said, apologizing for his inability to be more helpful.

"But did you see him?" Celiese grabbed André's hands, pulling him near so she might question him fully.

"Yes, he came to my home and left another large bag of silver, I—"

Surprised by that remark, Celiese interrupted quickly, "What do you mean another bag of silver, has he given you some before?"

"When you left here I found the coins at my door and knew they could only have come from the two of you. Did he not tell you how generous he'd been with me? I thought the money was meant for all of us, to help the village as a gift from you."

"He apparently neglected to mention it." Celiese did not know what to think now. That Mylan had wanted to help the peasants pleased her very much, but why had he not told her of his generosity? Returning to their present problem, she continued, "You said he left more silver with you today?"

André chuckled to himself as he replied, "Yes, but this is for your house. He took a stick and drew an outline in the dirt so I would understand I am to use this money to help you rebuild your house."

Celiese slumped down in the sand, simply sank to her knees as she realized what Mylan had meant André to do. "I have no need of a house without a husband, André, and clearly the man has left me." She tried frantically to remember what he'd told her before dawn. He would work for Robert so she could keep her land, he'd rebuild her house but not live in it unless she promised, promised what? She brought her hands to her mouth to muffle her sobs. He had been so angry, bitterly enumerating each wrong he thought she'd done him, when she was innocent of every one of his accusations. She wept on and on, heartbroken that he had left her when she'd deserved none of his hatred. André squatted down beside her, gently stroking her silken curls as if he could soothe her misery, but he could do no more than provide a sympathetic ear as Celiese continued to cry, her heartbreak evident in the tremors that shook her slender body with unbearable sorrow.

When Celiese was finally exhausted by her torrent of tears, she looked up at André, embarrassed to have let him witness such a shocking lack of self-control. She wiped the last of her tears from her eyes with trembling fingertips, then rose gracefully to her feet. "Please forgive me, I did not mean to burden you with my unhappiness."

"But dear lady, I want to be of service in whatever way

I am able." André struggled to stand, pausing to brush the sand from his trousers. "Your husband left something at my home, clothing, I believe it is."

"How considerate of him." Drained of all emotion, Celiese did not care what he might have left behind when he'd not chosen to stay himself. She preceded André along the path that made its way up the face of the cliff, then turned to wait for him. "I'll come get those things now, although I do not know where I shall take them."

Seeing a way to lift her spirits, André began to describe how her family home might be rebuilt. "While the weather holds, granite can be gathered from the mountains by the men among us who possess skill in working with stone. There are lush forests nearby, so timber can be found for the rafters. I know the work will progress slowly, but little by little we can transform what remains into a replica of the house that once stood so proudly upon the hill. The home of the d'Loganvilles can again be as beautiful as it once was."

Celiese listened attentively as they walked into the village, following the man's growing enthusiasm with a heavy heart. He seemed to think the project a most worthwhile one, since his memories of her family were as happy as hers. "I do not want to take any of the men away from their main task, which is to provide a livelihood for their families. That would be most unfair."

"Your husband left money enough to pay all those who wish to be employed in the project. You need not concern yourself with how the men will be rewarded."

After a moment's hesitation, Celiese explained her reluctance to begin the reconstruction. "Somehow when

Mylan promised to rebuild my home, I thought he would provide the labor himself. It seems I misunderstood all he said," she commented softly. "The men will have to understand the house will be his as well as mine, that it will be the home of the Vandahls, not the d'Loganvilles. Will they be willing to work for a Dane after what they have suffered?"

André frowned slightly as he considered her words. "If you can call such a man husband, we will not insult him in any way. Besides, you are the one who is here and in desperate need of a home. We have become very practical, and that will be the only consideration, I am sure."

As they entered the village, Celiese was again surrounded by the well-meaning residents as she had been on her previous visits. She attempted to smile bravely, then reassured them that she had received the promise of the duke that she would retain her estate and their lands would be safe for them to farm. The ripples of excitement that passed through the rapidly growing crowd lifted her spirits greatly, for her problems seemed minor when compared to theirs. For too many years they had been battling invading Danes, as well as the elements, in a valiant effort to survive. If she could bring peace to their troubled lives, at whatever the cost to her own personal happiness, she knew she would be willing to pay it. She felt foolish wearing brocade when the women around her wore such simple garb, but she knew she was different from the happy crowd in so many more important ways than her clothing that the extravagant fabric and style of her gown seemed insignificant. She politely refused their offers of hospitality and instead followed André into his cottage to collect her belongings. They were all there, still wrapped as they had been when they left Rouen. Placing the bundle upon his table she searched through it quickly, hoping to find the silver necklace among her things. But it was missing.

"Has something been lost?" André asked curiously.

"Why yes, my silver necklace. It was a present from my husband and most precious to me," Celiese explained sadly.

After a moment's thought, André began to smile. "Did this necklace have an unusual charm, in the shape of a hammer?"

"Yes, that's it, did you find it?" Celiese was delighted to think he had.

"I do not believe it is lost, unless there are two, for I saw your husband wearing such a charm this morning."

Gathering up her bundle, Celiese tried not to let her disappointment show in either her words or expression. "I am happy to learn it is not lost, then." She went toward the door, still uncomfortable in the close confines of the tiny dwelling, for it reminded her too much of the cell where she'd been held in the tower of Robert's mansion. "I want to be by myself, André. There are so many questions to which I have no answers, and I need time to give them thought."

"But you cannot live in the portion of your home that remains standing! It is filled with weeds, an unsafe place for a young woman as beautiful as you to reside alone!" André attempted to stop her, but Celiese gave his weathered cheek a light kiss and with a sad, sweet smile was gone.

Walking up the hill, Celiese forced herself to concentrate upon purely practical matters. When she reached the ruins of her house she decided that what she needed to do first was to change her clothes, for she could not work in so fine a gown as she was wearing. Sorting through the few items she had, she selected the linen gown Olgrethe had given her as being the most practical. Then she walked slowly through her home, trying to decide what should be done first. As if weeds were her only problem, she began in what had been the kitchen, and with vicious yanks grabbed handful after handful of the weeds that had grown up between the smooth stones that had been the floor. The chimney was still standing, the stones of the hearth in place, so after she had gathered firewood she would be able to cook her own meals. With winter approaching and no store of provisions to see her through the cold months, she had not a moment to lose. Her mind preoccupied with the basic requirements for survival, she spent the entire afternoon doing what she could to make livable the corner of the ground floor the kitchen had occupied.

At dusk, André joined her. He was carrying a small basket filled with food, which he hoped Celiese would accept as a gift. When she was most reluctant to do so he offered to dine with her, and, since they would then be sharing his provisions, she agreed. When she had finished the bread and cheese he'd brought and reached for an apple, he hoped perhaps she would enjoy having his company for a while longer. "Were you able to solve those problems of which you spoke?"

Shaking her head sadly, Celiese explained, "No, I have decided to devote my attentions to merely rebuilding a small portion of my home, so that I will have a place to spend the winter. I will still need food, of course. Do you find the fishing good from the beach?''

Surprised that the delicate young woman would consider such a pastime, André described his own luck. ''Some days I am fortunate, others I am not. I go out very early in the morning when the fish are hungry, but sometimes I am there all day before I have any luck. In cold weather I dare not go out upon the beach, for I am clumsy and too often become wet, and I have no wish to risk illness.''

''Well, then, when the weather is too poor for fishing I will have to hunt,'' Celiese decided thoughtfully. ''I know how, my husband taught me all that my father didn't.''

''But that is ridiculous!'' André replied in horror. ''You can not creep through the woods searching for game!''

''And why not?'' Celiese laughed at his disdain. ''My life has been very different from the one I knew here as a child, André. I have learned that a woman must be able to provide for herself. In Denmark, since the men are so frequently away from home in the summer, the women supervise the work upon the farms themselves. They are much more independent than the women here in France, and I think happier for it.''

Aghast that she would describe the lives of her captors as if they should be admired, André stuttered nervously, ''But you are a Frenchwoman, how can you even think such things?''

''Thinking is not the difficult part, André; living as I wish to is what will provide the challenge.'' She looked away then, unable to accept the fact that she would have to spend even one more day of her life without Mylan at her side.

The elderly servant watched his companion's expression change to one of such abject sorrow that he was moved to tears himself. Drying his eyes upon his sleeve, he attempted to offer the only encouragement that came to mind. "I cannot believe your husband has left you here like this; surely he means to return soon. I must have misunderstood his meaning this morning, for I cannot believe any man would be so great a fool as to leave you."

Celiese reached out to pat his hand lightly. "My husband is a proud man, André, and a determined one. Everything continually went wrong for us, and, while I did not think I was to blame, he did."

"Then he is a fool!" André criticized sharply.

"No, he is no fool." Celiese gathered up the remains of their meal and packed it away into the man's basket. "Thank you for this wonderful supper. I was more hungry than I realized, but I'd worked all afternoon without once thinking of food."

André was wise enough to know Celiese had changed the subject for a reason and he did not make any further comments about her husband, but he had meant precisely what he'd said about the man. "If you would not mind, I would like to bring you something each day. I have no skill as a farmer after spending my life raising horses, but I manage to trade for what I need. Our numbers are so few that we take care of one another, and all will want to see you have to neither hunt nor fish to live among us."

She knew she had shocked the man with ideas she thought only reasonable, but rather than argue Celiese thanked him for his generosity. "I will be delighted to share your meals whenever you wish, and as soon as I am able I will contribute something too."

André bid her good night and started down the path to the village, then recalled something he'd not thought to offer and walked back to speak with Celiese once more. "Whenever you wish to visit your mother, I will escort you. Simply tell me the day before, and I will have the horses ready at dawn."

Not knowing what to say to that suggestion, Celiese thought it best to smile warmly, as though she were pleased. "Why thank you, but I think I will be busy here for the next few weeks, and another visit to her will have to wait."

"Whatever you wish." Thinking he had pleased her, André smiled to himself as he walked home, but he was afraid Lady Marie would not approve of the life her daughter planned to lead now that she had returned home.

Once the sun had set, Celiese's courage deserted her. With Mylan, sleeping under the stars had been an adventure; alone it was misery, an oppressive reminder of the vastness of the heavens and her own pitiful insignificance. She rolled over upon her stomach and propped her chin in her hands and closed her eyes to shut out the brightness of the nighttime sky. If only Mylan had given her an opportunity to speak with him that morning. There must have been some way for them to reach a compromise, but they had had no chance to talk over their situation, and it had changed greatly since their arrival in France. They were again husband and wife, but not friends; lovers whose passion for each other was insatiable, but two proud people who could not seem to agree on how their lives should be lived. "Together," she whispered softly to herself. That Mylan had deserted her, left her sound asleep dreaming only of him, had been unspeakably cruel, but she knew someday he would have to return. If only because Robert demanded to speak to both of them together, but eventually he would come back, and she wanted him to be astonished by how successfully she'd managed to live without him. She'd see their house was completed, the gardens replanted, the fields sewn with grain. She'd do it all by herself if she had to, but do it she would, simply to make him realize the chance for happiness he'd thrown away when he'd left her with little more than the earth upon which she lay. Sleep was a long time in coming, but she was too tired to dream that night, and Mylan's taunting smile no longer haunted her as it had when she had been held prisoner. His presence had left her dreams as suddenly as he had left her life, but that did not lessen the aching need she still felt for him, nor ease her sorrow in the slightest.

When she awakened the next morning, a thick blanket of fog hovered over the land, shutting out the light of the rising sun and covering the ground with a damp mist. She shivered and wrapped her now damp blanket tightly around herself as she wished she had some way to light a fire. Knowing André would have one burning and thinking how cozy and warm his small cottage would be, she quickly got dressed, donned her long cloak, and made her way to his home.

Hearing the knock at his door, André rushed to admit

his visitor. "I was just coming to get you! Come in and warm yourself by the fire." The elderly man moved one of his benches in front of the hearth and gestured for her to be seated. "I had awakened to find the day a poor one for venturing out, but I knew you could not be allowed to remain out in the elements."

"I want to thank you again for your hospitality, André. This fire is delightful. I will gather wood today so I can have my own fire tomorrow." Celiese held out her hands to warm them in the fire's glow.

Looking askance, André decided not to comment upon what he thought of her gathering her own firewood. He was certain there were several young boys who would be grateful for the opportunity to be of service and decided he'd send for one later to spare her that labor. "You must have some breakfast, for you ate little last night." He busied himself preparing a thin porridge, apologizing that he had so little talent as a cook.

"Please do not trouble yourself for me. I have not felt well enough to eat for several mornings, and today is no exception." Indeed, her stomach lurched as she spoke of her problem, and she feared she might again become ill.

"I will brew some herb tea for you, then, as you must take no chances with your health. If the weather permits travel later in the day, will you not consider making another visit to your mother? We can accomplish little if there is rain, and nothing at all should you fall ill." André was greatly worried, for Celiese's fair complexion had grown pale, making her green eyes appear enormous, and her hair, which fell in damp ringlets about her shoulders, gave her the appearance of a neglected waif. A sorry image he hoped to change for the better with a warm meal.

"I am not ready to visit her yet, truly I am not." Celiese could think of no way to please her mother other than by staying away.

"I am merely being practical." He explained. "You could reside with her while a portion of your home is made ready for you to occupy." Seeing another important point, he offered helpfully, "A place such as the Convent of Saint Valery would afford you the solitude in which to consider those problems you mentioned yesterday."

"Yes, both your points are well taken." However, the memory of the austere atmosphere of the convent sent a chill up her spine and she drew her cloak more tightly around her shoulders. "I do not want to leave the rebuilding of my home entirely up to others, though. I think I should be here to help in whatever manner I may."

André chuckled at her determination. "You are a very proud young woman, my dear, and while that is an admirable quality, you must not allow it to cloud that fine mind of yours and prevent you from observing what must be seen."

"That is the way you used to speak to me when I was a child, André. When I'd come to the stable to give our horses treats, you always had some word of advice for me." She'd found his instruction useful then, but she was reluctant to accept it now.

"That was not so many years ago, although it seems like a lifetime to me now." André placed two bowls of steaming porridge upon the table and invited Celiese to join him. They ate quietly, both far more hungry than they cared to admit.

When they had finished, Celiese sipped the herb tea and asked skeptically, "What is it you think I do not see?"

André leaned forward as he whispered, "The secrets you have hidden in your own heart."

Confused, Celiese nevertheless began to argue. "I've no secrets of any kind, André, not hidden from myself or anyone else." That he seemed to think her so devious a creature as Mylan did hurt her badly, for she was quite fond of him.

Frustrated that she did not see his point, André spoke more harshly, "Of course not, but are you certain the fact your husband chose to leave without bidding you good-bye was as unexpected a shock as it appeared?"

Blushing brightly with embarrassment, Celiese looked away, unable to think of any way to express how she felt about that betrayal other than what he'd observed the previous day upon the beach. "I would rather discuss the plans to rebuild my house, if you don't mind. That is what matters most to me now."

"You cannot mean that!" André responded angrily. "It is obvious to me it is Mylan who matters most to you, but if you will not admit that truth to yourself, how could you have communicated that important point to him?"

Stunned by the clarity of his observation, Celiese realized that the depth of her feeling was not something she'd ever attempted to put into words. She'd tried only to express those tender emotions with all the imagination and devotion she possessed. "You do not understand how things were between us, André, there is no way that you can."

"It is not necessary that I understand anything, it is only you and Mylan who must seek that accord."

"The man is gone, André, there is nothing I can do now to make him see what he refused to accept when we were together. It was hopeless from the beginning, for my love was never returned. He did not even want a wife when we first met, and most especially he did not want me!" Celiese fought back the tears that threatened to overwhelm her again, tears of anger as well as sorrow. She had no desire to put on another pathetic display. She lifted her cup to her lips instead, and finished her tea, grateful to have that distraction.

André waited until he was certain Celiese again had her emotions under control, for he had not meant to upset her, only to assist her in finding her own truth. "If your husband were to return today, what would you tell him?"

Puzzled by that question, Celiese refused to speculate on so unlikely an eventuality. "He will not return for a very long time, if ever, André."

"Indulge me then, for I am an old man, and should I not live until his return, what will you tell him?" André smiled in his most charming fashion, hoping she would play his game.

Celiese frowned, remembering only how she'd wanted to show Mylan how well she could live without him. "I am afraid I would say all the wrong things, André. He'd become angry with me as he always does, and then he would probably just leave me again."

"I am pleased to see you understand far more than I thought you did. You are correct when you say you have many questions without answers, but you will gain nothing by avoiding them. I think the fog has begun to lift. I will saddle the horses while you gather your belongings, for surely your own inner peace must be found before you can devote your attentions to supervising your estate. I will take you to the convent for the time being, while we begin work on your home, and perhaps when I come for you you will have thought of a thousand ways in which to greet your husband without angering him. What do you say? Is that idea not a fine one?"

"Do not saddle the horses as yet, André. Let me think about this a while longer, please." Celiese tried to smile, for she knew he was being kind. He was as fond of her as she was of him. She left his home to wander slowly back to the ruins of her own, choosing this time to walk down the overgrown paths that had once been part of her mother's beautifully tended garden. Here and there a flower remained, growing wild now amongst the weeds, and she bent down to pick up a handful of soil as she'd done on her first visit there with Mylan. It had only been dirt, he had said, no more or less than the rich soil that covered his farmlands. "It is not a question of land, though, but of what a person loves as his home." She knew that, even if he had not, but was her loyalty to the place where she'd been born and surrounded with love no more than pride of the most foolish sort? She was more confused than she had ever been, but if the answers to her problems lay within her own heart, as André had said, then she knew she would be a fool not to seek them. Gathering up the few things she owned, she made her way back to his cottage, ready to join her mother in the Convent of Saint Valery for however many weeks or years it took her to find the secrets she'd hidden even from herself.

Chapter Twenty-Six

Mylan spent the day forcing himself to concentrate solely upon maintaining a firm grasp upon the tiller, giving his full attention to successfully making the voyage home, but his thoughts betrayed him time and again. "Home." He spoke the word softly to himself as if it were a curse, for he wanted only to put France far behind him, rather than having any great desire to return to his native shores. Winter was coming, its chill already in the air, and he knew he would merely be marking time until spring when he could again set sail in the Raven. He'd go to his farm and hunt when he could, but the weeks he'd spent alone there after Celiese had gone had not provided him with the peaceful solitude he'd expected. He'd been far too restless, and none of the activities that had consumed his time as he'd prepared for the harvest had held his interest. He had no qualms about facing his father after taking a voyage the man had forbidden. He'd tell him the truth of why he had left so hastily, but he still shuddered to think how close Celiese had come to falling victim to the Torgvalds' lust for revenge. His anger rekindled at that memory, his handsome features set in a deep frown. No, he had no apologies to make to his father, but the man he had once respected so completely owed him an apology he was uncertain he would ever accept.

Despite Mylan's preoccupation with his problems, the Falcon's progress was swift, but when they went ashore to make camp for the night he found himself the object of many curious stares. He had no explanation he cared to give as to why he'd left his lovely bride behind, and so he offered none. The men of the crew were strangely silent, none wishing to begin the lively exchange of jokes and laughter that usually filled their evenings. Knowing his solemn mood was the cause of their discomfort, Mylan finished his supper in a few hasty bites and excused himself, leaving their midst to search out a place where he could be alone with his thoughts.

Finding a small clearing nearby, he stretched out on his back and propped his head upon his hands as he looked up at the shimmering stars. He knew their patterns well, and how to use them to plot an accurate course, but it was not a question of navigation that plagued his mind that night. He'd made his decision to leave Celiese in the heat of anger, but he had given her the choice. It was better to end their marriage after no more than one day than to continue to bear the agony she'd made him endure in the months since they'd first met. He hated her in that instant, despised her for twisting his emotions until they were no more than tangled shreds. Yet even as he lay surrounded by the peace of the night, finally rid of her maddening presence, he missed her so terribly he could scarcely stand the pain that pierced his heart with an unbearable loneliness. No matter how fierce their perpetual arguments might have been, she had made a paradise of his nights, and it was the memory of that sweet pleasure that tormented him unmercifully now. He knew he would never find her equal, nor did he even wish to begin a search. He was exhausted both mentally and physically, his courageous spirit as well as his powerful body drained of energy, and he began to repeat the prayers Father Bernard had taught him in hopes of lulling himself to sleep but each word reminded him of Celiese and how desperately he'd tried to win her love and how miserably he had failed.

The next morning they had done little more than make their way through the surf and head out into the open sea when the fog overtook them. The thick mist obscured the horizon as well as the coastline, sealing them in a blanket of gray, shutting them off from all contact with the physical world as surely as if they'd been wrapped in a giant cocoon. Mylan slackened their pace until they were barely moving, taking them close enough to the shore so they could hear the waves breaking upon the rocks. It was a difficult task, requiring the utmost precision, for should they venture too close the Surf Falcon would be dashed to bits upon the jagged rocks, and if he held their course at too great a distance they would miss the curve of the coastline and find themselves far out at sea. *Hafvilla* would be the word for their situation then: lost at sea. He was not overly concerned with that dire possibility, as he'd always had good luck using a *solarstein*. The sunstone was a dull gray until the invisible rays of the sun were focused upon it, then it glowed a bright blue, making navigation as simple a matter under an overcast sky as it was on a cloudless day.

They were all tired, worn out from the strain of trying to maintain their course, but finding a good spot for the night was nearly impossible without the benefit of sight to assess the shoreline. They had made such little progress that Mylan hesitated to stop, hoping for a clear night in which they could make up for lost time, but the fog became increasingly dense, until they were all drenched to the skin. He had to continue to depend upon his skill at listening to the force of the sea as it met the land to judge where a safe harbor might lie. He took the Falcon in close, and two men swam ashore, searching for signs of a settlement they'd not wish to disturb, but finding none they shouted for the others to drop anchor and come ashore.

Mylan stayed near the fire that night, not wanting to stray from its warmth after having spent such a cold and fruitless day. The men belonged to his brothers' crew rather than his own, but he knew them well enough now to sense their mood, and the chill of their apprehension was a tangible force, despite the comforting warmth of the fire. "If this is the worst day you have ever spent on board the Surf Falcon, you are fortunate men indeed," he told them. Then, with the most vivid description he could summon to mind, he proceeded to relate a spellbinding tale of a fearful storm he'd encountered off the coast of Iceland in his own ship, the Raven. The tempest had raged for more than two torturous days, the waves cresting at heights above their mast, and only by furious bailing had they managed to remain afloat. The fascinated men listened with mouths agape. Knowing by his very presence among them that Mylan had survived the horrid ordeal, they wanted to hear every agonizing detail of how he had succeeded in escaping so harsh a fate as had nearly overtaken him. By the time he finished his story, a day or two of fog seemed so minor a hazard that they yawned lazily and went to sleep without the slightest fear their captain would not see them safely home regardless of how uncooperative the weather.

Mylan closed his eyes too, an amused smile curving his lips as he recalled the storm, which had been anything but entertaining when he'd been caught in its midst. It was a memorable adventure, however, when seen in retrospect. With a stab of guilt he recalled that Celiese had once asked him to recount some of his adventures, and he'd refused her request as a ridiculous one for a man to grant on his wedding night. She had never inquired about his past again, and he was saddened to think how many opportunities he'd missed to relate stories of his life and travels to her. Andrick had chided him for not courting Celiese, but surely no man need court his own wife! As he lay there in the darkness he could see her face so clearly in his mind, her delicate features filled with concern on their wedding night as she'd cautioned him that they were strangers who had to be patient with each other, that misunderstandings were inevitable between them. Rolling over on his side to get more comfortable and to shut out her tantalizing image, he realized her advice had been sound. Unfortunately their second wedding night had ended no better than their first. "Mis-

understandings" was an understatement of gigantic proportions. Frowning unhappily, he fell into a troubled
sleep, his whole body aching not only with fatigue, but
with want of her.

When they found the fog had not lifted the next
morning, the men awakened reluctantly. Mylan had
gotten up first, added wood to the fire, building the
gleaming coals to a cheery blaze, but he was no happier
than they with the challenge the weather continued to
present. While the fog was no worse, its very presence
had such an ominous quality that it took considerable
courage to face another day of sailing when their sense of
sight would be so useless. Far from being discouraged,
however, Mylan was merely resigned to their continuing
difficulties, and with a few well-placed slaps had his crew
up and ready to begin the day as if it were going to be a
most splendid one.

Thinking the fog might be hugging the coastline,
Mylan set their course for the open seas. But it was soon
clear to him that if the dense mist had an outer boundary,
he could not find it. Returning to skirt the shoreline,
they made no better progress than they had the previous
day, and by late afternoon they had all grown weary with
the effort. With extra rations of ale, the crew's mood
improved somewhat, but Mylan felt as though he were
battling an enemy who could neither be seen nor heard,
and, frustrated by his own inability to proceed with his
customary swiftness, he strode off down the beach,
trying to walk off the nervous tension that he knew
would never permit him to sleep.

Once alone he admitted to himself that he had been

completely unsuccessful in keeping thoughts of Celiese
out of his mind that day. Her delightful presence seemed
to swirl about him with the persistence of the mist, until
it seemed she had created the fog herself simply to torment him. "Lady Celiese d'Loganville," he whispered
softly, and, letting his thoughts come freely without
restraint, he began to wonder what their life would have
been had he never discovered her true identity. Would
the sweetness she'd shown him upon their first meeting
have continued? She had told him that that was her true
self—the one in which he had believed for all too few
hours before Raktor and his sons had plunged his life into
chaos. What if that dear creature were the wife he should
have had? Would she ever have told him who she really
was, or asked for his help in returning home? Somehow
he thought not, for when she'd first told him of her past,
her home and family had seemed lost to her, gone forever, and she'd had no hope of returning to the land of
her birth. It was much later, only after he'd sent her
away, that she began to dream of her homeland, and with
Hagen's encouragement had sought a way to return to it.
He scuffed his toe in the sand, finally digging a hole with
vicious kicks as he acknowledged that he'd seen from the
behavior of André and the others that she was exactly
who she'd claimed to be. Indeed, Robert's fear of her
influence confirmed her bloodline, as well.

Certain he had discovered an important truth, Mylan
continued to walk slowly along the damp sand, remembering each gesture she had made, each nuance of
expression he'd seen and loved. It still hurt to remember
that she had heard him shout to Andrick that he did not

love her, for that had been his pride not his heart speaking, and yet that was a cruelty she'd endured without comment.

He suddenly saw it all then, with a clarity that astonished him. Celiese was, most significantly, a young woman who had in the worst of circumstances been forced to learn how to survive on her own. A dear and pampered child, she'd seen the home she loved put to the torch, while all around her the bodies of those she'd adored lay in bloody heaps. As if that horror were not enough to endure, she'd been kidnapped and cruelly abused, and yet she had lost neither her sense of her own identity nor her pride. Time and again he had seen that very pride that made her so magnificent a creature as being the cause of all their problems, but it was suddenly plain to him that it was her very determination to live her life to the fullest that he admired most. She had accepted him as he was; knowing little of his past, she'd wanted to share his future, not as the slave he'd made of her, but as the equal she demanded and had every right to be. Appalled by the enormity of his countless errors, he knew without question that whatever happiness the fates had planned for them to share had been thrown away by him when he'd left her. All he deserved was to sail on forever surrounded by an impenetrable fog, for truly even when the skies were clear he saw nothing. As he turned to walk back to his camp, he saw no way to right the many wrongs he'd done his beautiful bride, none at all, but he hid his depression from his crew just as he'd hidden his love from Celiese. He was too proud a man to show any sign of emotion in front of them, but he knew that the price he'd paid for that pride had not been worth the pain.

Celiese waited anxiously in the small parlor of the Convent of Saint Valery, uncertain what her mother's reaction would be to her this time. The fire upon the hearth was most welcome, but while it provided an outer warmth, her heart still held an unshakable chill. When, after a long wait, her mother appeared, she rose to meet her, her smile wavering as she greeted her. "It is good of you to see me again, Mama. I am sorry I had no way to tell you I was coming."

"You are alone this time?" Marie asked suspiciously. In her long gray habit she appeared to float across the distance that separated them, but her green eyes were cold, devoid of any welcoming sparkle.

"If you are referring to my husband, he has left me, so I am quite alone," Celiese explained calmly, none of her intense sorrow evident in either her tone of voice or her expression.

Intrigued, Marie came closer. "You have come to join us then, as I asked you to?"

"No, that is impossible, for Mylan has become a Christian and we were married again. I doubt that this order or any other would accept a woman whose husband is still living." At least she had never heard of such a thing.

Frowning, Marie took a place upon the bench opposite the fire and patted the cushion beside her. When Celiese sat down, she laced her fingers in hers. "If the man has deserted you, perhaps an annulment can be arranged."

"No, I'll not ask for one." Making every effort to gain her mother's understanding once again, Celiese asked only that she might be permitted to stay at the convent for a brief visit. "I need time to collect my thoughts, for so much has happened since we last spoke together that I have had great difficulty placing it all in its proper perspective. I will work at whatever chores you wish to assign me; all I ask is that I be given some time each day to be alone with my own thoughts."

Marie was puzzled, for her daughter's mood was too subdued. "Our door is open to those who wish to seek God, Celiese, not to women searching for an easy escape from a life they find too difficult to live. The challenges presented here are far greater than any you will ever confront in the outside world."

"You are speaking of understanding the mysteries that lie hidden within the human heart?" Celiese asked softly.

"Why, yes, that is one way to state our quest," Marie replied with surprise.

Celiese responded with an enchanting smile. "That is precisely why I have come."

The changeless routine of the convent was soothing in itself, for Celiese found the choices as to how she'd spend her days had already been made for her. The sisters were either in the chapel or working at their assigned tasks. An introspective group, they were silent during meals, but their food was plentiful, providing a variety of vegetables and grains, butter and cheese, if little meat. She had her own room, a tiny one, so the nausea that continued to plague her mornings went unnoticed, but it worried her greatly. For the rest of the day she found her appetite voracious and was embarrassed to think she might be eating more than her share, but the sisters were generous and did not seem to mind, if in fact they had even noticed.

They complimented her upon her delicate touch with needle and thread and provided her with a large basket of garments that needed repair. Far from being insulted by the humble task, Celiese found sewing as pleasurable as it had been when she'd been with Olgrethe. With her hands occupied in useful work, she was able to contemplate her future without being rushed to make any decisions for the present. But it was Mylan who occupied all her thoughts. She soon realized she'd been a poor wife to him, for she'd failed to make him understand how dearly he was loved. Something else had always taken precedence: winning her freedom, coming home, regaining her estate, all important quests, but empty victories when he was not there to share them. More often than not she found herself in tears, upset at the slightest obstacle, even if it was no more than a broken thread, or the fact that she was late to chapel. Her thinking was becoming more clear each day, but, sadly, her emotional turmoil had not lessened. She missed Mylan too greatly to concentrate on any task fully without his handsome face's filling her thoughts. The memories of his smile and his kiss were most precious, but they brought an agony, as well, for they were a continuous reminder of what she had lost.

Finding her daughter seated beneath a window to take advantage of the sunlight while she did her mending, Marie sat down upon the bench beside her to talk for a moment. After mentioning several other topics, she came to the true reason for their conversation. "You are happy here, aren't you? Content with the life we live?"

Attempting to be as tactful as she could, Celiese agreed. "Yes, your hospitality is most gracious, and I am more than content." As content as possible without Mylan, she did not add, but that was the truth of her situation.

Clearing her throat nervously, Marie continued quickly, hoping to convince Celiese to accept her suggestion without argument. "Mylan is a Dane, Celiese, his conversion quite recent, and from the way in which he deserted you I'd say it was most insincere. When you are certain you are not carrying his child, I think we should seek an annulment of your marriage so that you might join our order."

At the mention of a child, Celiese blushed deeply. "It is too soon for me to be positive, Mama, but each day I grow more certain, and an annulment would be most inappropriate if I am to bear Mylan's child."

Devastated by that possibility, Marie was near tears as she rose to her feet. "We must pray such a travesty does not come to pass, for now that you are free of the man, the last thing you need is the responsibility of rearing his son."

"He would be my son as well, or perhaps I will have a daughter, Mama, your grandchild. Can you not think of a babe in those terms?" Celiese hardly dared hope she was pregnant, but if she were, she knew she would love Mylan's baby as dearly as she'd loved him. With a smile she thought how shocked he would be to hear he had an heir; it was an even better surprise than she'd hoped to give him by completing her house without his help.

Before Marie could respond, the stone walls of the ancient convent reverberated with a din as deafening as thunder, growing in intensity as the small wooden door at the entrance creaked and groaned under repeated blows from a battering ram. Celiese lay her mending aside as she leapt to her feet. With her mother's help, she managed to wrench open the narrow leaded glass window so they could look down upon the scene below. Marie was terrified at the sight of the six muscular Danes who were moving back with carefully measured steps, preparing to strike the splintered door another fearsome blow. Celiese, however, called down to the tall blond man standing to one side who had been shouting directions. This time she remembered to use his Christian name. "Michael, if you wished to see me, you needed to do no more than ring the bell and I would have come to the door."

"That is your husband?" Marie gasped in horror, her fair skin growing deathly pale. The young man had not only height and obvious strength, but the beauty of a god, as well. The sun sparkled upon his tawny curls, and his light eyes glowed with the golden gleam of a wildcat's as he looked up at her. He was the most attractive of men, but that did not diminish her fear, and she gripped her daughter's arm tightly, "Do not let him break down the door! Send him away at once, he must not be allowed to enter!"

The terror in her expression was too real for Celiese not to readily comprehend its cause, and she hugged her mother warmly as she attempted to reassure her that there was nothing to fear. "Mylan has come to speak with me, Mama, not to harm you or any of the other dear sisters. You will see, please have faith in me if you cannot as yet have any in him."

Looking out again, Celiese saw the young men had dropped the log they'd carried and had moved back to stare up at her. Waving, she called to her husband, "I will be but a moment, please wait for me." Stopping to be certain her mother had recovered from her initial shock at finding so threatening a group of young men at her door, she ran from the room and with flying steps hurried down the winding staircase to reach the first floor. Several of the younger sisters were working together to push heavy pieces of furniture behind the battered door in an attempt to keep the men outside from forcing the entrance, and Celiese had first to convince them to move the makeshift barricade aside before she could leave.

Once unlocked, the old door dangled precariously on its hinges, but with the assistance of the sisters she was able to open it wide enough to slip through. She smiled at the men she recognized from the Surf Falcon, and they grinned sheepishly in return, obviously embarrassed to have been involved in so unnecessary an assault. Mylan, on the other hand, seemed merely astonished, and none of the pretty speeches she had been rehearsing in her mind to greet him seemed appropriate when he'd arrived bent on storming the walls rather than politely requesting she speak with him. Thinking she should hear the explanation for the violence of his action first, she held her tongue and waited for him to speak.

Mylan could not believe the ease with which Celiese

515

had simply walked out to meet him as if he'd knocked in a gentlemanly fashion upon the convent door, and he felt utterly ridiculous for having behaved in so outrageous a manner. She looked even more beautiful than he had remembered, which he had not thought possible. Her smile was enchanting, her fair complexion glowing with the bloom of health, her shimmering curls falling loose about her shoulders, and as always the desire she inspired overwhelmed him and he blurted out the first thought that came to his mind. "They allow you to wear your own clothing rather than requiring you to dress as the others do?"

Celiese glanced down at the pretty silk gown, pleased by his admiring glance. He apparently still thought her attractive. "Why yes, of course, for I am no more than a visitor here." Suddenly realizing the nature of his concern, she inquired softly, "Is that what you thought, that I'd entered the convent?"

Mylan glanced up at the frightened faces peeking out of the narrow windows of the upper stories of the large stone edifice. He attempted to give the ladies a reassuring smile, but none of their expressions changed to more friendly ones, which didn't surprise him. He'd undoubtedly scared them all nearly witless, and he could think of no suitable way to apologize for mounting such a senseless attack upon their home. "I had expected to find you at your house. André was there with some other men who were gathering stones. He said only the name of the convent, and I remembered your telling me that when women entered the order they remained inside forever." While his mistake was an understandable one, he was appalled by the enormity of his error.

Celiese wanted only to throw her arms around Mylan and cover his face with lavish kisses, but she waited patiently for a more appropriate time to display the affection that filled her heart to overflowing. "I can see now you misunderstood his message, and I am certain if you and your men would be so kind as to repair the door, you will be forgiven for the rashness of your actions. I will explain to the sisters that you did not realize my stay here was only temporary, and they will then understand why your reaction was such a desperate and reckless one." At least she hoped they would be sympathetic, but she knew she would have to use her most forceful arguments to convince them her handsome Danish husband had only the purest of motives when he'd mounted such a furious assault upon the residence they considered sacred.

Blushing with embarrassment, Mylan pointed to the damaged door. "What is left of that door is beyond repair; we will have to make a new one."

"That will be even better. I am certain they will appreciate it," Celiese offered agreeably. "Now would you care to walk a few paces into the woods with me where we can discuss the reason for your visit without attracting so much attention?" Taking his arm, she gestured toward the forest that surrounded the convent walls, and he readily accepted her suggestion. But once they could no longer be observed, he seemed unable to find any explanation for what he'd done, so she attempted to prompt him. "You frightened my mother, as well as all the others, quite badly. Perhaps after she has had time to

517

regain her composure, I can convince her to come to the entrance so that I may introduce you to her."

"I doubt she'll want to bother after that ridiculous display of stupidity!" Mylan was furious with himself, but he'd thought her lost to him forever and he had gone after her in the only way he'd known how. However, his deed had not been the heroic one he'd imagined, but merely foolish, and he did not like that feeling one bit.

Seeing a fallen log, Celiese sat down upon it as she continued to give her husband her full attention. "I am not angry with you, please don't be so mad at yourself. We are quite alone here; now what was it you wished to say to me that was so urgent? I will be happy to listen for as long as it takes you to explain."

Since her expression held only concern and no ridicule, Mylan went to her side, but he sat down upon the carpet of fallen leaves and leaned back against the log, hoping his task would be an easier one if he did not have the distraction of her beauty with which to contend. "You told me once that I should be patient, that even as man and wife you and I were strangers still, and that misunderstandings were sure to occur between us. Do you recall that conversation?"

With a sweet smile, Celiese recalled the exact time and place. "Yes, we were in your father's home, in your room, in fact. We had just gone there after leaving the party celebrating our marriage." His marriage to Olgrethe, she was tempted to say, but thought better of it.

"Yes, and I had only one thought on my mind. You were a far more lovely bride than I'd dared hope to have, bright and so considerate, but you were right in saying we were strangers. I thought we'd have a lifetime to become well acquainted, but that one night was all we had. I did not mean to be such a poor husband to you, to accept you that night and then turn my back upon you at dawn."

Surprised by his candor, Celiese reached out to give his shoulder a comforting pat, and he took her hand in his, bringing her palm to his lips for a sweet kiss. "We have never had the time to become friends, have we? So much has happened to us, so many terrible things, and we've never had the time to simply get to know one another as we should have in the beginning."

"It might have happened when we were on my farm, if only I'd not kept insisting you were my slave. I was such a fool then, and obviously I am still one today."

"You are no fool, Michael, please don't even think that, for the evidence was always against me, and you cannot help that your mind is a most logical one."

That she would not insult him even when he deserved it pleased Mylan greatly, and he reached up to pull her down across his lap where he hugged her tightly. "I should not have left you as I did, but I thought it was my only choice that morning. You seemed to delight in tormenting me with problems I thought you created yourself, but when I finally decided to leave you I found it was impossible for me to go."

"What do you mean? You were gone, when I went down to the beach your ship had simply vanished." Celiese knew that for a fact.

"That's true enough, but the second day of our voyage we ran into a fog bank that seemed endless. I tried not to think about you, but I couldn't keep your striking beauty

519

from filling my mind. Finally I gave in to my memorie
and began to wonder how things might have bee
different for us. When it dawned on me that if I ha
accepted all you told me as the truth from the beginnin
then everything would have fallen neatly into place.
came back as fast as I could make the Falcon fly throug
the waves. I swear to you that in the very instant
decided to change our course the fog lifted and the win
grew brisk, to give us the speed we'd need. A very min
miracle perhaps, but one for which I am sincerely grat
ful."

Celiese hesitated to comment for a long moment. Th
silence between them was not an awkward one, howeve
but quite comfortable. Finally, she spoke. "Please do n
misunderstand me, but I think the days we've been apa
have helped us both to see our lives more clearly. I ha
been a very poor wife; whether you considered
married or not, I failed you in so many important ways.

"Oh, Celiese," Mylan argued impatiently. "The fau
was all mine, every damn time."

"It takes two to argue, Michael, and you must admit
had fights aplenty." Celiese was ready to argue this poin
too.

"At least you remember my name now, that is a
improvement." He had missed her so terribly, and y
now merely holding her in his arms filled him with a co
tentment he'd thought he'd not ever experience agai

"I am attempting to change for the better, truly I am.
know I do need to be more thoughtful, and to curb m
temper. You were the one who convinced Robert to l
me have my estate again, and I did not even take the tim

520

to thank you for your help. That was why I came to the convent, to learn how I might be a better person, because I knew you'd come back some day and I didn't want to lose you again."

Mylan pulled her close, kissing her temple softly, "Would you have remained shut up in that drafty old place until I finally had the sense to return?"

"The convent is far more comfortable than it appears to be from the exterior, but no, actually I did not plan to stay much longer." Celiese began to blush, her cheeks filling with a burst of color she couldn't suppress, but she could think of no way to confide her suspicions.

"Celiese?" Mylan wound his fingers in her lustrous curls to force her gaze up to his. "What is it, tell me. I don't care what you'd planned to do, it could not have been nearly so silly as battering down the door of the convent was. You were sweet enough not to laugh at me for that folly, and I will not laugh at you now, I promise."

Celiese looked down at his hand, which held hers so firmly. His skin was deeply tanned, his grasp warm, as comforting as his words, but her eyes filled with tears as she explained, "No, I am not afraid that you will laugh, nor be angry; it is only that I did not want a child until you were proud to call me your wife, and I was uncertain that day would ever come."

Mylan turned her gently in his arms, kissing her damp eyelashes sweetly before he spoke. "Are you still thinking about what Raktor told you? Why is it you remember that one insult of his rather than being impressed by all I have done to win your affection? That you were forced to submit to the lusts of the Torgvalds pains me greatly, for no woman should ever have to suffer what you did, but it does not diminish your value to me, Celiese. I adore you and will never call another woman my wife." Seeing the light of hope fill her emerald gaze, he sought to end her needless torment with a question. "I want only to know how many men you have truly loved with all your heart as I love you?"

Celiese began to smile, her eyes sparkling with the affection she no longer had to hide. "You are the only man I have ever loved, Mylan, only you, and no matter what you choose to call yourself, I will love you still!"

Mylan hugged Celiese tightly, returning her enthusiastic embrace with a satisfied grin. "Now is there still some doubt as to the depth of my pride in you, my beloved bride?"

Celiese shook her head, too happy to respond in words when she knew she would be moved to tears with the joy he had given her. She kissed him instead, her obvious pride in him making her gesture irresistibly appealing.

"I hope this babe is only the first child of many for us, Celiese, for I know a woman as loving as you will be the best of mothers. Since I helped to raise my three younger brothers, I don't think I'll do too badly as the babe's father, do you?"

Astonished that he would ask such a question, she hastened to reassure him. "I know you will be a marvelous father, since you are so very clever. You have sailed to so many exciting places and know how to raise abundant crops, as well as hunt with a skill any man would envy. I could ask for no finer man to help me raise a family and rebuild my home. Our home." She corrected herself quickly and was relieved to see by Mylan's amused glance that he was not offended by her unintentional slip.

"The first thing I am going to do is teach your countrymen how to use a sword effectively, for I certainly don't want to have to depend upon them to form our defense armed with no more than their pitchforks!"

Surprised by that prospect, Celiese gripped his hand tightly, "Do you think we will need to defend ourselves now that our province is the property of a Dane? Surely Robert's name alone will keep other Vikings from attacking us."

"I am certain it will, but skill with weapons will give the men the confidence they lack, and they'll be better farmers as a result."

Celiese understood his reasoning well, for in the months they had been together Mylan had again become the man he'd once been, courageous and proud, and she liked to think it was her belief in him that had made the difference in his attitude toward life. She reached out to touch the shiny silver hammer he wore suspended around his neck, but did not ask him to return it, for she wanted it to again be his gift to her.

As if he could read her mind, Mylan took the silver chain from around his neck and slipped it over her head. "Forgive me for taking this, since it was a present. I think only that I wanted something of yours to keep."

Celiese gripped the tiny hammer in a firm grasp. "Thor has brought us both good luck today, hasn't he?"

With a deep chuckle, Mylan helped Celiese to rise, then got to his feet and brushed the leaves from his clothes. "Well, let us hope his magic works with my mother-in-law, as well. I will have to rely upon you to translate my words into something she will understand and admire, and then I will see to that door." His mind suddenly filled with tasks that needed to be accomplished without delay, and he continued, "When we get back to your home, I think we should give the reconstruction of the house more thought. I think we should build a larger one." Mylan took her arm, hurrying her along toward the convent. "I do not want our children to lack for room in which to play and grow."

"Larger, Michael? It was of considerable size; perhaps you cannot visualize it as well as I can, but it was an enormous house."

"You were a child when you last saw it, Celiese, and I'm certain houses must seem larger to children. No, I am right, you will see."

Celiese opened her mouth to argue that the proportions should not be changed, but then she began to laugh with a delicious giggle that made Mylan laugh as well. "I am certain you can build a magnificent home, and as long as you agree to reside there I will be content. You have changed your mind about not living with me, haven't you?"

"You must have known I could never have kept that vow," Mylan admitted with a rakish grin.

"I only hoped that you would not wish to," Celiese teased playfully. "May I tell you again that I love you? I know I can not hear that too often from you."

Mylan pulled her around to face him, his slow, deep kiss the only response he cared to give. She truly had changed, but so had he. She was no longer the high-spirited young woman he'd wanted to tame, but the wife he adored. He pressed her supple body against the length of his, wanting only to savor her nearness to the fullest before they joined the others, but when he drew away, Celiese's eyes were bright with mischief, not tears.

"My mother was so terribly frightened by your arrival that I doubt she has had sufficient time to recover, and I can hear the sounds of hammering, so your men must already be working upon the door. Must we go back just yet?" She raised her hands to his chest, then his neck, pulling his mouth back down to hers as she whispered seductively, "Must we?"

They had made love in the forest near his farm, as well as all along the coastline on their journey to France, so it seemed quite natural to Mylan to take her hand in his and lead her back to the soft bed of leaves in the small clearing where they'd stopped to talk. "I think I fell in love with you the moment we met, and if it takes the rest of my life to make up for the fact that it has taken me so damn long to admit that truth, I will gladly do it." His lips moved hungrily down her throat as he peeled away her silken garments. She was so precious to him, and he'd had no hope the reception she'd give him that day would be such a warm one. "Had I known how dearly you love me, Celiese, I would never have left you, never."

Celiese returned his playful kisses before she replied, "Well, now you do know, but I know how much you love to sail, so I do not expect you to be content to stay at home. All I ask is that you make your journeys brief ones, so I do not perish of loneliness while you are away."

"That is a risk I'll not take." Mylan pulled her into his arms, lost in the enchantment of her tender affection, and he knew, even though she did not, that he had sailed solely for the thrill of discovering new worlds. It had been an exciting quest, but it was over, for no adventure he could have would ever equal the thrill of knowing her love. That was a secret he'd keep for the moment, but with one thing or another, he knew he would be unlikely to have the time, let alone the inclination ever to leave her side. He would be more than content with being a husband and father for the time being, and perhaps he might even learn to love farming with the assistance of his charming bride. Hagen would be eager to help him handle Robert's trade, and his brother was clever at arranging high profits, so the duke would present no more problems.

Celiese snuggled against him, her fingertips tracing the scars that crossed his chest, as she wondered what he might be thinking. "Do you realize that had that bear not cut you to shreds you would be married to Estrid? And I shudder to think where I would be at this moment."

"I will remember to thank God for creating bears every night in my prayers, Celiese, but for the moment you are with me, and I plan to make the most of it."

Celiese purred softly as she wrapped her arms around his neck, and she was soon lost in his delicious kiss, for she planned to make the most of each and every moment they had the good fortune to share.

THE BEST IN ROMANCE FROM ZEBRA

TENDER TORMENT   (1550, $3.95)
by Joyce Myrus

Wide-eyed Caitlin could no more resist the black-haired Quinn than he could ignore her bewitching beauty. Risking danger and defying convention, together they'd steal away to his isolated Canadian castle. There, by the magic of the Northern lights, he would worship her luscious curves until she begged for more tantalizing TENDER TORMENT.

SWEET FIERCE FIRES   (1401, $3.95)
by Joyce Myrus

Though handsome Slade had a reputation as an arrogant pirate with the soul of a shark, sensuous Brigida was determined to tame him. Knowing he longed to caress her luscious curves and silken thighs, she'd find a way to make him love her to madness — or he'd never have her at all!

DESIRE'S BLOSSOM   (1536, $3.75)
by Cassie Edwards

Lovely and innocent Letitia would never be a proper demure Chinese maiden. From the moment she met the dashing, handsome American Timothy, her wide, honey-brown eyes filled with bold desires. Once she felt his burning kisses she knew she'd gladly sail to the other side of the world to be in his arms!

SAVAGE INNOCENCE   (1486, $3.75)
by Cassie Edwards

Only moments before Gray Wolf had saved her life. Now, in the heat of his embrace, as he molded her to his body, she was consumed by wild forbidden ecstasy. She was his heart, his soul, and his woman from that rapturous moment!

PASSION'S WEB   (1358, $3.50)
by Cassie Edwards

Natalie's flesh was a treasure chest of endless pleasure. Bryce took the gift of her innocence and made no promise of forever. But once he molded her body to his, he was lost in the depths of her and her soul. . . .

Available wherever paperbacks are sold, or order direct from the Publisher. Send cover price plus 50¢ per copy for mailing and handling to Zebra Books, 475 Park Avenue South, New York, N.Y. 10016. DO NOT SEND CASH.